From that bend, the road descended quickly and she felt the car picking up speed as gravity and its powerful engine propelled it downhill. As she approached the next turn, Amanda realized she was coming in a little too fast. She slid her foot to the brake. Her concentration on steering the twisting road ahead, at first it didn't register. She dared to take her gaze off the road and look down at her feet before she understood. When her right foot depressed the brake, the pedal glided all the way to the floor. No friction. She pulled her foot back and slammed on the brake again. The pedal slid all the way down. Unbelieving, she pumped it, again and again.

There was nothing there.

She jerked her eyes back. The hairpin turn hurtled at her. On instinct, she kept jamming on the pedal. It was supposed to work. She turned the wheel wildly. The big car shuddered as it tried to negotiate the turn. The two rear wheels slipped off the pavement, spinning in space. With the front wheel drive, the front two tires managed enough traction to catch. The car veered around the curve and headed down the next straight incline. The heavy vehicle rolled faster again as gravity pulled it down the hill.

Amanda's mind reeled. What was she supposed to do?

Praise

Advance Praise for Randy Overbeck's *Cruel Lessons*

"A thrilling murder mystery…with an immersive plot, steady pace and stellar character development…one of the best mysteries of 2023." ★★★★★—ReaderViews

"Brilliant from start to finish…Impressive storytelling left me with a racing heart and shivers. One of the best thrillers I've ever read." ★★★★★+++—N.N. Light's Bookheaven

"Masterfully written…Each new revelation adds to the suspense and keeps the reader on edge, eagerly anticipating what further secrets the story holds…A gripping crime thriller and amateur sleuth mystery."—Literary Titan

Praise for Randy Overbeck's *The Haunted Shores Mysteries*

"A tale to be savored in a darkened room, with an eye to all the possibilities lurking just out of sight."—William Kent Krueger, NY Times bestselling author of Fox Creek

"A rollercoaster of a mystery, hurtling up and down hills and sharp corners until the very end, when the reader is left slightly breathless, waiting for their hearts to beat back to a normal rhythm." ★★★★★—ReadersView. Silver Award—Mystery of the Year

"Masterly spooky adventure …an accomplished work of haunting mystery fiction that fans of the genre won't want to miss out on. Highly Recommend." ★★★★★—ReadersFavorite.com

"An absolutely chilling ghost story wrapped around an even scarier piece of history—or perhaps the other way around. Recommended. BEST BOOK" ★★★★★—Chanticleer Reviews and Media

"Timely and original, this contemporary ghost story is genuinely entertaining …a terrific one-sitting read." ~Hank Phillippi Ryan, USA Bestselling and Award-Winning Author of *The House Guest*

"Overbeck intrigues the reader with a tantalizing mystery, cleverly drawn characters, haunting paranormal activity, and a great story steeped in contemporary social issues and interests."—Recommended Reads

"Overall, a fascinating mystery and I was pulled in with trying to solve it."—Musings from an Addicted Reader

"A suspenseful paranormal novel with compelling characters and an enigmatic mystery that drives the story to a riveting conclusion." ★★★★★—Literary Titan, Gold Award

"A thrilling whodunit with a supernatural edge. Delightful and engrossing."—Futures Mostly Mystery Magazine

"A mesmerizing story which consumes the reader from

the very first page…Overbeck is a fantastic storyteller…perfect for those readers looking for a mystery that will keep them on the edge of their seats and up until the wee hours!" ★★★★★ "Crown of Excellence" award—InD'tale Magazine

"The plot is so engrossing it had me hooked from the very first page." ★★★★★—Ioanna's Reviews, Greece

"A definite purchase for lovers of mysteries. This is at times light and fun, and other times, dark and disturbing. But it has a satisfying ending. Recommended."—Sparkling Book Reviews

"A ghost story with a twist, *Scarlet at Crystal River* is a bestseller in the making. Brilliant descriptive narration sucks the reader in and doesn't let go until the end of the story. If you're looking for a spine-tingling mystery, Highly recommend!" 5+ Stars—N N Light Bookheaven

Cruel Lessons

by

Randy Overbeck

Cruel Lessons

COPYRIGHT © 2023 by Randy Overbeck

Cover Art by *The Wild Rose Press, Inc.*

The Wild Rose Press, Inc.
PO Box 708
Adams Basin, NY 14410-0708
Visit us at www.thewildrosepress.com

Publishing History
First Edition, 2023
Trade Paperback ISBN 978-1-5092-5213-8
Digital ISBN 978-1-5092-5214-5

Published in the United States of America

Acknowledgments

This novel has a particularly long history. The earliest draft of Cruel Lessons was written in 1994, though it took numerous rewrites, revisions and reimaginings to arrive at this finished product. As such, over almost three decades, there are many friends, colleagues and family who never gave up on the narrative and who encouraged me to give it life. The first of those is, of course, my wife Cathy and my extended family. From the beginning, colleagues and friends in the teaching profession have been expressed their belief in me as a storyteller and their faith over the years has inspired my work on this mystery of deaths in a school district.

I want to offer special thanks to my two very talented editors, Jaden Terrell and Dianne Rich, who helped make this story the very best it can be. I also owe a special debt to a tremendous group of beta-readers who read the manuscript as it evolved and provided me with important feedback. Perhaps, most critical to making the story come alive was the work of my writers' group, talented authors and poets themselves who unselfishly spent hours helping me make A Cruel Lessons as engaging as possible. Other specialists, from mechanics to policemen to drug experts, helped guide my research for this narrative to make the story as realistic as possible and I'm grateful to them as well.

I believe all of this demonstrates that writing is definitely not a solitary activity. Without the support, encouragement and expertise of the individuals above, A Cruel Lesson would not be the gripping mystery you will read in the following pages. In fact, it probably wouldn't exist at all.

Chapter 1

October, 1995
12:20 a.m.

"You guys ready for the wildest ride of your life?" James Clayton whispered, his breath making small white puffs in the cool night air.

James and his buddies, Chad and Robert, stood outside the Boys Cabin No. 2, the three figures little more than silhouettes in the dim porch lamp. Bouncing on their feet, they hunched around the corner, just out of sight from the door of the cabin.

James flexed his abs like he'd watched his brother do, stretching his white tee shirt with the words "JUST SAY NO" across his chest. How perfect was it the school had given these out just last week? Holding a clear plastic bag, he dangled it in the faint light. The other two boys leaned closer, trying to peer as James swayed it back and forth in a slow arc like he saw a hypnotist do on TV. The two guys looked like they were drooling. James grinned. Pulling his other hand from his pocket, he brandished a set of car keys with the Chevy logo.

He said, "First, we're going—"

"What are you guys up to?" squealed another voice at the cabin door.

James jerked around to see Justin Waycross, little,

puny, nosy Justin, standing in the doorway, gawking at them. Just what he needed, some runt screwing up his big plans.

He muttered, "Nothin'. We're ain't doing nothing," and stomped toward the other kid.

Justin flinched but then his eyes went wide. "Hey, what are you doing with my dad's keys?"

"I said nothin'. Now get over here and shut up." James took three quick strides and, grabbing Justin by the arm, dragged him over to where the other two boys huddled in the corner of the rustic cabin.

James was thirteen, two years older than the other kids in his class, having failed second grade and then held back another year. An inch or two taller than the others, he'd started to sprout a few bristles above his top lip. Couldn't call it a mustache, not even enough to shave yet, but it was something. He had cold blue eyes, which he inherited from his father—one of the few reminders of a man who left him, his brother, and his mom years ago. James had learned how to use those cobalt eyes for a hard, angry stare when needed, like now.

Justin cowered then seemed to recover. He nodded toward the cabin behind them. "We're supposed to stay in the sack until six. Nobody outside. Those are the school rules." His glance darted from one boy to the other. "You guys are going to screw up science camp."

In a low squeal, James mimicked, "You guys are going to screw up science camp."

Robert Hayes, James' number two, pointed a pudgy finger at Justin. "What are we going to do now? I mean with the narc here?" He bumped his considerable bulk into Justin.

The intruder squealed, "Hey."

James hissed, "Shut up. Why don't just crawl back into your bunk and go nighty-night before I beat the crap out of you."

He watched fear ignite in the boy's eyes, but the kid said, "You do and I'll scream. Then my dad and everybody will be out here."

Chad Hayes, the third member of the trio, spoke up, his voice a bit squeaky. "Wait a minute. Hey, James, how about we let the kid in on this one?" Chad was smaller, about the same size as Justin. He moved next to the newcomer, putting a hand on Justin's shoulder. "You want to hang with us? If we let you come along, you won't go squealing to your daddy, will you?"

"What *are* you guys up to?" Justin's gaze went to the keys James still held. "And what are you doing with my dad's car keys?"

The original trio had snuck out of their cabin a few minutes earlier, right under the nose of the chaperone, Mr. Waycross, Justin's dad, who snored loudly in his bunk. Then, as part of his brilliant scheme, James had lifted the keys to Waycross' cool car, sliding them out of the pocket of the man's pants hanging on the peg. Pretty slick. The car, a Camaro Z-28, sat parked just beyond the cabin, its metallic black paint gleaming in the moonlight. James planned to *borrow* the car.

He said, "We're just going for a little ride. No harm. No foul. We'll have it back before anyone knows it's gone." He watched Justin's face and thought he saw an opening. He moved closer and wrapped an arm around him. Squeezed once. "I'll tell you what. I'll let you join our little group if…if you promise to keep your mouth shut." He flashed a smile, the one that got his way—at least most of the time.

He studied Justin's features as thoughts seem to race across them—first doubt, then hesitation, then curiosity.

"W-w-what are you going to do?" Justin stammered.

"Like I said, we're just going for a little ride and have a little fun." Giving Justin another squeeze, James eyed him up and down. "That is, unless you're too scared."

Justin strutted his shoulders. "I ain't scared."

"Okay, then." James nodded at the three boys and pointed to the car, gleaming in the night light. "Let's take this baby for a little ride."

The four of them made their way down the long gravel sidewalk to the small parking lot, their feet making crunching sounds on the stones. When they got to the Z-28, Robert claimed the shotgun seat and Justin and Chad climbed into the back.

"Have you ever driven a car?" Chad asked in a voice with equal measures of fear and excitement, as James slid behind the wheel.

"Sure," James said, as he stretched his legs to reach the pedals. He was pissed he still hadn't grown like his older brother but tried to hide it. "I've driven my mom's old car plenty." He had too—at least around the driveway.

"This is gonna be great," Robert said from the front seat, his big gut shaking with laughter.

"Fuckin' A," Chad added.

James threw the car in reverse, spinning the steering wheel, and almost backed into a post. He jammed on the brake, just short of the white and gold painted marker. Turning the vehicle, he pulled it out of the parking area and drove it a little to get the feel, playing with the steering wheel, his fingers exploring the texture of the smooth plastic. He managed to get it across the gravel drive and onto the county road.

The heavy suspension of the muscle car made maneuvering tricky, and James kept swerving, having to overcorrect to keep the car on the asphalt. The narrow two-lane road was blacktopped, the surface built up with steep gullies on either side leading into the black woods beyond, skeletons of trees jutting out of the ground. When the headlights lit up another parking area off to the right, he pulled over. As the Z-28 rolled to a stop, James eased out the plastic package and held it up to the dome light. Grinning, he turned toward the others. "Magic time."

"What's that?" Justin asked, the squeal in his voice betraying his fear.

James' grin widened. "*Some of us* are goin' to take another ride."

Chad asked, "So, how does it work?"

"These here"—James pointed to the package—"are Zip Tattoos and my brother says these things are to die for."

The other three boys strained to get a good look. Robert edged across the front bucket seat, the fabric of his wide shorts making swishing sounds on the tacky vinyl. From the back, the other two stretched forward, moving their faces close to the light.

Justin asked, "What'll they do?"

James slid back the sleeve of his tee, extracted one, peeled off the backing, and applied it to a spot high on the exposed arm. He held his work up the interior light. "That oughta work." He flashed his smile again. He knew it would take a few minutes for him to feel the juice. "Like I said, these just give you another great ride. Hey, but you don't have to…if you're scared. No one's makin' you."

"I'm in," Chad said. Leaning over the front seat, he brushed his errant black hair out of his eyes and pulled up the sleeve of his tee shirt, offering a bare arm.

Taking the next paper off the pile, James held it between his two fingers and peeled off the protective backing. He gripped Chad's arm and applied the patch to the skin about halfway between the shoulder and elbow. Done, he held the kid's arm up to the bare light bulb and, satisfied, let go.

"I don't feel nothin'," Chad said.

"You gotta wait a while," James said. "My brother's been on this ride and said it takes a bit before it hits you. Okay, who's next?"

"I'm game," said Robert.

With his horned-rim glasses and chunky body, he was the dorkiest of the bunch but James knew better. Robert was always game. Leaning across, Robert extended an exposed arm. James repeated the process and soon had another tattoo applied. Robert drew his arm back, examined the patch, and then pushed his glasses up his nose again.

"Okay, Justin, decision time." James eyed the small figure in the back seat, clutching the door handle.

Justin appeared to be second guessing his decision. He had blond hair and a baby face, which matched his disposition. "W-w-what do those things do?" he stammered.

James grinned and patted the plastic wrapper. "These are going to give you the wildest ride you've even been on."

James studied Justin's face in the dim light and read fear. "If you don't want to, that's okay. If you're too chicken to try, we'll understand, won't we, guys?" James' gaze went to Robert, then Chad, then back at Justin.

At the mention of the word "chicken," both Robert and Chad began making loud clucking sounds.

Justin's glance darted from Chad, next to him in the back seat, to Robert up front, and then to James. No one said anything but the clucking sounds from the two boys continued. James thought Justin was going to start crying…or bolt out the door.

Instead, the puny little guy let go of the door handle and thrust a skinny arm across the seat back. "Here."

James did the honors.

Here they were, four guys from some podunk little town, waiting for the magic juice to hit them. For a moment, James imagined he could sense it, the drug flooding into his bloodstream. He swore he could feel his heart beat faster, stronger. And, if his brother was right, this was some powerful shit and would flow to his brain, setting off neurons or synapses or whatever they were called. He could hardly wait. For now, he sat back in anticipation, a smirk on his face.

For a few moments, the entire car was quiet. The night air was cool and with two of the car windows halfway down, the slight chill slithered into the interior, but no one noticed. The only sound, beyond those of insects and animals, came from the tense breathing of the four boys.

In the silence, James asked, "Have you guys ever tried a little acid?"

In response, the other three boys shifted in their spots and Chad said, "Well—"

James laughed. "I didn't think so. I have and it's something else. These things"—he pointed to the patch on his arm—"ain't LSD. Jack says they're some new concoction and a helluva lot wilder. You just got to wait a bit to let it hit you."

Another longer silence descended on the car, except for the crickets and the frogs. Inside the car, each of the four boys shifted in their spots, trying to find a more comfortable position, their clothing making quiet whispers against the vinyl.

James stared through the windshield and watched a blanket of fog curl across the pavement and flow into the woods, graying the trees and shrubs, though it could have been his imagination—or the drugs. The aromas of the woods surrounded them, dead leaves and trees, soil and mulch, seeped through the open windows.

Minutes ticked by, the passing of time marked by the staccato of loud breathing inside the car. James could sense the other boys' impatience growing. Finally, Chad said, "I don't feel nothing. How long we supposed to wait?"

"Give it a little more time," James said.

Robert said, "Well, if we gotta wait, we might as well do a little road trip."

"Road trip. Sounds good to me," added Chad. "Better than sitting still."

"Sure, why not?" said James. "Let's do what we came to science camp to do. Let's go explore Cape

Haven…on the road." He slid around in his seat and thought he felt the first twinge but wasn't sure.

He reached down for the key ring. As he turned his head and stared at the ignition, the ring of keys seemed to pulse in and out, receding every time he tried to reach for them. He tried three times. Each time his fingers came away empty, grasping only air. For some reason he found his failures hilarious and hooted again and again, his whole body convulsing in spasms of laughter.

"What's so funny?" Robert asked from across the front seat.

"Nothing," snickered James. "I just can't seem to catch the keys." He pointed at the ignition and laughed again.

Robert stared at the keys and started hooting too. In the back seat, Justin and Chad slid forward to see what was going on. James turned and couldn't control himself, laughing at them too. After a few seconds, first Chad and then Justin joined in and soon, all four were giggling uncontrollably.

James took a deep breath and, on the fourth try, he grabbed the dangling keys and turned the ignition, the huge engine roaring to life. All four boys made imitative engine sounds, chortling again at their own noises. James backed around on the gravel of the parking area, the stones making loud crunching sounds in the night. Turning to focus his eyes on the highway ahead, he saw no signs of any traffic.

He steered the muscle car onto the asphalt and down the road, the lumbering weight of the vehicle bearing down upon the blacktop. Camp Haven stuck out in the country. With no other lights on the road, the only illumination came from the Camaro's headlights. James drove on, feeling exhilarated as he mashed down the accelerator. The powerful Z-28 engine responded with a surge.

"Yeah!" James squealed.

The other three joined in with their, "Vroom, vroom, vroom."

"Shut up, you dumbass and listen," barked James as he turned and cranked his window all the way down. The cool night air oozed into the car along with the nocturnal sounds of the forest. "Can't you hear that?" The others leaned toward him. "Hey do-da-do-da-ach-ooh." James crooned in an incoherent babble, singing more loudly than he ever did in music class, as the sounds of crickets and frogs were transformed into mismatched notes in his head.

From the back seat, Chad called, "Hey, we're supposed to 'get back to nature' right?" He made air quotes. "I want some fresh air, so I can drink in this nature-loving shit." He rolled his window down all the way and pulled himself up to the edge of the frame. He sat, his torso out the window. "God, this is beautiful, James, just beautiful. Hey, Justin, get your scrawny ass up here. The weather's fine."

Justin hesitated at first, then followed Chad's lead. He rolled his window down and perched his butt on the other frame, his hands pounding the roof of the car. He laughed and soon all four boys were chortling again, uncontrollably. As James moved the car around a wide turn, both boys in the back had to hold on as the car swayed and Justin yelled, "Whoa, boy!" They all giggled again.

As they came out of the next turn, some lights

shone at them from the far end of the straight stretch of highway, another pair of headlights. As the lights grew brighter, they struck James' now-fractured sense of sight. To him, the lights glowed and became kaleidoscopic beacons. "Shit, will you look at that?" he yelled to the others.

"What?" Robert squealed and turned to see the vision. "Oh, shit, yeah."

In the driver's seat, James stared ahead, mesmerized by the light. Fixated on the hallucination, he let go of the steering wheel, muttering, "Ain't that fuckin' cool?"

As he relaxed his grip on the wheel, the Camaro began to veer to the right, pulled by the unaligned front right side. So captivated by the drug-induced image, James didn't notice as the wheels on that side bumped off the pavement onto the gravel of the narrow shoulder. Both tires on the passenger side bit into the loose stones on the incline, pulling the car farther to the right. Intent only on the vision, James took his foot off the accelerator, but the muscle car barely slowed. Propelled by the weight of the heavy frame, the sleek, black Camaro rolled on. The front right tire hit a rock in the slope and the suspension bounced over it. The swerve angled the Z-28 off the road and down the shoulder, heading for the woods.

There was still time, but James, steering wheel before him, was caught up in his own wonder world. The vehicle moved on its own, an evil predator, bouncing over the edge of the roadway into the woods.

Chapter 2

Stacy Thompson sat on the hard wooden bench, both hands grasping the coffee mug. The first to arrive at the teacher table, she stared out the tall lodge windows and watched the rising sun ignite the brilliant hues of the leaves, the forest beyond exploding in reds, yellows, and oranges. She counted her blessings for being here at camp with the kids on this glorious autumn morning…rather than stuck teaching inside the walls of her classroom.

When she got the urgent call yesterday, Stacy had only a few minutes to wrap things up at school, jump in the car and drive up here, all to make sure the students were covered. Thank heaven she'd had everything packed. She even got here in time to take an afternoon hike with her kids, managing to squeeze in a little teaching about native insects. Then, along with her twenty kids, she navigated the ropes course, though she almost fell off near the end.

Last night she bunked with the girls in Cabin No. 3. While the girls showered and got ready for bed, a few students had "secrets" they needed to share with Mrs. Thompson in the tiny walled-off sleeping area—secrets which turned out to be normal pre-teen stuff, like James Clayton had something sneaky planned. Like what else is new? At ten, lights out, once the girls stopped their chattering, she'd collapsed into a deep sleep.

A few minutes ago, the rising sun had peeked through the small window over her bed, its rays brushing her face. After rousing the girls in her cabin, she threw on some sweats, dragged a brush through her hair, took the path to the lodge and grabbed some coffee. Now, alone for a few precious moments, she immersed herself in this incredible view.

She counted backward. This was her sixth year serving as one of the school chaperones for the Fifth Grade Science Camp. While other teachers did everything they could to get out of coming up here for an overnight with the kids, she treasured these days, when she could get some down time with her kids.

"Oh, there you are," called a raspy voice from the doorway.

Her friend and teaching partner, Dawn Hatcher stomped her feet and stepped inside onto the wooden floor. A few students, still with sleep in their eyes, wandered in behind Dawn and shuffled over to the serving line. Stacy noticed the ones filing in were only girls and wondered where the boys were. They had fifteen minutes until chow time. Usually the boys were first in line, sometimes shoving their way to get to the front. The smells from the cooking breakfast floated across the large space—the sweet scent of syrup and the aroma of crispy bacon—making her stomach rumble.

Dawn hustled to the coffee station, filled her mug, then returned and plopped next to Stacy on the teacher bench, a bit aways from the kids' tables. This morning, Dawn wore an oversized and wrinkled Notre Dame sweatshirt, baggy blue jeans, and a strained expression. Her shoulder-length brown hair had been brushed back off her face and she held a mug that read, *The three best reasons for becoming a teacher—June, July, and August.* She took a long drink and pronounced, "That's better."

Stacy pointed to Dawn's mug. "You always bring your own?"

Dawn used her mug to indicate Stacy's chipped cup. "Can't be too careful. Never know where those have been." She gave a throaty laugh. "I heard from the kids you came up yesterday, but I didn't see you. When did you get in?"

"I wasn't planning to come until the night shift," Stacy answered, "but Rachel called, said she was sick and had to go home. So I headed up here early, right after school."

Dawn whined, *"Rachel Bedinghaus.* Every time it's her turn to chaperone a group of our kids for science camp, she gets *sick.* I think she didn't want to deal with the class we brought up here this time, that's all." She took another sip and shrugged. "Well, my stint here is almost up, so I guess these hellions are all yours tonight."

Stacy glanced across at her friend. "Give them a break. They're just eleven-year-olds with a lot of baggage. You know how many of them come from broken homes? Not easy for them, I can tell you."

"Still," Dawn objected. "Just two names. *James Clayton* and *Chad Thorton.*"

The head camp counselor, Dan, a twenty-five-year-old with red hair and freckles, stepped to the front of the lodge and cleared his throat. He did his welcome piece and reviewed the activities for the day. While he talked, Stacy zoned out, thinking about the kids again, her kids.

Sometimes out here, kids let their guard down and opened up and she found ways to reach them, all while hiking through the woods, doing some nature observations or making s'mores. The past few years, she found if she could spend some down time with them here, outside the structure of the classroom— talking, joking, and learning alongside them—she'd have a chance to reach a few more.

Okay, she'd been teaching long enough to realize it wasn't that simple. She'd yet to discover any magic formula for working with troubled kids. "Problem" kids were as different as everyone else, each with his, or her, own set of difficulties. But Stacy was never satisfied until she tried everything she could think of to get through to them.

At least, that's what she told herself.

Every time she looked into one of the forlorn faces of her students staring back with that curious combination of cockiness and pleading, she imagined she could see Brent looking back. *Her* Brent. He'd be not much older than these kids and she couldn't stop herself from wondering what he looked like now. The only reminder she had of him was a small, faded Polaroid, its edges wrinkled, taken right after he was born. She could still remember, as she held him in the delivery room years ago, the snap of the shutter and the whir of the gear as the photo emerged from the slot. Back then, she should've taken more pictures and held onto more memories, but she been too stupid to understand how precious those times were. She'd had *other* priorities—really lousy priorities then. Now, in each mischievous grin, in each pair of haunting eyes, in each neglected face, she saw her past staring back at her. She saw one more chance to set things right, to atone for prior sins.

Who was she kidding? Redemption was never that easy.

"Where are the boys?" Head Counselor Dan asked, coming over to the table.

Stacy shot a look at the lodge clock, 8:03, and then exchanged glances with Dawn. Sliding her legs out from underneath the picnic table bench, she said, "I'll go check and see what's keeping them. Probably overslept. They have a parent chaperoning."

When she opened the door, she almost ran into a tall man with disheveled black hair, a two-day stubble, and bloodshot eyes, which looked left and right. The man stepped through the doorway, several boys squeezing past. Stacy had to step aside as the boys made a beeline for the food.

The man asked, "Have you seen my son, Justin? Justin Waycross?"

Stacy said, "No, we hadn't seen any of the boys until now." She pointed to the stream of boys filing through the door opening. "We wondered what was keep—"

"He wasn't in his bed," Waycross cut her off. "I went in this morning to get everyone up and going and saw his bunk was empty. I thought maybe he got up early to get a jump on breakfast. You sure you ain't seen him?"

Dawn now stood next to Stacy. "I know Justin." She looked into the man's eyes. "He's a good kid. I'm sure he's around here someplace."

"I looked all over." He shook his head. "I don't get

it. I made sure they were all down for the night, like I's supposed to. I asked the kids and they ain't seen him either." His gaze searched the spacious lodge, as if he could locate his son among the kids now mulling around the chow line or at the tables.

Stacy reached a hand to his arm. "Could he be off doing an early morning hike?"

Waycross shook his head harder. "That ain't Justin. He's not the nature type." He cleared his throat. "Three other kids didn't answer roll call either." He scanned the sheet he was holding. "James Clayton, Robert Hayes and, uh…Chad Thorton. You seen them?"

Stacy felt her stomach lurch.

Chapter 3

As he sipped his tea, Ken Parks studied his wife across the table. Amanda had her nose buried in the newspaper, a very pretty nose on a quite a lovely face, with just a touch of makeup this morning.

"Our timing's perfect, you know that?" she said, her blue-green eyes glancing over the top of the paper. "Mullins has a special on kitchen cabinets. And with the sale I made last week, we can use my commission to pay for the upgrade."

As she folded the paper out of the way, Ken served the omelet along with two slices of bacon he'd prepared. Bringing the pan back to the stove, he pointed to the lighter wood cabinets that came with the house several years ago. "I think they still look okay, but if you want to get new ones, that's fine with me."

Amanda took a small bite and smiled, nodding at the eggs. "Really good." Setting down her fork, she made an expansive gesture with both her hands. "Can't you see it? The new cherry cabinets will give the kitchen a whole new look."

Ken shrugged. "If that's—"

The phone on the wall rang, interrupting him. Ken walked to the wall, finishing, "What you'd like, it's fine with me." He grabbed up the receiver. "Parks."

"Mr. Parks? Ken? This is Stacy Thompson…from Foster," said a shaky voice.

He could hear the woman take a breath and then she started in, her words tumbling out. "Ken, I'm out here at Camp Haven. I'm one of the school chaperones. Something's happened…I think. Four of the boys have gone missing."

His stomach tightened, considering several options, some bad, others not so. He asked, "What do you mean *missing*?"

"Nobody's sure. When Mr. Waycross—he's the parent chaperone with the boys—when he did roll call this morning, four of them weren't in their bunks. The camp counselors and Dawn are out looking for the boys, but so far no luck." She took a breath, and added, "Our instructions were to notify you if there were any problems."

Ken was nodding, even though Stacy couldn't see him. "All right. I'll be out there as soon as I can. Don't worry. We'll find the kids." He glanced at his watch. "I'll be there in about twenty minutes, say, nine o'clock or so."

Hanging up the phone, he returned to the table. "Four fifth graders from Foster Middle have gone missing at the science camp. Didn't show up for roll call." He stuffed down a few bites of eggs.

"Missed roll call?" Amanda frowned. "Jeez. You know how kids are. They probably wandered into the woods and fell asleep. They'll probably find them in some secret hideaway or someplace." She sat back in her chair and flipped one hand at him. "Can't the camp staff handle it?"

He watched her eyes narrow over the top of the mug. He'd seen that look before and knew Amanda resented that he felt his first responsibility was to the students. They'd had this *discussion* more than a few times. He tried, "Maybe, but they're our kids."

She pointed the mug at him. "Yeah, well, why does the *curriculum* guy have to handle missing kids?"

Stepping over to the coat closet, he pulled out his brown blazer. "Walters is on vacation this week, remember?"

Amanda set her mug down on the table a little hard. "But you took a half day off so we could go to Mullins and pick out the cabinets together."

Ken gave his wife a quick peck on the cheek. "Maybe you're right and we'll find the boys quickly and I'll be back in time to do some shopping with you." He stepped through the door to the garage and hit the button for the opener. He called back, "I'll do the best I can."

She mumbled something but he couldn't hear it over the grinding of the springs on the heavy garage door. He'd been married long enough to guess what Amanda said. He'd have to smooth this over when he got back. Maybe he'd get her new countertops as well.

Twenty-five minutes later, he turned his Taurus onto the gravel driveway to the camp. He had to slow the car on the uneven surface and read the carved wooden sign as he passed, CAMP HAVEN: ENVIRONMENTAL CAMP FOR YOUTH. His gaze roaming the area, he didn't see anyone yet, on foot or in a car, so he kept rolling as fast as he dared on the roadway. A few minutes later, he caught sight of the large lodge ahead and saw a figure pacing out front. As he got closer, he recognized Stacy Thompson, a frantic look on her face.

By the time he'd rolled to a stop and had his door

open, Stacy came up beside him. "Thank God you're here."

"No news yet?"

"They haven't found any sign of the boys." She shook her head. "But we may have another problem."

"What?"

"Mr. Waycross's car is also missing." She took a quick breath. "In all the confusion when the boys didn't show up, he asked Dawn and me if we'd seen them. When he went back to the cabin and to take another look, he noticed his car was gone. The parking lot is a little ways away from the cabins and he didn't noticed it missing at first."

"So they think the boys *took* his car and went joyriding." Ken frowned. "You think one of these kids would try to drive a car?"

Stacy stared at Ken. "One of the boys is James Clayton."

"Oh, damn." He pointed to the passenger door. "Well, get in and we'll go looking."

As she hurried around the front of the car, she said, "Dawn is out driving, and Mr. Waycross and two counselors are doing a walking search. Dawn called Bart and he's driving the cruiser, checking the roads too."

Ken felt a little better—and a little more panicked—to know his friend and DARE officer, Bart Callahan, was joining the search. Stacy slid inside and he did the same, both belting in.

She held up a black object. "The counselors passed these out. I knew you needed one so you'd be in the loop." She pushed the button on the unit. "Ken just got here." She glanced over at him and added, "Over."

Bart's voice crackled over the walkie-talkie. "Have him drive 128 west. I'm heading east now, and Dawn took the north fork. Radio back if you see anything. Over."

Ken drove the car around the circle driveway and took the gravel roadway back to the county road. He did a quick check and put the rising sun behind them and headed west. Moving slowly on the blacktopped road, he searched left, while Stacy kept watch on the right. A tense silence invaded the car. Ken drove slowly to give them time to search the copses of trees that bordered each side of the road. The only sound came from the hiss of the tires on the blacktop.

"Ken, you don't think—"

"I don't know what to think." He took his eyes from the side and met hers. "I hope and pray—"

"Attention all searchers, this is Callahan," Bart's official police voice snapped through the walkie-talkie. "Return to the lodge."

"Did you find them? Are they okay?" Dawn asked over the frequency, her voice tight.

"All searchers return to the lodge…immediately," Bart commanded.

Staring ahead for a place to turn around on the narrow two-lane highway, Ken accelerated and found a rutted driveway about a half mile down. Performing the tight maneuver, his gaze swept both ways on the highway, but it was hardly necessary. No vehicles either way.

Stacy whispered, "Does that mean—"

He shook his head. "Let's not get ahead of ourselves."

A bleat erupted from beneath the console, making

Ken and Stacy both jump. Then he remembered the new car phone he'd purchased last week. His boss wanted him to get one so he could be reached anywhere in the district. It'd only rung once before, and it took Ken a second to realize what it was. Keeping an eye on the asphalt road—still no one coming either way—he reached down and grabbed the handset off the cradle. "Parks."

"Mr. Parks, this is Joyce, the dispatcher. I just heard from Bart, I mean, Officer Callahan. He asked me to relay a message to you."

"Okay."

"Officer Callahan said he wants you to drive east on 128, about two miles past the lodge."

Ken nodded and said, "I'm on my way."

The dispatcher added, "Oh, and Mr. Parks, he said to ask you not to tell anyone else. Bart's afraid they'll just trample the scene. The EMT's have been called and they're on the way, but he said there is no need for the emergency team to hurry."

Ken caught her inference. "Thanks, Joyce. I'm on my way."

He hung up the phone and saw the questions in Stacy's face. He couldn't figure out what to say, so he just said, "It's really bad."

Stacy started crying, tears edging down both sides of her face, shaking her head back and forth. "No. No. No."

The miles seemed to drag by, even though Ken hurried as best he could on the curvy highway. A half mile out, he saw Bart's cruiser parked on the side of the road, emergency lights flashing. Ken pulled behind and got out.

He turned to Stacy. "You might want to stay here." He strode over to where Bart was placing flares on the road surface. "Where?" Ken asked.

The cop turned and pointed past the cruiser and Ken gazed in that direction. He stepped up alongside the police car. Staring into the woods, he saw it, about a hundred yards ahead down the ravine. The tail end of the black car stuck out of a thicket of trees. Almost without willing it, his mind replayed the horrific scene. The car, out of control, left the road and smashed through growth down the slope, small trees snapped off and wild grasses crushed. Those kids had to be terrified.

His heart stopped for a bit and his throat went dry. He struggled to get the words out. "You already went down there…and checked? All four are there?"

Bart nodded. "Yep. It's way too late for them."

God, only eleven years old. How can their lives be gone, just like that? He stared, not wanting to believe, and heard Stacy come up behind him. As he turned, his face must have shown it all because she broke down weeping. Her gaze went from him to the wrecked car and back to him. "No…it can't be. I just saw them yesterday."

Ken wrapped his arms around her, holding her and letting her cry, her tears wetting the shoulder of his jacket. He felt the sobbing wrack her frail body and he fought to keep his own tears from leaking out.

"Was this…our fault?" she managed between sobs.

"No," he said, patting her shoulder, doing his best to assure her, although her words provoked his own question—Whose fault was it?

After the worst passed, Stacy settled down and he led her back to his car, helping her collapse into the passenger seat. He reached past her and pulled out tissues from the console and handed them to her. Her response was understandable and—though he tried to be calm—it only ratcheted up his anxiety. His mind, trying to prepare himself, ran through several scenarios, all of them ugly. His next thought was that he and Bart would have to tell the grieving families. He wasn't sure he'd be able to hold it together to do that. Sometimes he hated this job.

When he closed the door, Bart came up alongside him and said, "Come on. I'll take you down. Before everyone gets here, there's something I want you to see."

Together they stepped off the curb onto the gravel shoulder and started down the slope. It was slow going, having to maneuver around broken stumps of trees and large rocks so as not to trip.

Without looking back, Bart said, "I got to warn you. This is really bad." He led the way through the trampled growth and cracked tree limbs, Ken careful to follow in his footsteps. Halfway down the hill, Bart stopped, turned, and said, "I mean *really* bad but you need to see this." He turned back and headed the rest of the way down, Ken right behind him.

As soon as they were close enough to see the bodies, Ken started breathing through his mouth. Oh, God. It was worse than he thought. Two kids had been thrown from the car, their bodies ending up ten yards away on either side of the car, like obscene markers. They lay crumpled in the weeds, their arms and legs at contorted angles. He took two more steps, peering. Another body, some overweight kid, was stuck halfway through the windshield, congealed blood smearing down the glass. A fourth kid sat behind the steering wheel, the engine pushed back on him.

Him, Ken recognized. James Clayton.

He couldn't handle it. He ran into the weeds, away from the scene. He leaned over and retched, glad he hadn't eaten more earlier. After the spasm passed, he took out a handkerchief and wiped his mouth, the ugly taste still clinging to the inside of his throat.

His friend asked, his voice kind, "You going to be okay?"

Ken found it hard to talk so he nodded.

Bart walked over to the closest body, one of the boys thrown from the car, now face down on the grass. He pointed to something on the boy's bare arm, a smeared image of reds and yellows. "See that?"

"What is it?" Ken croaked.

"One of those new drug tattoos. And it looks like each boy is sporting one."

Breathing through his mouth again, Ken peered a little closer, still being careful not to touch anything. Hell, just like the ones Bart had warned them about at the administrative meeting last month.

Chapter 4

"The Lord is my shepherd. I shall not want. He maketh me to lie down in green pastures; he leadeth me beside still waters." The resonant voice chanted above the crowd in a stirring baritone, but Ken Parks was not sure many were listening.

To Ken's amazement, life in the town, his town, had turned ugly seemingly overnight, even transforming the weather into something foul. A chilling frost and a frigid wind had replaced the almost balmy, Indian summer weather earlier in the week.

He stared out at the crowd. Bundled in bulky coats, the mourners stood motionless, numb to the stinging autumn wind, the cemetery crowded. From the gravesites, throngs of people stretched out in all directions as far as he could see, long lines of disconsolate grievers snaking around markers and tombstones all the way back to the black-topped lanes. Everyone in town appeared to be here—children, parents, teachers, shop owners, ministers, teens. The deaths of the four boys were so horrific, so traumatic, most of the small town had the same reaction—shock and disbelief.

According to the locals he'd spoken with, when news seeped down from the community hospital in Shelby early Wednesday morning, word of the deaths spread like some horrible plague, the tragedy shared from shop to shop, street corner to street corner. In the barbershops, no one talked about the foibles of the football coach. In the salons, few gossiped about who was cheating on whom. In all the town businesses, the words varied but the sentiment was the same—how could this happen here? Nothing like this had ever occurred in the small town before.

The small cemetery had not been designed for this. The stream of cars stretched so long they had to be double-parked on the narrow lanes. Halfway through the procession, the funeral director had run out of magnetic purple flags, but it didn't matter. There was little other traffic on the town roads. School had been canceled, businesses closed, and most matters in the small town were simply put on hold for the day.

Ken stood to the side of the mass of mourners, trying to listen to the minister's words, but too stunned by the shocking death of four of *his* kids to draw much solace. The families were so traumatized, they consented to have this shared service, perhaps hoping to draw comfort from each other and the town's embrace. Tightly clustered around the coffins, each boy's family huddled together, clinging to each other and the casket, trying desperately to hold on to their child for a few more precious minutes. As the minister mentioned the boys' names, two mothers crumpled like large rag dolls and collapsed beside the coffins.

Studying the distraught parents, Ken noticed the grief of the parents of the "bad kids" seemed just as raw and cruel as that of Mr. and Mrs. Waycross, whose son had never even been sent to principal's office. Ken wondered how Justin got sucked into the whole thing. He stared at the distraught faces of the Waycrosses.

That didn't matter to them. Justin was just as dead as Chad or James or Robert.

As he surveyed the mourners, some motion caught Ken's attention and he noticed a teenager leaning over one of the caskets, his face scowling. He recognized the kid, Jack Clayton, James' older brother. Ken had presided over two, no three suspension hearings for Jack Clayton. As he studied the lanky teen, he watched as shadows of emotions seem to play across Jack's face, what looked like grief, then anger, then guilt. Ken wondered about the relationship between the two siblings.

Standing behind the grieving parents were the school leaders, led by Dr. Mark Walters, the district superintendent, who'd interrupted his vacation and returned to Portsmouth. Walters stood tall, with handsome, chiseled features and a full head of dark, flowing hair. A powerfully-built youth, Walters had excelled as a star football and basketball player at both the high school in town and later at a private college in Pennsylvania. Even in his fifty-some years, he still carried that build, fit and strong. As always, he wore a starched white shirt, finely tailored black suit, conservative tie. Even with the chilling temperatures, he'd disdained a topcoat.

Next to him, in an impeccable, Italian-styled, charcoal suit and overcoat, stood Dr. Everett O'Brien, physician and school board president. He was almost as tall as Walters, though the physical similarity ended there. His physique of more than forty years still possessed the structure of the lean, lanky youth who had found his athletic niche on the track field. His body had filled out some since, but his face still carried a boyish look and charm. Behind designer, wire-framed glasses, steely-gray eyes peered out at the crowd. From time to time, he leaned over and whispered to the superintendent, who nodded solemnly.

As he stood there in the cold, Ken couldn't help but compare himself with the other school leaders. And he didn't measure up. He knew he projected an image less formal, less polished—his own topcoat slightly rumpled and his brown hair not gelled into perfect place. Unlike Walters and O'Brien who both wore looks of detached, formal grief, he couldn't keep from his face his own sense of deep, personal pain—red-rimmed eyes, lines on his cheeks furrowed from tears. He'd not gotten much sleep the last few days.

In his position, he'd met three of the dead boys more than once, much as he interacted with other students who strayed into trouble from time to time. He had to admit he didn't know any of them well, but these four were more than simply names to him. Knowing them was enough to make the deaths real, raw and painful.

Ken surveyed the rest of the crowd. He recognized the teachers, over a hundred all together, some huddled in small groups and others scattered among the students, parents, and townspeople. He watched a few teachers glance his way, meet his gaze, and then avert their eyes.

In his job, he'd come to know every staff member and had personally worked with most. Recognizing teaching is arduous and often stressful, Ken worked to project the image of a positive, optimistic leader, hoping to inspire the same. He tried to find the brighter side of school challenges, whether a new state testing requirement, an angry and demanding parent, or the newest dictate from the Board. Known as a "glass half full" kind of guy, he was proud of this reputation. But not today. The dark cloud of the tragedy hung heavy over him, resurrecting a depression he'd experienced years earlier and thought he'd buried.

The reverend finished his pastoral words, and anointed the coffins, the scent of incense drifting outward from the gravesite. The crowd stirred as the numbed mourners began their final pass by the caskets, which sat side by side. Later, each casket would be moved to a different family section of the small cemetery, but for now they were huddled together to give the small community the chance to grieve together.

Ken prepared to take up his position along with the rest of the school group. Off to his left, he noticed Stacy Thompson, the teacher who accompanied him to the site of the accident. Shuddering where she stood, tears dripped down her cheeks and dropped to the grass below. He glanced over and her green eyes, now red and swollen also, met his gaze.

As Ken watched the other middle school teachers throng together, Carla Michaels, their principal, stepped up and cut in front of him to fall in line behind the board members. Any other day, her move—scurrying to appear close to the district leaders—would've bothered him. But today, his grief and fear made him realize such issues were unimportant. Michaels shook and wept, mascara running in tiny blue rivers from the corners of her eyes, and erupted in small, repeated sobs. She kept muttering, "I just can't believe it. I just can't believe it. Those poor boys." As she stumbled past the caskets, Ken pondered her expression of grief. As far as he knew, Carla had never showed much of a connection with the boys, when alive.

Behind her, the teachers from Foster Middle filed by, with Stacy Thompson and Dawn Hatcher, two of the chaperones from the camp, joining their colleagues. Each stepped haltingly, seeming to wait their turn to take one last glimpse at death.

In his turn, Ken stepped up to the line of bereft parents, immeasurable sadness in their faces. Grasping the hands of each distraught mother and father, he stared into their eyes, nodded solemnly, and mumbled, "I'm so sorry for your loss." He realized his words were inadequate, too stiff—he had been there—but he could come up with nothing better. As he filed past the last closed coffin, a wave of anger at the four senseless deaths swept through him, intermingled with his own personal grief.

As he turned to take a final look at the coffins, his eyes blurred, tears dripping down his cheeks onto his lapels. Through his blurred vision, he saw—or thought he saw—not four coffins, but a single, silver casket, sitting alone above a freshly dug cavity, the pouring rain running off the sides of the metal. Ken knew it couldn't be and shook his head to shake the image, but it would not go. A shiver sliced through his body. The buried guilt of his past, somehow tethered to his gnawing fear about these new deaths, fought to overwhelm him. Light-headed, he staggered forward.

He knew he had to keep moving…or collapse.

Chapter 5

Amanda, dressed in a slim black outfit, emerged from the crowd and grasped his arm to steady him. "Are you okay? You look pale."

With his coat sleeve, he brushed the tears off his cheek. "I'll survive." He glanced back toward the gravesites. "That's more than they did."

Together, he and Amanda trudged away from the gravesites toward the line of cars. As they neared the sidewalk, they approached Walters and O'Brien, huddled together and talking quietly. Ken halted so he could exchange a few words with his boss and Amanda slowed and stopped beside him. Milling around the four of them, the other mourners took little notice and headed to their own cars.

Shooting a glance at Ken, O'Brien looked agitated. His gaze returned to the superintendent and he continued, "Look, Mark, I feel terrible about this. The deaths of those poor boys is the worst tragedy I can remember happening here. This must be impossibly hard on the parents…and the other kids." He shifted his weight from foot to foot. "The board members have received good comments on how the teachers have helped the students cope with this tragedy. The board appreciates your leadership on this."

His eyes darting quickly to both sides, O'Brien paused. His next words came out in a harsh whisper.

Ken, still a few feet away, had little trouble hearing. "Mark, what I want to know is, what is our liability here? I mean those boys did die on a school outing. Are these parents likely to sue us over this?"

Walters paused before answering, as if weighing his words. "Well, Dr. O'Brien, I don't know if we can answer that yet."

O'Brien shot Ken a brief look and uttered, "I don't need to tell you the Board doesn't like having our collective butts hanging out." He focused his gaze back on the superintendent. "Now, I want to be clear about this, perfectly clear. The Board wants you to do something to protect us and to do it quickly."

O'Brien buttoned one black button on his overcoat and strode toward his polished, silver Mercedes at the curb, where his wife and daughter waited for him.

Walters' eyes met Ken's and the superintendent shook his head, the corners of his mouth turning down. "Sometimes I hate this job. We need to talk." He took a step to the side to indicate he wanted privacy.

Ken released his wife's hand and whispered, "I'll meet you at the car."

Amanda hesitated at first, then turned to go. Ken could tell she didn't want him to linger, even to speak with his boss. She probably wanted to put all this tragedy behind her. He couldn't blame her, though that was hardly a possibility for him.

They'd been in this situation often enough before and he realized she knew the drill. That didn't stop her from rolling her blue-green eyes and curling her lips in a grimace. She edged away, merging with the stream of people making their way silently. For a few seconds, Ken studied his wife, in her sleek black formal outfit, and realized she looked good, attractive, professional, understated—a plus for him. As he watched, Amanda stepped alongside Alex Hardcastle, their family doctor. The two exchanged nods and some quiet words.

"I guess you heard what O'Brien said?" Walters asked, dragging Ken's attention back to his boss.

"I could hardly help. I think he wanted both of us to hear."

"Yeah, I think he did."

Ken whispered, "I don't get the urgency, why he had to do this here, now."

Walters shook his head again. "Well, he has a point. The Board has reason to be concerned. And so do we...don't we?" the superintendent asked. "You're the district expert here, since you took the grad class on school law last year. How do you read this?"

"Look, Mark, this isn't the place to discuss this," Ken protested, glancing around as a family of mourners passed, and then noticed Amanda and Hardcastle still talking. "Can't we do this tomorrow—"

Walters cut him off. "Ken, answer the question."

Ken shrugged and examined the well-trimmed lawn, sliding the toe of his shoe across the blades. Even in the frigid air, the odor of freshly cut grass drifted up. "Well, the parents can always sue. Anyone can sue."

"That's not much help," Walters snapped.

Ken looked up and met his gaze. "We have no control over what some lawyer might do. The real issue is whether they could win or not. Mainly, that would hinge on the question of negligence. Did we provide adequate supervision for the students? Did we have anything to do with the drugs? Did we do what should have done to prevent their distribution?

Questions like that."

"Well, then, we need answers," demanded Walters. "And since you're our expert on the law here, I'm putting you personally in charge of this. Talk to the kids and the staff. I know you have a good relationship with many of the teachers. Maybe they'll talk to you." He nodded. "Work with the police. I don't care what you have to do, but get to the bottom of this. Let's see if we can stay one step ahead of the money-hungry lawyers." He released a long sigh. "Besides, I really want to find out what happened. See if you can find out anything about who's pushing these drugs. If you can get a handle on that, maybe we can distance the district from this thing."

Walters glanced around at the thinning crowd. "And, yes, O'Brien has a point. We do need to see what we can do to protect *our* respective asses! Not to mention, we've got the tax levy in seven months and we can't afford to have this hanging over our heads then."

Did he want this problem dumped in his lap? Ken waited a few beats before he spoke. Maybe it would give him a chance to redeem himself after he'd failed his brother. "Okay, Mark, I'll take this on, but...I've got to do it my way. You'll have to take care of my other responsibilities and give me a free hand in this." He stared straight at his boss. "And I don't want to worry about board interference...or whose toes I might be stepping on."

Walters nodded. "Agreed. Do it your way. Put what you can on hold. If it can't wait, give it to George. If he can't handle it, let me know and I'll deal with it, but get on this. We need to get some answers...for lots of reasons." He turned and headed toward his dark blue Seville, his long, purposeful strides covering the distance quickly.

Ken ambled over to where his wife waited, now alone by their car.

"He had to do business here, at a time like this?" she snapped.

"Well, you know Mark Walters."

"Yeah, I know Mark Walters." Amanda gave a quick chortle.

Holding the door open for his wife to slide in, he cast one last glance back at the four metal caskets, now sitting side by side, untended and isolated from the rest of the world. The image ripped at his heart. Damn, he'd find out what happened, no matter what.

Chapter 6

Earl Staunton studied his *domain*. He liked that word. He glanced out at the sign, which swayed slightly in the brisk morning wind, *Earl's Place*. True, it didn't look like much to others, but he knew better. He'd turned his expertise working with engines into quite a business—well that and a side hustle or two. The service station may have looked like a giant junk pile from the outside, but that appearance simply kept others from asking questions. Since he'd inherited the place from his dad, he'd managed in the past ten years to turn a tidy profit from his repair work …not to mention his other sources of income. The work was hard and physical—he had to crawl under cars, lift heavy engines and twist his body into contorted positions—but it kept him in great shape, without ever having to step inside a gym. And that served him well with the ladies, like the one he had lined up for tonight. He even enjoyed the strong smell of the grease and oil of the place.

When a set of large tires crunched the gravel in the parking lot, he glanced out through the bay door. A shiny black Sonoma 4-by-4 stopped in the drive, its oversized wheels spraying gravel in all directions, swirling the stirred dust into a milky, white fog. Two strutting teenagers emerged from the cloud. He'd seen them before and recognized them. The first, Vince, was a tall, tough teen with a body developed most likely from hours at the gym, rather than any real job. The kid tied his long hair into a black ponytail—he said he thought it made him look like a young Steven Seagal—and wore some stupid gold earring in his left ear. The other, Jack, walked a step behind and tried to pull off a similar swagger, but Earl thought the kid just came off like a smaller, weaker imitation of his friend.

The morning air was quite cool but these two wore only white sleeveless "wife-beater" tees over weathered jeans with those idiot rips. Earl didn't get that. Why was it cooler to have all these rips in your pants like some bear had clawed the legs? Not to mention, it would make your skin cold on a day like this.

The kids strutted in with those damn high-top Air Jordan basketball shoes, untied and left open at the top. Not cheap. Their business must be doing okay. On both right arms, the teens sported identical tattoos, drawings of a single barbed wire which encircled their skin right below their biceps. Supposed to make them look tough, he guessed.

As the two teens came across the service station lot, they jostled each other. "Can you believe people actually bring their cars here to get them fixed?" Vince asked, his arms making a wide swath at the cluttered service station.

Earl knew what the kids were looking at. On the left side of the garage was a pile of old, worn tires almost eight feet tall. When Earl threw the last one atop, he wasn't sure if the entire heap would collapse. In the front corner of the station lot, where others displayed some manicured flower border, he'd pitched a bunch of old car parts—rusted fenders and bumpers, twisted exhaust pipes and brown mufflers with jagged holes. As the teens walked by, Vince kicked a small, broken piece of tailpipe lying in the gravel and sent it flying across the lot.

Jack said, "Oh, I don't know, Vince. You know what it says on the radio commercial:

"Earl, Earl, the car doctor
Whatever ails your truck or car
Bring it to Earl first
It will feel better by far!"

"I don't know how you could fix 'em, Earl," called Vince, fingering his gold earring. "In the mess around here, you couldn't even find 'em." Both boys convulsed in laughter, slapping each other's shoulders.

"Shut up, ya assholes," Earl shouted back from the garage, his tone laughing at the same time.

Wiping his hands on an orange shop rag, Earl stepped from behind the upraised hood of a '93 Jeep Cherokee. He was even taller than the older teen and looked down at the kids. His calloused hands brushed the brown hair out of his gray eyes. Over the years, he found his natural good looks, even camouflaged with grease, often surprised female patrons, who would lose their train of thought when describing their automotive issues. A situation he wasn't afraid to exploit. Today, he'd chosen a pair of worn, brown overalls, deliberately revealing his heavily-muscled, tanned chest. You never knew who might stop by.

Earl decided he needed to get something out of the way. "Jack, I'm awfully sorry about your brother. Terrible, the way he went."

"Yeah, whatever," the kid muttered. "I really don't want to talk about it."

An awkward silence filled the air.

After a bit, Earl said, with forced enthusiasm, "Hey, you guys haven't seen my new wheels." He strolled past the filthy glass windows in front of the building and led the teens around the corner of the structure. "Voila!" he said, opening his arms wide to indicate the car nestled close to the rear wall.

He enjoyed the boys' reaction. They stared wide-eyed, their mouths falling open. Vince found his voice first. "Jeeee-sus H. Christ, Earl. That is a beaut. A Porsche 670, ain't it?"

"Hey, Vince, pretty good. You know your cars," said Earl.

"God, this car repair shit must pay real good," said Jack.

"Oh, I do okay. But sometimes you got to cultivate other sources of income."

"Speaking of which, what's your pleasure today?" Vince asked.

"Not here, dumbass. Let's get inside," Earl commanded, eyes darting around the area. Then he turned back to Jack, who was using his fingers to feather the new car's expert paint job. "Hey, don't mess with the finish, school boy."

"Shit. I bet you can really pick up the babes in this thing," Jack said, as he hurried to catch up.

"You forget I'm a happily married man." Earl grinned.

"Yeah, right," both boys said together.

Laughing, the three figures ambled around building and followed one after the other through the narrow glass door. They walked through an unkempt, crowded front room, cluttered with racks of odd items to purchase, from potato chips to maps to cassette tapes to key chains. Jack brushed the packages on the racks as he passed, causing them to swing back and forth in odd, syncopated rhythms.

After the three had reached the cramped space that served as an office, Earl closed the door and turned on the light, bathing the small room in dingy white from the lone suspended bulb. So close together, the odor of some overly strong cologne—some cheap drugstore brand, he guessed—reeked from both boys and he fought down a gag.

He'd seen the stacks of invoices stamped "Earl, the Car Doctor" strewn in piles on the Formica desktop and reminded himself to get to them. On a rusted nail embedded in the cheap wood paneling, he kept a car part calendar—the one with the most revealing female models—open to his favorite page, now two months old. Beneath the calendar, along the sidewall sat his gray computer and printer and a small black fax machine.

Eying the equipment, Jack said, "Shit, Earl, you've gone real high tech, huh?"

Earl ignored the question and turned to Vince. "Okay, whadda ya got?"

Vince presented two clear plastic bags, each bulging with their contents. "I've got some of the tattoos everybody's talkin' about and some great fuckin' crack. Take your pick. For you, ten bucks for the tattoos and five dollars for the crack. Both are guaranteed to blow you away."

"Tattoos?" Earl tensed. "Aren't those the damn things your brother was usin', Jack, when he …ya know?"

Jack snapped back, "Shut up. He wadn't supposed

to be drivin' no fuckin' car when he did it!"

"Easy, Jack. Easy," said Vince. "Well, Earl, whadda ya want?"

"Gimme a couple hits of crack. I got this broad lined up for tonight and I wanna blow her mind so she'll be hot to blow me."

"Ten dollars is a helluva deal for that," Vince said, extracting the coke and setting clear baggies on the metal desk. Earl peeled off a ten-dollar bill, which disappeared into the front pocket of Vince's worn jeans.

The bleat of a bell erupted in the confined space, making the three jump. As one, they turned toward the sound and watched as the fax machine shuddered slightly and started spitting out a thin white paper.

Earl's gaze flicked from the fax to his guests. He hustled over to the door. When he opened it, the morning light flooded in, momentarily blinding all. Raising his left arm to block the light, he turned back to his guests as his right hand flipped off the light switch and gestured out the door. "Okay, boys. Some of us have real work to do. I've got to transport the Hotchins kid over to the hospital for O.T. in about fifteen minutes."

"C'mon Jack, we got other customers and we don't wanna keep 'em waitin' ." The taller youth hurried through the front room and seemed to be swallowed up by the bright sunlight. Jack followed behind, hurrying to keep up, puppy-dog style.

His fingernails toying with the shoulder straps of his Dickies, Earl watched the boys climb into the cab. The shiny truck squealed out of the driveway, shooting gravel in its wake, raising the white cloud again.

Earl hurried to the back room, flipped the light

back on, and tore the fax off the machine. His gray eyes squinting at the page, he already knew what it would say.

10/24/95 10:01 4197464246 Kinko's

The next shipment of special parts is ready for pick-up today. Same arrangements as before, costs as agreed.

Then he noticed a new note added and the hairs on the back of his neck stood on edge. He swallowed.

Remarks: *We know competition is tough in this business so we are willing to do what we can to keep our competitive edge. So, we thought you'd like to know we had a nice conversation with Miss Tricia. As always, it's a pleasure doing business with you.*

Catching the word "Tricia," his whole body flinched.

He wadded up the thin paper, using both hands to smash the wad smaller. He raised his right hand to dunk the paper ball into the small, dented metal wastebasket next to the desk, but stopped. Then, using both hands again, he pulled the paper wad apart till it was almost flat and reached into the cavernous, front pocket of his overalls. His fingers fumbled a bit and then produced his expensive gold Zippo lighter with the company's logo emblazoned upon it. For just a moment, his thumb caressed the engraved words "Earl the Car Doctor" and then he flipped open the top, lit the flame, and moved it to the corner of the paper. The yellow-blue flame licked the wrinkled paper. Staring at the fire, he held the paper for a bit then dropped the burning piece into the old wastebasket. Inside the dented gray can, the flame consumed the white paper, leaving only a pile of gray ash.

Chapter 7

Ken and Amanda sat at the dinner table, eating late as usual. Amanda was a decent cook—the aroma of tomatoes, garlic, and oregano drifting up from the dish would normally make his mouth water—but tonight Ken didn't have much of an appetite. Numb, he stared at his food, using his fork to push the corkscrew pasta around on his plate.

"I ordered the cabinets…the cherry ones I told you about," Amanda said. When Ken glanced up, she went on, "Well, it's obvious you're not going to have time to do much shopping…until the investigation is over. Maybe I should have checked with you first, but you've been so busy."

Ken nodded. "Good. I'm glad you got what you wanted." He looked around the room. "Hope it makes this kitchen looks new, like you like. I'm glad you didn't wait for me." He dropped his fork and met her gaze. "I've no idea how long this is going to take. I've already been investigating a week. I've learned some but haven't been able to put much together."

"Don't put your fork on the placemat, *please*. How many times do I have to remind you?" She pointed to the braided "work of art" she'd bought at the artisan fair last summer, but dropped her hand when Ken glared back at her. He moved the silverware to the plate, though. She said, "Anyway, you need to give yourself more time. Have they figured out if the drugs had anything to do with the boys' deaths?"

"Not certain yet. We're pretty sure all four took something through those damn tattoos on their arms, but we don't know much else. The lab results on their blood aren't due back until tomorrow. They'll confirm then."

"Six days? Does it typically take that long for lab tests?"

"Bart says it usually takes much longer. But they put a rush on them…because of the kids' deaths. This is the biggest problem ever to drop in Hardcastle's lap. He's concerned and doesn't want to screw—"

Amanda dropped her own fork on the plate, the clink interrupting Ken. When he looked up, her face reddened and she muttered, "Sorry." Her fingers pick the utensil up. "Go on."

"Well, anyway, what I discovered so far doesn't amount to much."

"Why don't you share what you've learned and maybe together we can sort something out."

Sometimes, his wife would listen as Ken would reconstruct events from work. On occasion, his retelling and her questioning would prompt a new revelation. Their twenty-two-year marriage, though hardly romantic these days, was at least practical.

He realized Amanda was right. Most times he shared easily, but the boys' deaths had unsettled him, unearthed a buried guilt. He'd become withdrawn, meditative and quiet, even at home. He poked more at the rotini.

A tense silence gripped the room.

Ken knew he could use his wife's help, but felt her

heart wasn't in it. He was hurting and she kept telling him to let it go. She seemed…callous almost. He stared at her frown across the table. She's changed, he told himself, or maybe he'd simply been working so much lately he hadn't had enough time for her. He gave in.

"Okay," Ken said and took a slow breath. "First of all, the four dead boys were all in the same class, Stacy Thompson's class."

"Thompson? Isn't she the teacher Steven had?" Amanda asked.

"Yeah, sure."

"You know, I told you I was never quite sure about her. Wasn't she the one who did all those bizarre things with the kids? You know, breathing exercises and stuff?"

"Amanda, don't start on that," Ken snapped.

She raised both hands in surrender. "Okay, okay, sorry. Go on."

Ken continued, "Anyway, according to their student files, they'd gotten into some trouble before, but nothing serious, only detention and in-school suspension offenses. There is nothing in any of their records to indicate any connection with drugs before."

"Weren't these boys young, eleven and twelve? Awfully young to be mixed up with drugs. What about the boys' families, their brothers and sisters?"

"The police are checking on that now, but so far no record of any drug dealing. I picked up a rumor about James' older brother and I'm going to check it out. I also talked with the counselors at Camp Haven. They weren't much help."

"They didn't notice anything?"

"No, they said they had to correct the boys a few

times, but that was all. They didn't catch any hint about the drugs. But the counselors are all so young. I don't think they could be much older than nineteen or twenty. I'm not sure they even know what to look for. Bart said they will check them all out, but my instinct told me they didn't have anything to do with it."

Amanda said, "Still, something might turn up when the cops do the background checks."

"Maybe, but I doubt it. Those young counselors seemed genuinely horrified. Nothing like this has ever happened at the camp." Ken shook his head. "Then I interviewed every single student in Thompson's class who went on the science trip. Nothing substantial. The other boys in the same cabin said they didn't see or hear anything. Judging from when it all went down, the four kids must have waited until everyone else fell asleep."

"I'd guess the girls couldn't have seen anything," Amanda said. "Don't they still keep boys and girls in separate cabins?"

"Yes, and no. The girls were in a different cabin. But one girl, Tina Simpson, claimed she overheard James and Robert saying something about 'scoring big time.' But she didn't say anything because James and Robert were always bragging and planning something.

"Anyway, then I checked the school discipline records and I found little drug activity in the middle school. *Very* little. In the past three years, the cops have done four locker searches and they have come up with practically nothing."

"You mean, the dogs didn't sniff out anything in the school? Well, maybe there weren't any," suggested Amanda.

"Oh, there must be some drugs. We simply can't

find them. The students I've talked to—who will say anything—tell me there is plenty of stuff being sold in school."

"In the middle school? So, how are the students getting them? And why don't they turn up in the searches?"

"I don't know."

Amanda stared across at her husband, her understanding dawning. "You think someone on the staff is involved?"

"Maybe. I don't know. It's as if someone is tipping off the dealers ahead of time."

"Oh, God. Ken, if that's true, this could get hairy." Amanda shook her head twice. "Maybe you shouldn't get involved in this. Maybe you better let the cops handle it."

"I'm in it now and I *have* to find out. I'd think you understand why."

Amanda shook her head. "*That* was all a long time ago, and it wasn't your fault. You told me the cop cleared you back then."

"Yeah, but back then I could've done something and I didn't. I'm not about to let that happen again."

As the promise came out of his mouth, Ken could feel the memory nudge at him again, clawing, struggling to get out. He shook his head, massaging his temple.

He pressed on. "Even if I wanted to drop it, I couldn't. O'Brien and Mark are really hot on this one. I've never seen them so worked up, especially O'Brien. Our esteemed board president told me I'd better find someone to hang this on and soon, so the district can get off the hook. He said I'd better come through on this or else."

"Or else what?" Amanda's eyebrows raised.

"Oh, you know O'Brien. He was smooth about it. He said if this thing goes sideways, it's going to hurt the district and our levy chances next May. Then he happened to mention that my contract was up next year."

"He always was an arrogant bastard."

"Yeah, well, now he's an arrogant bastard who happens to be board president. Anyway, tomorrow, I'll start interviewing some of the adults, the teachers and the principal. Maybe I can piece something together from what they tell me. Walters and O'Brien may be all worried about lawsuits, but that's not what I'm concerned about."

He held Amanda's gaze. "Somebody killed those four boys, just as surely as if they had put a gun to their heads and pulled the trigger. Four boys from my school, four boys *I* was responsible for." He stabbed the air with his fork. "These kids may not have been from *good* families, but they deserved better. Walters and O'Brien can make all the noise they want about protecting the district, but I swear I'm going to expose whoever did this to those kids…regardless of what it takes."

Chapter 8

"Who wants to bet me they'll blame this one on us too?"

Stacy Thompson looked up from the papers she was grading to see Chris Goodman, resident staff rebel, offer the challenge to his colleagues, one hand out in invitation. She knew he was getting ready to unwind and she tried to steel herself, glancing around. Though teachers had crowded into every seat in the small lounge this morning, no one seemed willing to take the proposed wager. Inside the cramped space, the odors of burnt coffee, duplicating fluid, and perspiration lingered in the air.

"Anyone? I didn't think so." Goodman pushed the green button on the copy machine, which began spitting out duplicates. "Like always, it doesn't matter what the problem is, society is going to dump it on the schools. Smoking, teen pregnancy, now drugs." He turned and leaned back against the machine. "And then they'll blame public school teachers when it's not solved." When the machine signaled, he grabbed the copies out of the receiving tray, stacked them on the red Formica-topped table, and set them down. "Right now, I can picture it." Pivoting, he faced the group, and his hands made an impromptu frame. "Walters and Parks huddled in the admin office, scheming, figuring out how they can make one of us goddamn peasants the scapegoat for these kids' deaths…so they can get the district off the hook. Probably on the phone with the district lawyer right now."

"Come on, Chris, that's a bit much," Stacy said. "We all know Walters can be a bit…" She paused a moment, searching for the right word. Unlike Chris, who never seemed to care how he came off, she often worried she might be overheard saying the wrong thing. She had her own share of, uh, skeletons. Though knew her colleagues, she wasn't sure how many she knew well enough. "He can be a bit expedient," she finished, "but I'd hardly put Ken Parks in that category."

"Expedient! Great fuckin' word choice, Stace. According to Webster's, 'based on what is of use or advantage rather than what is right,' " quoted Chris, his fingers making motions in the air as if he were opening a page in the dictionary. "You got Walters pegged all right." He laughed at his own wit.

"Chris, how do you do that?" Stacy asked.

"Oh, I don't know. It's a gift," Goodman said, with a grin reminiscent of the Cheshire cat, from *Alice in Wonderland* Stacy was reading to her class. "Anyway, we all know Walters' number one directive is CYA." This drew a few puzzled looks from the others sitting around the table.

"Cover Your Ass," explained Bill "the maestro" Daniels, in a didactic tone, as if he was explaining a point to the simple minds of his second graders—again. "Yeah, I'd agree that's how Walters operates, but I think Stacy's right about Ken. He's never struck me that way."

Daniels ran his wrinkled hand through what was

left of his silver hair. Today, Daniels wore a flamboyant, bright yellow shirt and a navy tie with musical instruments dancing down it. Staring over the top of his jelly donut, he lectured his colleagues with his mouth full. As his lips moved, Stacy couldn't help but watch the pieces of jelly and dough roll around in his mouth. She tried to ignore the sight.

Being the seasoned member of the staff—thirty-three years, Stacy thought—he took a different tack. "You worry too much about everything," he mumbled. "Give it enough time and it'll blow over. It always does. I've seen it plenty of times before." In a gulp, he swallowed the last of his impromptu breakfast.

Goodman shook his head. "I don't think this one is going to blow over." He walked across the small room, paper in hand. Wadding it up, he tossed it in a perfect arch into the wastepaper can. He stood there, staring at the others at the table, in his weathered jeans and wrinkled golf shirt, his only concession to convention the brown string tie around his neck. His dress constantly infuriated Walters and his other bosses and Stacy knew Chris took immense pleasure in the deliberate aggravation. His dark brown hair was long—though not the shoulder length he favored a decade ago—today, tied in a tight ponytail.

Stacy found Chris an interesting colleague. In the fifteen years he'd been at Foster he had built an enviable reputation as an effective and inspiring English teacher. He'd pretty much earned the self-proclaimed moniker of "English teacher extraordinaire" and she herself had recommended him to parents often. That stellar reputation had generally insulated him from attacks of his supervisors. Not to mention, Chris had pressed before, and the previous superintendent had granted him tenure. Something Stacy wasn't courageous enough to do yet. Maybe this would be the year.

Dawn Hatcher, Stacy's teaching partner, got up from the table and walked over to the brewing coffee pot. As she waited for the machine to fill her mug of the day, which read *I don't love money, just spending it*, she added in her raspy voice, "I know people don't like to hear it, but those kids were simply headed for trouble. For kids like James, it seemed like he was on a downhill speeding train. We spent most of our time trying to keep it from derailing."

Stacy noted Dawn had dressed up a bit, a new flowered blouse and a flared navy skirt with large white buttons down the side. Dawn stirred a little cream into her cup and stared as the white liquid swirled and disappeared.

Dawn continued, "But to go out like that, wow. Thinking about that car crash creeps me out. I feel so bad about what happened. I can't get the picture of those four coffins out of my head." She shuddered, even though the drink steamed hot. "But I don't see how they are going to lay this problem on us. Look at some of the homes those boys came from."

"I'm still waiting for someone to take my damn bet," Chris said.

"Oh come off it, Chris. You're always imagining grand conspiracies," said Jacqueline Highstreet. As the woman emerged from the restroom adjacent to the teachers' lounge, the heavy scent of some expensive perfume followed. Using a handheld mirror, she checked her hair and applied a bolder shade of lipstick, her bright red lips puckering. Finished, she said, "Maybe Walters and Parks are as torn up about the kids' deaths as we all are." Apparently satisfied, she put away the makeup and glanced up at the other teachers. "You know, it's been really tough trying to help the kids cope. I believe we need to simply focus on how we can help them deal with the deaths. I know I'm going to try to get my girls to concentrate on the competition next week."

"Oh, gees-el," the music teacher said.

Jacqueline continued as if she didn't notice. "I know, I know, it's no big deal to you, but our team has won the regional for the past five years and we're not going to miss number six." She snapped the purse shut with a click. "I've already decided we're going to dedicate the competition to the four boys."

Stacy looked at Jacqueline and inwardly shook her head. She always looked so "put together." The woman was, among other things, the middle school cheerleading advisor and her girls were *the best*. The "other things" were math teacher and counselor and, even at forty, still a knockout. With a well-sculpted figure—far better than her own, Stacy admitted—she carried herself with class, and taught "her girls" to do the same. Her strawberry blonde hair—probably tinted some—still looked radiant, and framed an attractive face with perfect teeth and confident hazel eyes. Her posture conveyed a certain savior faire, something she had learned in the finishing school where her father, the publisher of *The Boston Observer,* had sent her—she had once shared over drinks on a Friday. After a few margaritas, Jacqueline had even confided she had been married to someone rich even, but a divorce and an unfortunate prenuptial agreement had "forced her to go into teaching." Stacy chafed when she'd heard that but didn't say anything.

"I will say I'm glad my cheerleading practice kept me from volunteering for Camp Haven last week," Jacqueline said.

"Gee, thanks for sharing that thought," Dawn rasped over her coffee cup. "Stacy and I really appreciate it."

"If I hadn't gotten sick, I guess I might've still been up there when it all—" started Rachel Bedinghaus, snatching out a handkerchief and sneezing into it. Rachel, the third fifth grade teacher, had a red nose and a doozy of a head cold, one of the many she seemed to contract lately. Standing a mere five feet and weighing barely a hundred pounds, she was more than simply petite. With her auburn hair curved into a pageboy style, parents sometimes mistook Rachel for one of the middle school students.

"When I was up at Camp Haven, the night air in the cabin must have given me this cold. I haven't been able to shake it since." As if to prove her point, she issued another loud "Ach-choo."

Dawn quipped, "Jeez, Rachel, could you watch the spreading of the germs? You've proven your point, all right." Dawn handed her a tissue from the box on the counter. "But it sure seems strange that you always get sick when you're supposed to chaperone the kids."

Rachel blew her nose again, this time into the offered Kleenex. "Well, excuse me for living."

Stacy decided to step in. "Rachel, it's no big deal. I didn't mind coming up a little earlier." She shot a look at Dawn, who shrugged her shoulders and sipped a little more of her morning caffeine.

The four boys' deaths still haunted Stacy, all the more so because she was there. She remembered what little she saw of the wrecked car and crumpled bodies. She couldn't get those images out of her mind. She said, "Maybe we're looking at this wrong. The death of the boys was, oh, a horrible tragedy and we all feel terrible. It's natural, with the possibility of a drug connection, there's going to be a lot of questions. They've got to be worried about the students, especially those as young as ours, getting hold of those drugs. Jacqueline's right. We should be focused on the kids. They're the ones who are feeling it the most—well, besides the families of the boys—and they're the ones who need our attention. We're not going to be very good for them if we're busy looking over our shoulders all the time."

This drew a few silent nods. No one spoke for a bit.

In the silence, Dawn strolled over to the three rows of wooden cubicles that passed for mailboxes. As she retrieved the few items, she pointed to the mailbox marked Goodman. That cubicle was stuffed so full of papers half of the contents spilled out, obscuring the name on the box below. Turning back, she asked, "What gives, Goodman?"

"Hey, I never touch the damn thing," Chris said. "I learned a long time ago, since the checks go straight to our bank accounts, there's nothing important in there anyway, only memos, rules, and directions. So I don't even bother." He flicked his hand as if to dismiss the topic. "You're right about the kids, Stace, but all the same I'm going to watch my backside. I know Walters would love to lay something like this at my doorstep."

Rachel started to ask a question when the door to the lounge opened, and the teachers turned at once, waiting.

"Morning, everyone," called Robyn Boyle in her quick, businesslike tone. She pulled a paper from her folder and, withdrawing a blue pushpin, she attached it to the large "National Education Association" bulletin board. Without waiting, Boyle said, "Sorry to interrupt, but I only came by to share an announcement as president of the Portsmouth Teachers' Association." Boyle was dressed smartly this morning in a blue pantsuit, the one she called her power suit. Boyle had started her career a little later in life and had only eight years' experience, but her self-assurance and passion convinced her fellow teachers she could handle the job of president. So far, Stacy thought, she'd proven them right.

"The Association is setting up a scholarship fund for students going to two-year or technical schools in honor of the four dead boys," she explained. "As always with these things, contributions are voluntary, but I do think it's important that we step forward and show the organization cares. Think about it, okay?"

Boyle started to head out the door and stopped, turning. "I've been informed they're going to interview staff members today about what…happened at Camp Haven." Her gaze flicked on the faces in the room. "You probably heard Ken Parks is doing the interviewing. He's coming to see Rachel, Stacy, and Dawn." She stopped and looked at the three women in the room. "Well, thought you'd like to know."

With that, she stepped through the door and out. It closed quietly and no one spoke till it clicked shut.

"And so it begins. Mark my goddamn words. You heard it here first. They're coming for us," said Goodman, fingering his brown ponytail. His next words were cut off by the bell, which clamored loudly, making further conversation impossible. All the teachers moved as one, picking up books, grabbing files, and shuffling toward the door. As soon as the noise subsided, Chris added, "Stacy, Rachel, Dawn, all you guys, watch your backside," patting his own tight buttocks on the way out the door.

Chapter 9

Ken drove up Broadway, cresting the hill and watching the sun climb over the tile roof of the old high school, all the while struggling with conflicting feelings. He loved being here, with the teachers and students—it was why he got into this profession. But today he hated it, his dread eating away at his insides. He tried to steel himself.

The old high school.

Most everyone in town called it that, though that had changed years ago. Seventy-two years of heritage had proven hard to get past, even with a remodel and a new name. Four generations of the small town had been cheered on the basketball court and at commencement ceremonies in the old high school and to many it seemed blasphemous to think of the building as anything else. But, eight years ago, with the third attempt on the ballot, the conservative taxpayers of Portsmouth had agreed to build a new high school and the old building had officially become Foster Middle School. The renovation updated and modernized the interior systems but somehow maintained the traditional appearance of hallways, offices, and even the exterior, with the final result that the building appeared almost untouched, frozen in time as in the photographs of 1917.

The building stood all granite and brick, perched at

the top of the hill, guarding the town like some stoic, ancient keeper of tradition. A stone courtyard splayed out in front of three floors of classic schoolhouse-red brick, sealed into position with traditional whitish-gray grout and bordered by fitted corners of carved yellow-white rock.

Even in the middle of the current tragedy, Ken couldn't help but admire the educational heritage. Lives had been changed here—most often for the better, he hoped—and he'd been a small part of it. But the responsibility which brought him here today weighed heavy and ominous.

He turned his Taurus into the driveway, catching the sign perched on the verdant grass. In large, block letters, it read:

FOSTER MIDDLE SCHOOL Grades 5-8 and then in faded red script below: *A National Drug-Free School*.

He frowned. Not so much.

Settling his car into a visitor's space, Ken cut across the lawn, noting the white tops of grass left icy fingerprints on his brown dress shoes and released the harsh scent of fertilized turf. After holding the door open for two girls he'd guess to be eighth graders, he started down the old hallway, his leather soles slapping the tile floor. Staring ahead, he was still amazed, with the renovations, how well they managed to maintain the look of the classic high school. Simply peering down the school's main corridors brought to mind the term "hallowed halls." There, stretching down the central passageway, hung the photos of seventy graduation classes. The display started at the one end with the eight boys and two girls who were "awarded diplomas" in

1917 to the last class that graduated from the building in 1987, boasting "104 fine young men and women of Portsmouth." The photographs hung in their stately positions, high on the wall, as if standing guard over the present students. The collection was meticulously cared for, dusted on a regular schedule, and even taken down and cleaned twice a year—much to the chagrin of the building janitors. In Portsmouth, each photo collage of the youthful, eager faces served as one critical part of the small town's history.

As he strode down the corridor, Ken was struck by the incongruity of the polished faces in the solemn graduation poses and the restless, rushing preteens who now inhabited the halls. The middle school students had long since become oblivious to the honored graduates overhead. In fact, the only time it seemed these students paid any attention to the row of photographs was when some young man, in an effort to impress his friends, would make a running jump to slap an unlucky frame, ten feet off the ground.

"The whole thing is over their heads, ain't it?" said a wry voice. Ken looked up to see Wally Kowalchek leaning on a broom, glancing at him. Wally always seemed to be leaning on a broom or a mop. A fixture in the building for more than ten years, he served as head custodian. Wally, a balding, overweight figure with an unkempt, bushy mustache, wore a sneaky smile that made you think he just got away with something. "Them grad photos. They're over the kids' heads."

"I think that's the idea, Wally, so the students don't vandalize them."

"Naw. I mean these here middle schoolers are too far away to understand the honor of gettin' a diploma."

He and Wally performed this routine on a regular basis. Wally would say something, well, mildly funny and Ken would feign ignorance, smiling all the while.

"Oh, over their heads. I get it," Ken answered, as if enlightened.

"What brings ya by today, Mr. Parks?" asked the janitor.

"I'm here to interview some of the staff about the boys' deaths."

Wally let out a slow whistle. "Man, now that's a tough one. Ya know, them boys wasn't the most popular kids 'round here, but you'd never know it from how some people been carryin' on. The only time some teachers paid 'em any attention was to yell at 'em. Now they actin' like they lost their own sons. Mebbe they just feel guilty, I dunno." Wally moved his broom around, attempting to corral some dust. "I know them boys were a problem some, but I kinda liked 'em, 'specially that James and Robert, always hanging around talkin' with me. Sometimes Chad, he'd asked how sumpin worked. I didn't really know that Justin kid. Still, their deaths and all, a real shame."

Ken stood there, listening. In his work with staff, he'd learned a long time ago, many simply wanted someone to listen. And Wally loved to talk. Ken couldn't help liking the old guy, even if Wally's work performance sometimes lacked commitment.

The janitor said, "I heard you got the investigation job for the boys' deaths. I don't envy ya that one. Have you found much out yet?"

"Not much." Ken made a mental note to take time to talk to Wally later, alone. He'd been in the school business long enough to know janitors are the eyes and ears of the building. And he seemed to know the three boys. Wally might very likely have some idea about what was going on with the drugs. "Is Mrs. Michaels in her office?"

"Hey, I dunno. I just work here," Wally said, as he half-pushed and half-leaned on the broom down the hallway, whistling as he left.

Ken glanced across the way at the sign he'd seen often. On a fake-antique wooden plaque, the words "Administrative Offices" were carved in ornate letters, with an arrow pointing down the hall. Heading down the corridor, he passed a pair of seventh grade girls, so deep in conservation they didn't even notice him. Looking across at the glass-enclosed office, he read once again, "Foster Middle School, Office of the Principal, Carla Michaels, Principal," the lettering stenciled on the glass in an embellished, flowery calligraphy.

Ken rolled his eyes and pushed the door open.

He enjoyed working with the principals, at least, most of the time. He knew how hard their jobs were and how much they needed an ear. He'd been there. He was pleased to be able to help them solve problems and secure much needed resources.

But Principals Michaels sat in a class all her own. Ken thought her picture might appear next to the dictionary definition of "needy"…or at least "loquacious." Anytime he entered a building he checked in on the principal, but today, he dreaded making this visit.

"Good morning, Martha," he said to the diminutive, older woman on the other side of the counter.

The secretary looked up with a brief start and flashed a wide grin. "Good morning, Mr. Parks." He knew she was too "old school" to call him Ken, even though he'd asked. Several times.

"I'd like to speak with Carla, if I may."

"I'll let her know." The secretary disappeared into an interior office. A few seconds later, she reappeared. "Go right on in." Then, in a whispered voice, she added, "She's a little frazzled today."

Ken feigned surprise. "What, again?"

Martha grinned at him.

When he walked through the door, Carla Michaels, on the phone, glanced up and made a tiny wave with her left hand. As she concluded her conversation, trying to get off the phone, he glanced around. The office, like her attire, looked immaculate and professional. Behind the principal's desk hung a tasteful print of children sitting attentively at their desks in an old school room. Flanking the picture on both side walls of the narrow office were Michaels' degrees and certificates, each professionally framed. In the small window to the right was the familiar "Just Say No" sticker. The office held little personal character, no photographs or other personal mementos. A sculpture of a little red schoolhouse sat alone on one shelf, bearing the inscription, "To Mrs. Michaels from your staff."

Closing the door behind him, he took one of the two chairs facing the desk. Carla Michaels looked striking this morning in an aquamarine dress suit and white blouse with a classic gold chain and heart pendant around her neck. Though not married, she wore an expensive ring on the pinkie finger, some rare blue stone in a small diamond setting, she'd once told him.

Her clothes and jewelry always appeared high end. Someone on the staff told him her family had money.

Though he knew her to be nearing fifty, she didn't look it. Her makeup, as always, appeared perfect, lipstick and eyeliner accenting her refined Roman features, and her blonde hair danced with highlights. The light scent of some perfume Ken couldn't recognize—probably too expensive for his budget—drifted across the office.

"I'm sorry, Ken. That was Mrs. Haywood, and I couldn't get her off the phone." Michaels began even before the black receiver hit the cradle. "She said her son is being picked on by some older boys and the bus driver's doing nothing about it. I had to assure her we'd take care of it so her little Shawn will be safe from the wrath of eighth graders." She uttered a loud sigh. "It all takes time. *Time* to work with the kids in trouble, *time* to talk to the parents, *time* to write up the discipline forms." She pointed to a pile of paperwork on her desk. "These are the discipline forms I've filled out this quarter alone. It's too much." She shook her head, her smile fading.

Ken waited, and only half listened. He knew the principals' jobs were hard—too many responsibilities and never enough time. Normally, when he stepped into their offices, he tried to remember what the principals were up against, but he found listening to Carla Michaels' rambling hard to endure. Especially this morning

"What can I do for you?" Michaels said, finally finishing her digressions.

"I need to talk to you about the four boys who died last week," Ken said. "You probably heard Walters asked me to look into the whole thing. He's quite concerned…for lots of reasons."

Ken watched as a cloud slid across her face, darkening her features. The professional composure seemed to crack. "I-I-I tried to work with those boys. I really did." She had difficulty getting the words out at first, a rarity for her. Then she started babbling, the words rushing upon themselves, coming in waves. "I feel like it's all my fault. I was afraid something would happen. Ken, do you know how many at-risk kids we have here?" She turned in her chair and deftly hit a few strokes on the new computer. "In the last two months we've handled ninety-three referrals for kids in trouble. For James Clayton alone," she typed a few more keys, "he had fifteen office referrals since the start of the year, and this is only the end of October. Fifteen! I guess I won't have to worry about more referrals for him, will I?"

She turned back, her blue eyes moistening. One drop slid from her mascara, creating a tiny pale blue streak down her cheek. She fought to control her composure. "Ken, there are too many of them. With these boys, I was afraid something was going to happen, but not this. Oh my God, I still have to write a note to their parents." At that, the damn burst and tears flowed down her face. She didn't try to hold them back, sobbing twice. Before Ken could offer a handkerchief, she retrieved a tissue and dabbed her cheeks.

Watching her struggle, Ken realized she had a point. He made a mental note to talk to Walters about getting more help for the principals. But he had a job to do today.

"Carla, I checked the four boys' disciplinary

records, but I didn't find any mention of anything having to do with drugs. In dealing with them, or their friends, did you come across anything? Anything that would've given us a clue about this?"

Sniffling, Michaels peered through her tears. "Nothing." She shook her head. "I've asked myself a hundred times since last week. I've gone over every conversation with those boys, searching for something, anything I might have missed."

"I know we haven't turned up anything here in the last few locker searches," Ken added, hoping to help the principal focus. "Do you have any ideas where the boys got the drugs?"

"I don't know, Ken. I assumed from someone out at Camp Haven. What have you learned from the students?"

"Not much. I'm still trying to put the pieces together. A few of them knew Robert and James were up to something, but that was nothing new. And they think the kids are getting the stuff here at school."

The comment appeared to rattle Carla Michaels. "Oh my God, who said they got them at school? I hope not," she blurted, her tone now adamant. "We try so hard here to keep drugs out with the DARE and the Just Say No programs. Who told you that?"

The tears had vanished and she transformed into the *Principal* again, defensive, ready to protect her turf.

"I don't know, Carla. I'm simply trying to find out," Ken answered. "Either they don't know or they're not talking."

"Ken, can I ask you to keep me informed? After all, it is my building."

"I'll do what I can," Ken said. "I need to talk to a

few teachers to see if I can learn anything. Will Martha have their schedules?"

"Sure, she can get you whatever you need. If there's anything else I can do to help, let me know. Stay in touch."

Ken walked over to the office door, opening it. "And Carla, that goes both ways. If you learn anything, pass it on, okay?"

"Count on it," said the principal, but Ken thought her features betrayed her candor.

Through the doorway, he shot a last glance at Michaels and saw the woman's attention was focused back on the reports on her desk. For a few seconds, he stared at her, gripped by the suspicion she knew more than she was saying. She was holding something back. He ought to push her but didn't have time today. As he left the office, he jotted a quick note on his pad to check back.

Chapter 10

Tricia Holloway decided she couldn't take it another minute. Mr. Goodman thought he was so cool, and usually she could hang with him third period, but today he was so bor-r-ring. Who really cared about participles anyway? When he started the lesson and mentioned "dangling participles," she thought he meant something else. Boy, was she wrong!

Tricia pulled on a stray lock of her hair and then drummed her fingers on the desk.

Mr. Goodman shot her a look and Tricia's face reddened. Then he continued on, without missing a beat. "Participles are verbs we've added an 'ing' to and use them to describe a noun, like barking dog and…"

Blah, blah, blah. Tricia thought she couldn't stand it any longer. Casting a sideways glance, she tried to catch the eye of Damien, who sat one over and one back from her. Now, Earl was nice and everything—even if he was much older—but this guy was hot. He slouched in his desk, his muscular arms resting on the top, his hair slightly messy and a crooked grin on his face. She tried to flash a smile at him. But, as she watched, she noticed whenever he thought Mr. Goodman wasn't looking, Damien would lean over and whisper to Brittany, one of the *cheerleaders!* Gag!

Searching for another distraction, Tricia's eyes wandered the room and caught some action at the front.

Mr. Goodman was swooping a camouflage jacket like a cape and putting it on. "Participles work like adjectives in camouflage. Okay, let's review, what do adjectives do in a sentence anyway?"

Of course, Erica, the brown-nose and another *cheerleader,* was the first with her hand up and of course, Mr. Goodman called on her. *This is so lame.* Her gaze wandered the classroom. Ever since those four stupid fifth graders crashed that car at Camp Haven, nobody's even interested in partying. What kind of idiots get stoned and then go driving in a car? She felt bad about the boys too, but they were dead now.

She glanced around, searching for anyone worth taking along. After a few seconds, she gave up. *They're all losers.* She'd do this alone. Reaching into her purse, her fingers felt around and brushed the plastic bag. It was there, all right. Without thinking, she raised her hand, interrupting Mr. Goodman mid-sentence.

He immediately called on her. "Miss Holloway, I see you would like to take a stab at the $1000 question."

Tricia had lost track of the lesson and didn't have a clue what Goodman had asked. "No, uh, sorry," she managed, feeling her face turning red. "I, I, uh, just wanted to ask permission to use the restroom." As a few snickers erupted around the room, she lowered her eyes to her desk.

Mr. Goodman didn't miss a beat. "Hey, cut that out," he blurted and cast a glance at Tricia. "We only have a few minutes till the end of class but if you need to, you know where the hall pass is. Don't forget to sign out." Turning to the rest of the class, he asked, "Anyone else want to hazard an answer to my question?"

Tricia got up from her desk and padded up to the front of the room. Mr. Goodman was okay. He let her off the hook and he cut off the other smartass kids. She hated to ditch him, but she *had* to get out of there. Before she could change her mind, she stepped out the door, her right hand dragging the hall pass.

Five minutes later, Tricia stared at her reflection in the old mirror, turning a little from side to side. She didn't much like what she saw. She knew she was taller than most of the boys and way too skinny and her face looked like the pictures of the moon's surface from science class. She glanced down at the faded Ohio State sweatshirt she wore and the stupid, cheap jeans her mom had bought at K-Mart.

"No wonder Damien doesn't even give you a second look. Why should he?" she asked aloud of the visage in the cloudy mirror. She wasn't worried about anyone hearing. Instead of using the restroom down the hallway from Mr. Goodman's room, she had headed back the other way and down the stairs to the old restroom in the basement by the locker rooms. This place was grimy with old, stained toilets and cracked sinks, and hardly any kids came down here during school. Of course, it stank with the odors of piss and mold, but that was a small price to pay for a little privacy. Just to be sure she was alone, she'd checked inside every stall.

Her reflection didn't respond and she thought, *at least I'm not answering myself yet*. She pulled her purse off her shoulder and set it on top of the "hall pass," which was really a stupid, dinged up hubcap balanced on the edge of the sink. The purse jostled the hubcap, making it fall to the floor with a loud clang. Shit. Tricia glanced around the bathroom and then ran to the door and checked both ways down the hall. No one.

She let out a breath. Easing the door closed, she went back inside.

Tricia stared at the banged-up piece of metal on the concrete floor. Mr. Goodman thought it was so funny you had to carry the stupid hubcap when you want to go to the bathroom. Ha-ha. Well, today, she didn't care. She reached inside her purse and, moving aside the tube of lipstick and wrapped tampons, her fingers grabbed the clear plastic sandwich bag. Holding it up, she examined the small, square sliver of paper with the bright colors reflecting the harsh fluorescent lights. "Looks like the head of some animal," she said and held the baggie up to her mirrored reflection. "She told me it'd make me howl. I hope it doesn't bite." Tricia laughed at her own joke.

She'd told Tricia not to use the thing at school. Tricia didn't care. She needed *something*. No longer willing to wait, she started to bunch up the sleeve of her sweatshirt and realized it wouldn't work. She'd been told to stick the tattoo on her arm, just below her shoulder. She couldn't get the fabric up that far. So she dragged the gray sweatshirt over her head, stripping down to her bra, another stupid K-Mart buy. She extracted the blue, yellow, and white tattoo and peeled the backing off. Her fingers shaking, she almost dropped the tattoo—shit—but managed to adhere it to her bare left arm, exactly like she'd been told. See, she *was* a good learner.

Turning her left side to the cloudy mirror, Tricia studied the image of the wolf's head on her arm. She squinted at the reflected image and giggled again. Was the wolf's teeth grinning? She shivered a bit.

She glanced around and decided she wanted some privacy, just in case. Going to the final stall in the row, she moved inside, then closed and locked the door behind her. She didn't want anyone discovering her and interrupting her trip. Leaning against the wall, she felt the soothing, cool concrete against her back. She slid down to the floor and stretched her legs out.

She tried to slow her breath down and breathe in and out, in and out, enjoying the ride. Tricia thought she could start to feel it now, though she said the trip would take a little while. Tricia smiled. She could wait. She had nowhere to go. Besides, no one would miss Tricia Holloway anyway.

She closed her eyes and waited.

Chapter 11

Ken walked back out to the secretary's desk. "Martha, I want to see"—he glanced down at his note—"Dawn Hatcher, Rachel Bedinghaus, and Stacy Thompson, the teachers who were on duty at Camp Haven last week. Could you check their schedules and see when they're free?"

"Be glad to, Mr. Parks. Let's see," said the secretary, "today is Wednesday. According to the grand Foster master schedule, Ms. Bedinghaus is on her planning time right now for another twenty minutes. Ms. Hatcher will be free next period. Her students have music right after Hatcher's class. Then Mrs. Thompson has her free time the period after."

"Thanks. Martha, I have one more favor. Could you pull the permanent records of the four boys who…I need to look them over and see if anything jumps out."

The woman shook her head. "Already pulled them." She pointed to a small pile of manila folders sitting on the back counter. "Damn shame. Anyway they're here when you get a moment."

Ken glanced at the files and nodded. "Thanks. Where will I find Ms. Bedinghaus, do you know?"

"Most likely in her classroom

"Thanks again."

As Ken stepped out into the hall, the bell rang, classroom doors opened, and the restless bodies of

75

students flooded the hallway. He stood to the side, watching the students as they passed. They paid him little heed and were using these few moments to do what they liked most, socializing.

Most days, Ken enjoyed visiting and observing the bright, active faces—even the obnoxious ones at this age—with their hormones starting to take over. Being here, with the students and in the classrooms, reminded him of the important aspects in his job. He was in service of children. And this was one more reason he found the deaths of the four boys so hard to take.

As long as he would live, Ken would never erase the dreadful images from his brain, images of the blood-smeared windshield and the small crumpled and broken bodies. Each night this week, he'd dreamt, the horrific visions returning, and each night he'd awakened from the nightmare, drenched in sweat and shaking.

Now, watching these students hurry into classrooms, he anguished at the thought those four boys would never walk down these halls again. He peered and, for a moment, he could almost picture their ghosts strutting across the floor.

The memory of the death of another young man, years earlier, tried again to creep around the corner of his mind like an unwelcomed spirit. For a second, Ken thought he saw *him,* too, among the students, but the rational part of his brain told him it couldn't be. He shook his head and the gossamer image dissolved.

Ken made his way down the end of the hallway watching the lines of students disappear through the classroom doors, like separated streams of water into disparate drains. The bell rang and suddenly the hall became quiet, leaving Ken alone with his thoughts again.

As the last bleat of the bell echoed through the hallways, Ken walked down the now deserted corridor on his way to the classroom of Ms. Bedinghaus. A second beep erupted from the speaker and he paused to glance up at the white box.

"Please give me your attention for today's announcements," came the melodious voice of Carla Michaels. "As always, we'll start with the pledge of allegiance."

Chairs moved inside the classrooms as children shuffled to their feet.

"Now, begin. I pledge allegiance," intoned the principal and scores of voices took up the lines in sing-song unison and Ken, without thinking, uttered the same quiet words.

When the pledge concluded, the sounds of the students repeated in reverse order, first the shuffling, then rustling of chairs. After a brief pause, Michaels continued, "Today is Wednesday and sixth graders will have a special DARE program with Officer Callahan today. Preparations for the science fair will begin…"

Ken remembered Carla Michaels liked to interrupt the day with announcements now, rather than first thing in the morning. He stopped listening and strolled down the hall toward Bedinghaus' room. In Carla Michaels' building, it was an unwritten rule you didn't interrupt students or staff during her announcements. Ken simply wanted to use the time to get to his destination. As he arrived at room 245, the principal said, "One last thing. Teachers, please log into your workstation and retrieve your messages. Next week, I'm planning to send all communication via email only and you'll need to be comfortable with the system by then. If you need help, simply ask." A brief pause followed, then, "Have a great day, drug free and happy!"

When Ken peered in the doorway of room 245, Rachel Bedinghaus sat at her desk alone, her kids already deposited in the music room. When he walked in, she rose quickly and shook his offered hand, her palm a little clammy. From an almost invisible side pocket in the trim slacks she wore, her small hand extracted a white tissue.

As he stood across from her, he towered over her and had to look down to meet her gaze. He noted the red nose, spoiling an attractive face, a face so petite it still held a childlike appearance. The teacher managed a demure smile, revealing two rows of perfectly straight, white teeth. Her dark auburn hair had lighter highlights sprinkled throughout and her pageboy bangs hung over normally azure eyes, now swollen and red-rimmed. As they talked, she moved her weight from foot to foot.

Ken said, "Rachel, I'm sorry to drop in on you like this. It looks like you have your hands full with your kids' papers"—he nodded at the desk—"but I'd like a few minutes to talk to you about the incident at Camp Haven."

"I understand, Ken," she said in a tone that bore little understanding. "My students just handed in their science reports and I was trying to—" A loud sneeze erupted from her small nose and, in a lightning move, her hands produced the white handkerchief again, her polished, cinnamon fingernails holding it to her nose.

"I'm sorry. Last week when I was up at Camp Haven I caught this horrible cold and haven't been able to shake it." Twice more she blew her nose, her eyes tearing in the process. "I understand it's important. What'd you want to ask me?"

"Dawn told me you left the camp early last Tuesday and came home. What happened?"

"This," Rachel said and blew her nose again, the sound loud coming out of the petite face. "Only last week it was much worse. I could hardly breathe. I guess it must've been the cabin or all that damp air in the woods. I don't know, but I got really sick. So I called the school and asked if Stacy could come up early and she said she'd be up right after school. When the counselors took the group after lunch and I knew the kids would be covered, I took off and went home to bed."

At first, Ken didn't say anything. Staring across at the small figure in front of him, he tried to weigh her words. Apparently uncomfortable with the brief silence, Rachel hurried to the wooden chair behind the cluttered desk, leaving a whiff of floral perfume behind. As he took the molded student chair across from her, he noticed her face all but disappeared, hidden behind towering piles of student reports. He looked over the papers and asked, "Did you notice anything wrong with the boys before you left? Anything going on?"

Rachel laughed out loud. "Are you kidding? With James and his gang, there was *always* something going on. You had to stay on top of these guys every minute to keep problems from happening. I can't tell you how many times some of the other students came in from recess crying. Most times, all I'd get out of them was that James or Robert had stolen their ball and wouldn't let them play or Chad was bullying some girl."

"Thinking back now, did you see or hear anything that could've been a tip off about the drugs?"

"I didn't see anything or hear anything about any drugs. Don't you think I would've said something about it if I had?"

"I know that, Rachel. That's not what I meant. You said you were with the kids during lunch on Tuesday. Maybe there was something you might've heard from these guys and didn't think much about it at the time. Could you just take a minute and think back?"

Rachel blew out a breath and did a short eyeroll. Then, she stared up at the ceiling. When she met Ken's gaze she started to shake her head and stopped. She closed one eye and Ken thought she looked like a small pre-teen trying to concentrate.

"Toward the end of the lunch period, when the kids were pretty much done, I heard James say, 'The Doctor said these are going to kick ass,' or at least I thought I did. I stopped and said, 'James, what did you say?' and he said 'Nothing' and gave me this fake innocent face of his." She did a quick imitation, complete with drooping eyes. "Then I told him we don't use that kind of language here." She looked across at Ken. "I have no idea what he was talking about and don't see how it could have anything to do with…with what happened to them." Her eyes got hard. "With the way these kids are, it was only a matter of time before something bad happened. You know it's not our fault. The teachers' fault, I mean. What happened to them."

Ken let her challenge go unanswered and made a note on his pad of what she'd heard. When he finished, he said, "Look, I know these kids were no star pupils, but it eats at my insides they died like that. And what's worse, some of the kids are telling me James and his gang got the drugs tattoos here at school." He studied her face for any response. "What do you think?"

Rachel turned away, busying herself with her students' papers. "I wouldn't know anything about that."

Right then, a tall, overweight student strolled into the classroom, as if in some pleasant fog.

"Kyle, what are doing here? You know you're supposed to be in music," she said, her voice shifting into an accusing teacher tone.

The heavy-set boy lowered his head. "I'm sorry, Ms. Bedinghaus, but I got in trouble in music and Mr. Daniels sent me back to get a pencil for time out."

"Okay, hurry up and get your pencil and go." The teacher issued the command in a clipped tone and the young student waddled to his desk, retrieved a broken nub of a pencil, and headed out the door.

As Rachel turned her attention back to Ken, the classroom door bounced open again and the boisterous laughter of three other fifth graders spilled into the room. Then the three boys saw their teacher and a boss at the front of the room. The laughter halted. Embarrassed expressions replaced the looks of merriment.

"Okay, what are *you* guys doing here?" the teacher barked.

The student in the middle, a fair-haired boy with brooding eyes spoke up. "Mr. Daniels got us into trouble and sent us to time out. We gotta get our pencils first."

"I *doubt* that Mr. Daniels got the three of you in trouble. You seem to be able to do that all by yourselves. Hop to it, get what you came for and get to the detention room."

Released for action, the three miscreants scurried into the room and soon had hands buried in their desks. As Ken and Rachel watched, loose papers and partially covered books landed on the floor around the desks with slaps. The teacher turned toward Ken and rolled her eyes. He simply nodded in recognition.

"Okay, boys. Take any pencil you can find." As if enlightened, two of the boys suddenly found a writing instrument and jammed the dispersed contents back into their small private space. The third student, the earlier spokesman for the group, got more frantic, his nimble hands pulling more and more items out of the small cavity in his desk.

Rachel got up and walked over to where the boy knelt. "Dennis, you can't find a pencil, can you?" she asked.

The boy's eyes got big and he shook his head, his limp, blond hair dancing in the motion. "No'm."

"Maybe I better help," she replied, her voice showing the first hint of compassion. The teacher sat down next to the slumping student. Then, remembering Ken, she said, "Mr. Parks, could we continue this later? I guess this could take a while."

Ken stood up. "No problem, Ms. Bedinghaus. I'll catch you later."

Not waiting for Ken's reply, the teacher started dislodging every item from the student's desk and depositing items on the floor. As she extracted textbooks, used candy wrappers, worn erasers, dog-eared folders, and wrinkled papers from the shelf, she lectured the student on the need to keep his desk organized.

Even as he studied Rachel trying to help the troubled student, Ken was still not sure. Something in his gut told him he wasn't getting the whole story, that Rachel knew something she wasn't telling him. Based on how she acted earlier, she had seemed…well, a little too eager to help out the student. As he stepped back through the doorway, he made another mental note to follow up with Rachel Bedinghaus.

Chapter 12

Ken didn't know Dawn Hatcher that well. He hadn't yet worked with her on any committees or projects, but he remembered her anyway. She was one of those teachers who left an impression on you. When he opened the door to the lounge, he saw her at the table, drinking coffee in a slow gulp.

As he entered, she glanced up and flashed him a small grin. "Good morning, Mr. Parks. Can I pour you some?" Dawn asked in that hoarse voice of hers. She held up a mug, which read *Teachers do it with class*.

"It's Ken, Dawn, and sure I'll take a cup if you're pouring."

"Would you like hi-test or decaf? We have both here in the full-service lounge."

"I probably better go with the decaf the way my nerves have been lately." Ken glanced around, glad to see they were alone. Unlike the cops, he didn't have any legal authority, but he needed to talk with these teachers and felt he'd better keep these interviews confidential. He checked the clock and hurried on. "Dawn, I need to talk to you about the four boys who died last week. Dr. Walters has asked me to look into what happened."

She brought him the brew in a chipped mug with the logo of the local insurance company. He inhaled the pungent aroma of the coffee and set the mug aside.

Dawn rasped, "Oh, I heard about your newest assignment. Don't you ever get tired of all the lousy jobs? Any dirty task Walters wants done he hands to you."

Ken wondered before about her scratchy voice. She sounded like a life-long smoker, though Ken had never seen her huddled with the staff members puffing at the side of the building. He knew some guys found that kind of raspy voice alluring, but that hardly jived with her looks. He took her in. Dawn wore a roomy top, dark blue with flowers, and flared skirt to match. Her brunette hair was cut somewhere between long and short in no particular style and framed a full face. Easing back in the chair, she gave off an air of nonchalance and looked what his grandmother would have called "frumpy." Still, the times he'd seen her, she seemed comfortable in her own skin. And she had a reputation as someone not afraid to speak her mind. That was what Ken was counting on.

He said, "Well, this is one job I want. The fact those kids died on *our* field trip haunts me. Now we know those damn drugs were involved and I intend to find out who's poisoning our kids." He heard the anger climb into his voice, but seeing Dawn's reaction, he took a slow breath and then asked, "What can you tell me about what happened that day at Camp Haven? Weren't you there all day Tuesday?"

"Yes, I was, but I don't know how much good I'm going to be. You see, Ken, I'm a good employee, or try to be. When Carla said she needed staff to go up to the camp to serve as back up to the camp counselors, I said sure, which is more than I can say about some male teachers in this building." The rasp became louder and more pronounced as she finished the last sentence. Bill Moore, the phys. ed. teacher, stuck his head in the door, looked around, and ducked back out.

Ken wasn't sure whether Dawn's last comment was for his benefit or for her colleague's.

She continued, "Anyway, I was glad to pitch in, so I went. But I need to tell you I'm not much into that nature stuff. My idea of getting back to nature is resting my legs off the balcony at the cabin. I'm not into hiking the way Stacy is, so I spent almost all of the day in our cabin or the canteen. I really didn't see the kids much that day."

"Who else was out there from school?" asked Parks.

"Well, Stacy came late afternoon, right after from school, I think, but I didn't see her till later. She said she was hanging with the students. And we didn't have a chance to talk until the next morning." Dawn shifted in her seat. "You see, Rachel was there earlier, but she got sick and went home. You know, she pulls something like that all the time. Anyway, Stacy wasn't due till that night, but she came up early to cover for Rachel. That was all for our group—except for John Waycross, Justin's dad. He came in that evening and was staying with the boys when they…snuck out." She let her voice trail off.

Though Dawn was a little brusque, Ken couldn't help but like her for her candor. He had trouble seeing her involved with the drugs. But what did he know? He asked, "You didn't see anything out of the ordinary that day?"

"No, like I said, I didn't spend much time with the kids. So, even if something was going on, I probably

86

wouldn't have seen it. Besides, the camp counselors are with the kids all the time, not us. I think they'd notice if anything was up." She paused and then went on, "Oh, you might ask Stacy. She said she hung out with the kids after she arrived. She's always trying to do things, to get through to the kids, and she likes to be around them."

"About what time did Stacy get there?"

"I don't know. I think she told me she came right after school, so probably around four, but you need to ask her."

Ken nodded and jotted a few notes on the open page of his clipboard. Glancing up, he stared across at Dawn Hatcher. "Can you just think back over the day before…before the boys died? Did you hear something, anything from these kids which might help us?" Dawn started to answer, but Ken cut her off. "Maybe something you overheard and didn't make anything of it at the time?" He waited.

Dawn didn't answer right away and appeared to be thinking. He liked that. She slowly shook her head. "About the only times I was around these kids was at mealtime. Tuesday, the day we arrived at Camp Haven, Rachel and I had lunch duty."

Ken nodded.

"You know how it goes. While the kids eat, we roam around and make sure everything is okay, until the camp counselors take over." She stared up at the ceiling, as if she was trying to recall something. "I remember going past the table where James and Robert were sitting together. Those two were always together."

"Were Chad and Justin at the same table?"

Dawn took a slow sip of her coffee. "Chad, yes, but

I don't remember seeing Justin with them."

"Okay." Ken drank some of the coffee and found it on the bitter side.

"The only thing I remember—" she said and stopped.

Ken put down the mug. "Yes?"

"It's probably nothing, but I overheard James say he'd gotten some help from his brother, er something like that."

"So? I don't get it."

Dawn smiled a grim smile. "I had James' brother Jack and he was—and no doubt, is—a real selfish jerk. I never knew him to care about his brother…or anyone else but himself. I thought it was off, Jack helping James."

Ken jotted another note on the page but had no idea if it mattered. When he finished, he asked, "Dawn, did you know the boys? I mean, was this thing with the drugs a surprise to you?"

"Oh, I knew those boys all right, but not that well. I know I'm not supposed to say this, now that they're dead, but I didn't really like them. Never speak ill of the dead and all that." She glanced around the room and brought her gaze back to Ken. "Well, that's not exactly true. Justin was a good kid, I think. Just really quiet. Not sure how he ended up with the others." She shook her head. "But the other three. Robert had quite a mouth on him and liked to bully the other kids. James sometimes got this look in his eyes. Gave me the creeps. Like he was planning something nasty. And I think Chad just went along and ended up in trouble." She pointed the mug at Ken. "I don't care what most teachers around here are telling you, hardly any of them had a decent word for those boys when they were alive…except Stacy."

"Did she like them?"

"I'm not sure you could say 'like.' Stacy seems to connect with a lot of these kids," Dawn continued. "I don't know if it's her experience or something, but she thinks she can save them."

"What about these kids and drugs? They're pretty young?"

"Well, they were in trouble enough. I didn't know them well enough to say, but today, with what kids are up against, who knows?" Dawn shot a glance at the wall clock. "Oh jeez, I didn't notice the time. I'm late and I've got to pick my kids up at music. The maestro's going to be mad. Well, life's tough all over." She took one last gulp, plopped the mug down, and fled out the door.

A few minutes later, he arrived at Stacy Thompson's classroom—the third teacher he was supposed to interview—and glanced at his watch. According to Martha's notes, he had a few minutes before her students would go to gym and he'd be able to talk to her privately. Rather than disturb her class and interrupt her teaching, he decided to wait. Through the window in the closed door, he watched her and part of the class, but couldn't hear the discussion. The students sat with their backs to the door, unaware of his presence. Mrs. Thompson, facing the class, glanced up to see him standing at the door and smiled. As she made a move to come to the door, Ken put up a palm and shook it side to side. Satisfied, she went back to the class.

Ken stared through the small rectangle of glass and

studied Stacy Thompson, still an attractive female. In his job, he worked with a number of good-looking women. It came with the territory, and it was one part Ken didn't mind at all. Carla Michaels was certainly striking in her own way and even Rachel Bedinghaus was pretty, in a petite, little girl next door manner. Beauty was one thing, but he had learned a long time ago beauty and virtue in women are not always the same. He'd seen enough of the first without the latter to know.

As he stood there staring, he'd found this woman a bit different. Unlike other attractive women on the staff like Jacqueline Highstreet or even Carla, Stacy didn't do glamor. Rather, she seemed to possess a natural, graceful beauty. She wore a small, strained smile and her carefully chiseled features were framed by shining, chestnut hair, now curled on each side of her head like a set of parentheses. Today, she wore a red pullover, cashmere sweater.

Since he had a few moments, he took a few slow breaths and, bending his neck, tried to release some of the tension. The deathly fate of the kids and the search for the person behind the drugs so haunted him, he needed to think of something else, anything else. He recalled his first meeting with Stacy Thompson, ten years earlier, at a much better time.

Chapter 13

"I think you better meet with Steven's teacher, Thompson," Amanda had said, right as Ken was drifting off to sleep. "I'm afraid of how I might react when she starts in on our son."

Ken turned in the bed to face her. "You know as principal, I've got a whole building of conferences going on tomorrow. Besides, I thought we agreed Steven needs to learn that actions have consequences."

"I know we said that but…I'd rather not have to face this Mrs. Thompson. From what some of the parents told me, she's a little on the strange side and I don't know what she might do."

Now, he sat up in bed. "Strange how?"

"Oh, I don't know. Steven says she has the kids do calisthenics at their desks and something she calls yoga breathing." Amanda turned both hands up and out. "The parents I talked to said she's too lazy to do her own bulletin boards. She makes the kids do them."

He'd never heard a teacher do that. "Are you sure? That sounds like sour grapes from a few disgruntled parents. Besides, I'll have a school full of parents tomorrow, some certainly upset, and I'll be putting out fires most of the day."

"Don't you think maybe this teacher will go a little easier, if she has to deal with a principal as the parent?" Amanda laid a hand on his bare chest. "Are you going to tell me you can't spare a few minutes tomorrow for our son?"

"You simply don't want to deal with it." Ken cocked his head and gave her a small grin. "How much is it worth to you?"

Her fingers did a come hither gesture and she purred, "How about I show you."

If her enthusiasm was any indication, she really, really didn't want to do the conference. So he called the middle school office in the morning and reserved one of the few remaining slots. Midday, he'd left Tom in charge at the high school and explained he'd be back as soon as he could.

So he stood there, outside the classroom, his son's classroom. Glancing at his watch, he noticed he was late, as usual, but it looked like Thompson was running behind anyway. He shifted from foot to foot, nodding at the other parents roaming the hallways, searching for room numbers.

This was hardly his first parent-teacher conference as a parent, but still, Ken had mixed feelings about this conference. Having been on the opposite side for years, first as an English teacher and then as a principal, he knew conferences between staff members were awkward, at best. Amanda thought it would go easier because he was an administrator, but he knew his role as principal would only make the whole thing more complicated.

At the same time, he had to admit he was looking forward to meeting this Mrs. Thompson. He had checked. She was in her second year at Foster and was a few years younger than he. But that was not all he'd heard. Some of the male teachers had said Thompson was a looker—sometimes in colorful, even crude, language—and he wanted to see for himself. After all, he was married, not blind. Besides, Amanda had asked him to meet with this woman, hadn't she?

Too nervous to take one of the chairs in the hallway, he ambled around, his glance landing on the bulletin board beside the classroom door. Indeed, the printing across the top did appear to be done by children, the words "Exemplary Work By Mrs. Thompson's Class" in large, boxy lettering. Ken scanned the attached papers—essays on the kids' heroes—searching for his son's writing, but he didn't find it. Given the year Steven had had, Ken was hardly surprised.

In the bottom right-hand corner was a small, typed paragraph. "The arrangement and content of this bulletin board has been designed by students. They even decide which assignments get displayed. The young men and women in Mrs. Thompson's class are empowered to make their own decisions whenever they can, hopefully making good choices most of the time."

All in all not a bad idea. So much for the parents' complaint about Thompson's bulletin boards.

Standing there, waiting and more than a little nervous, Ken got why Amanda had begged out of this. No parent liked to hear their child has been a problem, even if it were true. No, especially when it was true. He was no exception. This fall had been a challenging time for their son. Steven had made some poor choices in friends and, by October, had already earned special notice in the middle school principal's office. More than once, Harold, the Foster principal, had given Ken a heads up on the issues, as a courtesy. Ken took a slow breath and steeled himself against what he anticipated would be a deservedly bad report on his son.

"Thank you for coming, Mr. Hampton. I promise I'll keep working with Christopher. We'll get those grades up," a soft, feminine voice said. He hadn't heard the door open and turned to see the teacher escorting a rough looking man into the hallway.

The man gave a gruff "Thanks," and stomped away, his heavy steps echoing down the nearly empty hallway.

Mrs. Stacy Thompson turned his way, studying a sheet in her hand. "Who's next? Mr. Parks?" She extended her hand.

Ken took it and looked down at her. Her grasp was firm, but soft at the same time. The teacher beamed a broad smile and radiated a comfortable manner. He noticed Stacy Thompson had a shapely form, not entirely hidden by the dark green professional suit.

Yoga breathing? She didn't look flaky.

"You're Steven's father. I'm so glad to meet you." She led the way back into the classroom. Over her shoulder, she said, "Aren't you the high school principal?"

She took a student chair and he slid into the one opposite her, his knees almost touching his elbows.

"Guilty as charged." Ken shrugged and gave a small smile.

"Big responsibility," she replied, and it sounded like she meant it.

Long, flowing brunette hair brushed her shoulders, the lighter highlights reflecting the overhead fluorescents. When she glanced up to him, her emerald eyes sparkled. The teachers had not lied.

Well, he was married, he reminded himself…and a boss.

"So, let's talk about Steven," Stacy Thompson said and blew out a breath and he caught a hint of mint, wintergreen he thought.

"First of all, I apologize for my son's behavior. My wife and I have sat down with him and let him know that is not what we expect out of him. And he's promised to do better."

The teacher's smile returned. "He already has. I admit, if we'd had this conference a few weeks ago, our conversation might've been quite different. But I've seen a real turnaround in Steven's behavior in the last two weeks."

"You have?"

"Oh, yes, Steven has started making better friends and I've seen much more effort in his assignments. I think your parenting skills might be working."

Hardly what Ken had expected. "That's good to hear."

"He'd made some bad choices earlier, but I think he's learning from them. He's a smart boy. And I'm sure you know Steven has a really creative mind. You know, he is one of the best problem solvers in my class—when he chooses."

Ken hadn't thought about Steven as a problem solver and was surprised this teacher fostered abilities in his son Amanda and he hadn't even recognized yet.

"I saw you looking at the students' hero essays on the bulletin board. Didn't see Steven's up there, did you?"

"Well, with his behavior, I didn't really expect to find his work displayed, but a father can hope." Ken gave her another weak smile.

Reaching over to her desktop, Stacy pulled a piece of paper from a manila folder and slid it over to him. "I kept it for the conference. I thought you or your wife might want to see it."

Ken looked down at the sheet of notebook paper with a handwriting he recognized. He read the heading aloud, "My Dad, My Hero by Steven Parks" and saw the mark of a B+ in the top right corner. He glanced up at the teacher and then back down at the paper, trying to decipher the scribbling. He read "works harder than anyone" and "keeps his word" and "really cares about the students and teachers." Afraid now to look up, he could feel the tears forming in the corner of his eyes.

Stacy Thompson either didn't notice or pretended not to. She continued, "You know, I see the qualities of a leader in Steven and I'm enjoying having him in my class."

Her compassion for their son left him speechless that day and her words stayed with him for years. Since then, Stacy Thompson worked with him on several school committees, earning his respect, and the intervening years had moved them from colleagues to friends.

As that school year progressed, with his teacher's careful prodding and guidance, Steven blossomed and by fourth quarter had even brought his grades up to A's and B's.

Now, ten years later, their son was in college and successful.

Chapter 14

"Do you have a few minutes to talk to me?"

Stacy Thompson looked up to see Ken in the doorway once the last student had exited.

She turned her eyes from her cluttered desk. "Sure, Ken, come on in. I need to find one thing and get a book from the locker for the next class. If I don't do it now, my distracted brain will forget."

Her hands moved quickly across the desk, checking under piles and folders. Although the desk was a mess, she knew her way around the scattered papers and folders. "Here it is. I knew it was right here, but it was easier to find before my students put ten stacks of papers on my desk." She held up one finger. "Now, hang on a second." She stepped around the corner into the workroom and stooped to open the locker.

She fumbled with the dial for a few seconds. "It would help if I could remember the combination. Oh yeah," she said aloud and spun the dial. She opened the locker door and slid out the book she was looking for. She brought it back into the classroom, setting it on her desk atop the papers, the cover showing *Dream Keeper* by Langston Hughes.

"Okay, I'm all yours." Stacy folded her arms and smiled at him.

Stacy didn't want to admit it earlier in the teachers'

lounge, but she *was* nervous about this interview. More than a week after the incident, the guilt about the boys' deaths still weighed heavy on her—she was the teacher in charge, after all—and she was afraid it might show. But she realized this was difficult for Ken Parks, having to ask what had to be very uncomfortable questions, and she wanted to be supportive.

As she sat across from him, the warm gaze of his blue-green eyes and his sad smile eased her anxiety some. He'd chosen a navy blazer and yellow shirt along with one of his trademark children's ties, his choice for today a child's drawing of kids from different countries holding hands against a sky-blue background. The tie hung slightly askew on him. Without thinking, Stacy reached over and straightened it, her fingers tingling at the touch. She quickly withdrew them and looked down, suddenly embarrassed. Close in, she caught a mere whisper of some masculine cologne.

Ken began, "I was standing outside and couldn't help but notice how involved your students seemed to be. I couldn't hear much of the discussion, but it was obvious you had your students with you. They didn't even move when the bell rang."

She flashed a half smile to cover her embarrassment at the compliment. Then it occurred to her he was probably trying to make her a little more comfortable and said, "Thank you. It's what they call a teachable moment, a lesson on drug abuse. It wasn't originally in my lesson plans this week, but I thought my students needed this lesson now." She pointed to the desks to her right.

Ken's gaze followed her outstretched hand and his eyes widened in recognition. The four desks Stacy was indicating were clustered in a tight group at the front of the room. On the top of each lay a single sheet of black construction paper, dark and in stark contrast to the blond Formica top. Glued to each black paper was a small oval photograph of a boy, crudely cut from a class group portrait, and the boy's name, scrawled in a fifth grader's handwriting.

She released a deep breath. "The students decided they wanted to keep the four boys' desks here. And they wanted to do something to remember them. This is what they came up with."

Ken nodded at the desks. "Looks good. I can't imagine how hard it's been to teach this week, after—" He didn't finish the sentence. "No one would've blamed you if you needed time off after what you experienced at the camp. It looks like you're exactly what these kids need, though."

Grateful for his support, she said, "After viewing that horrible death scene, no way could I abandon these kids. Ken, you know for many of them, this is their first encounter with death. The counselors have helped, but most are still not coping very well."

Ken said, "I get it. You and I are two of the only staff who witnessed what really happened to those boys."

At the image of the death scene, with the crushed young bodies and the sickening smell of blood, she felt a shudder run through her.

Ken met her gaze and continued, "Anyway, you've probably heard Dr. Walters has asked me to look into what happened, to see if I can find out how those children got their hands on those drug tattoos. He's really worried about possible consequences. I'm hoping *you* can help. From what I've heard, you're one of the only teachers who had any kind of relationship with some of the boys."

Her eyes tearing up, Stacy let out a long sigh. "Well, I'm not sure you could call it a relationship. Sometimes I couldn't stand them, pretty much like everyone else." She used a sleeve of her blouse to wipe her eyes. "But there were other times, times when they would let you get past their false bravado and their insecurities. You could *just* get a glimpse of their potential, you know."

Ken shook his head. "Not really. I usually only get to meet the kids when they've crossed the line and they're up for suspension."

Stacy said, "Well, like this one time, I teamed James up with two struggling students for this session we were working on math problems. I was going around the room, checking how the groups were doing and when I got to James' table, he was showing the other two a new way to solve the problem. All three students were leaning together and the other two were hanging on James' words. I complimented him on how well he was doing and he grinned back at me. Then, like the flip of a switch, his eyes got hard and he quit working, right then and there. Wouldn't even talk with the other two kids in his group."

Stacy felt a lump form in her throat and finished, "I knew where these kids were coming from—at least, more than most teachers—and, yeah, sometimes I wanted to take them home. And then the next minute I wanted to kill 'em." She shrugged, embarrassed. "I'm not sure if that qualifies as a relationship."

A brief pause followed as if Ken didn't know how

to ask his next question. After a bit, he got out, "Did you know any of the boys well enough to know if they'd experimented with drugs before?"

"Yes and no. As far as I knew, they weren't into drugs—I mean they're only eleven, except for James—but I wasn't totally surprised either. Wait, that's not true about Justin. I don't understand how he fell in with the other three. Justin is…" She stopped, feeling the tears welling up again. "Justin *was* a sweet, quiet kid. But the other three boys were always on the edge, led by James. I think *he'd* try about anything, and the other two would follow along. For some of these kids, it's a pretty lousy world, and almost anything is worth trying." She heard the bitterness in her voice. "I simply wanted to make my classroom a safe place, a place where they felt welcomed."

"I know this isn't easy for you and I know you cared about these boys. I understand. I didn't even know the kids that well and *I* can't sleep at night when I picture those small four gold caskets. This whole thing is driving me crazy. I want to…no, I *have* to figure out how our fifth graders got their hands on those drugs."

As Stacy looked across the desk to her boss, she was struck by his expression. She had noticed before Ken was not like most administrators. He didn't go by titles—he insisted you call him Ken—and he almost never pulled rank or lorded his authority over the teachers. If anything, maybe he cared too much about the students, rather than the teachers. At least, that was what some teachers complained about him. He always put kids first. Seeing the anguished look in his eyes, she could tell this wasn't merely another job handed to him by the superintendent. She sensed he had some personal stake in it but knew it wasn't her place to ask.

He said, "Dawn told me you were with the boys for a while the afternoon and evening before they died. Have you thought of anything you saw or heard that might help me?"

Thinking for a minute before she answered, Stacy shook her head. "No. I wish I could think of something and man, how I've tried. That afternoon when I caught up with them, the boys were arguing, which was nothing new. They were out on the trail and the argument could have been about the drugs, I don't know. It could have been about anything. When I got there, it was obvious the camp counselor had his hands full, so I tried to intervene and distract the boys. I guess it worked because they stopped arguing and we all marched back to camp together."

Ken nodded and then stared at her, rubbing his chin. He looked as if he was trying to decide something. "Do you have any idea where they could've gotten the drugs?"

"Why, no. What makes you think *I* would know something?" She heard the anxiety in her voice and tried to tamp it down. "Is there a particular reason you're asking *me*?"

"I'm asking everyone, but I mean, since you seem to be closer to these students, I thought they might tell you something they wouldn't say to anyone else."

Stacy stared at her colleague and friend and read the frustration in his face. In that moment, as she pondered how to answer, she realized the grief and anger over the boys' deaths was a bond she shared with him. Ken's gaze stayed fixed on her, waiting. He didn't look away and she feared he was able to peer right inside her. Her embarrassment returned and she looked to the side. "You're not going to like my answer."

Ken didn't respond immediately, and Stacy was grateful for his patience. He sat there across from her, less than two feet away, his gaze never leaving hers. Finally he whispered, "Try me."

She sat there for a moment longer, deciding how much she was willing to risk. Staring into the pair of intense blue-green eyes still fixed on her, she decided to take a chance. "I don't know where the boys got the drugs." She paused, trying to decide how to phrase the rest. "None of the students ever told me directly, but I've overheard enough that I'm pretty sure they're getting the drugs, um…here at school."

Pausing, she tried to gauge his reaction but his features gave little away. "Oh, I know that's not a very popular opinion. After all, Foster is a 'National Drug Free School.' " She made air quotes.

Ken didn't respond the way she feared. He wasn't defensive of the school's name or reputation. He asked, "Is there anything in particular you can tell me that might help me know where to look, or at least where to start?"

"I don't know, Ken. I've only heard a few specifics. Often the talk of the boys mimics that of their older brothers. I've heard them say things like…" She hesitated, trying to remember the particular wording. "At Foster we can get whatever we want or Foster is like Meijer, you can find anything here." She waved her hands in front of her. "I know it doesn't sound like much. With this school's reputation, *I* probably sound nuts. But you'd understand if you had been there, if you knew these boys." Stacy's anxiety ratcheted up and her words tumbled out. She wondered if she'd made a mistake, said too much.

"I believe you," Ken said, clearly sensing her apprehension. "From what a few kids have admitted, I've had a hunch they were getting the drugs from here, but not much more than that. Over the years I've learned to trust my instincts, but for this, I need more, a lot more. At least what you've shared confirms my hunch."

He looked across at her and she saw him studying her, as if he were probing her. Quickly, she looked away and another awkward silence enveloped the room.

After a bit, he pressed, "Did they say anything that would give you an idea who was selling the drugs? Students? Adults here at Foster? Anything at all?" Before she had a chance to answer, he asked, "Why didn't you report this before?"

Stacy's defenses went up. Maybe she *had* shared too much. "Report what? A couple of kids making fun of their older brothers? And besides, I tried. About four weeks ago, I went and reported it to Mrs.—"

Before she could get the rest of her sentence out, the deafening beep of the intercom blared. The screech was followed by a tinny female voice. "Mrs. Thompson, is Mr. Parks down there?"

"Yes, Martha. Mr. Parks is here," Stacy answered.

"He has a phone call from his office," the tin voice responded.

Ken intervened, "Martha, will you ask them if I can call them back? We'll be done here in a few minutes."

"Mr. Parks, I already tried that. Vivian said you needed to be interrupted. She was pretty insistent."

For a few seconds, both Stacy and Ken stared at the

white box speaker. Then Stacy said, "Martha, transfer the call to the workroom here."

"I'm already doing that, Mrs. T."

Stacy said, "The phone is right on the far wall."

Ken took his time moving from the chair to the connected workroom. He exchanged a glance with Stacy, and she could tell he was perturbed at being interrupted.

The phone rang and when he picked up the receiver, he snapped, "This better be good, Vivian." It was all he got out.

As Stacy watched from the doorway, chewing slightly on her lower lip, she saw shock register in his eyes, the color draining from his face. She had no idea what news he was getting, but she could see some new tragedy invade his features.

He let out a whispered "Oh my God!" and then, "I'm on my way." He hung up. "It's another student, a seventh grader named Tricia Holloway. Know her?" Ken fired the words quickly and Stacy nodded. "Looks like the same thing as the boys," he said, pointing to the shrouded desks. "They found her in the basement girls' bathroom, one of those damn tattoo patches on her arm exactly like the dead boys."

"Oh, no," Stacy gasped.

Chapter 15

Ken hated hospitals, always had. Hated the nauseating smell of disinfectant, the sterile whitewash of the walls, the constant undercurrent of Muzak and intercom announcements. He went only when he needed to and stayed only as long as he had to.

No doubt, this aversion went back to having to watch his father die in a hospital bed when he was four. Even now, almost forty years later, he could still remember coming, day after day with his then pregnant mom to the great, gray leviathan of a hospital building. In his nightmares, he still pictured that hospital room and the snaking equipment hooked up to his father's motionless body. At the time he didn't understand what was going on and thought, in his young brain, the machines were sucking the life out of his father—day by day, little by little, stealing the light out of his dad's eyes, till there was no light, no smile, no father. With the exception of the birth of his son, his only encounters with hospitals had been occasions to have life snatched away from him. He didn't know how to cope with this repulsion, but he did what he always did with something he couldn't or didn't want to deal with. He shoved it to the back of his mind and moved on.

He hated hospitals, but he was here anyway, at Portsmouth Memorial.

Shortly after being found, Tricia Holloway had

lapsed into a coma, probably brought on by a severe reaction to the drugs according to the EMT's. Though she had uttered a few incoherent syllables when they discovered her, the medics said they couldn't make any sense of what she said. Tricia had not awakened since.

Since he couldn't talk with the student yet, Ken decided he needed to speak with Tricia's parents. Maybe they knew something. And maybe they'd be so devastated, their defenses would be down. One more part of this job he detested, asking parents of a comatose thirteen-year-old if they had any idea where their daughter might have gotten the drugs.

When he first heard what happened, Ken hoped the student's bout would be short-lived. He thought, perhaps, the whole experience might be so unsettling, she'd come out of it and give up some answers about where she got the drugs. Now, he simply prayed she'd wake up.

On his trip to Portsmouth Memorial, Ken reviewed his conversations with the teachers. Not much. The disruptions in his interviews with both Rachel and Stacy bothered him. True, he hadn't gotten anything useful from Bedinghaus, but he had the gnawing feeling she was hiding some secret. Of course, he had no idea what it could be. It may have nothing to do with the boys' deaths, but he felt certain there was something.

With Stacy, it was different. When they talked, it seemed more like conversations between friends, or at least colleagues. And he realized he had to be careful to not let their friendship blind him. When he thought back to her explanation of what happened at the camp, he remembered seeing her expression change. Her face darkening, her green eyes seemed to surrender their light like the horizon succumbing to the twilight. The spark he'd seen earlier was replaced by something else. Grief, anger, guilt—Ken wasn't sure, but he was haunted by what he saw in those eyes.

He needed to sit down with both teachers again, and soon.

Pulling his Taurus into one of the visitor parking spots, he strode in through the yawning glass doors. His secretary had told him Tricia was in room 226 and he glanced at the signage, trying to determine which way to go. His eyes focused on the wall, he bumped into an empty, gray gurney, sitting discarded in the hallway like an old, abandoned car on the side of the road.

As his hand grasped the stretcher railing, the cold, metallic touch stirred his subconscious, briefly strafing the hidden memory. Ken sensed it more than remembered it. The guilt, still deeply buried, threatened to escape and consume him.

He stopped. "I can't deal with it now. I can't," Ken heard himself gasp aloud and looked around to see if anyone had noticed. They hadn't. Relieved, he shoved the gurney away and felt the icy fingers of the memory release their cold grip.

He hurried down the hallway.

Glancing along the wall, he read the room numbers printed in antiseptic white numerals with the obligatory Braille bumps below. The odd mixture of cloying disinfectant and fresh cut flowers assailed his nostrils. When he arrived at 226, he peered around the door jamb. He saw Tricia, lying on the white, sterile bed, eyes closed, breathing gently, a top sheet with small geometric designs in primary colors up to her shoulders. When he saw her face, he remembered her somewhat, a slightly tall adolescent, awkward, shy, but boy crazy. Her face was fighting a miniature war with pimples and losing, and her dark hair was brushed back out of what would eventually be a pretty face. No machines were attached to her except the clamp on her finger taking her pulse. She could have been merely sleeping.

At the foot of her bed slouched a man Ken took to be Tricia's father. His hair disheveled, the stubble of a heavy beard shadowing his chin, his face bore long lines of weariness and worry. A dog-eared, hunting magazine dangled from two fingers of his left hand. His long, lean figure slumped in the chair. He'd drifted off, no doubt exhausted from the cruel waiting. Ken did not want to intrude, so he paused, lingering right outside the doorway.

Peering into the small hospital room, Ken caught sight of a worn green-and-brown Eddie Bauer backpack sitting atop the chair right inside the door. He reached down and grabbed the strap to lift the bag. It gave way in his hand, exposing the tattered end of leather ripped from age and use, and dumped two schoolbooks onto the cushion of the chair, making a bumping sound. Checking the sleeping figure, Ken saw the slight noise hadn't awakened the man and exhaled.

He reached down to pick up the texts, his eyes scanning the two books as he stuffed them back into the bag. Both textbooks were wrapped with school-issued, maroon-and-white book covers, the red "Portsmouth Warriors" logo printed in large letters across the front. Every available white space on both books was covered with the scribbling and doodling of a teenager. Ken's eyes took in everything from tiny hearts colored in a deep blue, to various boys' names, to intricate, abstract patterns—but he found nothing particularly revealing.

As he was stuffing the texts into the worn bag, something near the back of the science book caught his eye, a flash of color he hadn't seen before. Picking up the text, he noticed a pink slip sticking part way out of the pages. When he opened the cover, he found it. Sticking to the last page was a pink Post-it note with the saying "When the going gets tough, the tough go shopping $$$" printed across the top. He peeled the note off. Studying the small slip of paper, he read the words written below in a vaguely familiar script, though he couldn't quite place the feminine handwriting:

If you need anything just call.
972-9499

He folded the note, the rubber cement of the two halves sticking together, and replaced the book. Turning the small paper over in his fingers, he read and reread the message in halves. First "If you need anything, just call." Then "972-9499."

He slid the paper into his shirt pocket.

"I haven't watched her like this since she was a baby," said a quiet, tired female voice behind him.

Ken jerked and turned, feeling like a burglar caught in the act.

Chapter 16

"She simply lays there. The doctors 've run tests, that CAT scan, some EE something." The woman wept, crying large tears, her small body trembling. "They don't know if there's any brain damage yet, and they don't know how soon she's going to wake up."

Ken tried to slide the book back into the worn backpack unobtrusively. Feeling guilty and moved by her worry and concern, once again the fury inside him rose like bile in his throat and he had to choke it back.

Turning away from the room, he looked into the pained face across from him and waited patiently for her to gain her composure. The visage was one of a fairly young woman, Ken would have guessed about thirty-five, who at an earlier time had certainly been attractive, but a broken nose had spoiled a once lovely silhouette. Today, her face bore the deeply etched lines and swollen, bloodshot eyes that made the woman age at least ten years.

"Mrs. Holloway?"

She nodded, handkerchief to her nose.

"My name is Ken Parks. We haven't met but I'm Assistant Superintendent of Portsmouth Schools."

He peered into the face to gauge if his words registered. Staring back at him, her eyes looked like hollow sockets with two small black dots in a double sea of red and white, the blue color almost eclipsed.

He went on, trying to draw some recognition. "I work for the school district. I'm trying to find out something about the drugs. About what happened to Tricia." He glanced from the still figure on the bed to the mother. This time she nodded in understanding, still clutching the small, white cloth next to her crooked nose.

Ken gazed across at the strained face before him and decided to press on. "I'm trying to learn where the students are getting these drugs, how the kids are getting the drugs. I wondered if you knew anything, if you'd ever overheard Tricia say something about someone selling her drugs?" When this elicited no response, he asked, "Had you ever had problems like this before with her?"

"Well, no—"

Before she could get more out, Ken felt his left shoulder shoved roughly. He staggered sideways into the corridor. He turned to see the tall, haggard figure of Mr. Holloway, his grizzled face scrunched and his eyes wide. The man shook a gnarled fist at him as if threatening with a gun. "What's the matter w' ya? Can't ya see she's in a hell of a lot o' pain right now? Damn education bureaucrats ain't got no sense." The stink of unwashed sweat and dirt came off the man in waves.

"I'm, sorry," Ken answered, working not to hold his nose. He raised both hands, palms out in surrender. "I understand your worry."

"Ya don't understand nothin'," the other man replied.

Ken hated hospitals, hated this task, and was furious himself. His normal, calm diplomacy deserted him and he shot back, "Look, Mr. Holloway, I know you're under a lot of stress here and I feel for your pain, but *I* am not the enemy. I'm only here because I'm trying to catch the scum who did *that* to your daughter." Ken's arm shot out and pointed at the still figure on the bed.

"Henry, settle down," Mrs. Holloway spoke up, suddenly animated in an obvious effort to calm her husband. "Mr. Parks is only doing his job and we want to help." Then to Ken, "This is driving us both crazy."

"I understand, Mrs. Holloway, maybe better than you know," Ken said, choking down his own personal guilt. "For the past week I've thought of little else. I've interviewed parents and classmates of the four dead boys, teachers and counselors still in shock. I haven't been able to sleep. I want to catch the person who did this…and make sure it doesn't happen to any more students like Tricia."

He paused, letting his words register. "Look, I know you don't want to talk to me right now and I'm sorry I can't wait till your daughter is better. If I do, what happened to your daughter or those boys might happen to more kids. I don't want to take that chance…do you?"

"What do you want to know?" asked Mrs. Holloway, her voice quiet.

"Is there anything you can tell me, anything at all, that might get me closer to who's doing this?"

"Well…"

"Clarese!" commanded her husband. "That ain't none of his biz'ness."

Man and wife eyed each other, engaging in one of those tests of wills so common among couples. The wife, though a little battle-scarred, Ken thought, would not relent and eventually won. "Henry Holloway, your daughter's layin' in that there bed in a coma and you're worried 'bout what's not his biz'ness. We can stand a little embarrassment and mebbe spare somebody else this grief."

Ken waited and, listening to the exchange, hoped he might learn something, anything. Maybe if it was a big enough secret, it might be of help to him, he thought desperately. At the same time he hated himself for wishing they had bad news to tell him. "Mrs. Holloway, is there anything you can tell me that would help us learn where the drugs are coming from?"

"We've had a little problem with Tricia before." Clarese Holloway stared at the dull, gray floor beneath her feet. "We caught Tricia with some drugs once before, about three weeks ago."

"Rese, it was just a couple o' joints," interjected her husband.

"Of marijuana?" asked Ken.

"Yeah," responded Mrs. Holloway. "I found them in her room when I was cleaning. When we asked her about them, all she would tell us was that she got 'em at school, from some other kid. No matter how hard we pressed, she refused to tell us who that was."

"I wanted to hit her, but I didn't," added her husband, raising the gnarled fist again. "So we grounded her for two weeks. Didn't do much good, did it? She still had to go to school and that's where the problem is, ain't it, Mr. Parks?" The bitterness in his voice was raw-edged, like broken glass.

Ken met his gaze and empathized with the frustration and anger in the man's eyes. "To tell you the truth, Mr. Holloway, it's beginning to look that way."

Ken could already hear O'Brien rail about lawyers, and liability, and money, because of his candor. He didn't care. "If it is, I give you my word, I'll find a way to stop it. When your daughter does wake up and you think she is up to it, please talk to her about the drugs. She's bound to be scared and maybe she won't be so anxious to protect who's selling this poison."

Both parents nodded in agreement.

"I'll be back soon. If she awakens before that, please let me know." He reached into his vest pocket, pulling out a business card. "Here is my information. My number at the office is printed on the front and I've written my home number on the back. You can call me at either. And again, I apologize for intruding. I know you have enough sorrow without me adding to it. But I need your help to stop this madness."

He extended his hand and Henry Holloway hesitated at first. Then, very slowly, the tall man raised his calloused palm to meet Ken's. The two hands met and held briefly, suspended in air.

Leaving the anguished parents alone, Ken headed down the hall, hurrying to escape the hospital. As he stepped out of the elevator into the lobby, he walked straight toward the large glass exit doors directly ahead of him. He had to get out of here. As he stepped up to the automatic doors and heard the quiet swish of the rotors, his peripheral vision caught sight of something on his left and he halted. Hesitating—torn between wanting to leave and needing to learn something, anything that might help—he stared at the bank of three pay phones pressed against the wall, phone books hanging below on dangling lifelines.

Glancing around, Ken saw only an empty lobby,

save for a janitor lazily emptying a trashcan. Maybe the number would get him something, get him to someone connected with the drugs. On impulse, he stepped up to the first phone in the line and inserted a quarter. Pulling the folded, pink Post-it from his breast pocket, he carefully punched in the number written in the distinct feminine script. He listened. He held his breath as he waited for four rings, then he heard the clink of an answering machine and a bright, familiar voice.

"Hi, this is the Thompsons. Sorry we can't come to the phone right now, but we're a little busy. Please leave us a message and we'll get right back to you."

Stacy Thompson? What the hell was going on?

Ken slammed the phone down and strode to the nearby exit, where the electric eye opened the glass doors. For a moment, in Ken's tortured imagination, the exit waited for him, like a yawning mouth of some carnivorous beast.

Chapter 17

The door to the office had been shut for a while and Ken could feel the temperature within the small room rising. This made the four occupants even more uncomfortable and tempers even shorter.

"*You* are responsible for his death. You, Dr. Walters, and you, Dr. O'Brien," railed an angry Samuel Hayes, father of one of the dead boys.

Having declined the chair offered to him, the parent stood in wrinkled pants and a red and black flannel shirt. He pointed at the two men with a hairy hand with dirty split fingernails. When he spoke, he practically hissed the words through crooked, tobacco-stained teeth, his acrid breath spilling out into the room, fouling the air.

"For Christ's sake, it was a school outing. You guys are s'posed t' take care of our boys. If ya hadn't taken him to that goddamn camp, my Robert would still be with me today, wouldn't he?"

Ken stole a glance at his watch. 7:45 a.m. The day had barely begun and already looked bleak. At ten last night, he'd received a call and his boss told him to be at a meeting with the board president in the morning. When Ken arrived a few minutes early, he found Walters and O'Brien already in deep discussion. Shortly after, the man forced his way into the office. Samuel Hayes, a small, distraught figure, demanded to talk to them about his son's death.

"Look, Mr. Hayes, please sit down," said Mark Walters in his most reassuring voice, gesturing to the open chair in front of his desk. Reluctantly, the man accepted his offer and sat. Behind the big oak desk, Walters straightened in his chair, both arms resting on the desktop encased in the perfectly starched sleeves of his white shirt. "I know this is very hard for you and your family. We all share your grief. We're as concerned as you are about your loss."

"Bullshit!" Hayes' fist slammed down so hard on the desk, the others in the room jumped. "You didn't give a damn 'bout my boy when he was alive. Nobody here did...except for one or two teachers. You didn't care then. How am I s'pose t' believe ya care now? My guess is, since these boys was not from some big, important families, since everybody calls 'em troublemakers, nobody here really gives a damn. Well, I'll tell you what. I ain't goin' to let ya sweep this under the rug."

"I understand how you could feel that way," Dr. Everett O'Brien responded. His voice sounded quiet, even penitent, the essence of calm. He hung his head a little, his face a picture of contrition. "If we have not treated your son right in the past, *I* personally apologize, Sam. Is it okay if I call you Sam?"

The head on the unkempt figure nodded once in agreement, the matted gray hair following a little behind.

O'Brien continued, "We are very disturbed by your son's death, by the deaths of all four boys. You have my personal assurance the board is making this its highest priority." He paused, meeting the visitor's gaze, as if trying to gauge his reaction. Hayes seemed to relax a bit, so the board president continued. "I want to make this clear to you, perfectly clear. We have really worked hard to stop kids from getting drugs here. Hey, I know how hard it is to be a parent today. I have an eight-year-old myself and I'm scared about what's out there. Bringing up kids has never been harder."

"You can say that." Hayes nodded in agreement.

"I know you did what you could, Sam. We try to protect our kids from tragedies like this, but today's world is terribly cruel," O'Brien went on, his voice a soothing tone. "For the past few years, we've prided ourselves on our great reputation for fighting drugs in our schools, you know that. Well…maybe we've gotten too smug. Your son's death—and the other three boys' deaths—they are going to be an inspiration to others. Maybe help keep other kids off drugs."

As Ken studied the man, Samuel Hayes seemed to have simmered down a little, no longer so agitated, his hands almost quiet now. He appeared to be contemplating O'Brien's little speech. A short pause of quiet followed. Finally, he looked up.

"I'm grateful to ya for your kind words, Dr. O'Brien, I really am." Then he looked from board president to superintendent and spoke the next words with steely determination. "But, uh…if I find out the school had anythin' to do with this, anythin' at all, I'll sue ya'll for every penny ya have. I don't care what it takes."

Chapter 18

The door to the outside office slammed shut. Mark Walters spoke first. "Well, that was not wholly unexpected."

"Unexpected, hell," snapped O'Brien. "That old alcoholic's been spreading it all over town he's going to get *big* money for his son's death." He waved both hands in front of him back and forth as if he was trying to dispel the nauseating stink left behind by the parent. "He cared more about his next bottle than anything his son did when he was alive. The only reason he cares now is because he thinks he can make money from it. That drunk doesn't care about anyone or anybody other than himself. Hell, he's already hired some shyster lawyer who's anxious to get his hooks into the school budget and my pocketbook."

O'Brien pulled his Mont Blanc pen from his shirt pocket and began to fiddle with it as he talked, twirling it between his fingers. "Well, Ken, what the hell *have* you found out about the boys' deaths?"

"Not that much yet, at least not for sure," Ken began. "According to the autopsy, all four boys had high doses of some exotic drug I've never heard of. This particular version appears to be extremely potent and concentrated."

"Did the drugs cause the accident?" asked Walters.

"Probably, we don't know for sure," Ken

continued. "Doc Hardcastle said the amount of drugs in their blood was extremely high. High enough to cause major hallucinations and disorientation. He thinks it probably led to loss of control and the accident. All four died from injuries sustained in the collision. I have copies of the four autopsy reports, if you'd like them."

O'Brien said, "Yes, thanks. I'll take a look at them."

"What else have you learned?" asked Walters. "Who all have you interviewed so far?"

"I've talked with everyone at Camp Haven, from the boys' camp counselor to the camp director," replied Ken.

"Any chance we can hang this on the camp? You know, on their property and all?" raised O'Brien.

"I don't think so," Ken said, eying the board president. "They check out clean. Seems the camp has a very stringent policy on drugs. Employee urine tests, random searches, thorough background checks. Anything's possible, but I doubt it."

"Okay, who else have you talked to?" asked Walters.

"I've interviewed each one of the students who were at the camp with the boys."

As Ken talked, he slid his right hand inside his navy blazer. Reaching in to retrieve a pen, his index finger and thumb touched the small, folded paper he had stuffed into his breast pocket, and he pulled it out. Half listening to his own recounting, he glanced obliquely at the pink note again, reading its message in split halves.

"I've spoken with the three teachers who were on duty that day, Dawn Hatcher, Rachel Bedinghaus, and

Stacy Thompson, and I touched base with Carla, their principal."

"And Ken, what about the teachers?" pushed O'Brien.

"Well, basically, no one saw anything," Ken said, refusing to be ruffled. "The boys were into a few scrapes and Mrs. Thompson had to break up an argument between two of the boys, but that was nothing new. One of the students said she heard them planning something, but that wasn't unusual either."

Mark Walters sat and listened quietly. O'Brien glanced back and forth from superintendent to assistant. "Is there anything else?"

Ken studied the faces of the two men across from him. His gaze went from the folded Post-it note to his two bosses. He got ready to tell them about the message on the paper but stopped himself. Turning the pink half-slip over and over in the three fingers of his right hand, he held his tongue. Something, some caution made him hesitate. He needed to talk to Stacy first, to give her a chance to explain. There was probably a simple explanation, maybe a coincidence …he hoped. Besides, he didn't want to give O'Brien anything that would set him off. Looking up at the two men, he said, "No, I guess that's about it."

"Ken, that's not a whole hell of a lot, is it?" barked the board president.

"Oh, perhaps, one thing more," Ken said, letting a little steel in his voice. He refused to do what most of the staff, including his boss, did. He refused to defer to the board president and call him doctor. He called him by his first name. "According to what I've learned so far, Everett, it looks like these kids might be getting the drugs inside the school."

"Holy Christ, Ken!" O'Brien was up out of his chair, his tall, lanky figure strutting around the room. He shoved the expensive pen in his shirt pocket and the fingers of his right hand moved to his Cartier watch and he twirled the band around the wrist. "Do we know for sure or is this some conjecture of yours?"

"No, we don't know for sure, but it's not merely a conjecture of mine," Ken stated, looking evenly at his two bosses. "For right now, let's call it a partially substantiated hunch."

"Well, that's great!" O'Brien snapped. "That's all we need. Let's see if I can be clear about this." Ken felt O'Brien's gaze bore down on him. "Listen, until we know for sure, I mean for-absolute-goddamn-ironclad sure, keep this 'conjecture' of yours quiet. That's probably all the lawyers will need to hear and they'll be hauling our collective asses into court. And, gentlemen, you better listen to me. If word of this gets out, we can probably simply get out our checkbooks." He spit out the last phrase like venom.

"Easy, Dr. O'Brien. I think we should all settle down here," stated the superintendent, obviously trying to regain control. "Ken, can you bring us up-to-date on the other student?" He consulted his notes. "Tricia Holloway?"

"Like the boys, no one saw what happened to her either," Ken explained. "They found her in the basement girls' bathroom, the one that's not used very much. She went down there between classes, and it took a while to track her down. When the EMT's arrived, she was already out of it. But so far she's still hanging on, at least for now."

"Thank God for that," Walters said.

"But she's in a coma and the doctors are doing no predicting about when or if she's going to wake up," Ken continued.

"Is it the same drug that the boys had?" asked O'Brien, subdued again.

"She was wearing the same patch—the kids call it a drug tattoo—as the boys were. At this point, the doctors are not sure what they can do for Tricia."

Silence followed Ken's comments. The possibility of another dead youth sobered all three men in the small room. After a moment, O'Brien seem to regain his professional composure and spoke again.

"Look, Ken, I'm sorry I jumped on you before about the drug pusher being one of ours." He twisted his watchband again on his wrist. "I guess I don't want to believe it could be one of our employees. That's way too scary." He shook his head slowly. "What makes you think it could be one of the staff? You must have some reason for suspecting."

"Well," Ken said, "the kids are really scared on this one, even the tough ones. They won't say much, but they've admitted that the drugs are coming from the inside, and not from other students."

"If that's true, and I hope to God it's not. I only wish—" O'Brien paused, returning to his chair. "I wish there was a way to catch the low life in the act. Hey, Mark, isn't there any way we could tap the phones and eavesdrop on conversations and maybe catch them making a drug connection?"

"You've got to be kidding, Dr. O'Brien," Walters said. "I'm sure there's a right of privacy issue and, anyway, wouldn't the union have fun with that one?

Not to mention how many phone lines we have in this district."

"Yeah, but I wish we could catch them in the act." The board president mused aloud. "Ken, isn't there anything we could do with all this new technology? After all, the board spent more than a million dollars for all those new computers and the district network. Is there anything we can do to try to catch someone if he's using the email to make their drug connections?"

"You know, Everett, you might have something. It's a long shot, but it's possible," Ken said, thinking out loud.

Both the president and the superintendent leaned forward in their chairs.

"It's possible to take a look at all the emails of any staff member, through the administrative override. I'm not sure we'd find anything though or even know what we're looking for."

"Sounds like it might be worth a try," said Walters. "But aren't there the same privacy issues?"

"Not with the email," Ken answered. "Every staff member signs an agreement acknowledging all transmissions are the district's property and agrees to have them checked. It was a provision we put in to guard against anyone conducting inappropriate forays into the internet with school equipment, but the agreement should cover us here as well."

"Good. Since you're the one with system administrator override, why don't you get with the police?" said Walters. "We might as well let them comb through the email records. Besides, they're more likely to know what to look for. Maybe it will give us some place to start."

"I wouldn't get your hopes up," replied Ken, "but it's worth a try. I'll call Bart and Garcia and see what they can do."

"Look, Ken, I know this is not an easy job I'm asking of you," Walters said. "I appreciate everything you're doing on this. Do it your way, and do *not* let up. We need to know where these drugs are coming from. We need to do everything we can to protect these kids *and* this district. The sooner you can get to the bottom of this, the sooner we can keep more kids from getting hurt and put this ugly episode behind us."

He stood up to indicate Ken was being dismissed. "Let me know if you come up with anything."

"Sure," said Ken, heading for the door.

O'Brien stood up also and added, "That goes for me too. Thanks for what you're doing. Oh, sorry about giving you a hard time."

"We're all pretty uptight about the kids' deaths, Everett." Ken said and exited through the now open door. When he left the inner office and walked to the secretary's desk, he turned and glanced back. Walters and O'Brien sat huddled next to each other, in matching, starched white collars and blue and gray power ties, talking in hushed, anxious tones. Like two conspirators, Ken thought and dismissed the thought.

O'Brien got up and closed the door.

Chapter 19

Stacy Thompson studied her class carefully. She'd decided it was time. A week had passed since the funeral and her students were still struggling to adjust but didn't know how. The past few days, ministers and counselors had been available in the building and some of her students had gone to talk with them. But for most, she could see it in their faces, the gnawing pain of sudden death. She read it in their eyes every time they passed the four empty desks at the front of the room.

Probably, the love-hate relationship many of the students had with the dead boys made the pain of grief worse. A few kids had told her they were relieved at not having to put up with the taunts and bullying by James and Robert. Then, when their young minds realized the boys were really dead, her students were embarrassed and ashamed at their relief, bursting into tears.

Stacy understood, only too well. She shared many of the same feelings. If she were honest, she'd have to admit the dead boys had been a real challenge—no, make that a pain in the butt—almost every day. She wasn't sure how yet, but she'd deal with her own grief and shame later. Last night, as she was reviewing her lesson plans, she decided she couldn't simply let her students' grief and fear fester. She had to do something. So she'd come up with an idea she thought might help, perhaps a little.

"This morning, we're going to do a special writing activity," she announced to the class. "I know you've all had practice in writing letters. I was very pleased with the letters we sent to town council members about your ideas for improving Devoe Park."

At her compliment, several students brightened, shifting in their seats, hopeful faces turned toward her. Stacy paused before going on, studying her class. She wanted to be sure she handled this right. Usually, she didn't need to be cautious with her words to her students. Most days, she simply spoke from her head, and sometimes her heart, and the students seemed to understand. But this lesson was different. It was important she chose exactly the right words.

"Today we're each going to write another letter, but this one will be a little different." She looked out at the room of expectant faces. The students seemed to sense her anxiety and waited quietly, their postures frozen in their chairs.

"Today we're going to write letters to James…Robert…Chad…and Justin." She uttered the four names slowly and walked to the four shrouded desks as she spoke. "Each of you can decide if you want to write to one of the boys or all four. We're not going to concentrate on the form or mechanics, so we'll use a simple form, like the one I put on the board up here." She pointed behind her to the whiteboard.

Stacy paused, waiting for a response. Most of the students looked confused. Scanning the puzzled, young faces, she could tell they had several questions, and she expected that. She preferred to let her students voice their own concerns, thought it important for them to be able to find words for their own questions. She knew they would, so she waited. For almost sixty seconds, no one spoke, an eternity of silence for fifth graders. The students glanced at one another and at their teacher, confusion etched in their faces.

Finally, Laura, the loveable brown noser, raised a timid hand. Stacy knew she could count on Laura to say something. "Mrs. T., if we write letters to those boys, who's going to read them? I mean the boys are…dead." When she spoke the last word, her typically loud voice shrunk to a whisper. Under her blonde curls, the normal golden face turned red.

"I know, Laura," her teacher said with a sigh. "That will certainly make it a different letter, won't it? As we learned last time, one of the most important things about a letter is who it's going to. But I think, for this letter, we can simply read it ourselves and, if you want later, you can share with each other." Stacy let her gaze roam around the class, meeting every pair of eyes. "I want the letter to be a chance for you to put some of your thoughts and feelings on paper. I'm not sure, but I think it might help." She paused. "This is one assignment I'm going to do myself, as soon as I get all of you started. I think it might help me too."

Stacy read other questions in their eyes. She nodded at one student.

"Well, what do we write? I mean, what do you want us to write about in the letter?" Tanya asked, her dark, expressive eyes mirroring her puzzlement.

"Whatever you would like," Stacy answered. "Maybe it would be easier if you'd simply write some things you'd like to tell the boys or wish you had told them."

"What if we want to tell them we're glad they're

dead?" This came from Clark, a spoiled boy from one of the "better" neighborhoods. Clark wore matching designer clothes and often made fun of some of the poorer kids.

The class bristled at Clark's question, as Stacy expected. Another student announced, "My mother says it's not polite to speak ill of the dead." Then after a brief pause, she added, "Besides, Clark, you're no prize." More murmurs followed.

Stacy interjected, "Usually, I would agree with your mom, Tina, but today this is a little different. I want you to write down whatever you feel, even if that's angry or glad. Okay?" She stared back at the class and this time all twenty-one heads nodded. "Okay, try to get started and I'll come around in a minute to see if you need any help."

In near perfect unison, the students took their notebooks out of their desks. For a moment, the hushed classroom got loud with the sound of books falling, slapping onto the flooring. Five children rose and crossed the room to sharpen pencils, with the familiar, metal-grinding-wood sounds emerging from their cranking, sending the odor of pencil shavings across the room. But no one talked. Their teacher waited, watching and, in a few minutes, all was quiet again, each of the twenty-one students writing or thinking.

At that point, Stacy remembered she hadn't finished checking one of her morning tasks—checking off her students' names on the PTO sales slip. Someone was due by any minute to pick it up. Standing and keeping one eye on the kids, she leaned over her desk, checking down the roster so she'd have it ready when the student helper came around. Before she got to the end of the list, she heard a solid knock at the door.

"Hang on, I'll be done in a second," she said, without looking up, confirming the last four names on her list. She grabbed the now complete form and headed to the door.

When she got there, she was surprised to see, not a student assistant, but rather Tony Garcia, the town police chief, in the window of the door. Dressed in his usual brown uniform, his large frame filled the entire window and his sober face bore a look of angry determination. When she opened the door, she noticed Bart Callahan, the school's DARE officer, standing next to his boss, one hand gesturing. As she opened the door, she heard Bart's part of an obvious argument.

"—Not here, Chief, not in front of the students," Bart said in a loud whisper. "Can't this wait a few minutes till the kids are gone?" His voice sounded desperate, but his boss didn't even acknowledge his question. Bart looked up at Stacy and shrugged. "I'm sorry."

Stacy looked into Bart's face. His normal good humor, which made him so popular with the students, had fled. Instead, he stared at her with a look of desperation. A swelling panic rose inside her. Glancing from Bart to Chief Garcia, she saw the chief's wrinkled hand holding a folded, white paper. His hard blue eyes remained fixed on her, his cold stare boring into her.

Garcia stepped inside the classroom and stood next to the cluster of the dead boys' desks. He glanced down at the four photographs and then back up at her. "Are you Stacy D. Thompson?" he asked in a formal tone.

At the sound of the unfamiliar voice, the students looked up from their desks to watch the scene. The chief studied the twenty-one young faces, their eyes fixed on him. He hesitated, and for a moment, appeared to be reconsidering. Then he glanced back at Stacy and shrugged. "Good for them to see this anyway." He handed her the paper and intoned, "Mrs. Thompson, I have here a warrant for your arrest for the murder of James Clayton, Justin Waycross, Chad Thorton, and Robert Hayes."

Chapter 20

The chief's words shattered the quiet atmosphere of the small classroom. Several children erupted from their desks, pleading, crying "Mrs. T! Mrs. T!"

Stacy's eyes darted from the shocked faces of her students to the angry gaze of Tony Garcia. She couldn't believe it. This made no sense. Her mind grasped to seize some rational explanation. Then she saw her students staring at her in horror and fought her own escalating panic. "Chief Garcia, there must be some kind of mistake. Let's step out in the hallway so we can clear this up," she said, trying to sound calm to ease her children's fears. She pointed a finger toward the open door.

When she did, Garcia grabbed her wrist, his grip so strong she couldn't pull back. He didn't look at her but continued, his voice remaining a flat monotone. "You have the right to remain silent. Anything you say can and will be used against you in a court of law. You have the right to an attorney. If you cannot afford one, the court will appoint one for you." He looked into her face and finished, "Do you understand these rights as they have been explained to you?"

Too stunned to respond, Stacy opened her mouth, but nothing came out.

"Mrs. Thompson, do you understand these rights?" Chief Garcia repeated, forcing her to meet his gaze.

"Uh, yes…I guess so," Stacy managed, tears squeezing out the corners of her eyes.

Garcia removed the handcuffs from his belt and slipped the first one around her right wrist. She felt the metal clamp scrape her skin and she winced from the pain.

On instinct, she brought her left hand up to rub her right. When she did, the chief grabbed both hands, turned her around and slapped the second clamp around her left wrist. It connected with a loud clink, the sound stunning the students into shocked silence. Arms behind her, hands cuffed together, she realized she was quite a sight for the students. They stared in disbelief, weeping, two of the girls reaching out their arms.

The chief grabbed her by the arm and shoved her into the hallway.

As she passed the DARE Officer, Stacy managed, "Bart, watch my class until—" but was unable to finish because Garcia pushed her roughly down the corridor. She turned and saw Bart nod at her, enter her room, and close the door behind him.

She turned and glanced down the hall through her tears. It was fairly quiet, no students in sight. Stacy was grateful at least for that. Their footsteps echoed down the hallway, Garcia's large boots and her small flats, making slapping sounds on the old tile floor. Pushed roughly by the chief, Stacy passed the next classroom as Dawn Hatcher stepped from her room, this time sans coffee cup, her face a mask of shocked disbelief.

By the time Stacy stumbled a few more steps in the corridor, word was somehow beginning to spread. Doors on both sides of the hallway opened and, for a moment, she feared all the students would file out to stare at her, humiliated and disgraced. She lowered her head and kept walking.

As she passed the door to 205, she heard a familiar voice. "I told you so. I knew it." She raised her head to see the angry, blue eyes of Chris Goodman. Before he could say more, he had to turn and herd his students back into the room. "You're supposed to be in your seats working on your quiz. Let's go!" he barked, backing into the room and slamming the door closed.

Garcia forced Stacy to keep moving. To keep up with the cop's constant prodding, she tried to shuffle and stumbled again. When she caught her balance and looked up, Stacy met the gaze of another teacher, Jacqueline Highstreet. The math teacher's face was covered with her long slender fingers, the nails painted a bright red. The eyes behind the fingers went wide with alarm. Jacqueline's look of dignity and grace fled, replaced now by fear. Before either woman could get a word out, Garcia shoved Stacy again.

Stacy heard someone sniffling and she glanced across to see the small figure of Rachel Bedinghaus. Huddled outside her room, the door closed, Rachel watched like a stunned spectator. She wept audibly through bloodshot eyes, the sounds punctuated by the blowing of her swollen nose. As Stacy looked across, she thought she saw Rachel mouth the words, "I'm sorry," but she wasn't sure as Garcia kept marching her farther down the corridor.

At the end of the hallway, she saw her principal, the superintendent, and the board president, huddled together, observing the spectacle. At first, she thought it peculiar the superintendent and the board president would be here, but then she realized they'd probably been notified by the police department. As she passed, Superintendent Walters simply lowered his head.

Dr. Everett O'Brien wore a look of professional detachment and Michaels shook her head and kept muttering, "I can't believe it. I simply can't believe it." Stacy tried to stop to meet her gaze, but Garcia only kept shoving her, making her stagger to keep up.

When she caught her balance, she almost walked into the push broom attached to the arms of Wally Kowalchek. The janitor glanced at Stacy and then glared at the officer. The broom and his wide body blocked Garcia's path and he refused to budge. The chief had no choice but to slow down and maneuver around the big janitor and his broom. Wally eyed Garcia as the officer moved around the obstacle, pushing Stacy ahead of him.

When they got to the turn in the hallway, Stacy looked back once more and saw the figures, standing still, frozen in their places, staring in morbid fascination. Then Garcia shoved her around the corner and they all disappeared from view.

Chapter 21

Stacy worked to force her eyes to open. They were red and swollen and opening them hurt. Her tears had come, uncontrollably for hours, through the ride to the station, the booking, the questioning. She had never cried so much or so long in her life, tears of confusion, tears of embarrassment, and finally tears of anger. What was she doing here? her mind screamed inside her head. She must be going insane.

Why me…again?

Forcing her eyes open, her fingers came into focus. Turning her hands over, she examined the still lingering smudges of black left when they had fingerprinted her, smashing her hands onto the blotter. She had tried to wash it off in the little sink—more out of disgrace than a desire for cleanliness—but it did little good. When they booked her, the matron had barked, "Don't worry. The ink will wear off…eventually." Stacy looked away in disgust and tried not to think about the rest. It was no use.

The experience had seared into her memory like the blinding flash as they took her picture holding the board with her name, her number, and the charge— second degree murder. They had confiscated her purse grabbed by Bart and the few belongings she had with her, including a favorite pen, given to her by a class three years ago. She protested, but it did no good. The matron dryly assured her everything would be returned. Still unbelieving, she had watched as they placed the contents of her purse and even the small heart pendant she wore around her neck—the contents of my life right now, she thought—into a large manila envelope with "S. Thompson" written on it. Finally, they had given her a comb, a small bar of soap, a toothbrush, and a small tube of toothpaste and then brought her *here*.

She lifted her swollen eyes from her hands and stared. The cell she sat in was barren, gray, cold. Concrete walls surrounded the six by ten room on three sides and an oversized metal door covered the fourth side. The bed she sat on was little more than a metal frame anchored to the wall, its thin fiberfill mattress covered in a thick plastic, long since cracked and stained by former "residents." A bare toilet, old and stained, sat in the corner of the tight space. The minerals in the water had long since turned the metal an ugly brown, staining the small metal toilet with no seat. Stacy shuddered at the prospect of having to use it. The whole cell gave off an ugly smell, the odor a sickening mixture of day-old puke and weak disinfectant.

There was no privacy. The heavy metal door had a small window so the guard could keep an eye on her prisoners. Stacy had been here long enough to tell she came through about twice an hour, though she couldn't be sure since they had taken her watch along with everything else. Usually very modest, she liked to keep her private life *private*, but that was not possible here. Finally, her full bladder won out over her modesty, and she decided she could wait no longer. Besides there was no point in waiting. She wasn't going anywhere. She dragged herself over to the toilet, pulled down her slacks and panties, and sat down. The cold metal stung her skin and felt slimy as if she could feel the dormant germs crawling onto her flesh and she had to fight an urge to jump up. She finished as quicky as she could and got up. She washed her hands, repeating the process twice, but she still felt contaminated. Then she flushed the toilet and the water rushing through the metal bowl roared, the sound reverberating off the concrete walls. In the small room the echo seemed to go on forever.

The crash of the water, bouncing off the cold walls brought it all flooding back, unwelcomed, unbidden. Almost fifteen years had passed, and she'd thought she had forgotten it. She had tried to put it behind her, out of mind, as if it were a separate existence, not her at all.

She'd been so young then.

And now, it was happening all over once again. As the edge of the memory flashed by her consciousness, she felt the bile rise in her throat and vomited into the ugly toilet. She flushed it again, sending the deafening sound around her small cell.

The matron's earthy whistling in the hallway brought Stacy back to the calloused reality of the present. The guard started to walk away and then turned back, as if remembering something. "Hey, Thompson, I almost forgot. You got a visitor."

"Who is it?" Stacy asked quickly in surprise.

"Damned if I know, some guy. I'll be back in a minute to take you to the interrogation room." She disappeared.

Suddenly hopeful, Stacy fantasized some miraculous savior, someone who would help her wake from this hellish nightmare. Then she remembered some talk about an attorney when she was booked and figured some court-appointed lawyer had shown up. Her expectations plummeted. Staring into the small piece of metal fastened to the wall that passed for a mirror, she scrutinized at what she could see of her face and then stopped. What difference did it make now?

A metal jangling signaled the matron returning with the ring of huge cell keys. She fumbled for a while before she found the right one, inserting it in the lock of Stacy's cell door and turned. Earlier, Stacy glimpsed the enormous keys, each one more than eight inches long and made of thick, black steel. The matron held the door and Stacy walked through the opening and down the small hallway. Hearing the heavy metal door slam behind her, Stacy cringed but didn't turn around.

"He's in that room over there," the matron said, one crooked finger pointing to the right. "You have fifteen minutes…and we have to leave the door open. House rules." She turned to head down the hallway, leaving Stacy standing there.

Chapter 22

Ken watched as Stacy came around the corner and peered into the interrogation room. He saw recognition and then relief shine in her eyes.

She simply said, "Ken," and walked in and took the chair opposite his. The space was tight, with barely enough room for a table and two old metal chairs.

When she came in, he rose in his chair, a little awkwardly, and knocked the chair backward. He caught it before it hit the concrete floor, righted it, and sat back down when she did. Settled into the flimsy chair, he turned to look at Stacy and her appearance stunned him, though he fought not to show it. Staring across into her face, he saw red-rimmed eyes, sunk into deep, empty pockets. Translucent traces of tears had dried in streaks down both cheeks. When she laid her arms on the table, he recognized the bruises on her wrists from the handcuffs.

"Stacy, are you okay?" he asked.

"Oh, peachy keen. Kinda like Club Med around here." Her eyes flared at him. "What am I doing here, Ken?"

He squirmed in his seat. "Look, I'm sorry, Stacy. I got down here as soon as I found out. I can't believe it but Garcia says they have a pretty strong case. He claims all the evidence points to you."

"What evidence?" Stacy asked.

"Garcia froze me out, so I didn't see any of this coming. He knows we're friends. So he's only willing to share so much." Ken shook his head. "I'll try to find out more from Bart. What did they say when they questioned you?"

"Almost nothing. Garcia kept asking me who I was buying the drugs from?"

"Oh, yeah, Garcia told me to tell you they're willing to offer you a deal if you cooperate."

"Oh, that's great! I didn't do anything. I don't even know why I'm here. And they want to cut me a deal if I *cooperate*? Ain't life grand?" Her hand slapped the table, the sound so loud the matron came to the door. He watched her glance into the room and then retreat, no doubt returning to the office.

Ken waited, not sure how to voice the rest. "Garcia did tell me they found a stash of those damn drug tattoos in your locker, same as the ones on the boys."

He watched as Stacy shook her head back and forth again and again. Staring across the table, she pleaded through her tears, "Ken, you can't believe this of me. You know me. How long have we worked together?" She sniffled. "You know how I feel about kids. For God's sake, I taught your son. I'm not into drugs. Please help me." The last three words came out in a whisper, a desperate plea.

Ken wanted to believe her. He knew her, didn't he? Still, could he trust his feelings? Could Stacy have victimized kids and be responsible for their deaths? He did not want to believe that, but he needed to be sure. "How can you explain the drugs in your locker?"

"I can't. I dunno, I-I-I guess somebody else could've placed them there." She reached one hand across the table. "Oh, come on. If I *were* selling drugs to these kids, do you think I'd be dumb enough to keep that, that junk in my own locker? For heaven's sake, Ken!" And then after a bit, "How did the sheriff know to look there, anyway?"

"An anonymous tip."

"Some coincidence." She raised both hands in the air.

"I said as much to Garcia. Then he told me they found a money trail."

Stacy shook her head. "Well, somebody should let me know. I think I have about two hundred dollars in my checking account and less than that in my savings. Some big drug dealer."

"No, Garcia said you used the money to buy a condo in Marco Island worth more than $375,000. The real estate agent even picked out your picture, conveniently faxed by Chief Garcia."

"What?" She shook her head, grinning. "Oh, please."

"What's so funny? The real estate agent even remembered you?"

"Now, that's not surprising, not if it's the same agent. When I was down there in August, it was so beautiful, I decided I wanted to go back again. So I checked with the agent about getting a time-share on one of the condos. You know, you get the condo two weeks out of the year. Well, the one I wanted was booked so she said she would call me back after January when new dates became available." She reached a hand across the table. "She knew I was a potential sale…for a time share. She'd better remember me. But *buy* a condo? On my salary? Give me a break."

Stacy shook her head again and then asked, "If I bought this place, how was it paid for?"

"According to Garcia, a money transfer," Ken said, "wired from your bank, right here in town." Ken stopped and then went on. "And Stacy, there's more."

He knew he was only making things worse for her, but he decided she needed to know the whole picture, at least as much as he knew. "Garcia says he has a record of transactions between you and what looks to be a supplier. He says it's all there plain as day."

He paused before he could tell her the last. His throat tightened. "Stacy, I'm sorry but it was my idea. I had no idea it would implicate you."

"What are you talking about?" Her brow furrowed.

"I came up with a way for the cops to look into the district email network. Garcia says he has at least four different, thinly-veiled exchanges between you and the drug supplier over a two-week period before the boys' deaths. He's already confiscated the email records for evidence."

At the last statement, she laughed, this time a short, high hoot. "Ken, I don't know how to break this to my administrator friend. I don't know how to use the damn email system. I've never ever sent an email, not one. I couldn't if my life depended on it,"—she barked another short, bitter laugh—"which I guess it does. Ask Dawn. She has to come into my room to get me straightened out all the time. I can barely get the attendance and lunch count on the system, honest."

Ken sat back in the metal chair and slowly shook his head. "Stacy, can't you see how it looks—the tattoos in your locker, this condo bought in Florida, the email messages. Stacy, I want to believe you, but if it's not you, it's one hell of a frame."

"Ken, you *know* me. These kids are my life. I could never do this to them, could never hurt them."

Trying to take it all in, Ken listened and studied her. He wanted to believe Stacy and his instinct told him he should, but still. These charges and the evidence simply didn't jive with the woman he'd come to know, a woman he'd worked with for more than a decade. But *something* was off, or maybe he was that poor a judge of character.

He slipped a finger into his breast pocket and fingered the Post-it note. He decided he had to know. He pulled out the folded small pink paper, its edges dog-eared from his constant handling it. Sliding it across to Stacy, he watched her reaction. "Okay, then tell me about this."

Stacy stared at the note and then back at Ken, her eyebrows narrowing. "I don't get it. I mean, that's my number and it looks like my handwriting, but I don't remember writing this. Where did you get it?"

"On a student's book." When this elicited no reaction, he asked, "Do you usually give your home phone number to students?"

"Of course not. I'm a little paranoid about that kinda stuff. My number's even unlisted. You said from a student." She paused briefly. "Which student? It must have been something special." Stacy shook her head, frowning.

"Tricia Holloway." As soon as he said the two words, he saw a flicker of recognition, an alarm race across Stacy's face. Then she turned away.

"Oh yeah, that," she said. "That has nothing to do with drugs."

When she said nothing more, Ken could barely contain himself. "Stacy, let me get this straight," he snapped. "You're sitting here in a cell charged in the death of four students using drugs found in *your* locker. Garcia has a list of evidence about a mile long, but you tell me I have to believe you had nothing to do with it. Then I tell you I found a message from you saying 'Call me, if you need anything,' in the book of *another* drug victim and all you've got to say is 'That has nothing to do with drugs.' "

"Well, it doesn't," Stacy said.

"Then what?"

"I can't tell you."

"Well, that's great! I'll tell you what," he barked as he snatched the paper back from Stacy. He slid the chair back, its metal feet grating across the cement. "How about I'll show this to Garcia and see what he thinks about it?"

"Please, Ken, don't do that. Please, I'm begging you!" Reaching across the table, she laid a hand on his arm. Her gaze darted to the door to see if the matron had overheard Ken's words.

"Come on, Stacy, what's going on? I want to believe you, but this all looks pretty damn suspicious. I need something."

She looked up at him, her large, expressive eyes so swollen the green had all but disappeared. More tears squeezed from the corners and dripped down her cheeks onto the scarred tabletop.

"Stacy, tell me about the note."

"Poor Tricia," Stacy managed between sobs.

Chapter 23

"Look, Stacy, no one else has seen this note *yet* and Garcia would probably get me for obstruction, so I need to know." Ken edged his tone from command to desperate plea. All the time, his gaze never left hers.

Stacy sniffled quickly, twice. She stared across the table for almost twenty seconds before she spoke. "Tricia came by to see me a few days ago, which wasn't that unusual. Ever since she moved up to the next grade, she's come back to my room every few weeks or so to say hi. But this time she looked different, edgy. She waited till all the other kids had gone and then she said she needed to talk to me."

She paused, as if gauging Ken's response. When he didn't say anything, she went on. "Tricia told me 'her secret'—those were her words—only if I promised not to tell anyone, which I did, of course. That's why I can't tell you."

"Tricia's lying in a hospital bed, comatose from those damn drugs. If sharing her secret might help get to the bottom of this, I'm sure Tricia would not mind."

"I don't see how it will help. Her secret has nothing to do with drugs."

"I want to believe you, Stace. I do, but—" He stopped and looked at Stacy. She stared back at him and then lowered her gaze.

Exasperated, Ken went on, "Look, maybe I should

simply give the note to Garcia. Amanda thinks I'm in over my head and I need to leave it all to the cops. Maybe she's right." Ken rose and turned to leave.

"Please wait! *Please* sit down and I'll tell you the whole thing. I'm going to have to trust somebody."

He didn't move, trying to make up his mind.

"Please, Ken, I need your help."

Sliding the chair back into place, he sat back down.

When Stacy spoke, her words were whispered so quietly, Ken had to lean across the table to hear. So close together, Ken could smell her breath, stale and sharp. "You have to promise me, if it doesn't turn out to be connected to all this, you won't betray Tricia's confidence."

"Agreed."

"Okay." She took a deep breath. "Well, I guess it started a few weeks ago. I don't remember when exactly. She would come into my room, all nervous. You know how you can tell when a student wants to tell you something but doesn't know where to start."

"Yeah, I know what you mean."

"Well, Tricia had that look, all right—but every time I'd ask her, she'd say, 'Oh, forget it, Mrs. T.' Then last week, she looked different. When she came in, she seemed agitated, really upset. When I asked her what was wrong, her response shocked me."

"What did she tell you?"

"It wasn't only what she told me. At first, she turned and walked to the window. When I went over to her, she snapped 'Don't look at me. I don't want you to look at me when I tell you this.' Then she told me she'd been molested, though she didn't use those words, of course."

"Did she tell you by whom?"

"She kept saying he would hurt her if she told. But, Ken, when I pushed her and asked a few questions, I'm pretty sure it was somebody at school."

Ken guffawed. "Alma Mater Portsmouth houses a drug pusher *and* a child molester. Oh hell, this is great."

"Can you understand now why I didn't want to say anything?"

"Yeah." Ken stared across at her. "Are you sure she didn't say anything to give you an idea of who?"

"No, I tried to press her, but she only clammed up."

"Did you try to get her to go to a counselor?" he asked.

"Of course. I tried to talk her into going to see her counselor right then, but she refused. Said she wasn't ready for anyone else to know her secret. I don't know if she ever did. I wanted to ask Jacqueline to see her, but Tricia made me promise not to say anything to Jacqueline or anyone. So I didn't."

"Jacqueline?"

"Jacqueline Highstreet. Remember she became a half-time counselor this year?"

"Oh, yeah. What about getting Tricia to an outside agency?" Ken asked.

"I tried to put her in touch with Children's Services, but she wouldn't go there either. That's why I gave her my number, so she could call me when she needed to." She stopped and looked down. "I guess now it looks pretty incriminating."

"Did you report it?"

"I tried. I called Children's Services yesterday and left a message for Mrs. Hicks, but she didn't call me back yet. Probably called me today after I got these new accommodations."

Ken pondered one more piece of the ugly puzzle. "Okay. Thanks for telling me all this, Stacy." He nodded. "I don't know what it all means, but at least I understand about the note."

"I'm sorry," she said quietly.

If everything she told him was true... Ken wondered about Stacy Thompson. *She sits here in a jail cell accused of second-degree murder and she's worried about keeping a student's secret.*

He was out of his depth here. How was he supposed to sort all this out?

"Is there someone I can contact for you, family, friends, anybody?" he asked.

"No, I don't think my friends are too interested in me right now," she joked with little humor. "And I don't have any family, at least not anymore."

"I'm sorry. I've never asked, but I figured with the Mrs. there might be someone."

"No, there's no one," she returned, her voice thick. "The marriage died a long time ago, thank God, and I've simply kept the Mrs. to keep the predators at bay."

The matron came to the door. "Time."

Ken rose to leave. "Is there anything I can get you?"

Stacy gave a small smile. "A hacksaw?"

A grin crossed Ken's face. "I'll be back when I can. I'll see what I can find out."

The matron stepped into the space and escorted Stacy back to her cell. Out in the hall, both Ken and Stacy stopped at the same time, turning and glancing at each other. He nodded and watched as she disappeared around the corner.

Chapter 24

The October morning had broken especially crisp and frigid. The brisk wind made the thirty-degree temperature feel like single digits and Ken's out-of-shape body was hardly ready for the change. Dressed in his warmest pair of sweats, he stood on the sidewalk, dancing from one foot to the other to keep warm, a heavy hooded sweatshirt layered over his running outfit. He blew into his hands to try to keep them warm and stared up and down the street, searching for trouble around the corner. This cold morning, most people were wise enough not to venture out. Standing on the corner, he received disapproving looks from drivers passing in their warm cars, heater vents on high, tailpipes belching curls of exhaust.

Maybe they were right, Ken thought. He must be an idiot to be out in this.

Swinging his arms across his body in an attempt to generate some internal heat, he started walking quickly, pumping his legs, struggling to keep warm. He had to cover two more blocks before meeting up with his jogging partner, if Bart even showed this morning. Ken kept moving, occasionally glancing down at his feet so as not to trip on the uneven concrete. As he ran, he inhaled, the morning air sharp and crisp.

Gazing around, he was struck by the bleak landscape surrounding him. Trees, so full of color a few weeks ago, now stood naked, barren. The last few days, the bitter, uncaring wind and rain had stripped them of leaves, revealing only empty, mocking skeletons of trunks and limbs. Cutting east, he turned onto Shore Drive and glanced out at the water. The bay had lost its alluring blue-green hue, surrendering to the encroaching gray. Waves made white slashes across the dark water and threw cold drops at Ken. He cut up Second Avenue to veer away from the ugly, angry water.

Much troubled him these days. Even as he fought it, he could feel his inner mood darken, the somber secret of his past conspiring with this present crisis to wage war on his psyche. Above, the sky, matching the desolation of the churning waves, displayed another murky shade of gray, the foreboding color predicting even worse weather ahead. This morning, all of nature collaborated to cast a pall of gloom over his senses. It was succeeding and Ken pumped his legs in a furious effort to beat back the sense of encroaching misery.

As he turned the corner past the old town library, he spied Bart ahead, jumping up and down in his own attempt to stay warm. He too was dressed in layers of sweats, head covered with his brown police cap inside a matching hooded sweatshirt. As Ken approached, Bart called out in a protest, "I need to have my head examined to be out here with you on a day like this. Why aren't we doing this inside the Y, where it's nice and warm?"

"What? And miss all this beautiful fresh air out here?" Ken asked, forcing a guffaw along with the white cloud of his breath. "It's not too cold for the tough DARE officer, is it? We wouldn't want it to get around school you couldn't take it, would we?"

Bart's exposed nose reddened and when he talked, the words emerged inside small, white puffs. "Okay, let's do this."

"Besides," Ken added, a little more seriously, "out here there are fewer ears to overhear our conversation."

Both men started together down the sidewalk at a brisk pace. Briefly, Bart moved out ahead with his longer stride but, after a bit, Ken caught up and the two jogged side by side. For a while, they ran in silence, letting their hearts rise to a manageable aerobic level as they steadied their pace. Finally, Ken broke the silence. "What can you tell me about the investigation?"

"Which investigation?" Bart got out between gasps.

"The investigation into who really killed JFK. Which do you think?"

"Ken, you know I'm not allowed to comment on ongoing police business. You wouldn't want me to break department rules, would you?"

"God forbid." Ken ran three more steps. "Does Garcia really think Stacy did this?" The question hung in the air while their feet slapped the pavement in a steady rhythm. "I mean, coming into her classroom and taking her out in handcuffs. Come on, that was pretty melodramatic, even for him."

"I did my best to talk him out of it. I did everything short of physically restraining him," said Bart, taking two slow breaths. "But you know Garcia. When he gets an idea in his head, it's impossible to stop him. He said he wanted to make a loud, public statement about what we do to drug pushers who deal to kids. Well, it was plenty loud. Probably thought it was a good way to score points for reelection next fall."

"Why Thompson? Why was he so hyped on putting her in jail?"

"Because he thinks she did it." Bart ran a while longer before he continued. "I know you and she are friends and I like Stacy. *I* have trouble believing it could be her, but Garcia has a pretty good case against her. He found the drugs in her locker." He raised one finger as they ran. "He thinks he's got a trail on the drug money." Two fingers. "He's got those damn email messages." Three fingers.

"Yeah, the email I put him onto."

They ran on. To an outsider it did look like a solid case. It had to, Ken admitted.

Together, the two men slowed their stride to time it so they wouldn't be stopped at the traffic light at the corner. They had to jog single file around a set of garbage cans, one of them overturned. Some rotting meat spilled out of the top and the stench floated up, even in the frigid air. They hurried past. By the time they were side by side again, Ken asked, "How did he happen on the evidence so quickly? How long did he have Stacy as a suspect?"

"A few days. As a matter of procedure, we were checking out everyone who had any contact with the boys in the last few days before their deaths. Or could have sold them the drugs. Stacy was only one of the persons of interest." Bart exhaled a few slow breaths as he ran. "But Garcia didn't really have any special interest in her until we got the anonymous tip on Thursday."

The slap of their feet on the pavement echoed off the closed-up buildings. Ken divided his glances between Bart and the broken pavement under foot.

After a bit, the cop went on. "Then, early Friday morning, they found the tattoos in her locker at school. He got a warrant to search her apartment, you know, after she left for school, and found the brochure on the condo. A couple hours of police work, the magic of the fax and he had a tentative ID from the real estate agent."

Bart fingered the rim of his cap and exhaled loudly. "And you know about the email. You're the one who got us into your system. Once Garcia was onto her, he had us check out her mailbox and we found the messages about the drugs. At least, that's what he thinks."

Another pause as the two ran around a corner, briefly separating, then coming up side by side again. Bart continued, "Hey, he didn't let me in on all of it until after he was ready to take her into custody. Guess he thought I might tell someone."

Ken pretended not to hear. "Doesn't it all strike you as being a little *too* convenient?"

"Could be."

"Stacy says she's being framed."

"Well, don't they all, after they're caught?"

They both ran a few more steps before continuing, their footfalls pounding staccatos in the quiet air.

Bart continued, "If it's a frame, it's a damn good one. And it wasn't done in a hurry. Some of the pieces had to be set up a while ago."

"Bart, you've taught alongside her for five years in that building. Do you think she could have done it?"

They ran for a while longer before Bart answered. "I'll say this. I've never seen a teacher who connects better with students than Stacy Thompson, especially those on the edge like James and Robert. I'll admit it doesn't fit. But, well, right now my hunches don't count for a whole lot down at the station."

"Is the department checking out any other suspects?"

"No."

"What?" Ken asked.

"Garcia says he has enough evidence to convict Stacy and he says the investigation is closed."

Ken ran and waited a while before saying any more, using the time to get some desperate breaths in. "I cannot believe Stacy did this. I plan to keep on digging. If I'm right—and my gut says I am—there is a drug pusher still out there poisoning our kids." He glanced over at the man jogging alongside of him. "I'd feel better if I could count on some help from you…unofficially, of course."

Bart didn't answer. He merely kept running, his breaths making more miniature white clouds in the cold air.

"Bart, are you going to help me or not?"

"I can see I'm not going to have much of a choice. I can't let my wimpy running buddy make a complete fool of himself, can I? But I'll have to do it off the record."

"Okay, thanks. I have a feeling I'm going to need your help."

"Sorry, buddy, but I learned a long time ago you're way past help." He barked a laugh.

After a few minutes more of silence, they came to the end of their three-and-a-half-mile loop around town and reduced their pace to cool down. They slowed, walking now, and Ken felt his heart rate come down to a comfortable level again.

Ken said, "Thanks. If you get any great ideas, let me know. Walters and O'Brien are on my ass big time to get this one out of the public eye, so I have to be careful."

"I'll do what I can." Bart headed back toward his car, to get warm no doubt.

Chapter 25

Amanda heard the ringing as Ken squeezed past her.

Hurrying through the mudroom and into the kitchen, he grabbed up the phone and called, "Parks." She came alongside him, setting her purse down on the counter. Ken listened for a bit and said, "We're only coming in from church." He turned to her and mouthed Bart and turned back to the phone. "You calling for business or pleasure?"

Amanda studied her husband's face as he listened. She knew that look. Something was about to screw up their Sunday. He nodded a few more times and gave some one-syllable responses and said, "I'll be right down."

He hung up the phone and turned toward her. She scowled at him, one hand on her hip. "Right down where?"

"I've got to go down to the police station. Bart's got the father of one of the dead boys down there and he's going to question him. He said he'd let me in on it."

"Why?" she whined. "And why on Sunday?"

Ken gave that dismissive head shake she hated. "Look, Bart's been checking on a few other 'persons of interest' as he called them, and he discovered this one father, a guy named Bill Clayton, James' dad, got out of prison a few years ago."

"So?"

"He was in for selling drugs." When she didn't respond, he added, "He could be the one behind the whole drug operation."

"Bart has to do this on Sunday? Why can't it wait till tomorrow?"

Ken shook his head. "Look, Bart's doing me a favor. Garcia announced the investigation is closed and doesn't want Bart spending any more time on it. Bart's doing this today to keep it under the wire."

"The only thing you think about anymore is this damn investigation," she snapped. "I'm sorry about the boys who died, I really am. But what about us? You ought to make some time for us. When was the last time you dropped everything to do something for me? For us?"

Ken lowered his glance to the floor. "I'm sorry. I didn't know you were counting on me for something." His head jerked up. "I thought you said you have an open house in about an hour?"

She shot back, "Well, you aren't the only one who has important work."

Ken raised both hands in mock surrender. "That's not what I meant. I figured I could slip down to the station and listen in on Bart's interrogation and maybe learn something. Then I'd get back here and have a nice dinner waiting for you when you got home. Anything special you'd like me to fix?"

"What I want doesn't seem to matter much anymore. Do what you want." She sighed. "Those poor boys are dead. What you're doing won't bring them back. I still say you're carrying this detective thing too far." He started to object, but she put up a hand, stopping him. "I wish you gave us this kind of attention."

He grabbed the hand she raised and kissed it and, in the same motion, slipped back into his overcoat. "You're right about not bringing the boys back, but *this* is something I feel I have to do." He walked out and into the garage. The door slammed in her face.

"Well, maybe there's something I have to do," Amanda muttered to the closed door.

She listened to the sounds of her husband's hurried exit—the whine of the garage door opener, the roar of the car engine reverberating off the confined walls, then dying away, and finally the garage door closing again. Angry, for the moment indecisive, she stayed rooted to the spot, staring at the geometric pattern on the kitchen vinyl. For almost thirty seconds she stood there, her body motionless except for the insistent tapping of her right foot, her fury mounting all the while.

Why does he always pull this stuff?

She made her decision. She strode to the kitchen wall phone and punched seven digits in rapid sequence. "Hi, Celia, this is Amanda. Celia, look. Something's come up. I need you to cover my open house for me this afternoon. Can you?"

"Sure. What time?" a cheery voice on the other end of the line asked.

"Two to four. The property on Wentworth, the two-family."

"No problem. Count me in," replied the other woman.

"Great, I owe you." Amanda released a short, tense laugh. "Well, maybe you'll pick up a few leads in the bargain. Hey, thanks. I'll see you later."

As Amanda replaced the receiver, she felt her pulse accelerate. She leaned her body against the sand-colored Formica countertop—the one she'd always hated. How many times had she asked Ken about upgrading it? It didn't make any difference to him. She pushed herself away and willed herself to take several deep, slow breaths. Then she picked up the phone again and dialed another number from memory.

"Come on...be there," she whispered, more to herself than to the phone. "Come on." Then she heard the click followed by a familiar voice.

"Dr. Hardcastle."

She stopped holding her breath. "Alex? Hi, it's Amanda. Can you talk for a second?"

"Sure, I remember that patient," Alex said.

"What? Oh, got it. Okay, just listen then. You'll know how to respond. I got myself free for a couple of hours. Can you get away?"

"Tell me what's changed about the patient's condition," his melodious voice said.

She loved the sound of his smooth baritone. "Ken took off for the police station to work on this damn drug investigation. Bart called him and he dropped everything and headed down there."

"I understand. That could be something."

She figured Alex's wife was probably within listening distance. Somehow, that made this even sweeter.

She continued, "That's all he has on his mind lately. He doesn't even care what I want. Anyway, I got Celia to cover my open house, so I've got a few hours to kill. Got any ideas?"

"I may be able to help. I'd need to examine her myself."

She could hear the smallest hint of a smile in his words, and she grinned in return, already feeling her body respond.

"I thought *you* might know how to treat this patient…being a doctor and all. I'll see you in a few."

She replaced the handset in the cradle and started up the stairs to change. By the time her foot hit the third step, she was singing to herself.

It took her only a few minutes to change. She reached into her small, black purse to retrieve that perfume—the scent he said made him horny—and spritzed it on a few strategic areas. She breathed in the delightful scent and started to get excited. When she tried to put the tiny bottle back into her purse, a small colored hotel keycard tumbled to the carpet. Picking up the thin rectangle, her fingers caressed the firm edges and the smoothness of the plastic. The sensations made her think of him…and that night. She smiled, her mind drifting back, tripping over the delightful memories again.

Chapter 26

Amanda had heard about Dr. Alex Hardcastle from some of her female clients. He swooped into town and purchased Doc Stone's family practice. Much to the surprise of finicky Portsmouth patients, including crotchety old Edgar Hawthorne, he quickly won them over with his bright smile, expert knowledge, and professional compassion. As she worked real estate deals in town, Amanda picked up a few stories about the new doctor, all of them good. And more than a few of her female clients had mentioned what a handsome pose the man struck as he examined them, what with his almost shaggy, brown hair and brilliant green-gray eyes. And they despaired he was already married.

At chamber events, Amanda had received a polite introduction or two to him—and she had to agree with her women friends—but she'd never had more than a passing acquaintance with him. And since both she and Ken were healthy overall, neither had need of his medical services. That was, until one frigid March morning.

Showing a split-level, she slipped on a patch of black ice and fell and, in a panic, tried to catch her weight on her right hand. The fall broke her wrist, shattering her bone, and hurt like hell. And damn, the couple hadn't even bought the house.

The husband, a thirty-something, surfer dude with

curling blond hair (at least that's how Amanda nailed him) said, "This place doesn't really speak to us." Then he noticed Amanda's wrist and added, "You better have that looked at," and he waved from his Mustang. She couldn't reach Ken, again, as he was traveling between schools, so she drove herself into the emergency room with one good hand. Dr. Alex Hardcastle happened to be doing a stint at the emergency room when she came through the automatic doors, her wrist throbbing.

She felt awkward, clumsy, and stupid, but Dr. Alex Hardcastle had been able to help her relax, set the bones, and ease her tension. Even as the pain wracked her wrist, he had made her smile with his humor during the examination.

"Ouch, looks like you wrenched this good. But not to worry, we'll get you as good as new." He traced the break, his fingers' touch feather-like. "You have such beautiful, delicate fingers. Oh, I love that nail color."

After a set of x-rays, a plaster cast, and a few strong pain killers, he even had her giggling at his terrible puns. She went home agreeing with her clients, both about his bedside manner and his good looks.

Even though he tried to make light of it at the time—she guessed to ease her anxiety—the break was pretty severe, making the healing process slow. When she returned for an exam a few weeks later, she and Alex (*not* Dr. Hardcastle) exchanged pleasantries, he asking about her work. Always on the hunt for new clients, she pitched him the idea of investing in some Portsmouth real estate.

He smiled at her and said, "You know, I'd not considered that. I'm fairly well invested in the market, but I suppose I could consider a little diversification.

Why don't you give me a ring when that heals?" He pointed to the cast.

So after the break mended and the cast came off, she lined up some perspective properties for him to check out. Together, they made several trips around Portsmouth and inspected a number of houses, always at night, after he was done seeing patients. Ken never objected. He understood her job required a good number of her evenings, not to mention he had evening meetings a couple nights a week.

But strange for her, she had little success. She couldn't get Alex to close on a single piece of real estate. One house needed too much work, another Alex doubted he'd make enough in the sale, and he discounted a third because he didn't want to be in the landlord business yet.

"I have enough trouble keeping track of my patients. I don't want to have to go chasing after some renters," he admitted one night.

All the same, she found she enjoyed her time with him, and as they rode together between stops, he had made mild, discreet overtures, complimenting an outfit, noting a new haircut, admiring her perfume.

Then one evening in the middle of a business discussion, his words made a smooth, subtle shift. He flipped his hair, just a bit and said, "Amanda, you have been so gracious with your time and I haven't bought a single property…yet. I guess I've had so much going on in my life, I haven't been able to give the time needed to really consider possible investments. I'm sorry."

She shrugged. "No big deal. I've learned it's all part of the business."

But Alex wasn't finished. "I'd like to repay your

kindness by taking you to dinner so I can spend some unfettered time tapping your…expertise." The eyebrows above those handsome green-gray eyes rose a bit. "Maybe, if we can take a little time to put together your special talents and what I'm looking for, we can come up with something which will reward us both."

Amanda was flushed, sensing but not sure of his real meaning and motive. Still, she said yes, even though she never knew why.

His *business dinner* had been at the exclusive restaurant in the new showcase Hilton out by the interstate, where they had dined in near dark anonymity. They both talked business sporadically—she reviewing still more listings for investment and him sharing a funny anecdote about one of his patients, anonymously, of course. They smiled at each other over crystal glasses of white wine, the fruity aroma tickling her nose in the bubbles. She realized she felt at ease in his company. It was as if his comfortable bedside manner had transplanted itself to the dinner table.

In the middle of one of their exchanges, he stood up, surprising her slightly. "If you'll excuse me, I need to use the little man's room." He grinned. "I won't be long."

Amanda watched Alex stroll down the aisle, admiring his surfer's physique and broad shoulders, then her gaze drifted around the dimly lit dining room. Subtle lights hidden behind gold sconces traced the outline of the restaurant. Pristine white tablecloths adorned each booth and table, with the silverware sparkling in the candles rested atop each table. Maroon napkins tied in perfect knots sat atop small china plates. Classy place. Her eyes roamed the room, but she didn't recognize a single soul and let out a long breath. That meant they probably didn't recognize her as well.

Glancing down the hallway where Alex had disappeared, she didn't see any movement. Her eyes returned to the table, and she saw it. Halfway between her plate and his, a hotel room key lay on the linen cloth, its blue and maroon colors in blazon contrast with the white. The room number was printed neatly on the folder beside it.

Her gaze flitted around the room and down the hallway where Alex disappeared. No one appeared interested in her. Good.

Was this what she wanted? Things with Ken had been deteriorating lately. Her husband was so committed to helping *the kids*, he seldom had time for her anymore. Why not?

In one easy move, she snatched up the key and rose from the table. She held her breath as she rode the elevator up six floors, alone thankfully.

"Come on, come on," she whispered aloud.

By the time she had the door open—with her hands shaking, it took three tries with the electronic key—her face felt flush. She hurried inside. Without thinking, she stepped into the fancy bathroom and stripped down to her pink silken bra and panties. Lying on the bed, she stretched herself across the king size bed atop the fluffy maroon and brown comforter as he came through the doorway, sporting a delighted grin. His eyes lit up and his smile broadened. Hurrying over to the bed, Alex's hands tried to undress in a flurry, struggling to open shirt buttons fast enough and undoing a stubborn belt buckle. He almost tripped on his trousers. Amanda couldn't help herself. She laughed and kept giggling until his mouth covered hers and his long, lean body smothered hers.

Chapter 27

When Ken arrived at the station, Bart was escorting Bill Clayton into the interrogation room, the same one where he met Stacy a few days earlier. Had that really been only two days? And he'd been able to accomplish nothing in those two days. Nothing for the investigation, nothing for Stacy.

"Have a seat, Mr. Clayton." Bart's voice wrenched Ken back to the present.

A short, squat man, Bill Clayton looked to be in his late thirties, though it was difficult to tell. Uneven stubble dotted the chin of a scraggly face, pockmarked with acne scars. A shock of matted black hair was mostly covered by a sweat-stained cap with a Boston Red Sox logo on it. He wore a faded T-shirt with large, ragged holes under his arms and a beer slogan across the front, from a local company. Below the shirt, his faded jeans looked as if he slept in them. Even from across the small room, foul odors of sweat, alcohol and something Ken couldn't identify—and didn't want to— washed from the man. Ken fought the urge to cover his nose.

Three wobbly, metal chairs surrounded the same scarred table, a microphone now in the center. Bill Clayton sat facing the microphone and Bart sat opposite him. Ken dragged the third chair away from the table and set it against the wall. With his record lately, he was glad to let Bart do the questioning. Glancing across the room, he saw the large plate of glass behind Bart's head and realized, for the first time, it was a two-way mirror. He didn't even remember it when he'd talked with Stacy here and then realized he'd sat with his back to the glass. They could see and hear everything, he thought.

"Mr. Clayton…Bill, is it okay to call you Bill?" Bart asked in a polite, unassuming, almost, but not quite friendly, tone. Clayton nodded and Bart went on. "How long have you lived in Portsmouth?"

"'Bout five years," Clayton quipped.

"What brought you here?"

"Wanted to get a new start."

"New start?"

"Look. You guys pro'bly know I did some time before I come here, so drop the bullshit, okay? Right now, I don't need this shit."

"Well, what were you in for?" asked Bart quietly, refusing to be ruffled.

"Dealing."

"What'd you sell?"

"Whatever. A lit'l crack, some weed, mainly cocaine."

"Ever sell to kids, Bill?"

"Hell, I don't remember. Shit, it was a long time ago, a lifetime ago," Clayton answered, a little too quickly Ken thought.

"Ever sell any acid back then?"

"Uh-uh, man. I can see where this is goin'. No way! You can't do this to me. I'm clean as a goddamn virgin. I did my time. I paid my fuckin' debt."

"Well, that's true, three-and-a-half years. Ken, did

you know he got out early for good behavior?" Bart turned to glance at Ken and grinned. "Bill, here, was a model prisoner."

Bart turned back to face Clayton. "But, Bill, when I ran a check, I found out we've been called to your house three times in the past year with complaints from the neighbors. Something about parties that got out of hand. Let's see," Bart checked a manila folder he held in his hand. "Well, says here there were complaints about alcohol and drugs. Something about kids and some underage partying."

"Hell no, man, we was only havin' a little fun and got a little loud, that's all. It ain't my fault I got some stuffed-shirt neighbors."

Bart kept on, "Hey, Bill, what'd you do? Probably think about going back into the old business? You know, great profit margins and all, and the parties are a good way to distribute. Is that it?"

"Hell, no, goddammit!" Clayton screamed and got up from the table, knocking the chair to the floor. The stench of sweat edged across the room. "I think mebbe I better git me a lawyer."

"Do you need a lawyer, Bill?" Bart asked, his voice the essence of calm.

"I ain't done nothin', if that's what you mean. Nothin' illegal, anyway."

Bart simply sat back, interlaced his hands behind his head, and looked at the standing figure opposite him. For a while, no one said anything. Finally, Clayton could keep quiet no longer.

"Look, okay. Sometimes I let my kids have a drink once in a while. They're gonna drink anyway. This way I can keep an eye on them, make sure they stay out of trouble. Anyway, it's my home, my property. Ain't it?"

Clayton stared across at Bart, the desperation showing in his withered face. Ken watched the scene unfold, intent on trying to look beyond the words, beyond the obvious. He noticed Bart purposely let the suspect wait, let him dangle.

"Actually, Mr. Clayton, it's against the law to provide minors with alcohol. But we're concerned with something a whole lot more serious here. Are you sure there wasn't a supply of other 'substances' available at your parties?"

"No, fuckin' way. Damn, I went that route once. I don't wanna go back. Besides, these are my kids we're talking about! What the hell you take me for?"

Bart waited a bit before saying any more. Ken could hear Bill Clayton's heavy breathing and smell his breath.

Bart held up both hands. "Okay, okay, let's say I believe you." A pause. "A man with your background, with your 'connections' has to have some idea where the drugs are coming from, you know?" Bart waited, but Clayton said nothing. "Where did James get the drug tattoo that cost his life, Mr. Clayton? Where'd your son get the drugs?"

"I don't know!" Clayton screamed at the officer. Two splotched hands seizing the table, he looked straight at Bart. "That's what's killing me. You're right. I should know, but I have no fuckin' idea. Not here, not in this town. I've tried to stay clean and look what it got me. My boy dead!"

"You got nothing for me, Bill?"

"My son Jack said the kids are gettin' it from school," Clayton said, shaking his head. "He said the kids talk about gettin' drugs from some dealer right there at Foster."

Ken remembered Jack as a sophomore at the high school, a dull lad who tended to follow the crowd. He spoke up for the first time. "Bill, did Jack say if other kids were dealing or if the drugs were coming from an adult at the school, like a teacher?" He got up and stepped next to Clayton. "I want to get the person who killed James, before more kids end up dead."

Clayton looked up and said, "He says it's an adult, but the kids aint talkin'. Scared shitless, I guess." Then he thought of something he wanted to add. "For what it's worth, I don't think it's that teacher you arrested, that Mrs. Thompson."

"Why not?" Ken asked.

"I don't know. Hell, she was the only one at school who gave a damn about my boy. It don't make no sense she was sellin' any drugs, that's all. It doesn't fit."

"Okay, I guess you can go...for now," Bart said.

Bill Clayton took a step to the door and turned. "I hope you catch the bastard who did this to my boy." He stood there for a moment, hesitating as if deciding. Then he seemed to make up his mind and said, "If I find out anything, I'll let you know. I'll ask around, okay?"

"Okay, we'll be in touch, so don't leave town," Bart answered without getting up. Clayton trudged out the door, his heavy footsteps echoing through the station.

Ken reached down, picked up the chair, and sat down opposite his friend. "Well, what do you think?"

"He could be involved, but I doubt it. On the one hand, he looks like he could be good for it, with the background, the parties and all. And his son Jack's already been through assessment once."

"But?" Ken probed.

"As far as we can tell, Clayton's been clean. He's got a job at the plastics factory, and he's been pretty regular. He's even got to pass drug screening once a month and does. And those parties get a little loud, but that's about it. The neighbors call and complain and yell about drugs, but we've never found anything. Only a bunch of guys having a good time, a little loud maybe, but mostly legal. I was simply pulling his chain a little."

"He did seem really distraught about his son," said Ken. "I guess he could have been faking, but it didn't look like it to me. After dealing drugs for years, it must have been something to find out his son died because of them."

"Yeah, what we might call poetic justice. I'll keep an eye on him anyway, just in case."

"Probably a good idea. Hey, as long as I'm here, do you think I could look in on Stacy?"

"Sure, as long as we can squeeze you in between room service."

"Very funny."

"Sorry, a little jail house humor. Let's go over and I'll talk to the matron for you."

Chapter 28

"Well, what *is* the union doing?" Dawn Hatcher snapped.

Chris Goodman watched the scene unfold and said nothing, at first, biding his time. He needed to see where this would go.

Even as chill as he was, he could slice the tension in this room. Nostrils flaring, Dawn leaned her head down so she stood nose-to-nose to Robyn Boyle, Portsmouth Education Association president. Dawn towered over the smaller woman. As he watched, everyone in the cramped room stopped what they were doing, awaiting the president's reply. The Foster teachers' lounge was packed and uncomfortably warm, especially for a Monday morning. Several teachers squirmed in their seats, and it was obvious they had more on their minds than lesson plans and student discipline. Even the Xerox copier sat silent, as if bearing witness.

The smells of burnt coffee and stale doughnuts flowed through the air, souring his stomach. That might have something to do with how much he had to drink last night.

Rolling her eyes, the exasperated president said, "First of all, for the hundredth time, we are *not* a union. We're a professional organization. How do you expect us to get any respect from the administration, if we act and talk like some redneck, blue-collar union?"

Chris noticed Robin Boyle had dressed up for the occasion, wearing an obviously expensive navy pant suit with a cream blouse accented by gold earrings and chain. Her power suit, he thought.

"Jeez, give me a break, *madam president*," Dawn said. "*What we expect* is for the old P E A to help us out when we're in a jam. Now, what *is* our organization doing to help Stacy?" Dawn didn't move, her height and bulk pinning the prez against the table, giving her no space to maneuver.

Chris grinned. That woman certainly wasn't his type, but he admired Dawn's chutzpah.

"Well, uh, I'm not sure there is much we can do…at this time," Boyle began.

He'd heard enough. "Oh, that's just great," he scoffed. Shifting his own slouched position on the worn, green lounge chair, he dangled his legs over one of the wooden arms. This morning, he'd left his cotton shirt open, a few buttons undone down the front. His dark slacks were wrinkled and looked like he'd slept in them—which he had. Who cares. He had a lot on his mind and didn't give a damn about any dress code. Not today.

Chris continued, "One of our members gets hauled off to jail, in handcuffs right in front of God and everybody, and our esteemed *union*"—he practically spit out the word—"is not sure if they can do anything. What the hell do we pay $400 a year for? I haven't seen any fat pay raises coming our way. Have you guys?" Chris glanced at the other teachers.

Before anyone could answer, Boyle said, "Well, we've arranged for a good lawyer for her. Tim Arnold."

Chris eyed the single bead of perspiration migrate through the cream foundation on the side of Boyle's forehead.

She hurried on. "He's local, but he's good and he handles criminal cases." Her gaze darted from Chris back to Dawn. "We can't do much more…at least not until we see how the investigation plays out."

Dawn jerked, thrusting her mug into the other woman's face. "To see how the investigation plays out? You can't tell me the *union*, in its infinite wisdom, thinks Stacy could *possibly* be guilty."

The P E A President didn't say anything.

Slumping into the only chair left around the small table, Dawn slammed her mug on the Formica top and spilled the hot coffee over the side, partially obscuring the words *Life's a bitch and then you die*. A few drops rolled onto her fingers, and she cussed, shaking her hand to cool it.

"I don't know," Daniels said. "Personally, I find it hard to believe Stacy could be involved in anything like this, but I understand the police have discovered some pretty solid evidence." Keeping his eyes on the table, he fingered the piece of sheet music in his hand, turning it around absentmindedly as he talked. "I mean, they found more of those tattoos in her locker, for God's sake. If she didn't put them there, how'd they get there? Don't we all keep our lockers locked?" He glanced up at the others, who nodded.

Chris looked around the room and shook his head. "Are you telling me none of you have shared your combination with another teacher? Or the custodian? Bill, how about you?"

Daniels looked down and straightened his music tie

of the day, black with trumpets parading down the center.

Chris added, "There are other ways those drugs could've found their way into her locker."

Daniels shrugged. "I guess."

Jacqueline Highstreet said, "Yeah, but I heard they found out Stacy bought a condo on Marco Island or someplace, worth more than $300,000. If Stacy Thompson is not dealing drugs, I ask you, where would she get that kind of money?"

Peering into her compact mirror, she checked her makeup once more and smiled at the result. She tilted the mirror so she caught Chris's face in the reflection. She gave him a discreet wink. He grinned back.

She sneered, "I mean, I could afford that, er, I mean my family can. But Stacy Thompson? I don't think so. I don't even know what family she has."

"Well, she was *there* at Camp Haven that night. I guess the cops think that makes her look guilty?" Bedinghaus offered.

"Yeah, the only reason she was there in time for the *big* event was because someone I know got sick. How convenient," Dawn shot back, her voice rising.

Bedinghaus seemed to shrink even smaller than her petite form. "Excuse me for living," she peeved and released a loud sneeze.

The lounge grew quiet. For a while, no one spoke.

After a bit, Dawn continued, "Look, Stacy Thompson is no saint. Nobody knows better than me what a pain she can be. She thinks she can save all these kids and is always giving me a hard time about not doing enough for them. But Stacy, some kind of big drug dealer? Come on, get real. She hates drugs. She won't even take aspirin. She's the advisor for "Just Say No" Club."

Chris decided to voice the question he figured others had to be thinking. "Stacy Thompson on Friday. Who's going to be next? You know, if they could get Stacy, it could be any of you—or me." Then he looked back at Boyle, while still not adjusting his position. He chortled. "And isn't it a great comfort to know the Teachers' Association will help you get a *decent lawyer*?" He looked back at the rest of the teachers. "I don't know about you guys, but I feel *a whole lot better* knowing that."

Boyle raised both hands, eyes darting around the room. "Look, guys, you don't mess with the law. I hated the way Garcia came in and practically dragged Stacy out of here Friday. That show of force wasn't necessary and he knew it." Her voice went up. "We've filed a formal protest."

Dawn held the back of her hand up to her head. "Oh, a formal protest. I think I'm going to faint."

"He had an arrest warrant," Boyle continued quickly, not wanting to be cut off again. "And he claims he has a pretty strong case against Stacy. Besides making sure she has good legal representation and protecting her job here, what else can the organization do?"

Before anyone could answer, the bell clamored, the loudspeaker on the wall erupting, and the teachers began shuffling out the door to get to their rooms, carrying on hushed conversations as they exited. Glancing at her Cartier watch, Boyle gathered up her folders and followed the others out. Lost her audience, Chris thought.

While the other teachers filed out the door, Chris watched Jacqueline move to the computer workstation, take off the plastic cover, and flip it on. He liked what he saw. He studied her slide her pretty derriere onto the mismatched, old chair in front of the new Mac G4.

He didn't budge, at first—if only on principle. But he only had so much time, so he figured he'd better get moving. He slid his legs off the chair arm onto the ground, stood, and stretched. Seeing Jacqueline alone at the computer, fingers dancing across the keys, he walked over and put his fingers on the back of her neck.

Jacqueline gave his hand a playful slap and darted a quick glance around the room. "Easy, tiger. Somebody could walk right in." She went back to striking the keys.

He leaned down and whispered in her ear, "That's part of the fun, isn't it?" He nodded at the computer. "You think you could give me a few personal lessons? You really seem to know what you're doing."

She stopped her typing and leaned her head back so she was looking up into his face, the enticing scent of her perfume drifting to his nose. "I'll be glad to. There's much I could teach you." She smiled, her beautiful painted lips parting, revealing perfect teeth.

"I bet there is. I bet there is." His fingers moved from around her neck and crawled down across the front of her expensive satin blouse. Both hands cupped her breasts and she purred. He kissed her and she looked surprised at first, but she rose to meet his lips for a second kiss.

He stopped and strode over to the door. "I've got to go. My gang will be waiting for me… and I wouldn't want Carla to come looking for me."

As he pulled the door open, she asked, "Chris?"

"Y-e-s?" Turning, he dragged the word out and he made his eyebrows dance like he knew she liked.

She'd turned in her chair, her face toward the open door. "Are we still on for tonight?'

"Count on it. My wife's going down to her mom's for the evening and I've begged off."

"I'll be waiting for you."

"I bet you will. Gotta go." He headed through the open door. Before it closed all the way, he heard Jacqueline pounding away at the keys, the clicks rapid fire. He took a minute to ponder what else those fingers could do.

He grinned.

Chapter 29

Ken eased back and settled into his large leather chair. Only 8:15 and he felt exhausted already. He'd always enjoyed this chair, savored the warm, soft feel of the old brown leather and this morning he surrendered to its soft embrace. Laying his head against the high back, he closed his eyelids and allowed himself to drift.

His secretary stuck her head in the office. "Good morning, Ken."

Vivian Coventry always projected a brightness in her voice and her smile welcomed him every morning. Ken had a reputation in the district for being positive, though he knew *she* was the eternal optimist in the office. He couldn't count how many times she buoyed him, her positive attitude a balm to ease his anxiety and calm his frazzled nerves. And on numerous times, Vivian's advance preparation often made him look good, both in front of his boss and in his work with teachers. He was lucky to have such a valuable assistant and he told her so often. Last year he'd even gotten *her* a card on boss's day and they'd joked about who was *really* the boss in the office.

"Good morning, Vivian," he responded in a quiet, slightly preoccupied voice. "Good to see you this morning." He attempted a wan smile.

Today she was dressed in her normal work attire, a

professional dress with a print pattern of colorful leaves across the front, the reds and yellows and oranges brightening up the office. With a heart-shaped faced, green-gray eyes, a small nose, and a mouth that smiled almost all the time, she carried the image of the kind grandmother, right down to the close-cropped hair edging from a brown to a silver.

"Is there anything I can get you or do you want me to leave you alone for a while?" she asked.

"I need to take some time to catch up around here." Ken stared at his desk, cluttered with piles of papers. "Maybe you better give me a little time this morning to do that and then we'll put our heads together."

Nodding, she disappeared without another word.

He stared at the small office. The dark wood paneling that surrounded him on all four walls had been the choice of a previous occupant and gave the room a dark, professional appearance. The scent of the lemon oil polish the staff used on the wood once a month still hung in the air. The room conveyed a more formal look than Ken would've preferred, but he'd grown to appreciate it. Trying to soften its appearance, he'd hung an original painting of children flying kites on the wall behind his desk and on the side wall he put up an art print of the interior of an old, one-room schoolhouse— or at least, what the artist thought it must have looked like.

Ken glanced around at the paneled walls, barely noticing the framed awards and plaques from grateful students and professional organizations. Not one for displaying such honors, he had conceded to his secretary who'd insisted on the need for "some decorum in here." Two large bookcases flanked one wall of the room. Binders bearing titles such as "Board Policy Book" and "Administrative Procedures" and scores of professional books and reference manuals filled the top shelves. Lower ones held file boxes filled to overflowing with professional journals, each labeled with the journal name and years.

He turned his chair around on its swivel and faced his new computer. Although clearly no "techie," he'd recently succumbed to the onrush of technology and brought his office into the computer revolution. The new computer, recently purchased with a sizable chunk of his office budget, sat waiting, staring at him. On the screen danced figures of clowns, smiling and gyrating around the display. Most days, he enjoyed their ridiculous appearance, but this morning their silly grins appeared to mock him. He hit a key to make them disappear and pulled up his schedule. Studying the calendar, he reviewed the activities for the day.

Vivian reappeared, a half-filled glass in one hand. "I thought you looked like you needed something, so I brought you some OJ."

When she set it on the wooden desktop, Ken reached for the glass and took a sip. "Thanks, you take good care of me."

"Somebody has to." Vivian grinned. After a brief silence, she asked, "Have you talked to Stacy? How's she holding up?"

"Yeah, I talked to her briefly yesterday and she's doing okay, though she's running a little low on hope." He paused for a bit and then said, "Hey, Viv, you're pretty plugged into the community. You've lived in Portsmouth all your life. What's the scuttlebutt about the kids' deaths, about Stacy?"

Vivian hesitated before speaking. "Like you said, I've lived here all of my fifty-five years and I learned not to put much stock into people's gossip. The boys' deaths have hit everyone in this town pretty hard. And, yes, now that she's been arrested, there are some people who'd like to believe it's Stacy, if only to get the whole thing behind them. Especially since she's not a *native*."

"What about you, Viv? What do you think?" Ken had learned long ago to value the opinion of his assistant and he sought it often.

She scrunched her nose before answering. "Well, I don't know all the facts, though I've heard most of the rumors." She shook her head. "But there's no way you'll convince me Stacy Thompson sold drugs to those little guys. That makes absolutely no sense. Has to be somebody else."

Ken nodded, glad to know Vivian held the same perspective on Stacy's situation he did. "Thanks, Viv, it's good to know. There is something you can do for me. Would you please go over to the middle school and pick up the permanent records of the boys who died? I forgot to get them when I was there, and I want to take a closer look at them."

"Will do." His secretary rose and left, leaving him alone with his thoughts again.

On the corner of his desk perched two family portraits. The first was a shot of Amanda and him with Steven, the toddler squirming between them. The second was a photograph of his wife and him seated, with their son, Steven, very much the young man, standing behind them, taken a year or two before he'd gone away to college. He kept both photos there on his desk because they captured better times, sweeter times.

Times he needed to remember. Glancing from one to the other, his memories flooded back.

****

In the hope of forgetting about his brother's death, Ken had thrown everything—focus, work, time—into his coursework. It had been almost two-and-a-half years but the cold, blue image of Dick's body on that gurney still haunted his nightmares. He'd punished himself, keeping everyone at a distance. Over that time, he'd dropped out of the fraternity, had no real relationships, and hadn't dated.

He prayed he could finally regain his balance his senior year. Overall, his college classes at UMass had gone well. By the time he started his fourth year, he'd completed nearly all his required classes, with only student teaching and a few electives left. He threw himself into his assignments and his teachers had commended his work and each compliment only confirmed he'd chosen the right path. He would dedicate himself to becoming a great teacher and save teens—like Dick.

Amanda was the one who punctured his armor.

Amanda and he attended the same elective speech class. The first couple classes, she flirted with him lightly, with a toss of her hair, a whispered word, and a light touch on his arm going down the row. He managed to ignore these early attempts, but Amanda was nothing, if not persistent. About the third week of classes, when he should've been concentrating on the speech being given, he *sensed* her looking his way and glanced over. She saw him watching and winked. Without willing it, his male instincts kicked in as he took in her shapely figure, enchanting hazel eyes, and long flowing brunette hair.

It was as if she'd flipped a switch in him. His carnal instincts and libido roared to life. Still, he felt paralyzed by his guilt about his brother's death and couldn't bring himself to ask her out. When the class ended, he mumbled a polite "See you," and then fled down the row past her and out the classroom. Afterward, his remorse flooded back with such force—he felt he'd betrayed his brother—that he almost didn't go back to Speech 310. But, of course, he did.

That next class, Amanda arrived before him and had somehow arranged it so the only seat he could take was next to her. As soon as he sat down, she turned toward him, extended her hand, and said in a breathy whisper, "Hi, I'm Amanda."

Ken had little choice. He took her hand—warm, soft, and smooth—and replied, "Ken."

Her eyebrows did a quick dance and her red lips parted into a wide smile. "I know."

Before he could respond, the prof entered and started the class. Ken tried to keep his focus on the teacher and the students doing the speeches, but found his attention pulled to the beautiful young woman sitting next to him. Today, she wore a bright, yellow, sleeveless tee with a wide scoop neckline, which revealed quite an enjoyable sight. He tried not to stare but it was hard. Below the top, she wore cutoff denim shorts, very short and showing off plenty of leg. Nice legs. The sizzle and aroma of cooking oil drew his attention to the front of the room, and he tried to concentrate on a less-than-riveting speech about "How to make French toast."

But Amanda was not to be denied. She leaned over

the top of her desk and, taking out a small notebook, she tore out a paper, scribbled down a few words and folded it in half. She slid the paper across the Formica top to him, brushing one finger across his arm, and left the note there.

Ken stared at the white, creased paper against the blond faux wood. Shooting a glance at the prof now in the back of the room, he grabbed it up, opened the note and read the feminine script.

632-1924 Call me. Let's grab a drink. Amanda

His gaze cut over to Amanda, who wore a delighted grin, making her features crinkle. She twitched her tiny nose a bit.

How did she do that?

He gave her a slight nod and stuffed the paper into his pocket. That night he caved and called her. He figured they'd go out once and she'd see his anxiety and move on. After all, she'd seen him make a fool of himself in speech class.

He couldn't have been more wrong.

He was nervous when they went out and tried to be the "perfect gentleman" like his mom had taught him and he treated Amanda Millner with courtesy and consideration. One date led to two, which to his surprise, led to three and more. Once he got past his initial apprehension, he discovered Amanda seemed to really like him and helped him become more comfortable and even relaxed—without the addition of alcohol. He took time to listen and learn about her and she seemed really interested to find out about him. Within weeks, he found himself recapturing his old self, complete with an intact sense of humor.

On occasions, his guilt and moodiness would

reappear and then she'd pressed him. After putting her off several times, eventually he caved and shared his ugly secret. When he told her, he sobbed, as they sat together in his car. She held him and let him cry, afterward telling him no one was perfect. Everyone has secrets. With his burden shared, Ken felt his foreboding sense of guilt lift some.

His jokes made Amanda laugh, a deep, throaty laugh that was infectious. She made people around her smile, including Ken. They had fun together and laughed a lot, and that seemed to redeem his soul.

Even a perfect gentleman can only be genteel for so long. About the third date, catching a late night showing of *The Way We Were*, a romantic drama about two college students in love, Ken got swept away. Their initial kissing migrated to more, *much* more. Once he started, Ken couldn't keep his hands off her…her admirable talents. Which Amanda didn't mind at all. One thing led to another and, before he realized it, they became quite the couple.

He went home with her over Thanksgiving and met her family. Even Amanda's mother proclaimed she loved Ken. Then Ken brought Amanda home to meet his mom over the holidays and the two women bonded immediately. So, while Amanda and he were on a Christmas carriage ride—during a light snowfall even—he asked her to marry him and she said yes.

They finished the year and married in the summer, with both moms collaborating on the planning and Amanda looking incredible in the flowing white dress. Since Amanda had one more year at school, Ken took a grad assistant job for the year so she could finish. Newlyweds in love, they spent every minute together, in bed in their tiny apartment, in the library, at the university theater and in the stands. He wished they could get those days back.

Shortly after she graduated, they moved to Portsmouth and he landed the job teaching English. Six months into their first year in town, Amanda got pregnant, then Steven came along. Man, those were sweet times. They *were* a truly contented family.

In the first few years, Amanda put her business degree to work as a manager in a small insurance business in town, working part time and caring for Steven. When their son started preschool, she decided she wanted something different and real estate seemed like a logical jump. The market was improving, and she read an ad a local firm was recruiting new agents. So he'd helped her study and get her license. She turned out to be quite the saleswoman, turning over properties and running up commissions. During the same time, he'd moved up the education ladder, first in the principal ranks and then as Assistant Superintendent.

Then, as life evolved, he had his world of the school district and she had hers in home and commercial sales. They both became so busy with work their lives together became…a second thought.

Chapter 30

Ken shook his head. When was the last time he'd made Amanda laugh, that wonderful, infectious laugh? He was ashamed to say he couldn't remember. When was the last time they made ardent love together, proclaiming their devotion aloud, like they used to do in his tiny apartment so many years ago? With Steven out of the house leaving the two of them alone, they should have plenty of time for each other, for listening, for sharing. for making love.

But that hadn't happened, not lately. They'd both been making other choices. Not good ones.

As he thought back over the past few months, or— if he wanted to be honest—the past few years, he had to admit he and Amanda had drifted far apart. So preoccupied with their own jobs, their own worlds, they made little time for each other. His school district responsibilities seem to grow each year and Amanda responded to his commitment by increasing her work selling houses. And they'd both had considerable success in their own professions, which only fed the loop of more work. There was always one more district task for him to tackle and one more property for her to move.

Ken still loved his wife and realized he was only making excuses. He resolved to do better, to take some time off and get away with her, take that trip to the resort, or better yet, to Hawaii like they discussed. He promised to try to make her laugh again.

Vivian reappeared, arms full of manila files, interrupting his reverie. "Here are the records you wanted." Then her tone changed. "It was chilling, asking for the files of those boys. I don't think Martha had made up her mind whether she was glad to be rid of them or felt guilty about giving them up. I didn't feel any too comfortable handling them myself."

"Sorry about that."

"Hey, that's okay. Such a tragedy about their deaths."

She pointed to the stacks of papers across his desk. "Ken, if you don't want to bother with all this, I placed the few things that need your immediate attention in the in-basket."

"Thanks, Viv, I may do that, but I have to get through some of this." He gestured at the accumulating paper on the wooden desktop.

Going through the mail was a chore Ken never relished, but this morning he found it especially grudging. Somehow, the special offers from publishers and the impassioned pleas from job seekers held little interest for him. Today, he simply couldn't tolerate the mundane tasks of his job. He had trouble focusing, his mind returning first to the image of the four metal caskets and then to the gaunt face of Stacy Thompson in her cell yesterday. Absentmindedly, he tossed the mail into piles, separating the pieces into junk, catalogs, and "keeper" stacks.

Then something among the papers caught his eye and he stopped. His attention focused on a plain white envelope. It sat amidst the pile, sealed, with the word

Confidential scrawled on it in a legible, boxy handwriting. The envelope stood out because his secretary normally opened all of his mail, except for the occasional confidential piece. Ken fumbled in his desk drawer, searching for a letter opener. It was there somewhere, but since he seldom used it, he had trouble locating it. Impatient, he gave up and shut the long drawer. He held the envelope up vertically and tore off the top edge. When he turned the envelope over, a small, white piece of paper, only about two-inches square, floated out and drifted onto the desk. At first, it appeared blank. Then, when he turned it over, he saw, scribbled in the same handwriting, the words *check out W K.*

He stared at it for a while, turning the paper over several times in his hand. He pushed a button on the desk phone. "Vivian, can you come in here a second?"

"Sure, Ken, I'll be right in." She walked in and slid into one of the two chairs opposite the desk. "What is it?"

Ken handed her the envelope first. "Do you remember this? When did this come?"

"I'm not sure exactly." Accepting the envelope, the secretary squinted at it, lengthening the lines in her forehead. "Oh yeah, when I went to get your mail out of the mailbox yesterday afternoon, I found it. Because it was marked confidential, I left it. I thought it might be another report of child abuse. What's up?"

Ken slid the paper across the polished surface. She turned it over and, putting on her half glasses that hung on a chain around her neck, examined it.

"What do you think?" he asked.

"Is this it? That's all that was in the envelope?"

"Pretty cryptic, huh?" Ken nodded. "Well, you're the great assistant, any ideas?"

"What is W K? Or maybe, who is W K?"

"Maybe. Just in case, why don't you check out the student files from the middle school and high school to see if we can come up with somebody with those initials who might tie into this whole mess. And while you're at it, check on the staff too and let me know."

"I'll get right on it, boss."

When Vivian left, Ken opened the student folders and thumbed through them. He'd gone over all the information when he was at Foster and he didn't really expect to find anything new, but he had to do something.

He paid special attention to the discipline referrals, reviewing each pink paper form. James' file was on top. The referrals were for pretty standard stuff for fifth graders—stealing, occasional bad language, even cussing at a teacher. He counted the slips and remembered Carla saying James had twelve referrals and that's what he found. As he examined the last few, he noticed something about the dates in the right-hand corner of the slips. Each one occurred exactly one week apart. The last seven happened all on the same day of the week. He turned his calendar to match the dates with a day of the week. October 12, 5, September 28, 21, 14, 7, he counted backwards on the calendar. All Fridays. "It seems James must have had problems on Fridays," he said aloud, having no idea what that meant.

So intent on his calculations, he didn't noticed his secretary standing in the doorway. She watched him, waiting. He looked up and saw the puzzled look on her face. "Did you find something?"

"Yeah," she said. "No students but one staff member with those initials."

"Teacher?"

She shook her head. "Custodian."

"Who?"

"Wally Kowalchek."

Chapter 31

Ken's sleeping had been tortured lately. Not a light sleeper under normal circumstances, the horrible deaths of the four boys and the mystery of the drug dealer had left him restless in bed, waking often to the recurring vision of the four gold coffins, interspersed with the suppressed memory of a single, silver casket in the pouring rain. When the phone rang, he was up with a start, grabbing it before it finished the first ring.

"Parks."

"Ken, this is Bart."

"Bart, do you have any idea what time it is? For God sakes, it's…" Ken scowled at the alarm clock. "…It's 2:23 in the morning. What are you doing calling at this time?"

"Drew another extra shift. I'm at the high school with Tom. It looks like you've had another break-in. Tom told me you're the one to call."

"Me? Oh, hell, I forgot George is out of town at the school board convention. What's going on? More vandalism?" Ken dropped his voice to a whisper, trying to not wake his wife. But, as he sat on the edge of the bed, he could hear Amanda turn and make barely disguised sounds of protest.

"Not much, maybe didn't have time," answered Bart. "It looks like they set off the silent alarm, you know, heard the cops and split. But they managed to take a few things."

"What'd they get?"

"We're not sure yet, but Tom says they took the three new laptops. We think there could be more. Tom's checking now."

"Okay, tell Tom I'll be out in a little bit, and Bart?"

"Yeah?"

"I have something I want to run by you when I get out there."

"Okay."

Ken hung up the phone and, for a minute, simply sat there. He calculated he'd been asleep for less than three hours. How long could he keep up this pace without his body collapsing?

In a voice thick with sleep, Amanda protested, "Do you have to go again? Buildings are not even in your responsibility. You can't keep doing *everything*. Why don't you let Walters handle it?"

"Amanda?"

"Well, then, at least try to be quiet. I've got a full day of work tomorrow and I need my sleep." She turned in the bed so she faced away from Ken and muttered, "Sometimes I feel like I'm married to the whole damn district."

Too tired to worry about what he was going to wear, he simply grabbed the pair of Dockers hanging on the hook in the closet and pulled a cotton shirt off a hanger. He stared in the mirror at the overgrown stubble on his face and disheveled hair. Dragging a brush through the hair, he fought the matted, uncooperative strands for a bit and gave up. He breathed into his palm and inhaled. Nasty. His gargled and swished with a bit of mouthwash. Staring at the mirror in the dim light, he shook his head. He didn't care how much the district prided itself on *image*—he could hear Walters' lecture already—this was how he was going. He slipped on his shoes, grabbed his keys, and headed out the door.

Fifteen minutes later he pulled up in front of the high school, next to the cruiser. He trudged past the flagpole and up the walk, his coat blown open by the cold night wind. Tom Samson was at the door, opening it for him and Ken greeted the principal, who looked as blurry-eyed and ragged as Ken felt. Tom's obese frame was silhouetted in the doorframe and the light of the fluorescent bulb reflected off his partially bald head. The white fringe that surrounded the top pink skin was even more disheveled than Ken's hair. Seeing the principal's slumping shoulders only seemed to compound Ken's exhaustion.

"Is this a great job or what, Tom?" Ken asked. "Where's Bart?"

"He's in the science wing. That's where we think they got in. Looks like somebody left a window unlocked and they simply slid it open. At least they didn't break anything." The principal's voice belied his exhaustion as the two walked down the half-lit corridor, their footfalls echoing.

"Do we know what all they took yet?"

"Damn it, Ken, I can't believe it. They took the three new Powerbooks we just got in," Tom said, his red eyes narrowing. The waistband of his wrinkled suit pants fought to contain the overweight figure, the pouch spilling over the worn leather belt. "They're worth almost $8,000! Do you know how long it took me to get that technology? Eighteen damn months. Eighteen months to lobby the board, plead our case to Walters, allocate the funds, and wait for the bureaucracy to get the computers in. And these guys steal them after only two days. You know, we haven't even had time to catalog and put the inventory stickers on them. That's on me." His shoulders slumped.

Ken wanted to say something but couldn't think of any consolation. Or maybe he simply couldn't think.

Tom drew in a long breath as they walked. "When they went into the hall, they must've tripped the alarm and took off. So far, that's all we can tell." He stopped and stared at Ken. "This is one hell of a job, Ken. And on top of it, we get to be here at almost three in the morning."

When they arrived at the opposite end of the building, they entered Coach Kellogg's room and found Bart. Another cop, Shaffer, stood over by the window, dusting it and examining the glass, metal, and ledge for fingerprints. Under the glare of the fluorescent fixtures, the room took on the strange, distant appearance of one of those crime scenes on TV, colors all washed out. Ken half expected to see an area cordoned off with the "Police–Do Not Cross" tape. Oblivious to their entry, Bart and Shaffer chatted and continued with their work. In Ken's stupor, they looked like the cops working in the background of some old black-and-white Perry Mason episode. Bart saw him there and came over.

"Never a dull moment around here, huh?" commented Bart.

"Not lately," Ken said. "Tom was filling me in on what was taken and how they got in."

"Looks like they backed a pickup with some of those wide tires around the corner of the building and simply carried the merchandise out through the window. Two of them from the footprints outside," Bart explained.

"Do we stand any chance of ID-ing the two who did this?" Ken pointed to the other officer. Shaffer finished with the window and moved his equipment to the counter where the computers had sat a few hours earlier.

"Probably, but not likely from this work." Bart pointed to the black dust. "There are way too many fingerprints from kids, teachers, janitors. It might be hard to even find one print that will stand out. Besides, if it is a student from here, he can always say he was in class."

"Then why go through all this?"

"Standard procedure, and besides we might get lucky. But I'll put my money on the fact these monkeys won't be able to keep their mouths shut and will brag about their big score. That's how we'll get 'em. Kids always have to talk about it."

"Can the other member of Portsmouth's finest spare you for a moment?" Ken asked.

"Sure. Jim, I'll be back in a few."

"Tom, would you keep an eye on Shaffer? We don't want him to break anything," joked Ken.

"Very funny," piped up the other cop.

Chapter 32

Ken and Bart walked out of the brightly lit room and into the darkened hallway. With only the illumination from the security lights to guide them, Ken led the way down the corridor, grateful for the shroud of semidarkness. In the dimness, his nose caught the pungent scent of cheese corn chips—a favorite among the students—and shook his head. The custodians must have missed sweeping this corridor. He figured the others guessed what they were talking about, but again had the feeling it was important they weren't overheard. Maybe he was merely getting paranoid, looking for conspiracies everywhere, but a gnawing at the back of his neck reminded him he had no idea who all the players were and he'd better be careful until he did.

"I couldn't find anything," Ken began. "There was nothing in Wally's file and when I called his references at the last place he had left, the new supervisor didn't know him. Maybe this is just another wild goose chase. I'm sure as hell getting tired of doing the chasing."

"Well, when I ran Wally Kowalchek through our computer, you know, I didn't find anything either," began Bart, "but—"

Too exhausted to play games, Ken growled, "Damn it, Bart, but what? Did you find something or not?"

"Not like you think. I couldn't find anything on

Wally Kowalchek. Not anything. No traffic ticket, no voter registration, no minor offense. Nothing." He paused.

"So?" Ken didn't appreciate the riddle.

"Well, I thought it was awfully strange that nothing showed up in the system. So I ran his social security number and came up blank there too."

"Bart, can we get to the point here?"

"Okay, okay. So I did a little creative investigation, you know?"

"A little what?"

"I lifted some prints from the janitors' closet, identified the other two—Janice and Big Al—and took Wally's."

"Wait a minute. How could you tell which was which?" Ken asked, now hooked.

"Figuring it out didn't take a genius. Janice is a petite woman and Big Al is, well, Big Al. It wasn't all that difficult to separate the prints of a hundred-ten-pound woman and a three-hundred-seventy-pound man from Wally's."

"Okay, what did you find out?"

"That the prints don't belong to Wally Kowalchek, but to Walter Kanelli. And Walter Kanelli not only has a past, but a fairly sordid one at that. Well, seems he did a little time in one of the fed's finest accommodations in upstate New York." He paused, grinning. "Guess what he did time for?"

Ken finally got the light of satisfaction in his friend's eyes. "Drugs," he said.

"Walter got out twelve years ago and a little while after that, skipped parole and simply disappeared. And presto, no further records of Walter Kanelli."

Catching on, Ken added, "And right about that time enter Wally Kowalchek, wise-cracking janitor for the middle school. Quite a coincidence."

"I thought you'd think so."

"When did you find all this out?"

"I got a call this afternoon from a friend in Pittsburgh. You know, I had him do the check, because he owed me a favor…and Garcia wouldn't find out about it."

"Are you going to pull Wally in and grill him?"

"No can do." Bart took his cap off and ran his hand through an oily mop of red hair. "You see, what I did was not exactly kosher, at least, not with the chief looking over my shoulder and so eager to lock up your Mrs. Thompson forever."

"She's *not* my Mrs. Thompson."

Bart ignored him. "Whatever. I don't think Garcia would exactly approve of my going against his orders, you know. He heard about me questioning Clayton and ripped me good."

"So, now what?" Ken's body reeled from the fatigue and his brain refused to function.

"I thought maybe you and I might simply have a nice talk with Wally. You know, nothing official. Maybe ask for his help with the case. Then, in the course of the conversation, we might just mention a few things and see what happens."

"Sounds like a plan. Besides, I don't have much else to go on," Ken said. "How about tomorrow, er, today right after school? Where do you want to do this?"

"Probably the more informal the better. How about if we catch him while he's cleaning one of the rooms in the east wing?"

"Wally actually cleaning a room? Now that really would be novel," said Ken. "I'll meet you around three."

"Sounds good."

The two made their way back to the lighted science room where Shaffer was finishing up, at the principal's urging. Ken checked with Tom who said he could handle it and made some comment about trying to salvage some sleep yet tonight.

As Ken headed out to his car, he wondered whether he'd be able to get any more rest tonight. He had to try. He hoped Amanda wouldn't be awake and then, in the same breath fumed that he felt that way about their relationship. He needed to do something.

He drove the car out of the parking lot and into the bleak darkness of the Portsmouth night. He yawned so wide his jaws hurt. Right now, he was so exhausted, he didn't want to tolerate Amanda's diatribe. Besides, he could tell her the details in the morning.

He decided to sleep on the couch.

Chapter 33

"Assis'nt Superintendent Parks, good to see ya," Wally Kowalchek hollered down the hallway and gave a quick wave of his hand. Flashing his trademark grin, Wally was, as always, half pushing, half leaning on his wide broom, his two-hundred-fifty pounds seemingly supported by the long wooden handle.

"I heard ya been keepin' busy investigatin' the boys' deaths," Wally continued as he reached down and wrestled with his old leather belt as it fought a losing battle to keep the shiny, black pants over his considerable stomach. "Ya gettin' anywhere?"

"I don't know, Wally," Ken said. "It's much harder than I thought, but I'm making some progress." Following Wally into the next classroom, Ken slid into a student desk.

The janitor made some half-hearted attempts to sweep around the rows of desks. Stooping, he picked up the waste can and dumped it into the large trash bag on his trolley, sending the odors of paper and pencil shavings across the room.

"You got a theory about what's going on?" Ken asked.

"Yeah, I got a few ideas…if you're askin'," Wally said, setting the can down with a clink and coming over to Ken. "First o' all—"

"Oh, there you are, Ken," Bart cut the janitor off

mid-sentence. "Martha said she thought she saw you go in here. Oh, hi, Wally."

"Hey, Bart. Wally was ready to share a few ideas of his own on the investigation. Care to join us?" Ken glanced toward the custodian for confirmation, who nodded.

"Glad to." Bart pulled a chair out from a student's desk, turned it around, and sat on it backward, straddling his legs around the back of the chair. Bart's right hand went to his cap. He removed it, ran his fingers through his auburn hair, and replaced the cap.

Obviously delighted with an audience, Wally started again. "First o' all, ya got the wrong person in jail." He looked straight at Bart. "And I think ya know it. The kids tell me it's not Mrs. T."

Bart said, "Well, Wally, I like Stacy too, but Garcia has a good bit of evidence pointing to her. How do you explain that?"

"Easy. She's been framed."

"Come on, Wally. Why was she framed…and framed by whom?" Bart asked.

When Wally tried to answer, the cop cut him off. "Besides, what would you know about anybody being framed?"

"Hey, look, I'm not as dumb as some people think and…I been around some," Wally said.

"Wally, no offense," continued Bart. "You're a nice guy, but you're only the janitor. What would you know about drug dealers?"

"It's Head Building Custodian, Bart," said Wally, punching the three words out, and then added, "and I wuddin' always a custodian. I know plenty."

Both Ken and Bart waited for him to say more, but

Wally turned away, making another half-hearted attempt with the broom.

Ken asked, "Wally, what did you do before you came to work for us?"

"Well…um, different things." Wally, suddenly evasive, sauntered away from the other two, guiding his push broom to the other end of the room.

Ken called after him, "Well, thanks anyway. I appreciate your interest. If you get anything from the kids that could help us, let me know, okay?" Then to Bart, "You learn anything from the prints you picked up last night?"

"The results on the fingerprints haven't come back yet," Bart said.

As he and Bart talked, Ken watched Wally out of the corner of his eye. On the other side of the room, Wally had stopped even pretending to work. He strode back toward the two of them and threw his broom handle against the wall to interrupt Bart. "Look, I know a lot more than ya guys think. Before I come here, well, let's jus' say I knew some real shady characters. Even knew some guys who sold drugs, so I know what them type's like." When neither Bart nor Ken responded, he yelled, "And I'm tellin' ya, ya got the wrong one in jail."

"Come on, Wally," said Bart. "You're kidding me. What'd you have, a former life or something?" He exchanged an incredulous look with Ken.

"Yeah…ya might say that," said Wally, tentative again. "Well, enough of a past to know somethin' about drugs." He looked at the two men who stared back at him.

They said nothing and waited, their gazes on him.

Wally glanced from Bart to Ken. He went on. "Look, before I came here I had some friends, the wrong kind of friends, ya know. They taught me more 'bout drugs than either of ya ever want to know." He waited and when still neither replied, Wally raised his voice, his face livid. "I'm tellin' ya there are some bad things goin' on here…an' it ain't Stacy Thompson!"

Ken and Bart glanced at Wally and at each other.

Bart raised both hands and said, "Hey, easy. We'd like to believe you, you know. We both like Stacy." He pointed one finger at Ken and then at himself. "But right now, who we like doesn't count for a hell of a lot. Now, if you have something more than *your opinion*, that would be something. You know, I can't go to my boss and say, 'Garcia, we have to let Thompson go because the janitor says it's not her.' "

Eyes darting from Bart to Ken, Wally hesitated. Ken figured the guy was weighing his options, deciding how much he could say. It was obvious Wally enjoyed commanding the attention of both the DARE officer *and* the assistant superintendent. When Ken and Bart didn't respond, Wally blurted, "A long time ago, I was…" He paused, searching for the right word. "I was involved with some drug dealers, so I know what I'm talkin' 'bout."

Bart looked up and asked, "Was that before or after you changed your name from Walter Kanelli?"

In an instant, the color drained from the custodian's face, his skin suddenly ashen behind the black, bushy mustache. "I dunno what you're talkin' 'bout," he mumbled. He turned, grabbed the broom, and made swirling motions around the desks.

"What?" Ken asked. "Wally, what's Bart talking

about?"

"He talkin' crazy, that's all," Wally snapped. He hurried to finish the room. "Look, I got to get goin'. Got more rooms t' clean," He maneuvered his broom toward the doorway.

In a quick motion, Bart rose from the student chair and stepped in his path. "Walter, I know," he announced.

The janitor's big form crumpled against the doorframe, his hands sliding down the broom handle.

"Know what?" Ken asked, playing along. "Hey, will somebody clue the assistant superintendent in? Bart? Wally?" He looked from one man to the other. The cop and the janitor eyed each other, Bart's face only a few inches away from Wally's.

"Wally, do you want to tell him or should I?" Bart asked in his flat policeman's voice.

"Go 'head," the janitor muttered. Collapsing into a student chair near the door, he let go of the broom handle, which slapped the tile floor.

"Well, Ken," Bart began, as he settled back into the chair as if he were beginning to spin a tale. He leaned back in the reversed chair and both hands removed his cap again, laying it in his lap. "It seems Wally here is not what he appears. Or to be more precise, he is a whole lot *more* than he appears to be."

Bart looked from Wally to Ken and then back at the custodian. Then he ran down the whole thing for Wally—the former life, the conviction, the name change. All the while Ken watched the custodian's face, studying it for any tell-tale signs. Wally said nothing and sat there, head bowed.

When Bart finished, Ken asked, "Wally, is all that

true?"

"Perty much," the janitor said.

Ken asked, feigned shock in his voice, "Don't you know withholding that information could get you fired?"

"Yeah, like you'd ever hire me in the firs' place if ya knew to begin with," Wally shot back and barked a harsh laugh. "Well, would ya?"

"I wasn't in charge of hiring when you started, but probably not," Ken said, trying to play out the charade. "But with what's happened, do you know how this looks?"

Wally shrugged.

Bart went on, playing bad cop again. "Look, Wally, or Walter, you were involved in drug trafficking big time before. You know, why should we think you'd stay out of this?"

When the janitor responded, it was with a different voice. Not the confident, kidding voice. This one was quiet, humble, and seemed out of place with the big body. "All that was a lifetime ago. That's why me and the Mrs. came to Portsmouth, t' get away. We wanted t' give our kids a clean start. Only way I knew to do that was t' change my name and start over."

He looked at Ken, but before Ken could respond, Bart pressed, "Look, Wally, everybody knows the dead kids hung out with you. And you clean up around Thompson's locker every day. Who's to say you didn't get the combination and plant those tattoos in her locker, you know?" He pointed at the custodian. "You're the one who said she was framed, maybe because you're the one doing the framing."

"Hold on, there, Callahan!" Wally shouted, his face

210

turning beet red behind the mustache. "Is this where you expect me t' confess or somethin'. Fat chance!" His laugh was brittle. "I'll admit I made some mistakes in the pas', but I paid for 'em. And I've been clean for twelve years! Twelve years, goddammit!" He threw his hands up. "Besides, I like Stacy and, if I was going to frame someone, I sure wouldn't pick her."

"Wally, we know some of these troubled kids like Robert and James talked to you a lot," Bart went on. "I thought it was because they related with you, you know, but maybe they were going to you for a little more than *conversation*. What do you say, Mr. Kanelli?"

All through this exchange, Ken studied Wally, trying to read the truth in his features. He was finding the truth more and more elusive in all of this.

"Look, I get along okay with some o' the kids. Mebbe it's 'cause I see me in 'em, I dunno." Wally shook his head. "But I ain't into no drugs, haven't been for twelve years. That stuff ruined my life once. I ain't about to let it happen t' these kids."

Bart didn't let up. "Okay, Wally, since you had a connection with these kids, give us something. If it's not you and you say it's not Stacy, who the hell is it? What are these kids telling you?"

"They ain't tellin' me much," Wally answered, his eyes darting from Bart to Ken. "The dealer for these drugs is the best goddamn secret I seen. All the kids are damned tight-lipped 'bout it. I think they're scared shitless." And then, as if he had forgotten something, "But they say it ain't Mrs. T. It's somebody else."

"Else?" Ken said. "Who else?"

Wally's glance shot around the classroom. He

whispered, "One time, when they didn't know I was around the corner, I overheard one of the boys—I think it was Robert—say 'The doctor's goin' to be pissed off if he duddn't git his money right away.' I stopped where I was, ya know, so I could hear 'em. Then James said 'My brother said the doctor once cut the balls off some kid in another school that didn't pay up.' " Wally paused, looking from Bart to Ken. "But when I come around the corner, they all shut up real fast, like I caught 'em at something. Then James said something he thought was funny and dumb, ya know, like he done and then they all split."

"Did they ever mention it again? Or tell you who the 'doctor' was?" Bart asked.

"I tried to ask a couple o' times, but they always acted like I was nuts or somethin', I couldn't git 'em to say any more," Wally added.

For a while, no one spoke.

Finally, Wally broke in, "Look, Ken, Mr. Parks, does this mean I lose this job? I still got two kids in school and Wally, Jr. says he wants to go t' college." His voice was pleading. "I'll do anything. I'll help ya, if I can."

"Frankly, Wally, I don't know," Ken said. "According to policy, you can lose your job, but that doesn't necessarily mean you have to. Let me work on it. I'll let you know." When Wally started to say something, Ken added, "I can't give you any better than that."

"We're not going to do anything right now," Bart announced. "But we want you to keep your eyes and ears open, you know, and let Ken or me know if you find out anything—I mean anything. Got it?"

"Sure. Sure. I can do that. I'll be glad t' do that."
Wally nodded a few times. "Besides, I kinda liked those
kids, 'specially James and Robert. I want t' catch the
bastard who did it to 'em." With that, he got up and
collected his broom off the floor. "If it's okay, I got t'
get going. I got more rooms to clean."

"Sure, Wally, you better get back to work," said
Ken. "But, Wally, I'm counting on you letting me know
if you learn anything."

"You can count on me, Ken." The janitor pushed
his broom out the door.

After a few seconds, Ken asked, "Well, what do
you think?"

"Uh, he knows more than he's saying," Bart said,
"I'm not sure what."

"You think maybe he's part of it?"

"Maybe, but probably not." He shook his head. "If
he is, he sure isn't making much money from it. You
know, he's driving a ten-year-old car, his clothes are all
nothing special, his wife and kids don't have much, and
you know where he lives, in Arrowhead. If he's in, he's
either on the short end of the deal money-wise, or is not
spending it." He paused a minute, pondering. "Okay,
your turn. What do you make of what he said he
overheard?'

"If he is part of dealing," Ken began, "he could be
simply covering up."

"Or?"

"Or, if he's telling the truth about what the kids
were saying, the possibilities make me real
uncomfortable. And remember I mentioned that
Rebecca Bedinghaus, one of the teacher chaperones at
Cape Haven, said she overheard the boys talk about

getting something from a doctor? She thought they might've been talking about the tattoos."

"That would fit with what Wally's saying."

"Yeah, but it doesn't narrow it much. There are plenty of doctors around town. Dr. Hardcastle, Dr. Fulmer, Dr Fannigan, old Doc Hart. And those are the ones I can think of right now."

"Don't forget the doctors at school." Bart raised one eyebrow and grinned. "This could get real interesting."

"Yeah, it sure could."

Ken, considering Wally's admission, didn't smile. They both untangled themselves from the small student chairs. As Ken slid the chair back into place, he stopped and looked at Bart. "If Wally's telling the truth, why did someone send me the confidential message?"

"Maybe to send you on another wild goose chase."

They headed out of the room, turning down opposite ends of the hall.

Bart stopped and said, "Oh, and Ken?"

"Yeah?"

"Watch your backside." Bart started walking again and then called over his shoulder, "In case it gets even more interesting."

"Always. Always," Ken said and headed down the corridor. He glanced at his watch. He had twenty minutes before his meeting with Superintendent Dr. Mark Walters.

Chapter 34

Ken scanned the hand-scribbled notes on his leather clipboard one more time. In his job, he had to balance a whole host of specifics in his head at once, with few notes. But he didn't trust his memory with these important details. Closing the pad, he made his way across the reception area to the superintendent's office.

"Do you need this?" his secretary asked in a quiet voice. Stopping mid-stride, he turned toward her, but didn't look up.

Vivian waited for him.

"I'm sorry, Viv, did you say something?" Preoccupied, Ken glanced up.

"I thought you might want the computer files you had me put together. I ran a hard copy so you could refer to it if you needed to."

Ken took the papers. "Is this the only copy?"

"Yes, except for what's on the computer. And that file's secured, like we discussed."

"Thanks, Viv. I don't know what I'd do without you. Gotta go. Don't want to keep the big guy waiting." Ken took two steps.

"Oh, and Ken?" When the secretary saw Ken turn back, she whispered, "O'Brien's in there, too."

"Again?"

Vivian nodded and Ken covered the distance,

knocking on the closed door.

"Come in." The clear, authoritative voice of Walters came through the metal.

Opening the door, he stepped inside and closed it again without being asked. The office of the superintendent covered a space twice the size of his own. Walters had recently refurbished the room, hanging cherry paneling on the lower half of the four walls, topped with a polished chair rail. He finished the upper half in wallpaper with an abstract design of the school colors, red and gray. Besides the large wooden desk and some chairs, the only other furniture in the office was a handsome credenza and a vertical file, both also in cherry. By most standards, Walters' office looked austere, the only item on the walls a framed, counted-cross-stitch wall hanging of a school bus by one of the district's drivers. Not a single personal item sat atop the desk. Walters said he considered such adornments unprofessional.

"Afternoon, Ken," Walters called. The superintendent leaned back in his large leather chair. Standing off to his left was Everett O'Brien, board president.

Ken could not help but notice both men facing him looked crisp, unfettered. Walters would say professional. Their starched white shirts and silk ties looked like they'd just come from the cleaners. He studied the two men. "The doctor"—his glance moved from one man to the other, from Dr. O'Brien to Dr. Walters—and his mind froze. Then he realized these were merely two of the doctors he knew…if he could even believe what Wally/Walter had said.

His eyes wandered from the stiff, one-hundred-percent cotton shirts across from him to his own wrinkled, pastel shirt with the sleeves rolled up, perspiration marking the folds. At other times, he knew his boss would've chided him for not conforming to the "starched-white-shirt-professional" look expected in the office, but today other matters demanded their attention. Frankly, being knee-deep in the investigation, he didn't care—at least that's what he told himself. Without thinking, he checked to see if the kid's tie he'd picked for today hung crooked. It did. He straightened it.

"Ken, Dr. O'Brien asked if he could sit in on your update," Walters said. "You know how concerned the whole board is about this and he thought he could better support you if he got the details firsthand from you." Although the superintendent delivered these lines in an offhand manner, Ken sensed his boss might *not* be that comfortable with the arrangement.

"Sure, good to see you again, Everett," Ken said.

Walters eased forward. "Okay, Ken, bring us up to date on what you've found out."

The board president moved from behind the desk to a chair off to the right and turned it so he too faced Ken.

Ken opened his notepad, gazed at his two bosses and began. "As you know, I've been working pretty closely with Bart. We think it likely Stacy Thompson is *not* the one selling drugs and we believe we may have uncovered two other possible suspects. In a routine check of all the boys' families, Bart discovered James' father, Bill Clayton, has a record. It turns out Clayton was convicted of selling drugs and did a two-and-a-half-year stint upstate."

"When was this?" Walters asked, animated.

Ken had to check his notes before answering. He thumbed through the computer sheets Vivian had readied for him, once again thankful for her penchant for meticulous preparation. "Convicted in 1985, served his time and released in 1988 and moved here shortly after." He paused and looked at his two bosses who both leaned forward. "The police don't have much on him since he moved here. Some of his neighbors have registered complaints about some drug and alcohol activity involving kids at his place, but nothing concrete."

"Ken, does Bart think it could be Clayton, one of the dead kids' fathers?" O'Brien asked.

"Clayton is certainly a person of interest, but Bart has some doubts," Ken said. "I was there when he questioned him, and the man seemed genuinely distraught about his son's death. Besides, as far as the cops could tell, Clayton has kept himself pretty clean since he came to town."

"Too bad," commented O'Brien.

"Why?" Walters asked.

O'Brien glanced down at his Rolex watch, his fingers unconsciously twirling the band around his wrist. "Oh, I was simply thinking of the district," the board president replied, with a shrug. "It would sure be better if we could move the focus of this investigation away from the school."

"Um…okay," replied Walters and turned back to Ken. "You said two suspects?"

"So I did," Ken said and grinned. "The second was uncovered by a little creative investigating by our same DARE officer. It appears one of our employees is not exactly who he pretends to be." Ken paused for a bit and went on. "One Wally Kowalchek has misrepresented himself."

"Wally, the custodian at Foster?" asked Walters, incredulous.

"The head building custodian," Ken said, mimicking Kowalchek's voice. "On a hunch, I asked Bart to run a check on Wally. When he did, he came up empty."

"So?" O'Brien was puzzled and not pleased about it.

"When I say empty, I mean nothing. Bart didn't find a record, a traffic ticket, even a voter registration for Wally." Ken enjoyed stringing his two bosses along, much as Bart had last night. God, was that only last night? He shook his head once. Then he went over what he and Bart had uncovered about the custodian.

When Ken finished, Walters said "Wally? I find that hard to believe."

O'Brien dropped his meek composure. "How did he get hired? I thought you guys did background checks on everyone before they were hired? Who screwed up?"

Ken thought, how typical. Uncover a possible problem and the board is looking for a head to chop off.

Walters turned to face O'Brien, but before he could get out a measured response, Ken answered, "Look, Everett. This was before I was here, before any of us were. We've only been doing background checks since '92 and Wally was hired twelve years ago. They weren't thinking too much about criminal records back then."

"So Wally—uh, Walter—is now a suspect?" asked the superintendent.

"Well, so far, Bart and I have questioned Wally and he was plenty nervous when he learned we had figured out his past." Ken looked down at his handwritten notes of an hour ago. "He claims to be clean. We're just not sure about him."

"So, he didn't put any of this on his application when we hired him?" O'Brien offered, his steel eyes lighting up.

"Of course not," replied Ken, "that's why we knew nothing about it."

"Isn't that cause for immediate dismissal, falsifying an application?" The board president directed the question at Mark Walters. It wasn't really a question.

Walters straightened up and answered, "It *can* be grounds for dismissal."

"Then let's fire his ass!" O'Brien said.

Ken said, "I wouldn't advise it, at least not yet."

"Why the hell not?" O'Brien shot back. The boyish demeanor had departed, his face muscles pinched.

"Bart doesn't think Wally is the source, but it's possible Wally may know something." Ken's instinct told him not to say anything about Wally's "doctor" comment. "Bart thinks we can keep a better eye on him if he's still working here." He looked from one boss to another. "And I agree."

"That sounds reasonable," Walters said.

O'Brien stared at Ken. "Okay, but I'm going to hold you personally responsible if this blows up."

"Take it easy, Dr. O'Brien," Walters said. "Ken is not the bad guy here. Let's remember we're all working for the same thing."

O'Brien's only response was to shift his lanky form in the chair.

The superintendent asked, "Ken, do you have anything else?"

"Well, you know Stacy Thompson is still in jail and Garcia thinks she's the best suspect. But I don't think it's her. Some things simply don't add up."

Walters leaned forward over his desk. "Chief Garcia told me he has a pretty convincing case on Mrs. Thompson, what with the drugs found in her locker, that new condo she bought, and those email messages. He's so certain he's closed the investigation…unofficially."

"Yeah, but—" Ken began.

"Look, Ken, I understand you like this Thompson woman," O'Brien interrupted, his voice regaining its calm, "but I think you may be letting your personal feelings cloud your judgment here. I've talked to Garcia at some length. He's told me he's convinced Thompson is guilty and the grand jury will indite her."

Ken wanted to object, but he didn't get the chance. He never saw the bomb coming until it dropped.

Chapter 35

The board president paused only briefly, glancing to Walters for support. The superintendent shifted his tall, muscular form in his chair, but said nothing. As if this signaled some unspoken agreement between them, O'Brien went on. "Mark and I have talked this over, Ken, and we've decided it's time for you to drop your investigation."

Ken's gaze darted from O'Brien to Walters, who stayed silent.

O'Brien continued, "You need to get back to the work the board hired you to do. After all, we know this has been really hard on you. Besides, so many other things need your attention. George has tried, but he's not you."

Ken read O'Brien's praise as insincere and tried to interrupt. He wanted to stop where this was headed, but O'Brien plowed on. "Look, it's not that you've done anything wrong. In fact, we're pleased with what you've accomplished with this investigation. You and Bart have found out about this parent and this custodian."

He looked to the superintendent who nodded his agreement.

O'Brien continued, his smooth tone returning, "But with Garcia's stand, we think it would be best for the district if things got back to normal. Ken, what we really need right now is for you to be a team player and help Portsmouth Schools get past this tragedy."

Before he answered, Ken weighed his words. While O'Brien spoke, his eyes never left Ken, and Ken stared right back. Now, Ken turned his gaze toward Walters and directed his response to the superintendent, ignoring the board president. "Mark, when you gave me this assignment, did you not give me free rein to take the investigation wherever I thought it needed to go?"

Walters answered, "Yes, Ken, but that was—"

This time Ken cut him off. "And you told me I was to do whatever I needed to do, *without board interference?*"

"That's true," the superintendent nodded and glanced over to the board president.

"Good," Ken went on, "For a moment, I thought you might've forgotten that." He paused, letting the sting of his words register. He noticed he'd caught both O'Brien and Walters off guard.

Ken continued, "And I don't care what Garcia says. I'm convinced—no, I *know* Stacy Thompson is not the one who's selling drugs to our students. I've worked with the woman for years and I know her." His index finger poked the desktop. "And that can mean only one thing. Some predator is still out there, waiting to poison and maybe kill more Portsmouth kids. Are you really willing to risk that, to save the district 'embarrassment'? I'm not going to walk away and let that happen. I plan to do everything I can to find and stop him…or her."

Ken stared at both men. Turning his gaze back toward Walters again, he said, "However, Mark, I understand you are my boss and you know I've always done what you told me …although I admit at times not without argument." Ken allowed himself the smallest hint of a smile. "And if you order me directly, I *will* drop the investigation officially."

Ken stopped and waited. For a while, no one spoke and O'Brien shifted in his chair. Walters, in his typical stoic manner, took his time answering. "Ken, over the years I've learned to trust you," the superintendent said. "You are right, I did say you could do it your way." He shrugged and shot a glance at O'Brien before looking back at Ken. "I don't see any reason to change now. I thought I could persuade you but, no, I am not going to order you to quit the investigation."

O'Brien turned in the chair, his back to Ken, and crossed his legs.

Walters went on. "But, Ken, Dr. O'Brien is right. We need to get this wrapped up. I will give you one more week." When Ken tried to object, Walters insisted, "One. Week. If you don't have any hard answers by then, I *am* going to pull you."

"O-kay," Ken said.

O'Brien jumped back in. "And, Ken, let me be clear about this. For your sake, crystal clear. If you're wrong about Thompson and this all comes down on us, I'm going to demand your resignation."

"Fine, if that's what you want, Everett. But I'm not wrong. I'll bet my reputation on it."

"You just did," said the board president. He focused on his Mont Blanc pen, which he pulled from his pocket. He clicked it several times. Then he asked, "By the way, what is Thompson's contract status?"

From the drawer, Walters pulled out the chart of staff contracts his secretary maintained and flipped through it. "Her contract is up this year," he read from the page.

Ken's gaze darting from Walters to O'Brien, he grasped the meaning of the inference. When he tried to interject, he was cut off by Walters.

"Perhaps we should announce we plan to non-renew her contract. *That* might help to distance the district?"

The board president sat back, grinning. "That's a good idea, Mark. It might help us out in the long run."

"It's a lousy idea," snapped Ken, unable to control his anger. Both O'Brien and Walters jerked toward him, eyes wide. "If she's exonerated—and I think she will be—she can sue the district for everything and win. You're the ones who were so worried about lawsuits. Do you want to risk that?" The surprised looks of the other two men were the only response. "Until we can get to the bottom of this, she is one of our employees and we have a responsibility to protect her. *I* have no intention of hanging her out to dry."

Ken closed his notepad and stood. "Well, Mark, that's about it for now. I'll let you know when there are more developments."

Ken exited the room and glanced back to see O'Brien and Walters in hushed conversation, eyes darting to him. "Nice career move, Parks," he grumbled to himself.

Then, one of his favorite Mark Twain sayings came to mind: "First, God created idiots; that was for practice. Then God created school boards."

Ken shot a glance back at O'Brien and muttered, "Twain got that one right."

Chapter 36

The blaring horn blew twice, jolting him. Ken looked up with a start, surprised to find the light had turned green. His foot jumped quickly to the accelerator and the car lunged, jack-rabbit-style, into the intersection and out into traffic. Totally preoccupied, his mind reeled, struggling to unravel the mystery of the culprit responsible for the four boys' deaths. He couldn't believe what all this had done to him.

Usually, in his job, he juggled a hundred details of twenty different committees and projects in his head, more or less simultaneously, and before the last few weeks, he could do it with ease. Walters had complimented him on this ability on several evaluations. But, ever since he had taken this on, the problem had consumed him. His waking and sleeping moments were haunted by the grotesque images of the boys' crumpled and bloodied bodies at the accident, not to mention, the tortured faces of the grieving parents— one of whom might be involved in the whole mess and another who was scheming to make money out of the tragedy.

Of course, his own buried guilt dragged behind him like an anchor.

And now, on top of everything else, yesterday he put his job on the line for this. Was he that convinced of Stacy's innocence? Of course, when he relayed the conversation and the consequences to Amanda, she'd gone ballistic. Why was he doing this, risking everything?

Even as his mind repeated her question, he knew the answer. He had to do whatever he could to save *his* kids. He could not stand by and watch more students poison their brains, ruin their lives. Not one more child will die…the way his kid brother had.

It was not about Stacy Thompson. He felt the district—read that as he—had a responsibility to protect their teachers…if they were innocent. Somehow, on some gut level, he knew Stacy could *not* be the drug dealer. He couldn't square the teacher who had pretty much rescued his eleven-year-old son years ago and who had been so dedicated to helping her students, especially the kids in trouble, with someone who would victimize kids simply to make money.

But no matter how many times he rolled it around in his head, he couldn't sort it out. Someone connected with school, someone the kids probably knew but were terrified of, some "doctor" was behind it all? He tried to come up with individuals who could fit that description and he could think of little else. With his regular school duties, he wasn't able to get much done, except keep the wheels from falling off.

Even things at home were different. Of course, things hadn't been great for a while. He and Amanda had been too busy with their own careers to make time for one another. Maybe they used their careers as an excuse *not* to have time for each other. He didn't like that thought, even as he figured it held more truth than he'd wanted to admit.

Lately, though, he realized he' d become

preoccupied—Amanda would say obsessed…and maybe she was right—he was so involved with this "assignment," he had ended up giving even less attention to her. And she resented it.

Ken felt guilty. Deep down, he knew it wasn't all his fault. After all, marriage was a two-way street. Amanda had been short and peevish lately, preoccupied herself as well. Was that on purpose? On too many days, they only saw each other in bed, and even that had been little more than slumbering coexistence. He couldn't even remember the last time he and Amanda had made love…or laughed together.

Still, given all that, she seemed especially annoyed since he took on this investigation. Ken had trouble understanding her resentment. She knew what this meant to him, why he was doing this.

He decided he needed to do something. The two of them needed to reconnect, to see if they could get back to what they had. Maybe, when this was over, he could book a getaway weekend at the great spa resort she had enjoyed so much last time. Something really nice for the two of them. He'd float the idea and see if he could get Amanda on board.

The thoughts about his troubled home life were short-lived. He couldn't help it. As he drove down Main Street and watched the students making their way to school, his mind reeled back to four dead boys, wolf head tattoos, and too many questions. Ken had trouble believing James' father could be involved in selling the drugs which ended up killing his own son. But what did he know? And Wally, good-natured, lazy Wally, had a secret life as a drug courier for the Mafia? And if before, why not now?

Nice little town, Portsmouth. And Walters and O'Brien seemed only interested in getting it all wrapped up so the district could *move on*. As he stopped his car at the crosswalk, watching four students amble across the street, he thought sometimes we forget we got into this business in the service of children.

Idling there, waiting, another thought struck him. Why had the dealer picked Stacy to frame? With her reputation, she did not seem like a logical choice. Why not Chris, the eccentric English teacher, or Jacqueline with her obvious money connections?

The questions nagged at him.

If he was right about Stacy—and his gut told him he was—then the answer to why they would frame Stacy might also give him the clue to the elusive shadow of the drug dealer. He pulled the white Taurus into one of the marked parking spaces. Sliding out of the seat, he grabbed his clipboard and stood by the car, watching scores of boisterous students file off the yellow buses into the yawning doors of the old, now new school building. Ken followed the droves of pre-teens into the building, some chattering, others shuffling by.

Inside the hallway, across from the principal's office stood Wally, watching the young ones hurry to their homerooms.

"Good morning, Wally," Ken said, forcing a little optimism into his voice.

"Morning, Ken," piped up the janitor through what Ken took to be a slightly forced smile. "Things seem a l'il quieter around here. Don't mind that. Quiet or not, these kids still make a mess. I tell 'em your mother don't work here, pick up afta yourself. It dudn't do much good, though." He moved from the broom handle and leaned over to pick up some stray notebook paper left on the floor. As he bent over his corpulent waist, he groaned slightly to dramatize the effort. "Oh well," he said, crumbling the dirty paper in his fist. "I guess this is job security. Right?"

Ken couldn't help himself and smiled. It was hard to reconcile the Walter Kanelli past with the wisecracking custodian in front of him. And after yesterday, Wally still managed to make jokes, at least what passed for his humor. Wally had either really put it all behind him or was giving quite a performance, Ken couldn't decide which, as he studied the lopsided grin on the old guy's face.

Stepping across the hall to the principal's office, Ken opened the glass door.

Martha smiled at him. "Well good morning, Mr. Parks. You're certainly here bright and early this morning." As she spoke, her face beamed and even her wavy, gray hair seemed to shine. Today, she wore a dark, conservative dress with a bright ceramic pin which read "Super Secretary."

Martha had been a fixture in the building a long time, even before it had become Foster Middle School. When most other staff had moved on to the new high school a few years back, she'd chosen to stay, claiming Foster was her home. She had made the office like a home, bright and cheery. She'd even brought in one of those new diffusers, dispelling the pleasant scent of vanilla in the space. And the secretary worked hard to make everyone feel welcomed, from the assistant superintendent to upset parents. Even though she was quickly approaching sixty and was a grandmother of six, she showed no signs of letting up. Ken knew she was the stable force behind the office. With her calm and even manner, she proved an effective counterbalance for her capricious boss.

"Let me guess," the secretary said, "you're here to see Mrs. Michaels? Lucky you." She grinned.

Not to be outdone, Ken chimed in, "Actually I'd rather see you, but Carla asked me to come by and see her. Something about a package of things from Stacy's class for her."

"Yeah, she said something about that to me. Let me see what she's up to and I'll let her know you're here. It wouldn't do for you to catch her napping, now would it?" She gave Ken a quick wink, her head of silver hair disappearing into the office maze. In a few seconds, she returned and escorted Ken back to the inner office.

As he stepped inside, Michaels was again on the phone and she waved him inside. Ken took a chair and was prepared to wait, but, to his surprise, the principal hung the phone up.

"Ken, thanks for coming over," Carla Michaels said. "Do you have a moment to talk?"

"Sure." The word escaped his mouth before he realized what he'd said. Ken appreciated the responsibilities the principals took on and tried to build a solid relationship with each one. He knew they often used him as a sounding board and needed someone to listen. He tried to fill that role when he could.

But, over the years, he'd learned, with this woman, no conversation took only *a moment*. Suppressing a desire to steal a look at his watch, he fixed his eyes on Principal Michaels. Her hair today was perfectly coifed and her make up looked professional. The exact right amount of liner, color, and lipstick. Ken wondered how long it took her each morning to achieve her look.

She wore a fashionable black suit, cut to render that "professional power woman" appearance. The green and white "Just Say No" pin stood out against the background of the dark lapel, the effect attractive and pleasant. But, as Ken stared at the face, he could barely make out the lines of age hiding behind the foundation, the applied colors a camouflage to what lay beneath.

"…ya can't believe how quickly things get hopping around here."

Ken heard her say and realized he'd already missed part of what she'd been telling him. He figured with Michaels, it didn't matter.

"No matter how early I come in here, the phone is ringing—students, parents, even vendors. You know, yesterday I got in here around six and when I walked into the office, the phone was ringing. It was a student calling, wanting to talk to one of our teachers. At 6:07, can you believe it?" she asked, but did not wait for an answer. Then an actual question. "How goes the investigation? Can you bring me up to date?"

"I'm working with Bart, but not that much to tell yet," he replied.

Obviously not satisfied, Michaels pressed. "What about the police? Where are they on this?"

"Well, Garcia is pretty confident about his case against Stacy but I'm certain by the time my investigation is over, she'll be exonerated."

She shook her head, blonde curls swaying. "Well, with Garcia taking such a hard stand, it can't be good for Stacy. Have you seen her lately? How she's doing? I've been so worried, we all have been," Michaels continued on, asking question after question, not allowing Ken to answer until the end.

"She's doing as well as can be expected," Ken said. "When I saw her a few days ago, she was going stir crazy and asked me if I could get her a few things, some books and things to take her mind off her…uh, current situation." Talking with the principal about one of her teachers sitting in jail made him uncomfortable.

"Well, anyone could see why, stuck in that cell all day. That's why when I covered her class the other day, I had the students write her some letters. I thought they might cheer her up." She leaned slightly across the desk, her whisper a quiet conspiracy. "But I had to take a few of the letters out, you know, so they wouldn't hurt her feelings. Kids at their age can be unbelievably cruel." She shook her head. "I hoped you might be able to take them to her."

She picked up a bulky manila envelope sitting on her desk and handed it to Ken. He opened the clasp and looked. Inside, he saw several loose-leaf papers, some with colored drawings, others with some scribbled handwriting. He closed the package and turned his attention back to Michaels, who'd not stopped talking. He forced himself to focus.

"…I know I should probably go to see her, but I'm afraid to. I simply feel terrible a wonderful teacher like Stacy was thrown in jail and I'm really angry about it. I'm afraid I'd only upset her if I went there. What do you think?" The principal seemed so emotional, even with her ramblings, he felt compelled to offer some comfort.

"I don't know. You're probably right, Carla. I'll pass on your good wishes when I see her."

"God, I hate all this," she babbled on. "Did I tell you they asked me to come down to the station to give a statement about Stacy? What can I tell them? That Stacy is a fine teacher and cares about kids. I don't think that's what they want to hear."

She took a breath and Ken wondered if this was his signal to respond. He didn't have to wonder long. "Well, maybe, if I go down there, I can help Stacy a little. That's how I'm going to look at it." She nodded twice. "With the reports that are overdue and all these discipline referrals from the teachers, I don't really have time, but you know I'd do anything for my teachers. They're the heart of this place…"

Michaels kept on, but Ken could not. He could tolerate her rambling for so long and this morning his limit was even shorter. His mind drifted to his next tasks, what he had planned for the day. That was the only way he was able to cope, to focus on the next item alone. Since he got started in this whole mess, he thought of his life as one long checklist and he moved blindly from one item to the next, checking each one off, without thinking long term. He didn't allow himself to look very far ahead. He tried not to think about what could happen to Stacy. As that thought attempted to intrude on his consciousness, he felt an urgency to move, to do something. He stood up, startling Carla.

"…and then I have this parent mad at me. Sometimes you can't please them, no matter what. Oh, I was digressing a bit, I'm sorry, I know how busy you are. Well, give my best to Stacy and tell her we're thinking of her." She smiled a saccharine smile. Seeing it, Ken remembered it looked like the smile of his Aunt Louise, the one with the beehive hair and beauty mark.

He couldn't stand Aunt Louise.

"I've got to get a few things out of Stacy's locker for her," Ken said as he moved to the door. "Who do you have subbing for her?"

"Mrs. Dickson is in there. She isn't Stacy, but she'll keep things together for us." Then she added, "Till Stacy returns, I mean."

"Thanks, I'll talk to you later."

"I'd appreciate it if you'd keep me informed if you learn anymore." Michaels' smile stayed wide as she held the door for him. "And thanks for taking those letters to Stacy. I do hope they cheer her up some."

Chapter 37

Ken's timing was perfect. He stepped back into the hallway, a hallway packed with hundreds of preadolescents—ambling, hurrying, clowning, cutting up. They were supposed to be changing classes, but their talk and minds were on other things besides science and social studies. Most days, Ken enjoyed this, watching the students interact, oblivious to his presence. Their manners were never rude. Except for stepping around him, the students simply ignored him. Continuing down the hall, he walked between pairs and trios of students, all in anxious conversation. He stepped around the corner and headed down the older corridor and, as he moved away from the junior high area, the noise level subsided.

Stopping in front of Stacy Thompson's room, he peered in through the small window, much as he had a week ago. The difference in the classroom was dramatic. The students hunched over their desks, pencils or pens clutched in tight fingers as they struggled through the black worksheet on their desks. He understood the looks of dejection on the fifth graders' faces. Mrs. Dickson, gray hair in a tight bun and half glasses perched on the end of her nose, paced the aisles, bent over, hands folded together behind her, the stereotypical image of the stern taskmaster.

As he opened the door and stepped into the

classroom, the students looked up from their papers, obviously glad for the possible interruption. However, Mrs. Dickson was not to be out-maneuvered. "Children, just because we have a visitor, does *not* mean you have an excuse to stop working. *Stay on task*." Her whining voice cut through the enforced silence of the classroom like a rusty blade.

At the mention of a visitor, almost every head turned toward the door, and then eyes quickly darted back to their papers, as if fearing some transgression. The classroom reeked of stale odors—bad breath, passed gas, and pencil shavings.

Ken reintroduced himself to the substitute and explained the purpose of his visit. Not to be distracted from her mission, Mrs. Dickson pointed to the connected workroom with a crooked finger and kept on patrolling the rows of desks.

As Ken strode up the aisle toward the front of the room, he saw the four desktops pushed together he noticed on his last visit. Only now, they'd been stripped of the names and photos of the four dead students. The desks still sat where Stacy had grouped them, bits of scotch tape clinging to the blond desk tops the only evidence of their former honors.

Ken intercepted the sub coming up the next row. "Mrs. Dickson, what happened to the photos of the four dead boys?"

"Mrs. Michaels and I decided they were too distracting for the students." Her voice was an attempted whisper, but it came out too loudly. Ken had never heard anyone give a whining whisper before, and his ears hurt listening. He suddenly felt sorry for the class. "We decided it was time to try to put the whole terrible experience behind us."

Ken fought to control his spiraling rage. Why was everyone so anxious to write it all off? Every fiber of his body cried to object, to scream out loud the senselessness of the tragedy, but then he glanced around to see every face in the room studying him. Instead, he hissed quietly, between clenched teeth, "Maybe it would help us all if we *didn't* forget." He glared at the substitute teacher, making sure she could read the message in his stare. He stormed into the adjoining workroom.

The locker was a free-standing gray metal cabinet, about twenty-four inches square, and stood in the corner of the small workroom. Walking over, he studied the front and stared at the combination lock.

Now, how was he supposed to open that? Standing there, he realized Stacy didn't think to give him the combination. He tried the handle, but the lock wouldn't budge.

Though frustrated, Ken tried to collect his thoughts. Stacy hadn't made a big deal about it, but he sensed it was important to her to bring back a few things, and he didn't want to return without them. Perhaps Dawn Hatcher, Stacy's teaching partner, might have the combination. He walked across the workspace over to the adjoining room.

Dawn's students were engaged in an activity known as "reading buddies" with the teacher observing from her desk. Having seen this activity in several classrooms before, he recognized the students reading to each other in pairs, along with the increased sound level in the classroom. He strode to the teacher's desk, eavesdropping on students as he walked.

Dawn rose to meet him. "Mr. Parks, welcome to Hatcher's reading corner." She lifted the coffee cup in her right hand to indicate the students at work. On this cup was written, *Laugh at your problems. Everyone else does.* Ken got a kick out of her mugs and even today, the lines on the cup helped a little.

Dawn continued, "This is one activity the students seem to enjoy, and it really pays off." She glanced over to the side and dropped her voice to a whisper. "See that pair over in the corner? When we started, Travis, the one in the blue tee shirt, struggled with almost every word, but since he's been working with Chris, he's getting individual help and doing quite well."

Both adults stayed silent for a few minutes and listened to Travis reading, sometimes easily, sometimes haltingly, but always with his friend's encouragement. When he finished, both boys beamed with their shared accomplishment.

Ken turned to the teacher. "It looks like the lesson is going well. I've seen it in some other rooms before, but not yours. Where did you get the idea?"

"Where do teachers get all their best ideas, from other teachers, of course. Actually, I got this idea from Stacy. She's been using it for more than a year." Then her voice changed and she asked, "Ken, how *is* Stacy holding up?"

"She's doing okay," Ken replied automatically and then realized he was talking to the closest thing Stacy had to a best friend and decided he could say more. "Actually, she's doing lousy. She's pretty frantic sitting there alone in jail. She asked me to bring her a few books and her journal so she can keep her mind occupied."

"You know, Ken, people around here are so weird. I can't believe the staff in this building who are ready to believe it could be Stacy. How could you be in this building for years and see her work with these kids and possibly think she could sell drugs to them?" Dawn threw both hands in the air. "Yeah, right, and I'll be the next Miss America! I don't care what Garcia or the stupid newspaper says. No way Stacy could ever do anything to hurt kids. I'd bet my next year's supply of coffee on it." She lifted her cup to punctuate her bet and the rich java aroma floated across to him. He needed some coffee too.

"I agree with you," Ken said. "But I've seen the evidence Garcia has against Stacy and it makes a damn good case." Dawn began to object, but he held a hand up to stop her. "Which means somebody has worked pretty hard to set Stacy up. What I want to know is, why Stacy? Someone around here is selling drugs to these kids. If we agree it can't be Stacy, then why did the dealer pick her to frame? You have any ideas?"

Setting her coffee cup down, Dawn put one finger to her mouth, displaying a pink garnet ring. "Good question…you know, I simply thought it was that idiot Garcia, but your point makes more sense. So somebody picked Stacy? Who would do that?"

"I don't know. Everyone expects me to be Sherlock Holmes around here, and I'm not. Right now, I'm trying to figure out *why* they would pick Stacy. Maybe if I can figure that out, I can trace it back to who. I thought you might be able to help since you seem to be a better friend to her than anyone else around here."

"Some friend! She's been in jail how long? Four days and I haven't gotten the courage up to go see her."

During the exchange the teacher's eyes had alternated from her boss to her students, making sure the kids were on task. Noticing one particular pair, Dawn said, "Excuse me" and walked over to the two girls, spoke quietly to them and then returned to her desk.

"Ken, I don't know why someone would pick Stacy, unless she was merely a convenient target?"

"What do you mean?"

"Well, Stacy is not real popular around here." Dawn paused and then said, "Well, I don't mean she's unpopular, only that she's somewhat of a loner. She does a few drinks with us on a Friday night every once in a while, but she doesn't hang with any particular crowd. Maybe someone figured she might be an easier target. I don't know."

"Sounds possible, but I don't know how that helps. Besides, I have another question."

"What?"

"Do you have the combination to Stacy's locker? She asked me to get a few books out of there and she forgot to give me the combination. I thought maybe she gave it to you."

"That sounds like Stacy, all right," Dawn said, "but I don't think I can help you. We talked about exchanging combinations, but never got around to it. Maybe you ought to check in the office. They might have it."

"You think so? I hope so. I'm going to try to see her later today and I didn't want to go without the books she wanted." He stood. "Thanks, Dawn, I'll check with Carla."

Chapter 38

It took Ken only a few seconds to retrace his steps to the office and find Martha working at her desk. "Is Carla in?"

"She just took off for her daily junket in town and central office. Won't be back for a while. Is there something I can help you with?"

"Maybe." He glanced down the hallway and then back at Martha. "Stacy asked me to bring her a few things from her locker, but she forgot to give me her combination. I was hoping you might keep a copy of it here in the office."

"I'm sure we do, Mr. Parks. We used to keep them in a file cabinet out here but ran out of room." She gave her head a shake. "Too much paperwork. If I'm not mistaken, they're in a drawer in the second filing cabinet in Mrs. Michaels' office. Let me go check."

Sliding her chair back, the secretary rose and headed down the small hallway to the inner office and Ken waited, tapping his fingers on the counter. He glanced around the front office, noting the several framed counted-cross stitch creations sitting on shelves in between photos of Martha with smiling young faces. Her six grandchildren, Martha had proudly announced when he asked.

In less than a minute, the secretary returned, white scrap of paper in hand. "Here you go. That should get you in. Anything else I can help you with?"

"Martha, you are a saint. Thanks," Ken said, as he stepped out and hurried down the hallway. When he arrived at Thompson's classroom, he opened the door, went in, and walked through the aisle, seeing the students still bent over their desks peering at a different worksheet this time. He exchanged a stern look with the sub and headed into the workroom. Leaning over, it took him two attempts with the dial before he was able to lift the latch and the lock came free.

As the door swung wide, Ken stared at the inside of the locker. Books, clothes, papers, pens, and other items were jammed into the small space. As he started pulling things out of the locker, he wondered why the police had not cleaned it out when they found the drugs here. And how did they find a few sealed drug tattoos among this mess?

As he extracted colored papers jutting out of every crevice, he recognized most as memos from the office, many weeks and months old, no doubt stuffed here and promptly forgotten. He grabbed as many of them as he could and stacked them on the workroom table in some semblance of a pile. He tried to sort things, setting them to one side or the other, rearranging so he could locate the books he needed to find.

He stopped mid-motion. He was intruding into Stacy's personal space. For some reason, he recalled the time in college when his then girlfriend, Gloria, asked him to check inside her purse for something. He did it, but felt strange sorting through lipstick, tampons, makeup, and keys. The same sense struck him now. Stacy and he had never been more than friends and colleagues and, even though she had asked him, he still felt like a trespasser. Still, he wanted to find what he came for.

Shaking his head, he returned to moving things around, fingering items. He was both embarrassed and now intrigued, exploring a side of Stacy Thompson he'd never known. The first thing he noticed was a postcard from Marco Island taped to the inside of the open door. The souvenir displayed a stunning sunset across a blue ocean, no doubt a reminder of her summer trip.

On a hook hung one of those colorful, button-down teacher sweaters, this one with a ruler, a little red schoolhouse, and the words "No. 1 Teacher" stitched on it. The hint of a fragrance clung to the cotton, some hint of a floral cologne. Sliding the sweater aside, he saw two large books lying on the bottom. He pulled them out, reading their titles, *The Insider's Guide to the Caribbean* and *Recommended Romantic Inns of America*. He guessed she and Mr. Thompson liked to get away, once upon a time. Also in the lower half, hanging on one of the other hooks, Ken fingered a long, gold chain with a small heart pendant. Curious, he picked it up, opened it and found the gold heart empty.

He moved his exploration to the upper shelves. On top, he noticed the yellow tape left by the police to mark where the tattoos were discovered. Strange, he thought, the police didn't even seem to bother anything else in the locker.

Along the edge of the shelf stood an old manila envelope. He pulled it out and peered inside. Bulging with so many papers stuffed into its narrow space, the envelope had split at the seam. Ken reached in and pulled out a few of the papers. They were letters, artwork, and handmade cards given to their teacher. He read a note, "You are the greatest teacher I have ever had, ever," and admired a rough, but colorful artwork of a teacher and her class with the inscription, "Mrs. T. teaching a great class—us!" As Ken thumbed through the mementos, he realized this must have been a collection Stacy had kept over time because he recognized the names of some older students, many other teachers called troublemakers.

The second shelf held more books, these smaller, paperback-size. He pulled them out and read their covers, Langston Hughes' *The Dream Keeper, Life's Little Instruction Booklet,* and Danielle Steele's *Secrets.* Next to these, he spied a small bound book covered in a green floral print, the journal she asked for. He reached for it. His hands full with the other books, he fumbled and dropped the journal. When the book tumbled to the floor, it landed on its edge and fell open, displaying lines of precise feminine script. Shaking his head at his clumsiness, Ken set the other books back on the shelf and bent down to grab the journal. He had no intention to read the writing—he already felt like a peeping Tom—and reached down to flip it closed. As he started to fix the clasp that had popped open, his gaze sighted his name written in her distinctive handwriting—Ken Parks.

He froze.

Chapter 39

Ken's battle between embarrassment and curiosity flared again. On the one hand, he respected Stacy's privacy, but he found himself drawn to the page, curious why Stacy would've written *his* name in her journal. And, if he were willing to admit it, he was glad for the distraction from the ugliness of the investigation, if only for a few moments.

His eyes darted around the small workroom. He felt like a thief worried about being caught. Raising the writing notebook close to his face, he sat down at the small table and began reading.

Tuesday, October 23

Ken Parks came to my room today to talk to me about the deaths of the four boys from my class. In the few minutes we talked I could tell he really cared about the boys. In his eyes I recognized the pain of their deaths, not unlike my own. Somehow, in the few minutes he was here, I sensed this was personal for him.

We know each other, but not that well. He sat close to me and looked me straight in the eyes and spoke directly, honestly. I was honest with him, too, and I told him about the day of the boys' deaths. He has no idea about the rest, though.

He stopped and re-read the last words, "He has no idea about the rest." What rest? About the boys…and their deaths? He pulled out his clipboard and jotted a note. He read on.

I saw his tie was crooked and while he sat there, I reached over and straightened it, a simple, friendly gesture. But as I touched his chest, my fingers tingled and my heart raced. I quickly withdrew my hand, but he was so preoccupied with asking about the boys' deaths, I don't think he even noticed. Thank God. He has no idea and I plan to keep it that way.

Ken slapped the book closed and glanced up. A small bead of perspiration crawled down the side of his head. Looking around, he expected to see the stern, hawk face of Mrs. Dickson peering in at him from the classroom door. He shot a glance that way. He was alone. He let out a quick breath. Grabbing up the journal, he couldn't bring himself to lock the clasp. Then he reached into the locker, retrieved a couple of books, and slid all the remaining items back into the locker. Stacking the books on the small table, he placed the writing journal on top and, balancing the four on his clipboard, walked out through the classroom. Preoccupied with Stacy's private thoughts—Ken couldn't shake the feeling he was eavesdropping, almost like stealing a peek at her undressing—he closed the classroom door quietly, backing into the hallway. He didn't see the person until they collided. He dropped his cargo, the books slapping the vinyl floor. As he scrambled to gather up Stacy's things, he looked across into the reddened eyes of Rachel Bedinghaus.

"Oh, sorry, Mr. P— er, Ken. I guess I wasn't watching where I was going." She giggled. "I was just coming out of the, uh, ladies' room and I guess I wasn't paying attention. Kinda lost in my own world." She flashed a vacant grin, looking like she were on another planet.

"It's okay, Rachel," Ken said. Kneeling down to try to scoop up the books, he stared into the face of the small teacher as she bent to help him. He stopped short. Something about Bedinghaus' appearance struck him, but when he glanced down at the floor, he saw the journal lying open among the scattered books. Not wanting Rachel to see the pages, he scooped them up.

"Ken, can I help?" she asked, fingernails pinching and massaging her nose.

"No, I've got them," he managed as he rose, books stacked again, the journal securely at the bottom now. Standing, he looked down at the smaller teacher and noticed the redness around her eyes and nostrils. "Rachel, are you okay?"

"This?" She brought a wadded tissue to her reddened nose. "Oh sure. It's only this damn cold I can't seem to shake." She gave a short laugh and veered off toward her classroom, small steps in a hurry. "See ya, Ken," she called without turning around.

For a moment, Ken stopped, standing there in the hall, the image of Rachel's face hanging before him. Something about it bothered him. He struggled, fighting hard to access the needed corner of his memory. Haunted by the icy memories of his past, the dread of a drug dealer running loose, and the thought of Stacy's life hanging in the balance—not to mention the disconcerting passage he'd read—he had trouble recently remembering even the simplest things. And yet, he nearly had it. He continued down the hall, trying to think.

Almost to the office, he stopped. "The drug seminar last spring," he said in a loud whisper right there in the corridor, his words startling him. He glanced around to see if anyone heard him. No one. In a flash, the proverbial light bulb coming on, he could see, could hear the speaker from the Delaware County Drug Prevention Bureau describe the symptoms of drug abuse. Standing alone in the hallway with the normal buzz of activity from the classrooms going on around him, Ken realized the speaker, six months earlier, had described the face he'd just seen. When he was telling the staff symptoms of drug use by students they should be watching for. Ken concentrated and recalled the slide of a young woman's appearance which looked very much like Rachel Bedinghaus' face. What drug label did the speaker put to it? In the middle of the hallway, the one-word answer popped into his head—cocaine.

Damn. Ken shook his head.

What was he supposed to do? Drag her from her room in front of her students? Like Garcia had done to Stacy? And he couldn't be sure it was cocaine. What if it really was a nasty cold? He decided he needed to talk with Bart, get his advice.

Although it was difficult to balance everything there in the middle of the hallway, he managed to get his clipboard open and jot down some brief notes—he didn't dare trust his memory. He closed it back up, restacked the books, and headed out.

He had to keep moving.

Chapter 40

Passing the front office, he waved a hurried good-bye to Martha through the glass and headed to the parking lot. Ken wanted to get to the safety of his car where he wouldn't be watched. Striding quickly across the parking lot, he arrived, his hard breath coming in clouds of white. Pulling the keys from his pocket, he fumbled with them, struggling with the lock before getting the key inserted and opening the door. He plopped the books on the front seat beside him and sat there, staring at the journal at the bottom of the small stack. Knowing he was prying inside Stacy's private world, he felt uneasy, like he was crossing some line, but the handwritten words beckoned. Perhaps, reading the entries could yield some clue to the kids' deaths he told himself, even as he realized that was simple rationalization.

Pulling the journal out from the bottom of the books, he flipped open the cover and it landed on the date he'd read before. He saw only a few entries after that date so he turned the pages backward, scanning the passages for any other mention of his name. Checking over several weeks, he didn't see his name again and found he was relieved…and disappointed. He felt like he'd gotten hold of a new addictive drug and wanted more. He had to keep looking and examined random sentences, skimming from page to page. He read on, catching Stacy's thoughts on problems she was having with her students, on her exasperation with how easily some of her teaching partners dismissed the problem kids. He knew he shouldn't, but he kept reading page after page, fascinated by the sketches of Stacy Thompson's private thoughts. Then something caught his eye in an entry. He read it carefully.

Wednesday, September 27

I attended a district meeting today on the new math curriculum and he was running it. It was a good meeting and we got some good ideas for our classrooms. But that's not why I'm writing.

Today, as I was sitting in a room full of people, I began drifting, enjoying the warm, rich sound of his voice. I started thinking of him in a new way. With his jacket off, I saw the strong square of his broad shoulders and his masculine arms. My mind floated down the rest of his frame and my body responded. Oh, God, my heart raced! I could feel the blood rush to my cheeks. My lips tingled. I haven't had that terrible aching down below in years. I can still feel it as I write this.

What? Ken felt his heart pound and stopped reading. He shut the journal. Pulling out the small calendar from his breast pocket, he flipped the pages back and found it. *Wednesday, September 27, Math Inservice, Media Center.*

He pushed his memory back, trying to recall the meeting held a month ago. He remembered a large turnout and working with the female presenter to give the staff teaching ideas for the new math program. He also could place Stacy there among the middle school crowd, but not much else. He didn't even remember paying any particular attention to her.

She must've been paying attention to him.

He couldn't help himself and opened the journal again, turning pages backward, reviewing the entries a little more carefully. Most of the captured thoughts were musings on troubled kids, on the absurdity of some of the practices at school, on her continuing struggle with her weight. He skimmed the entries, engrossed by the little details of the woman who apparently thought of him in a different light…and was now accused of murder.

One more entry stopped him.

Friday, August 26

Today was our first day back and again this year they gathered the whole staff in the high school auditorium. I know some of the teachers complain about this opening meeting (Dawn calls it the meeting of the mindless) but I rather like it.

Ken's eyes roamed over the rest, Stacy describing the speakers and even what *he* was wearing that day. Then his gaze went to the last part of the passage.

I was suddenly glad to be back in school. I am again free to enjoy watching him, like the sunrise, day after day.

Stunned, and yes, flattered, he eased back into the driver's seat and closed his eyes. How could he not have noticed? How naive was he? He and Stacy had been friends and colleagues for years, but his thoughts never went beyond that. Besides, he was married—even though things in that department were not great lately. And wasn't she married? She wore a ring, though he'd never heard her mention a husband or a family. Maybe this was merely her escape, her fantasy.

Opening his eyes, he saw the windows of the Taurus had fogged over. Feeling guilty now about his intrusion, he closed the book and began to lock the clasp.

Then he realized he hadn't checked the dates of the boys' deaths or their funeral. Not knowing what he hoped to find, he flipped the pages till he came upon the right dates. There, in her own distinct handwriting, her private thoughts stared back at him.

Friday, October 20

Today we buried four of my students—James, Justin, Robert, and Chad. All four of them died in a horrible automobile wreck.

Four young lives. Gone in an instant. I still can't believe it. I'm ashamed to say it, but I'm angry at them. All the times they came in upset or loud and made teaching them so difficult. The emotional energy it took to calm them, tease them, challenge them, and try to give them a drop of self-confidence. What was it all for?

And it gives the other teachers a chance to say, "I told you so. You were wasting your time on them. I knew they'd never amount to anything."

Why couldn't I reach them? It just wasn't enough. I'm, sorry, James, Robert, Chad, and especially Justin. How did you end up with the other three? God, have mercy on your souls. You were so young. Perhaps now you are at peace.

Ken closed the notebook again, mulling over Stacy's words. He glanced at his watch. Surprised, he found thirty minutes had passed since he'd talked with Dawn Hatcher. Absorbed with Stacy's private words, he had not realized how long he had sat there reading, skimming…intruding.

What was he going to do about it? Hell if he knew. Nothing.

He needed to be at the police station in fifteen minutes. Starting the engine, he turned up the defrost to clear the windows.

Chapter 41

"We may have a small-town operation here, but we do it right," Tony Garcia announced, as Ken walked into the squad room. "Mrs. Langford, if you'll step into this room?"

He led a woman into the area adjacent to the interrogation room. Ken didn't recognize the woman, who looked maybe thirty-five and dressed in an expensive professional suit. On the other side of the squad room, Bart motioned him over.

"Is this like one of those line-ups on TV?" asked the woman, her voice a little tinny and betraying a bit of southern twang. As she spoke, her mouth seemed to stay open longer on the long "i", drawing it out into a long, southern sigh. "I've watched them before but I've never done one."

"Well, it's a little like that," replied Garcia. "This glass is a two-way mirror. That means you can see in, but they can't see out. Do you understand, Mrs. Langford?" He paused long enough for the visitor to nod her head. "The room we're looking at is not that big, but we'll have four women sitting in there. All I want you to do is tell us if the person who purchased the condo we talked about is in there."

Squinting her eyes and concentrating, the woman stared into the "mirror."

Bart whispered to Ken, "This is Melinda Sue

Langford from Marco Island. She's the real estate agent from the condo company and she's the one who tentatively identified Stacy's picture from the fax. Garcia flew her up here. He's expecting her to ID Stacy in person."

From their angle in the room, Ken and Bart could see through the same mirror. Ken observed Stacy, the second one over, a consuming darkness on her face. Seeing her there among the suspects, he tried to reconcile the dark, almost haunting shell of a person with the spirit and vitality captured in her words on the pages of her journal.

It was almost as if this whole ordeal was stealing her life, robbing her soul.

His gaze shifted to the other three women sitting in the green chairs. He recognized one of them as Sylvia Thomas, one of the new policewomen on the town's small force. Although in "civilian" clothes, she was years younger than Stacy. The other two, Ken had seen before but did not know, figuring they were two other women from town. All four were dressed in simple clothes and had dark hair.

"I'm just not sure," the witness was saying, more to herself than anyone else, looking intently through the glass. "I'm just not sure."

"Take your time, Mrs. Langford," Garcia chimed in, his voice tense. "Nobody's going to rush you. Take all the time you want." His calculating eyes stared hard at his witness. Then Garcia said, "How about if I have each one of them say something?"

"I guess that might help," responded Langford.

Garcia leaned forward and pressed a button under the glass. "I'd like each one of you to say—" he paused, obviously searching for an appropriate sentence, and then went on, "I'd like each one of you to say 'How much is the townhouse condo?' One at a time please and in your natural voice. First, number one."

Each woman did as requested. When it was Stacy's turn, Garcia studied Melinda Sue Langford's face, searching for any sign of recognition. While Garcia paused, waiting for any possible reaction from the witness, Ken held his breath. When Langford made no sign of recognition, Garcia moved onto the other women in the small group and Ken exhaled loudly. He looked over and noticed Bart relaxing a bit too.

"I can't say," Langford drawled after an extended silence. "From what I remember, the woman who bought the condo looked a little like the second one here." She indicated Stacy. "I mean, same kind of dark hair and about the same age and height, but I'm not sure. But the voice doesn't sound right."

After another brief pause, the woman noticed all the heads turned toward her, and asked, "Chief Garcia, what's all this about anyway? What's this woman done?"

"We think she may be responsible for the death of four young boys," the chief answered with a clenched jaw. "And we think she may have bought the condo with profits from her dealings in drugs."

"Oh my God. I-I-I had no idea." Mrs. Langford said, the i's becoming multiple syllables.

"Please take another look," said Tony Garcia, his voice stern as if he could will her to respond. Everyone in the room fell silent waiting for the final judgment of the southern visitor. For a while, a long while it seemed to Ken, she stayed silent and it was clear, the longer she waited, the more flustered and unsure she became.

"I'm sorry," she said, "I can't say. It could be the woman who bought the condo, but I don't think so."

"That's enough, Garcia. Give the poor woman a break," said a quiet voice in the corner of the room. Ken glanced over and, for the first time, noticed the squat figure of Tim Arnold, Stacy's lawyer, leaning against the wall. He was dressed impeccably in his gray three-piece suit, white shirt with navy pin stripes, and maroon and blue tie.

"You gave it your best shot and blew it. The woman said she's not sure. Pressing her more won't help you in court and you know it." The lawyer spoke, self-assured, his voice almost taunting.

Garcia's frustration shone through his cold stare at Arnold. Then he turned toward the woman visitor and his demeanor changed, once again the professional cop. "Mrs. Langford, I want to thank you for taking your time to come up here and for trying to help us catch a killer. Officer Callahan here will give you a ride back to the airport." With that, he shook her hand, turned, and walked back to his office, disappointment obvious in his strides.

Bart walked over to the button under the glass, pushed it and said, "Ladies, thank you for your time. You can go now. Stacy, please wait a bit." He let go and turned toward Arnold. "Counselor, I figured you'd like a little time with your client?"

"Thank you. I have an appointment with a judge in fifteen minutes about getting her bail lowered," Arnold said and stepped into the small room. Ken watched through the glass as the lawyer spoke and Stacy nodded in agreement.

As Ken studied her in the semidarkness of the room, he found himself mesmerized by her appearance. He stood watching, unaware of anything else. He was taken in by her sad, deep-set eyes and was heartened when she smiled at one of her lawyer's obvious jests. As his mind raced back to her private words he'd read a little while before, he was enjoying watching her, but then felt embarrassed, like he was again intruding, trespassing without permission.

Then, as Ken watched, the lawyer finished, got up, and walked out. Now alone in the room, Stacy turned and looked straight at the mirror. Although Ken knew that she couldn't, he felt like she was staring straight into his eyes. He edged away from the glass.

When the figure of the lawyer came around the corner and headed for the door to the courthouse, Ken exited the observation room and stepped through the doorway of the interrogation room, struck immediately by the residue of stench of human sweat.

"Well, that went pretty well," he said to Stacy, who slouched in her chair. "The real estate agent didn't identify you as the condo buyer."

"Well, that does it," she said, straightening her posture. "That's the last time I do business with her. She couldn't even remember me." She glanced up and caught Ken's disapproving stare. "I'm only kidding. Of course, she didn't identify me. I didn't buy the condo. No way I could buy that condo."

"If we have a little time, I brought you a few things from school."

"We do until the old battle ax comes and throws you out." Stacy nodded to the door.

"Well, I raided your locker and brought you a

couple books," Ken said and reached into the canvas bag he had brought with him. "I tried to get you a few things for distraction. First, for a little inspiration, Langston Hughes' *Dream Keeper*. Then, for a little romantic escape, Danielle Steele's *Secrets*. And third, for planning after you break out of this place, *The Insider's Guide to the Caribbean*. And last, but not least, your journal."

"Very well done, Mr. Assistant Superintendent. I'd say I couldn't have picked better—" Stopping mid-sentence, she gazed at him, a puzzled look on her face. "I just thought of something. How did you get into my locker? I forgot to give you my combination."

"Oh, it took a little ingenuity," Ken said. "I didn't want to come back here empty-handed, so I asked around. When Dawn couldn't help, I went to the office and checked. Sure enough, Martha was able to get the combination from a file in Carla's office." Ken glanced at her. "Stacy, what is it?"

Her face held a puzzled look and then her features morphed into an ah-ha expression. "Ken, did you say Martha simply walked into Michaels' office and got the combination?"

"Yeah, she didn't have any trouble. She said they were in a regular file—oh, I get it," the thought dawning on him. "If she could get the combination—"

"—then anyone who had access to the office could get them. Carla or Martha—"

"Or Wally," continued Ken, "or maybe even any of the teachers or custodians."

"And any of them could have placed the tattoos in my locker. Do the police know about this?"

"I don't know but I'll make sure Bart knows when

he gets back this afternoon."

"Thanks, Ken," she said, her gaze drifting down the surface of the scarred tabletop.

Chapter 42

Stacy pointed to the large manila envelope he held.

Ken said, "Oh, I brought something else for you. It seems your students wrote you some letters. That taskmaster Mrs. Dickson was driving them without mercy when I was there, but Carla gave me these for you. From before, I think." He handed her the envelope bulging with student papers.

Stacy took it and began extracting the student letters out, her gaze skimming each as she pulled them free. God, how she missed "her kids." One by one, her eyes devoured the papers with ragged edges and small, scribbled handwriting. A few had carefully drawn pictures, some colored in with bright markers. With her fingers, she traced the outlines of a flower and a clown. Her eyes scanned each one quickly as if they would crumple in a second if she didn't, turning her head from side to side as if that would cover the words faster.

As she moved from letter to letter, one hand-scribbled message to the next, tears squeezed from the corners of her eyes.

Dear Mrs. T,

How are you. I'm awful without you. I wish you were here. Our sub is OK but your twice as good as her. Was all this a joke or real becuz I'm really worried about all this. I cant sleep all I do when someone menchins your name I start crying. Are you going to die for the crime people say you cumited. We really miss you so much.

Yours truly, Ashley T

Dear Mrs. T,

I think your were embarist for the police to arest you in front of the class. It looked like you were saying "Why are they arresting me? What did I do?" I felt angary because they arrested you for no reason at all. I bet those handcuffs hurt your rists when they put them on.

Sincerely,
Your student, Brian

MRS. T

IM SO SORRY YOUR IN JAIL. I KNOW YOU DIDN'T DO IT. SO I GOING TO TRY TO GET YOU OUT. IM NOT SHURE HOW YET BUT DON'T WORRY. IF YOU DID DO IT THOUGH ALL I WANT TO KNOW IS WHY. I MEAN HOW COULD YOU?
CURT

At first she used her arms to wipe away her tears, to try to keep them from blurring her vision or wetting the papers, but then it became too much. Her eyes flooded with tears and she dropped the letters, sobbing. She jumped up, knocking the chair over, and cowered in the corner of the room, weeping, face to the wall away from Ken.

She couldn't help herself. She couldn't stop crying, her whole body shaking, her quiet sobs the only sounds in the small room. Amidst her weeping, she felt a gentle hand on her shoulder, then heard Ken whisper, "It's okay. Let it out."

Without thinking, she responded to his gentle touch, the first human touch she'd experienced since the matron had searched and fingerprinted her, days ago. Until that moment, she hadn't realized how much she craved human touch. She turned and buried her face in the soft lapel of Ken's sport coat, wetting the material with her flowing tears.

"What have I done, Ken? How could I have let them down so? They were counting on me."

He took a deep breath and brought his arms around and patted both shoulders. She'd craved this touch, this embrace, but not like this. She started shaking her head.

Ken's quiet voice stopped. "You did not let them down, Stacy. You are not responsible for any of this and when we get you out of here, you can take care of those kids yourself again."

Staring back at him, she nodded and brushed the tears out of her eyes. "Thanks, Ken," she whispered. She appreciated his kindness but, as much as she'd dreamed of this, right now it made her uncomfortable.

She extricated herself from his hands and moved back to the table. She bent down and picked it up, setting it on the concrete. She sat. For a while, silence hung over the small room again and neither moved, Stacy in the chair by the table and he leaning against the wall behind her, his breath loud in her ears. Stacy busied herself with stacking the student papers, aligning them along two sides, tucking them back into the already torn envelope. She clasped the packet close to her chest, like a long-lost treasure and the tears started again.

Ken stepped over and joined her at the table. "I

need your help with something. Do you feel like talking about a few things?"

She used one hand to brush the tears out of her eyes. She nodded. "Sure. Shoot."

"Tell me about James Clayton."

"What do you want to know?"

"Oh, anything. What was he like? Family? What did he do in class? Anything you can think of."

"What was James like?" she mused and paused for a while. "In a word...angry. Sometimes it raged below the surface, sometimes it was at the boiling point, but I never knew a student who carried more anger than James. Lousy family life, you know with the father having been in prison and all. I think when his dad was home, he beat James pretty often."

"How do you know?"

"I didn't know, but you could just tell. There was a group of the kids who looked up to James, though. He knew it and loved it. He had a great sense of humor and when you weren't furious with him, you were laughing with him. One time, when we were working on this math word problem, James figured it out and then shared the answer with the others in his group. I complimented him but asked why he didn't simply help the two other boys figure out how he got the answer. He leaned over to me, rolled his eyes, and said, 'Mrs. T, I don't think Jeremy is ever going to get it.' Then he laughed. He's—was—something. Why all the interest in James?"

"I'm not sure. I've reviewed all four kids' records and James stood out. Did James get in trouble a lot on Fridays? Do you remember if anything happened to set him off before the weekend?"

"A lot of trouble? How much?"

"According to his discipline referrals, he was sent to the office seven times, all on Fridays, since September 1."

"That's a surprise. I only remember sending him a few times, maybe two or three times and I don't remember any special pattern on Fridays. Like most kids, he would get more rowdy as the weekend approached, but nothing special. Maybe he was referred by the music or P.E. teachers. He liked to needle them."

"Was James smart? His grades don't show it."

"Street smart, definitely. School smart, probably, but most times he didn't want others to know it. He did enough to get by, didn't want to do any more than he had to." She shook her head. "Why all the questions about James?"

"Like I said, I'm not sure. I don't know, I was simply wondering if there was a connection between his being sent to the office so regularly and using the drugs."

"Was there any record in his file of him using drugs? Selling drugs?"

"No. All the discipline entries were for other stuff." He shook his head, then changed the subject. "What did Arnold tell you?"

"He thought he might be able to get Judge Lewis to lower the bail, since Garcia's witness couldn't make the identification."

"So you may be checking out of this luxury hotel?"

"I'm not sure yet," Stacy said, frowning. Then her expression changed and she grinned. "I don't know if I can make bail. Remember, I just spent $375,000 on this condo in Marco Island."

"Stacy?"

"Only kidding. I hope the bail is reasonable. I really don't have much money. You know how little teachers get paid."

The gravelly voice of the matron interrupted them. "Stacy, I got to take you back to the cell. Sorry, Mr. Parks."

"That's okay, Mrs. Washburn," Ken called and then turned back. "Seriously, don't worry about the bail. We'll see it gets taken care of. You'll be back in your classroom before you know it." He laid his hand on hers and she felt the warmth of his touch. He rose and said, "Keep the faith."

Chapter 43

For a minute, Stacy stared at the doorway after Ken disappeared. She sighed and, rising slowly, preceded her jailer down the hall. It took less than sixty seconds to cross the space and, before she knew it, she heard the all-too-familiar sound of the huge keys turning, locking her cell door. She was alone again. Utterly alone.

She glanced at the concrete walls of her cell. How come none of her *friends* had come to see her? Why didn't her teaching partner, Dawn, stop by with some wisecrack to cheer her up? And what about her principal, Carla Michaels? Michaels liked to crow about how she had her teachers' backs. Where was she? Not to mention Chris Goodman, who was always railing against the system? Didn't he want to least bitch about how the system was treating her?

Could they all think she was guilty? Could Rachel or Jacqueline or any of them really believe she could sell drugs to her kids? She shuddered at the thought.

How come the only colleague who bothered to even step foot in the jail was Ken Parks? And he had no idea how she felt about him, did he? He claimed he was merely doing the decent thing—sharing letters from her kids, bringing books from her locker, and trying to let her feel less alone. Could it be more than that?

At least, he said *he* was convinced she was innocent. Stacy stared at the sheet of stainless steel above the sink that passed for a mirror, giving her face a stretched appearance, her hair hanging in stringy strands. And *this* was what he saw? She shook her head again. Tears squeezed out of both eyes and rolled down her cheeks.

From the psych class she took last year, she recognized the signs of a full-blown depression hitting her and she pulled her gaze away from the faux mirror. To calm herself, she did some yoga breathing like she taught the kids. Long breath in, slow breath out. It could be worse. The real estate agent didn't ID her. That ought to give Garcia a little more trouble with his ulcer. Maybe something was finally going her way. Still, someone flew down to Florida to make the purchase of the condo…and that person impersonated *her*? All to implicate her? Why?

Stacy sat on the edge of the hard bed frame, dropped the books on the floor, and stared at the gray concrete walls. A wave of exhaustion, no doubt from the tension of the day's events, washed over her. Even though it was only the middle of the afternoon, the tedium, worry, and stress of the last few days had drained all her strength. Stretching out her legs, she laid her head down on the thin, foam pillow and her back against the scratchy cloth of the cot. In a remarkable few seconds, sleep overcame her.

Her unconscious mind began to drift, darting back to earlier times and places. Images, isolated and broken, floated past on a memory path she was unable to control, her senses replaying the sights and sounds of her past.

In her dream, she saw her earlier, younger body, bronzed by the sun in a revealing pink bikini, lying on her back on a garishly colored towel on a beach, her face covered by a wide-brim hat. Her skin felt strong, muscular hands massaging, rubbing in the sunblock, smoothing out the cream against her stomach, his touch warm, sensuous, relaxing. In her sleep, she smiled at the memory.

The image dissolved, melting away like a neglected ice cream cone on a hot summer day, replaced by another. She stared at the same strong hands, but this time they didn't massage or caress. Instead, in her fractured memory, she watched, helpless, as the hands flew at her and struck her face, over and over again. It was a strange sensation, watching the hands hit and slap, knowing they were coming and being unable to do anything about it. In her disturbing nightmare, she flinched again and again on the cot, reeling from the imagined blows.

"No, please, no!" she heard a voice say. She jerked awake and saw she'd brought her arms up to shield her face, whimpering there in the cell. She sniffled to stop crying and, after a while, the fatigue overwhelmed her again and her body surrendered to sleep once more.

Before long though, the ugly nightmare returned, the fractured reel of memories moving to the next image of the strong hands with an offering. Two fingers extended a hand-rolled cigarette and a male voice laughed, "Go ahead, try it. You'll like it."

Compelled, fixated by the nightmare, she saw her small hand reach for the joint and, as she grabbed it, the substance changed, motion-picture-like, from the cigarette to a white powder, to red and blue pills. She took them, washing them down with a swig of liquor. It burned her throat. She knew she shouldn't, but felt she had no choice.

For a moment, her body began to relive the temporary euphoria and escape she used to get from them. Even in her memory, she felt the shift coming, as it had so many times before and she struggled to fight it. Without will or control, she was flung back there, years earlier, in that other cell, shaking, shuddering. The images of other gray concrete walls and another worn, metal bed frame came flooding back and her stomach tightened. The pain woke her again.

By the time Stacy rolled from the bed to the floor and crabbed the short distance to the toilet, she was already vomiting, heaving into and around the toilet. She retched over and over, until there was nothing left in her stomach.

The spasm finally halted, though it took her a bit before she realized it had passed. Exhausted and dirty, with bits of her own vomit still clinging to her clothes, her hair, and her skin, she dragged herself back to the worn bed frame and collapsed. She lay on her back and closed her eyes. She pondered the cruel twist of fate that had placed her *here* again.

Chapter 44

"Thank you, Officer Callahan. It's great tonight to recognize so many students in our 'Just Say No' campaign," Carla Michaels spoke into the microphone, her voice booming loudly like an off-key trombone, Chris Goodman thought. He thought she'd never finish. *That woman loves to hear herself talk.*

Sitting in the second row next to Jacqueline Highstreet, he turned and rolled his eyes at her. She smirked but tried to hide it.

The principal added, "He does such a great job for our students here at Foster Middle, let's give him another round of applause."

The ancient auditorium erupted with cheering and boisterous catcalls and Chris joined in the clapping, though not quite as enthusiastic as some of the crowd. He liked Bart. Many fifth and sixth graders had earned the award and had attended, along with parents and grandparents, and any other family members who could be talked into coming. He didn't have these kids yet, but he was here anyway.

Chris watched his principal survey her staff in the first few rows. His colleagues were pretty much all there, tonight, after school, *without pay*…as if they had a choice. In this afternoon's faculty meeting, Michaels had left little doubt.

"With the tragic deaths of our four students, not to

mention Tricia still in the hospital," the principal had said this afternoon, "I think it's really important we have a solid show of support for tonight's drug-free celebration. Besides, members of the Board and important community members have promised to attend." Then, standing there at the front of the classroom, she swiveled her head as if checking for eavesdroppers and lowered her voice. "I'm not supposed to say anything, but Dr. O'Brien is going to unveil a special memorial."

Chris noticed the shroud covering the thin object on the stage. Leaning over to Jacqueline, he whispered, "Think that's the big *memorial* Carla mentioned?"

Jacqueline said, "Sh-h-h," but strained to keep from giggling.

The eighth grade band started up again, the students struggling with a piece announced as "Tribute and Triumph", and Chris watched Maestro Daniels run one leathery hand through his thinning hair, while the other swayed his baton, pointing the stick at two kids in the back.

His gaze sweeping down the row, Chris took in his teaching colleagues. Jacqueline, of course, looked her stunning self in a tan skirt which hugged her hips and a white cashmere sweater covering a very nice chest, all accented with a lone gold necklace. What was he wearing? He hadn't even remembered and glanced down at his clothes. He settled for a clean pair of jeans and a long sleeve madras shirt. He knew Jacqueline liked whatever he wore and he didn't care about anyone else. Further down the row sat Dawn Hatcher in another frumpy outfit, this one some off-green color, and Rachel Bedinghaus perched in tan slacks and jacket, holding a handkerchief to her dripping nose. Next to them sat several others whose names he hadn't bothered to memorize yet.

When the band finished their number, Michaels returned to the microphone and glanced out at the audience. "Students, I know you're restless and I can't blame you. You've been wonderful and if you'll be patient a little longer, we're almost finished." She pointed to those sitting on the stage behind her. "We also want to thank some of the members of our extended school family who have joined us tonight for this special occasion. Our district is truly lucky to have the support of so many of the business and medical community and our children are the ones who benefit."

The principal nodded and went on, "Now, to make a special presentation, I'd like to introduce Dr. Everett O'Brien, school board president. Dr. O'Brien, the microphone is all yours." She handed the mike to the tall, lanky figure who had come up behind her.

Small smatterings of applause skittered out of a few places in the audience.

O'Brien nodded. "I appreciate the applause, but perhaps you should wait to hear what I have to say before you decide to clap." This brought a wave of mild laughter from the crowd. "Let me tell you the most important thing first." He paused a second and said, "I will be brief," then he flashed his boyish smile. This generated even louder applause.

Leaning closer to Jacqueline, Chris whispered, "Brief? That would be a first." Jacqueline gave him a playful slap.

O'Brien went on, his voice turning somber, "Tonight is a very important event in the lives of many of you boys and girls. By pledging to be drug-free, you have pledged to lead healthier, happier lives. In my work as a doctor, I have come to see the tragedy of drug abuse firsthand." He paused again, catching his breath. "This year I have been forced to witness that same tragedy as board president."

O'Brien put his hand over the microphone and swallowed as if he had a lump in his throat. "As you all know, we lost four of our students this past month in drug-related deaths. I have personally spoken with each boy's parents. Students, listen carefully."

Chris watched as the already still crowd seemed to freeze in their seats, waiting for what came next.

O'Brien continued, "Now, students, listen carefully because I want to be perfectly clear about this. I have promised these parents their children will not have died in vain. I've asked those parents to join us tonight for this special occasion and they are sitting here in the front row." He nodded solemnly to the parents immediately below him.

Chris studied the lined faces of the grieving parents who stared at the board president. They all looked distraught. Waycross even looked sober tonight. Chris frowned. Maybe he had to be clean if he wanted to proceed with his lawsuit against the district.

O'Brien continued, "It is perfectly clear they should be here tonight when we unveil this special brass plaque in the boys' memory."

He took two large strides from the microphone to a raised stand, sitting off to the right, the top part covered with a gold cloth. With a ceremonial swoop, O'Brien reached and pulled off the covering, revealing a large, wooden wall plaque with a brass front, rows of letters ornately carved into the surface.

O'Brien spoke again more loudly now without the mike, the natural resonance of his voice echoing in the still auditorium. "I know many of you are too far away to be able to read this, so I will read it for you. 'Robert Hayes, James Clayton, Justin Waycross, and Chad Thorton. We promise to remember your deaths, so our lives will be better.' And it is signed 'The students of Foster Middle School.' The money for this plaque was collected by our own Student Council and they chose what to put on it. I think they did a fine job and I want to congratulate the officers."

O'Brien strode to the edge of the stage and shook the students' hands, the two boys and two girls beaming at the attention.

Returning to the microphone, the Board President finished, "This commemorative plaque will hang in a special place in the center hallway here at Foster. As students walk past it every day, these names will serve as a reminder to lead drug-free lives. Now, please join me in a silent moment of prayer for the four students we lost and their families."

O'Brien stepped away from the mike, put his hands together, and bowed his head. The entire auditorium got quiet as the hundreds of students and parents followed the speaker's example, including Chris. After what O'Brien must've judged to be a suitable time period, he walked back to the microphone and said, "Amen." The crowd responded and Chris could hear the single word echoing through the rafters. Then the Board President added, "Thanks for coming. Please drive safely on your way home."

As the eighth grade band played the strains of the

school song, Chris watched as the O'Brien stepped down from the stage and solemnly shook the hands of each of the dead boys' parents, mumbling words of consolation. *Does he ever stop politicking?*

Chapter 45

Wally Kowalchek, head building custodian—now on overtime—stood alone, off to the side, watching the ceremony, waiting for the cavernous auditorium to empty so he could get to work. The place was packed with bodies and the smells of the crowd—perfume, hairspray, body odor—floated on the air to where the custodian stood.

As the long-still crowd stirred, the old auditorium echoed with the sound of chairs being moved, children running, and people talking. Wally watched as many of the adults gathered around the parents of the dead boys, extending their sympathies. A group of students thronged around the new plaque, admiring it, small fingers exploring its carved letters, while the kids exchanged a few comments with the Student Council officers.

Chatting among themselves, the teachers stood and strolled into the crowd. Like popular celebrities, several were surrounded by students and parents and Wally noticed the largest group around Chris Goodman—a half dozen, anxious preteen girls pressing close together. The teachers exchanged a few words with the students and parents, and then together ambled toward the exit.

Although some of the younger children were boisterous, most of the crowd was subdued, no doubt weighed down with the serious reminder of the evening. Wally glanced out among the crowd and pondered who to trust…and who not to trust in this whole thing. He gave a nod to Bart Daughterty, who held his gaze. Wally felt like the cop was saying "I'm watching you," without ever saying anything, of course. As Wally stared back, trying a small smile, Bart returned his attention to the students and parents.

As Wally stood, quiet, respectful, waiting, the crowd seemed to disintegrate in front of him, individuals congregating with their peers and making their way toward the exits. Teachers thronged with other teachers, parents with other parents, even visiting "town dignitaries" knotted together, apparently discussing the latest local issues.

Ken's wife, Amanda Parks, in a fashionable, red business suit, gathered up her purse and headed toward the rear. Looking ahead, she called to Dr. Hardcastle. "Alex, can you wait up a minute?"

As Wally studied them from the side, the handsome doctor paused, and Amanda came up beside him.

"I simply wanted to say thanks for coming tonight," Amanda began. "I'm sure if Ken were here, he would want to express his appreciation for you supporting the school, especially now. He had another meeting, *of course*."

"Glad to be here," responded Hardcastle, "and what a pleasant surprise to see you here. You standing in for Todd?"

"Yeah, our esteemed Chamber president was called out of town and he wanted somebody to represent the downtown businesses," Amanda said.

"If you're on your way out, let's head out together. I've got something I want to run past you," Hardcastle said.

"Sounds good," said Amanda, and as Wally watched, she flashed a demure smile at the doctor as they walked toward the hallway. Wally pondered what that was all about.

He had learned long ago to many others—school staff *and* parents—custodians like himself were invisible. Others acted and spoke around janitors as if they weren't even there. He'd overheard plenty in his time. Tonight, he only wanted to get to work to clean the big space and get home, though he kept his ears open. He still hadn't eaten any dinner. But he had to wait—and watch—until everyone had exited.

Two teachers, Jacqueline and Chris, moved to the stage and began taking down the decorations and Drug-Free banners. He remembered Jacqueline served as advisor to the Drug-Free club and figured Chris—who he knew was hot for her, even though they tried to keep it quiet—was helping out. At least he wouldn't have to clean those pieces up.

For a few seconds, Wally watched the exterior doors opening and closing repeatedly, each time the safety bar making a loud crashing sound that echoed into the hallway. He stood and observed as the teachers disappeared either through the swinging outside doors or down the hallway to their classrooms.

Stepping down from the stage, Everett O'Brien and Carla Michaels walked through the quickly diminishing crowd. Michaels was stopped several times by young students with questions, and O'Brien stood to the side, waiting patiently and watching her interact with the kids.

When the last student had finished and they were alone again, walking across the floor, O'Brien said, "I'm impressed with the way you handle those kids. You took time to give attention to each one."

"Thank you, Mr. Board President," Michaels said, a broad smile across her red lips. "Coming from you, that's quite a compliment." She laid a hand on O'Brien's arm. "And thank you so much for making time in your busy schedule to be with us tonight. I know you have many demands and a lot of other important places you're needed. I'm sure it meant a lot to the students and their parents that you were here to unveil the plaque."

"I'm happy to do it," O'Brien said. "As long as I'm here, do you have a few more minutes to take care of a couple of business issues? Might save me a trip, later."

"Sure."

Side by side, they reached the auditorium exit into the school hallway, passing Wally without even giving him a nod.

"Why don't we head over to my office," Michaels said, and they strolled down the same hallway as the teachers, the darkness eventually swallowing their figures.

Releasing a breath, Wally started in on the floor, his wide broom swinging through the aisles.

Chapter 46

Being the last two teachers to leave the auditorium, Chris and Jacqueline made their way down the darkened hallway. He knew the district only paid to keep the lights on when they had to, but they could find their way in the near darkness. It wasn't their first time. He knew it wouldn't be their last.

Jacqueline led the way with him following, carrying a stack of folded school banners, which had lined the stage. "Where do you want these?" he asked, the plastic runners proclaiming *Foster Middle—A Drug-Free School* piled up to his nose.

"They go in the closet in the workroom, second shelf. Here, I'll show you," she said, holding the door for him. When he was through the opening, she scurried across the workroom, extracted her keys, and opened the closet door for him. He liked her scurrying.

With their slippery surface, the banners started to slide off the pile and he struggled to keep them together and, with some effort, got them onto the only vacant shelf in the narrow closet.

"Thank you for helping," Jacqueline said, smiling at him in the dim light. "You know, I *always* appreciate your valuable assistance."

"You do? How much?" He liked teasing her like this…and always loved her response.

She stepped close to him and whispered, "This

much."

She kissed him long, with passion. His hands slid to her sides, his fingers already inside the waistband of her skirt, freeing the soft sweater from its confines. In seconds, his hands crawled up the inside of her sweater.

Chris was pleased to see Jacqueline enjoying his efforts as she leaned her head back, closed her eyes, and purred. This was going nicely.

Then, without looking at him, she asked, "Didn't I overhear the students calling you 'the doctor'? When did that start?"

Where did this come from?

"Oh that, Christ." Chris took a half-step back, frowning.

She has to ask that *now*? His growing desire pulsed in his pants…and he tried to tamp it down so he could think. What was he going to say? What could he tell her to get…back on track? He knew Jacqueline. He'd have to give her something.

"Um-m, a few weeks ago, I guess. You know, kids are always coming up to me with their problems because they think I can help them."

"I've usually found you can help me with my problems," she said as her fingers inched around his waistband.

"Anywa-a-a-ay." Chris backed away so he could finish his point. "Heidi Griffith in my seventh period class, do you know her?"

"Yes," she purred, making the one syllable sound sexy.

"Well, Heidi stayed after class and asked if she could talk to…me. Man, it's hard to concentrate with you doing that."

"It's going to get harder so you better finish," Jacqueline whispered in his ear.

He spoke faster. "Well, she had a few problems and wanted my advice so I gave her some. She said my advice was better than the expensive shrink her mom was sending her to and she started calling me 'doctor.' Before I knew it, the whole seventh period was going with the 'Doctor Goodman' bit and…I guess it spread from there."

"That's ver-r-r-y interesting, doctor. What I'd like to know is," Jacqueline said, both hands around his neck, "is the doctor in?"

"Yes, and he will have to do a careful examination." Chris drew up her skirt with his right hand and let his left go exploring.

Jacqueline squealed, "Chris, not now. Uh-h…not here."

His fingers continued their explorations. "Why not?"

"Oh-h-h, oh-h!" escaped from her mouth and Jacqueline moved a few inches away and let her breath out, carrying a hint of mint. "You know, someone may see us here."

"Isn't that part of the fun?" He closed the small gap again and raised his right hand to her sweater. His fingers snaked inside again.

He heard her breath catch in her throat. "Ah-h-ah," was all she managed and then whispered, "Look, at least go check to see if the coast is clear." She gave him a little shove toward the door.

Relenting, Chris backed out through the darkness of the supply closet into the workroom they'd just come through. Unlocking and opening the door to the hall, he stepped through the doorway and glanced in both directions. He studied the empty, half-lit corridor, listening for a few seconds. Then he re-entered the workroom, closing and locking the door behind him. The sparse light from the hall filtered through the slats in the door and, since his eyes had adjusted, he had no trouble making his way back to the closet.

"Well, what did you find out?" she asked.

"Nothing…" he began, and his voice was cut off by the sound of a zipper.

"Yes?" she asked, her tone matter-of-fact in the darkness against the quiet background of the metal teeth letting go.

"I didn't see *anything*," he said quickly, afraid he wouldn't be able to even speak soon. "All I could hear was the sound of some footsteps at the other end of the building." Then he smiled, even though he knew she couldn't see it in the dark. But she'd hear it in his voice. "I believe this doctor has to do a close examination here. Lucky for you, I'm used to working in the dark." He leaned close and kissed her, tongues touching. "But it's important the patient do her part."

"Oh, she'll be only too glad to." She laughed.

Chapter 47

As he watched the last two teachers exit the large auditorium, Wally griped aloud, "Took them long enough to clear out." His large, calloused hand reached into the worn canvas bag hanging on his cleaning cart and retrieved a black Walkman. Opening the door to examine the cassette tape, he grinned—he liked that tape—then closed the lid and pushed the knob marked PLAY. Slipping headphones over his ears, he listened a while and clipped the player onto his belt. With the sound of Alan Jackson blaring in his ears, he went about his task, sweeping the discarded printed programs and other papers into piles.

Glad to be able to bring this long day to an end, overtime or no overtime, he worked out the most efficient pattern to sweep between the rows of seats. With his years of experience cleaning up debris from school crowds, it didn't take long for him to corral all the paper, old gum, and even discarded certificates into a single mound at the end of the center aisle. With the huge pile collected, he ambled back to his cleaning cart to pull the garbage bags needed for the mess. When he checked the shelf where they were kept, he came up empty.

"Damn," he yelled, "Les didn't bother to refill 'em this afternoon. Lazy ass! Now I gotta walk all the way down to the closet in the fifth grade area, clear on the utter side of the building."

Figuring he had little choice, he shrugged and began the trek down the long hallway, half walking, half sauntering across the linoleum. As he turned the corner and headed down the side corridor, some sound caught his attention. With the music coming through his headphones, he wasn't certain what it was, not sure he'd heard anything, but on instinct, he stopped and listened, pausing the tape. He thought he heard the brief scream of a woman, but he decided it must have been a squeal from the song. Standing there, his eyes swept the corridor, looking for signs of any activity. Seeing nothing and satisfied there was no danger, he proceeded down the rest of the hall, singing along with Jackson's "Who's Cheating Who?" playing in his ear.

When Wally arrived at the janitor's closet, he sighed. Hell, starved and not able to eat anything for a while, at least he could get something to drink. He ambled around the corner into the teachers' lounge. The only light in the windowless room came from the pop machine, but it was enough for him to select his choice, pay, and retrieve a cold soda. Dropping his considerable bulk into one of the dilapidated, vinyl chairs, he collapsed and sipped. Glad to be off his feet, however briefly, he savored the syrupy taste alone in the dark room, his nose picking up the lingering odor of stale pizza. He wondered if Les had been too lazy to empty the trash can in here, but Wally was too tired to worry about it. The cassette came to the end, clicking the stop button, and he slipped the headphones off his ears. As he sat back, Pepsi can in hand, he heard something again. He thought it sounded like a woman's shriek, but shorter. Then it stopped.

Was he imagining it? Partly worried and partly intrigued, Wally pushed himself up from the chair to investigate. He exited the teachers' lounge and stepped into the corridor, scanning the hallway right and left, searching for a light or any sign of activity in one of the rooms. His heavy figure planted in the center of the hall, he waited and listened, which without his push broom wasn't all that easy.

Shrugging his shoulders again, he mumbled, "I must be going nuts." He headed back to the auditorium and his still-unfinished job. About three quarters of the way, he remembered he'd left the trash bags lying on the table in the lounge. "Shit," he yelled, the word echoing in the empty hallway, and he turned around to make his way back. When he got there, he went through the door, grabbed the folded bags off the table, and turned to head out, all in one motion.

Ready to round the corner back into the hallway, he spotted two figures, silhouettes only, emerge from up the hall. "Maybe I'm not so crazy after all," he whispered. He observed the two figures come down the corridor toward him, heading for the side exit. Anxiety now adding to his curiosity, Wally slinked back into the alcove, trying to flatten his bulk against the wall and disappear into the darkness.

His heart raced, even though he didn't understand his reaction. After all, he was supposed to be here. He stood still, frozen, certain any movement would give him away. Footsteps approached, the tap of a woman's heels and the slap of the man's leather soles. As they reached where the alcove intersected with the main hallway, opposite his position, he held his breath, staring. The hallway was darkened, but from his years on the second shift, he was accustomed to seeing his way around at night. With the light from the exit signs to make out a few details, he recognized both faces, smiling and dripping with perspiration.

His first reaction, surprise, migrated to uncertainty. Then, very slowly, as he began to piece together what he had seen and heard, Wally Kowalchek broke out in one of the widest grins he'd worn in a long time.

At the end of the hall, the sound of the bar on the side door opened and slammed shut.

"I'll be damned. I'll be damned!" He laughed out loud, a raucous laugh that reverberated through the empty building.

Chapter 48

The large leather chair engulfed Ken and he stared at the myriad of papers stacked in orderly piles on his desktop. Although his secretary had tried to take care of as many items as possible, a sizable number of problems still demanded his attention. He counted them. Twenty-seven yellow "While You Were Out" slips dotted the top of his desk, each one with a phone message, an urgent call begging to be returned. The requests came from impatient teachers wondering where their new sample textbooks were, from desperate parents pleading his intercession to keep their son from being suspended, from principals wanting help with a glitch in the new computer system. There were calls from six salesmen, from the high school counselor, from a building secretary, and from a local merchant who sat on the district Business Advisory Council.

Each slip had a hand scribbled note on it from his secretary relaying what she had accomplished about it or what needed to be done by her boss. Vivian had dispatched the salesmen till further notice and taken care of the building secretary's request. She had even solved the principals' computer problems. But that still left plenty Ken had to take care of and he felt he needed to do something, to get something accomplished.

Staring at the twenty-seven yellow slips, Ken thought, these represented what this job was supposed to be about. Solving district problems, planning long-term projects, putting out fires— that's what he was supposed to be doing, what he *was* doing before…before the boys' deaths. Seeing the normal, everyday work spread out on his desk, he felt an overwhelming desire to return to the routine tasks he'd complained of before. For most of two weeks, he had lived, breathed, eaten, and slept with the mystery of the students' deaths and the elusive trail of their drug supplier. He was tiring of it.

What was most frustrating was he simply didn't know. It couldn't be Stacy, it couldn't be. Garcia had all this evidence on Stacy but it simply didn't add up. Stacy was a friend and he'd always liked her, but was he letting feelings cloud his judgment? His gut told him it wasn't Stacy, though that didn't mean anything.

Or, maybe he didn't know her as well as he thought.

Could she be a patsy…and he her white knight? He rolled his eyes. Some knight, huh.

But if it wasn't Stacy, then who the hell was it? According to his and Bart's great inside source Wally— or Walter Kanelli, "retired" drug courier for the mafia—it was someone who called himself or herself "the doctor." Now that really narrowed it in this town…and what if it was merely a nickname? Oh yeah, and he didn't want to forget the kids were getting the drugs *right here* at school.

This sense of helplessness infected Ken with a growing cynicism. Could someone he worked with, some colleague charged with educating and caring for children, could he—or she—be selling drugs that already led to four deaths?

But that didn't make any sense. From what little Ken knew about drug dealers, they didn't kill their users, not on purpose. Dead users didn't keep buying. But four boys were dead, and Tricia was still unconscious in a hospital bed.

He shook his head.

All his checking, interviewing, reviewing, all this *supposed* investigating and he felt he didn't have much. He figured someone had targeted Stacy, had framed her, but he had no idea who…or why.

Vivian interrupted his rambling thoughts, bringing in the morning mail. She set a mug with steaming hot tea in front of him, the aroma of vanilla drifting in the steam.

"Thanks, Viv. I didn't remember asking for tea, but it looks good," he said, staring up at her face. On most days, Ken could count on her ever-present smile to bolster him and, regardless of the circumstances, she would be there, positive, upbeat. But when he glanced up at her, he saw a cloud over her features. "Viv, what is it?"

"I thought you might need the tea after you read this." She produced a folded up newspaper she'd cradled under her arm and opened it flat to the front page. "I'll be back in a minute after you have a chance to go through it."

Ken stared down at the morning edition of the *Cleveland Herald* with its name in the traditional, large Times font. Immediately below the day's date and weather hung a banner headline about more trouble in Central Europe, complete with a four-color photo of some of the latest carnage. Ken studied the newspaper, trying to figure out why Vivian had given it to him. He scanned the edition, examining a few articles and noting the weather forecast.

As he was ready to call his secretary back, his gaze caught it, the headline above the fold. He opened up the paper and laid it flat on top of the accumulated phone messages. Reading the printed words, he felt his stomach tighten, line by line.

Leading Suspect in Boys' Deaths Has Drug Past

Portsmouth, PA—It was learned today there may be a new breakthrough in a major murder case here. This small, quiet rural town was rocked by the deaths of four eleven-year-old boys in a tragic automobile crash more than two weeks ago. Autopsy results on the four youths turned up the fact that the four students, who were on a school camping trip at the time, were loaded with a powerful new drug. Apparently the boys had absorbed the drug through special patches called tattoos, still affixed to their arms at the time of their deaths. A fifth student from the same school is still hospitalized with a coma from an apparent overdose of the same powerful drug.

Within several days of the boys' deaths, the police arrested their leading suspect in the drug-murder connection, Stacy Thompson. Ms. Thompson is a fifth grade teacher at the school all five students attended and was chaperoning the trip the fifth graders were on at the time of their deaths. The police have made public little information on their investigation, but Chief Tony Garcia has said they have "a very strong case against Ms. Thompson." According to information uncovered by this newspaper, their case may have gotten a little stronger.

Through an anonymous source, it was learned the

leading suspect, Stacy Thompson, has had a "major drug problem" in the past and had been charged with child endangerment. In 1981, Ms. Thompson was admitted to the rehab center at the Seattle Clinic for treatment for chemical dependency. Officials at the Seattle Clinic refused to confirm or deny Ms. Thompson's status, citing the confidentiality of patients' medical records. However, this paper has learned from reliable sources Ms. Thompson was treated at the clinic for drug addiction.

When reached by phone, Police Chief Garcia commented he was unaware of any history of drug use by Ms. Thompson. "If the reports are true," Garcia said, "I certainly wouldn't be surprised."

When contacted by Herald *reporters late last night with the new information, Thompson's lawyer, Tim Arnold, replied, "My client has an outstanding reputation as a caring teacher who loves children and we'll stand by that."*

Stacy Thompson is due back in court today to request Judge Cassman to set bail in the case, something he was unwilling to do previously. Neither Garcia nor Arnold would comment on how this new information might affect the bail hearing set for 1:00 p.m. today.

Before he had read the last of the reporter's words, Ken called, "Vivian, can you come in here?" When he looked up, he saw his secretary already standing at the foot of his desk, steno pad in hand.

"I figured you might need me."

"As always, one step ahead of me. See if you can get me someone at the paper. I want to talk with the editor or the reporter who did this piece."

"Ken, do you think it's true?"

"I don't know. Either way, since it's in print, it'll drive the rumor mill wild. See what you can do about getting somebody at the *Herald*. I need to find out what kind of 'reliable sources' would give up such information about Stacy."

Turning on her low heels, Vivian was out the doorway in a second. Ken returned his attention to the article and began to re-read it. After the third time through, it hit him. *If* there was any truth to the story, maybe this was why Stacy had been framed. With this past, she made the perfect suspect.

Waiting impatiently to talk to the reporter, he rose at his desk and stood there, his fingers drumming on the glass top. Idly, he picked up some of the mail from the pile his secretary had assembled. Much of it was junk mail and he took a perverse pleasure in dropping a number of these pieces into the trash.

About ten items into this ritual, his fingers came up with a white envelope with district letterhead in the upper right-hand corner and his name "Ken Parks" typed in a large font in the center. Below the name, the word "CONFIDENTIAL" was stamped in red ink, using the kind of stamp available in every school office.

At first, Ken simply stared at the envelope in his hand, his mind still preoccupied with the article. Could he be wrong about Stacy? If she had some kind of drug past, what did that mean? O'Brien and Walters could be pompous and they were both obsessed with politics, but maybe they were right. Maybe he should simply walk away. Let the cops handle this? Is it possible Stacy could've sold drugs to the students? Maybe he *was* letting his friendship with Stacy cloud his judgment?

As Ken's thoughts drifted, doubting himself again, he bounced the sealed envelope against the desktop. Stopping the fidgeting, his eyes focused on the envelope in his hand again, his glance returning to the CONFIDENTIAL stamp. Not another report of child abuse, he hoped. Sliding the center drawer open, his fingers found the letter opener this time and he sliced the envelope. He pulled out the folded sheet to find a terse message in large black type.

The police already have the drug pusher. Back off before more die. Perhaps someone close to you.

No name or signature, of course. Turning the paper over frantically, he checked it and the envelope and found nothing. It was a damn threat. The precariousness of his position struck him once again. All of a sudden, this became not about politics, or reputation, or a job. His mind reeled, trying to focus, and all he could think was "someone close to you." He needed to call Bart and let him know. And he needed to check on Amanda.

As he reached for the phone, it rang and he jerked, his concentration broken. Vivian's voice came through the headset as he picked up, "It's the reporter from the paper, Mike Pander."

"Mr. Pander, this is Ken Parks from Portsmouth Schools. Thanks for giving me a few minutes of your time."

Chapter 49

Stacy sat in the tiny interrogation room, checking the three gray walls and the large two-way mirror. Her knees bounced up and down. When the matron came to retrieve her breakfast tray, runny scrambled eggs and toast, she said Stacy had a visitor. When Stacy asked who, all the stern-faced matron had said was, "Let's go." She followed the uniformed woman down the small hallway and into the cramped room. Stacy took *her* chair, the one facing the mirror, and waited. She figured most likely her lawyer would stop by to prep her for the bail hearing this afternoon. God, she wanted to get out of this place but was afraid to get her hopes up.

She heard the lock turn and the door open and then smiled. It wasn't her lawyer.

"Oh, it's great to see a friendly face again," she said as Ken walked into the small interrogation room. "That scowl of Mrs. Washburn was getting to be too much—"

Ken slapped a folded newspaper on the table, making her jump. She glanced from the paper to the man standing across from her. He looked like he was ready to explode, his eyes hard and narrow. Confused, she stared into the face of the man she so admired, her eyes searching for an explanation.

For a moment, neither spoke, the crack of the paper

echoing off the walls of the small room. He leaned over, moving in so close she could smell his musky aftershave. Bracing his frame on the gray metal tabletop, he stabbed his index finger at the newspaper lying in front of her.

"All I want to know is, is it true?"

Picking up and opening the folded paper, Stacy examined it. What had so changed Ken? She glanced back at perhaps her only remaining friend. His look unleased a panic in the back of her mind.

Oh, no.

That information was confidential. They said it would never be released and her record expunged. Her eyes scanned the headlines on the front page, darting from article to article, searching for something, anything to answer Ken's question. Praying it wasn't that.

Her hand moved to the headline and then, using both hands, she flattened the paper and laid it atop the small table. She started reading the article, already knowing what she would find there when she caught the words "drug past" in the headline. She scanned about half the article and stopped. Her fist came down so hard on the table the metal structure bounced against its bindings and the small room echoed again.

Her eyes narrowed and she spoke through tight lips, "How? Where did they get this information?"

"So, it is true?" Ken asked, the syllables harsh.

Stacy couldn't meet his gaze.

"I don't know how they got all this. I've already called the paper and talked with the reporter *and* the editor. All they would tell me is they had a source that was reliable…and they were ready to protect their source." He pulled the chair out across the table from her and lowered himself slowly, looking as if he were in pain. Sitting directly across from her, he stared into her eyes. It took all she had, but she didn't turn away. She looked back at him, her eyesight blurred as tears streamed down her cheeks.

Ken kept his gaze on her, though some of the fury seemed to have seeped out of his features. "Stacy," he said almost in a whisper, "is it true?"

The question hung in the air, waiting, becoming more oppressive with each second. At first, she said nothing and simply sat and returned his stare, looking deep into his eyes, trying to gauge what she could say, how much she could tell him. Finally, she couldn't hold his gaze any longer.

Lowering her head, she whispered, "Yes," and then, after a bit added, "I'm sorry." When these words escaped from her lips, the crying began, in quiet whimpers at first and then building till sobs racked her body, her whole face wet with tears.

How could she admit to all this…in front of *him*? A deluge of emotions bombarded Stacy—embarrassment, anger, fear, horror, self-pity. She covered her face with both hands and bumped her head on the metal tabletop again and again. This *can't* be happening. She didn't want anyone to know about that part of her life. Ever. That was why she traveled across the country to get a new start.

She didn't want *him* to know about this. She wanted to scream, to deny it all, say it wasn't true, it wasn't her. It wasn't her, not the new her…not that that mattered.

Through her sobbing, she heard Ken's next quiet

words, "What can you tell me?"

Though she still didn't look up, he must've leaned in closer because she picked up a scent of the vanilla tea he'd drunk earlier. Still, she didn't raise her head up, though her crying slowed.

"If you're able to tell, I promise to listen. Maybe I can help." Ken spoke so quietly she almost didn't hear him. "None of us are perfect. We all have secrets."

When Stacy raised her head and glanced into his face, the look of rage and betrayal that burned there earlier had vanished. In those blue-green eyes, she read…pain, as if he had some idea of what she was going through.

He repeated, "We all have our own secrets."

Him, secrets? It was hard to fathom. His words echoed in her mind, giving her a little courage.

Although her eyes still welled with tears, she ceased her weeping. She sniffled and used her arm to wipe her face. Taking a slow, deep breath, she began to talk and slowly, painfully let her dark past crawl out between her lips.

"It's been so long, I thought I'd forgotten. It seems now like a lifetime ago."

For the first time since he entered the room, Ken touched her. He reached across the gray table and laid his hand gently on her shaking fingers. "Begin where you want. I'll just listen."

Her eyes teared up again and her shoulders drooped. Lowering her gaze, Stacy began in a quiet voice. "I told you once I had been married, remember?"

Ken merely nodded.

She sniffed a few times and continued, "Well, it's not a part of my life I like to talk about, for good reason. You see, I married young. I was only eighteen and he was older, handsome, and I thought I was in love, and he said he loved me." She stopped and then said, "But we hadn't been married for only three months when Bill began to hit me."

She looked up again at Ken and thought she saw a shadow of doubt creep into his eyes.

"Oh, when we were dating, I never saw any of this. He was funny and attentive and even kind. But after we married, something changed. I never figured out what it was, but he became possessive, demanding. One time we were having an argument—I don't remember what it was about—something small I think—when I disagreed, he slapped me. I was so stunned, I didn't know what had happened, not at first. Then Bill hollered, 'You vowed to love and honor and *obey*, do you remember that?'

"I was crying by now and I think I said, 'I remember, but that doesn't mean I have to agree with everything you say.' He screamed, 'Yes, it does!' and he hit me on the side of my face with his fist." Her hand went to her right cheek as if she could feel the welt all over again. "I was terrified, but more than that, I was stunned. I didn't know what to do. I was ashamed, thought somehow it was my fault." She swallowed once and went on. "Later, he would apologize and we would 'make up'—his words for really aggressive sex—and I prayed it wouldn't happened again."

She glanced up at Ken again and shook her head. "Let's just say my prayers weren't answered."

Stacy stopped again, her breathing labored. This was even harder than she thought it would be. She sighed. Staring across the table and seeing the look of empathy from Ken helped. She inhaled again and pressed on. "You see, my parents had told me I was too young to get married and had tried to talk me out of it, but I kept insisting and in the end they gave in and went along. So when all this happened, I was too ashamed to even say anything."

Ken kept his gaze on her and said, "I can understand that."

Glad for even a little affirmation, she continued, "I tried to learn to deal with it. I was raised to believe when you marry, you make the best of it, no matter what, and that's what I tried to do. Even when his beating sent me to the hospital—twice—I covered for him, lied for him. Stupid me." She shook her head. "So, I learned to live carefully, trying to avoid anything that might trigger his rage. Sometimes it worked, most times it didn't. I thought maybe if I was very good and prayed hard, and tried very hard to please him, he would be happy and would change."

Ken didn't say anything, but she saw his eyebrows raise. She shook her head. "Oh, I know, I should have known better, but I was very young then. Finally, I got enough courage to do something and made up my mind to leave."

Stacy stopped and stared across the table. "And then I got pregnant."

Chapter 50

Stacy stopped, shaking her head again. She couldn't believe she was telling all this, reliving all of it. It made the pain fresh and raw. She could feel the tears returning, so she struggled on with the rest of it.

"I thought having a baby might make him happy, might calm his temper." She raised her palm. "And it did, for a while. Bill didn't hit me when I was carrying Brent—I told him I'd report him if he did—and Brent was born okay."

Her throat caught at the mention of her son's name but she managed to carry on. "But shortly after Brent was born, Bill started in again. He'd be upset because his coffee was too hot, because I burned dinner, or because I couldn't keep Brent from crying. He would hit me, and I would cower." The sobbing returned and she didn't try to stop it. "I'm sorry, you probably think I'm terrible, that I'm a coward."

"No, I don't." Ken said, his words crisp but reassuring. "I'm sure you did the best you could at the time. It's always easy to look back and criticize. We all have our past failures." He inhaled slowly and said, "Go on."

His encouragement relaxed her a bit. She took another deep breath and continued. "I know I'm going the long way around to tell this story. I'm sorry. Bill used to say I ramble like a brook. Probably one of the only things he was right about. It's simply hard to explain, to tell it all." She shook her head again and took a slow breath. "I've never told anyone the whole story."

"It's okay. Tell me what you can. Like I said, I'll listen."

"I don't remember exactly when the drugs started. Those times are all pretty hazy now. Bill had always been a drinker and I learned to stay out of his way when he had too much to drink. A mean drunk." She stared straight at Ken. "I know what you're thinking. You're thinking I should have seen that before we were married."

Ken shook his head. "I wasn't thinking that."

"Well, okay, then," Stacy said, a little surprised. "Well, Bill didn't drink before we were married. Er, I should say, I never saw Bill drink before we were married. I was so naïve, just like my parents said." She stared over at the two-way mirror and pictured her mom and dad in the glass.

Ken didn't rush her or interrupt. He simply sat and waited, his eyes on her. She brought her gaze back to him and went on.

"Where was I? Oh, yeah, a little while after Brent was born, Bill brought home some new *friends* and they sat around and smoked marijuana. At first, I didn't think it was that big of a deal. I mean, that was the seventies and there were plenty who smoked a little weed. I really didn't want to—not at first anyway, I think I was chicken—but Bill let me know I had no choice. And by this time, I was too beaten down to even question it.

"From there, it all went downhill. It wasn't too

long before we were into harder drugs—coke, hash, uppers, all mixed with alcohol, of course. You name it, we did it. Oh, we had some great parties, as they said." She laughed, a hollow, brittle laugh. "It's amazing, now when I think of it, that I didn't fry my brain. Or, maybe I did and don't know it." She rolled her eyes.

"Oh, don't get me wrong. It wasn't all Bill's fault. I have to take plenty of the blame. Some parts of it I liked. Bill almost never hit me when he was stoned and the temporary euphoria from the drugs allowed me to escape the hell my life had become, but only until I came back down. And of course, *I* got hooked, big time, much more than Bill. Different body chemistry, the doctors told me. I became a terrible mother and neglected Brent more and more.

"The problem was, coming down only got harder and harder and we had no money. Brent, my own son, was going hungry and Bill was buying drugs for both of us. I can't believe it when I hear myself say it. I'm so ashamed."

Stacy dropped her head and couldn't look at Ken anymore. Staring down at the old metal tabletop, she watched her tears fall and run into the carved lines. She felt Ken's hand under her chin, raising her gaze to meet his again. He let his hand drop and placed it atop her fingers. He didn't criticize and didn't turn away in disgust.

Stacy stared across at the man she was telling more than she'd told anyone in her life. He still sat motionless, his eyes on hers, his hand resting on hers. She took another long breath and plunged on. "One day while Bill was at work, I had been out shopping— which was my euphemism for connecting with our drug dealer." She shrugged. "I had Brent with me in the car. He was probably three at the time."

She starting talking faster now, afraid if she stopped, she wouldn't be able to continue.

"I was so desperate to get high that, when I pulled into the driveway, I slammed the car in park and ran into the house to get my fix. I don't even remember what drugs they were. I left Brent strapped in the back of the car in his child seat and I didn't even know it!" she screamed. "It was May, for God's sake, and I left my own son in a hot car while I was inside getting high."

She choked on the words and stopped, her voice filled with self-contempt. "Why am I telling you all this?"

Ken's voice was calm and his hand never left hers. "I guess, because you need to tell someone…and I care enough to listen."

Hearing his reassuring voice, Stacy paused a moment and went on. "Brent sat in the car for what I learned later was almost sixty minutes and screamed the whole time for his mommy. A neighbor finally rescued my son and called the police and they came. By that time, Brent had already suffered heat exhaustion, dehydration, and first-degree burns. They arrested me for child abuse and child endangerment and placed Brent in a foster home."

She choked as the words came out and started crying again. "Ken, I can't believe I did this!"

His only response was a slight tightening of his hand around hers. The gesture helped and, after a moment, she was able to continue.

"While I was arrested and sitting in a cell a lot like

the one I'm in now, I went into withdrawal. I had a terrible case of D.T.'s and they had to put me in the hospital. They told me later they were afraid they were going to lose me. I've often thought it might have been better if I'd died."

Another small laugh of self-derision.

"Anyway, by the time I was released from the hospital, I knew I needed help, big time. I was given a choice by the judge, prison or rehab, and when I entered the program at the Seattle Clinic, my son was ordered to stay in the foster home. It took me almost a year to get clean. I was not the most cooperative patient, but I finally made it. So that to this day, I will not take a drug, any drug, unless a doctor prescribes it and I'm practically dying. I could *never* sell any drugs to kids."

She searched Ken's eyes for any sign of what she was sure he was feeling—disgust, shock, disappointment—but didn't see any of that in his features. Instead, he whispered, "Stacy, what happened to your son? I've never heard you mention him before?"

At his question, her eyes filled with tears again and she lowered her head, shaking it back and forth. "While I was in the clinic, the court took custody away from me. I was charged with being an unfit mother. As a condition of getting the felony charges dropped, I signed away all my rights as a parent. I haven't seen Brent in fifteen years."

As she managed to get this last part of the story out, her eyes welled up again, flooding her face with wet, salty tears dripping into her mouth as she spoke. Stacy tried to wipe the tears away with a sleeve of her outfit, but it did little good.

"I divorced Bill while I was in rehab and haven't had anything to do with that part of my life since," she said, when she could finally go on. She yanked her hand away and climbed out of the chair, walking to a corner of the room. Crying again, she sniffed and said through her tears, her voice to the wall, "I thought I had put all that behind me, when I moved across the country and started my life over again."

She struck her head against the concrete wall again and again in a slow rhythm. A hand on her shoulder stopped her. Turning, she buried her face in the lapel of Ken's suit coat, sobbing still. She knew she shouldn't but couldn't help herself. After a few moments she was able to murmur, "I'm sorry, but now you know it all. I hope you don't hate me."

Both hands on her shoulders, Ken shook her slightly, forcing her to look at him. "I don't think I could ever hate *you*," he said, his voice compassionate, his stare unwavering. "Like I said, we all have parts of our past we're ashamed of. I'm sorry this has forced you to relive all this. It's got to be incredibly hard for you. No wonder you've been going crazy in here. All the more reason we have to do everything we can to get you out of here."

"Do you still think the judge will set bail after he reads that?" Stacy pointed to the paper on the table.

"Well, your lawyer thinks so. I talked to Tim before I got here and he said the judge really can't consider this kind of information about your past and, if he were to get tough now, well, it might look bad. That may be simply lawyer talk, but he sounded pretty confident."

The matron appeared and said, "Mr. Parks, five

minutes, then I'll be back to take her."

Awkwardly, Ken and Stacy separated.

After the matron disappeared, Ken said, "Thanks for having the courage to tell me all this." Though separated, their faces were only a few inches apart and his voice a kind whisper. "It makes my decision easier. You've probably heard I've been getting pressure to drop the investigation and feed you to the sharks, from O'Brien, Walters, even Amanda."

Her head shaking, she started, "Ken, I don't want you to take any chances. I would never forgive myself if something happened to you. Maybe you should—"

"Well, I was starting to think that too. Then this came in the mail." He handed her the white paper.

She read the threat in large, unmistakable letters and her eyes got wide. "Oh my God! I'm sorry, please, I don't want anything else to happen, not to you, or someone else!" She stopped and pointed to the paper. "Show this to the police. It might convince them—"

Ken cut her off again. "I already gave the original to Bart. This is a copy. Anyway, he says he thinks Garcia will simply say I made it up, but Bart's having it checked for prints. He said he'd let us know, but don't get your hopes up."

Stacy heaved a sigh again.

"But the more I think about it," he went on, "I'm making somebody nervous and that has to be good for you. I'm not giving up on you, Stacy."

Without thinking, Stacy gave him a hug and whispered in his ear, "Thank you, friend."

Right then Washburn returned. Dropping her arms, Stacy exchanged a brief glance with Ken and moved to the doorway where the matron waited.

Ken said, "Stacy?" and she stopped and turned to look at him. "Think positive and get ready. I'll be back tomorrow to take you home."

Before she turned to join the matron, Stacy managed a small smile. Walking with the matron, she heard another female voice call, "Mr. Parks?"

Stacy and Washburn halted, and Ken turned to face the voice and they all stared at the police receptionist.

"Mr. Parks, I'm glad I caught you before you got out the door. Your secretary is on the phone."

Ken walked down the hall and took the phone the woman offered, its long cord snaking out into the hallway. "Vivian? What's up?" He listened for a while and then turned to where Stacy and the matron waited. "It's Tricia. She's awake and I'm heading over there to talk to her. Maybe I can get a few answers."

He waved and turned back to the phone.

Washburn said, "Let's go. Garcia says time's up."

Stacy stared back at Ken in animated conversation with his secretary, his eyes bright. She wanted his image to be the last thing she remembered when the iron door swung shut.

Chapter 51

His mind reeling from all Stacy had shared, Ken drove on in a fog, going through the motions mechanically. While he drove, he replayed his conversation with Vivian.

"I just got a call from Mrs. Holloway at the hospital. Her daughter, Tricia, came out of her coma this morning. You know, she's the eighth grader who used the tattoo at school."

"Sure. It was great of her mother to let us know. Did she say if her daughter said anything yet about the drugs?"

"Not yet. She said her daughter only came out of it about nine this morning and she's still pretty groggy. But she wanted to get a hold of you right away." The secretary paused a few seconds and asked, "Ken?"

"Yes, Viv?"

"Maybe this is the break you've been waiting for." Ken heard Vivian's intake of breath. Then she asked, "How'd Stacy handle the news today?"

"Devastated, more dejected than I've ever seen her. There's a lot more to the story. I'll fill you in when I get back. I better get over to the hospital."

He thought of something else. "Tell Mark where I'm headed. I don't have time to—" He interrupted himself. "No, on second thought, don't. Does anyone else know about Tricia's condition yet?"

"I don't think so. The call from Mrs. Holloway came on our direct line."

"Good, let's keep it that way…at least for now. And Viv?"

"Yes?"

"Cover for me, okay? I have a feeling I may need to watch my backside on this."

"Got it, boss."

He was no longer sure whom he could trust.

Managing to maneuver through traffic only by instinct, he made the correct turns through the side roads of the small town. Once, waiting at a stop sign, a blaring horn from an annoyed driver behind him jerked Ken to attention. He hit the gas and jack-rabbited forward, realizing he'd been sitting there for a bit, thinking, reworking the events in his mind.

Clearly, someone had leaked the info about Stacy's background. And her earlier conviction for drugs looked pretty damning, even if he'd told Stacy otherwise. Still, she said she put that all behind her fifteen years ago and he wanted to believe her. When she started in the eighties, the district didn't do a record check, but, as far Ken knew, she'd maintained a spotless record here. If he didn't believe Stacy was selling drugs—and he didn't, did he?—then someone was working damn hard to set her up. Who was pulling the strings and how did they know about Stacy's past?

Before he knew it, Ken found himself in the parking lot of the cramped Bethesda Hospital of Portsmouth. With the front lot full, he had to pull around the building to the small parking area next to the emergency room entrance.

As he got out and locked his car, the sense of dread

washed over him again, a threatening, black storm cloud inside his head. His stomach knotted. His throat tightened, making his breathing labored. He froze in his footsteps and stood there in the middle of the blacktop, taking three slow, deliberate breaths. Battling his phobia—he recognized that was what it was, even if he didn't want to admit it—he tried to rationalize his fear and practiced some deep breathing. Still, as he stood there outside the hospital, struggling to manage his labored breaths, he could feel his control evaporating, leaking out like the helium from a punctured balloon. It left him in a dry, brittle panic. But he *had* to go into the hospital and talk to the Holloways—Tricia might be able to finger the dealer—so he willed his legs to take purposeful strides up the ramp into the emergency room entrance.

As he approached the electronic sensor, the two glass doors swooshed open like a huge mouth and he fought the eerie feeling of being swallowed whole by the forbidding building. Inside, the area buzzed with activity. A gurney rushed past him with a young boy lying on it, his head covered in blood, black hair matted in a dark red hue.

Twenty feet in front of him, the receptionist sat at a long desk and was interrogating patients, entering the essentials of their personal lives onto a glowing computer screen. At the end of the desk, a doctor stood, clad in a white jacket and clutching the familiar hospital clipboard. Shaking his head, the physician spoke to a man with glazed eyes and an expressionless face.

Ken turned and glanced around the waiting area. His gaze was drawn to a young woman, sitting alone in a blue, plastic chair, weeping silently. Cradled in her hands, her face hidden from him, he watched as tiny tears trickled down her cheeks and dripped noiselessly to the stained linoleum floor. Beside her, a toddler played with a broken, plastic workbench, pounding a red plastic peg into a worn hole. Above the boy's head, a small color TV was mounted on the wall, the sound muted while the on-screen announcer rattled on.

The images and sensations of the space flooded his senses—the sight of injured and anguished people, the sound of weeping and the mutters of grief and pain, the unmistakable odors of urine, disinfectant, and blood. Light-headed, he staggered once and then caught himself on the edge of a nearby chair. He managed the few, faltering steps to the receptionist's desk, grabbing the countertop for balance. Fighting to summon some semblance of control, he paused and cleared his throat to get the woman's attention. After a long moment, the receptionist glanced up from her computer screen, her brown eyes squinting at Ken over the top of her half glasses.

"May I help you?" she asked in a voice which offered little courtesy or help.

He stammered in his response, "C-C-Can you tell me how I can get to room 226?"

"Down the hall, round the corner, up the stairs," the receptionist answered rapid-fire, as her thumb jerked over her shoulder. She returned to the keyboard, her eyes scanning the screen, dismissing Ken.

He pushed past the desk and headed in the direction she'd pointed. When he made it down the end of the narrow corridor, he paused to read the words painted in stark, black letters on the dirty wall, trying to figure which way to turn.

A crash jerked his attention back to the ER entrance as a rushing EMT team slammed through the doors, pushing a hospital gurney. The sounds of colliding steel and glass echoed through the emergency room entry, riveting everyone's attention. Even the receptionist looked up from her screen.

Shoving the gurney forward, the medical team surged directly at Ken, hurtling straight at the corner where he stood. As he tried to flatten himself against the wall, the EMT's turned the gurney around the corner. While one med tech steered, the second perched atop the stretcher alternated between chest compressions and giving mouth to mouth to a young brown-haired boy whose once-white face had gone blue. As they rounded the bend, the drab blanket covering the body flipped open and a leg flopped out. As they passed, Ken caught sight of the ugly blue pallor of the boy's skin. He recognized the medical crisis. He had seen it before, once. And he didn't think the boy would survive.

Even after the medical workers had disappeared behind one of the pulled curtains, their disembodied legs making frenzied movements around the gurney, Ken stood, rooted to the same spot, his whole body trembling, shaking his head, trying desperately to hold off the wave again. But this time, it was no use.

The memories of that horrid night flooded back. In that instant, Ken was no longer in Portsmouth Hospital, but in University Hospital, twenty-five years earlier. Though he fought it, struggling to confine the memories to their special, locked compartment in his subconscious, the details exploded in his mind.

Chapter 52

"Hey, Ken!"

Even after all the years, he could still hear the clear voice, shriek really, of his kid brother, Dick, as he climbed out of their parents' car, all legs and arms bounding up the walk toward him. Only fourteen, Dick was thrilled to be visiting Ken for "Little Brother" weekend at college.

Dick, who adored his big brother, was fascinated with everything about Delta Zeta House, even Ken's cramped room, with stinky clothes strewn on the floor and the stack of textbooks in the corner next to the bed. Ken could picture the sparkle in his kid brother's brown eyes and, when he smiled, the front tooth chipped in football practice. Ken gave him an impromptu tour of the house and introduced him around. Dick hung on his every word. When they returned to the living room, the campus cops appeared at the front door in a raid of the house, they said based on a tip of a drug dealer working out of the frat house.

When the cops left—after not finding a stash and issuing a stern warning, but without arresting anyone—Ken laughed with the other frat brothers. "Damn stupid Keystone cops! They're lucky if they can find the keys to their car. We don't hurt anyone here, so why don't those jerks leave us alone."

Ken could still hear his younger brother laughing

in concert, obviously thrilled to hang with the older guys. Dick didn't ask any questions when he and Ken overheard two of the frat brothers planning to warn his absent roommate, Zeke, about the cops.

Together, Ken and Dick headed across the campus, visiting a few classrooms, the library, the Student Union, and the rec center. Later that night, Ken snuck him into two college bars which Dick loved. Ken checked out his tall but gangly younger brother and said, "You're a big man on campus now."

Dick's smile was huge. On Saturday, they went to the football game along with 50,000 screaming fans and they won, of course. Dick even liked the cafeteria food, eating as only a growing fourteen-year-old can.

By Saturday night, Ken decided he was tired of having his brother under his feet like a lovesick puppy. He said, "I got a hot date tonight. Do you mind hanging with some of the frat brothers?"

Dick's grin never even flagged when he said, "I'll be glad to hang with the guys."

It was funny, Ken could still even remember, the girl—what was her name? Naomi—was really hot that night. Her breath was slightly acrid, her eyes wide and her smile broad as they did it, a lot of it in the back seat of his old green Nova. Across this bridge of time, he could still feel the pleasant coolness on his neck when they cracked the windows enough to clear the steamed glass. Without wanting or willing, he could still smell their alcohol breath, feel their slightly sweaty skins as their naked bodies touch.

Of course, they stayed at it till late, their car wedged into a secluded spot he had discovered months earlier. He refused to go back there after that night.

After dropping Naomi off and returning to Delta Zeta, his frat brothers bombarded him when he walked through the door, five roommates yelling at him at once.

"Dude, we've been trying to reach you. We looked every fucking place we knew. Where the hell have you been?"

By the time Ken reached the hospital, he stumbled through the Emergency Room, grabbing a nurse to find out what happened. After she heard the name, Dick Parks, she shook her head and walked Ken to the elevator, even pushing the button for basement. The ugly gray elevator doors opened to a dark room with MORGUE painted in stark black letters. There, a lab-coated doctor pointed to his brother's body, already lying on a table in the morgue. Unbelieving, Ken simply stared at the thin, naked body, still holding a hint of blue from the freezing water. "Death by drowning" was listed as the official cause of death, though later Ken learned the rest of the story. All those years and Ken could still remember the doctor's words, spoken with a curious combination of regret and reproach.

"Your brother did die from drowning, but he had a high amount of LSD—you know what that is?—LSD in his blood. The boys who found him and brought him in, fraternity brothers of yours, I think, said they didn't know how he ingested the drug. Do you?"

Ken shook his head no, but he was lying, both to the doctor and himself.

"Anyway, from what we can piece together, he took this LSD and headed outside and somehow ended up in the lake." The doctor glanced hurriedly at his metal clipboard. "By the time the other students caught up with him, it was too late. I'm sorry."

Ken slumped against the corridor wall, silent, stunned, and the doctor left him there, standing alone with the lifeless form that had once been his kid brother, Dick. Then Ken started crying—angry, scared, ashamed tears. His weeping erupted in such uncontrollable spurts he gave up trying to contain and continued when he called to tell his parents. They blamed Ken but no more than he blamed himself. He couldn't control his tears when he moved out of Delta Zeta House even as his "brothers" tried to lie and absolve him, asking him to stay. For this, there was no absolution. Even days later, he was still crying when he stood in the freezing rain without a coat, watching as they lowered the silver casket into the open wound in the earth.

Of course, by the time Ken was able to pull himself together and go to the police, he was too late. From his other frat brothers, he learned Zeke had peppered Dick's Pepsi that night "just to see what the little guy would do." By the time the cops came looking for Zeke, he'd skipped town, leaving Ken alone with his own guilt.

Ken didn't want to catch him. He wanted to kill Zeke. Since then, the guilt had been killing Ken, little by little.

It had taken years, but Ken thought he'd come to terms with it...until the death of the four boys had ripped the wound open again. Through the past few weeks, the memory had haunted him, though he had struggled to keep it caged. Instead, he'd used the shadow of the memory, merely the briefest glimpse that flitted across his consciousness, to drive him on, in an anguished hope he could somehow, someday redeem himself for his hideous mistake. It was a foolish hope and he knew it, but he clung to it anyway.

Now, as the memories—full, poignant, agonizing—were released on him again, Ken collapsed to the floor, his body sliding down the gritty wall, weeping again, mumbling, "God…I'm so sorry, Dick."

Chapter 53

Ken had no idea how long he'd huddled there, collapsed against the filthy wall, tears wetting both cheeks.

An orderly tapped his shoulder. "Sir? Sir, are you all right?"

That contact broke the nightmare's grip and Ken, glancing around, realized where he was. "Having a really rough day. I'll be okay." He used a sleeve to brush the tears.

The assistant extended a hand and Ken took it, getting to his feet again. The young man asked, "Can I help with something?"

Ken nodded. "I'm here to see someone in room 226. I got directions but I think I got turned around." He glanced up at the words on the signs, which blurred out of focus.

"Sure. It can get confusing around here," the orderly said, his words kind and quiet.

After he listened to the directions, Ken willed his feet to take a few steps.

He had to keep moving.

As he wandered down the hallways, he repeated the instructions in his head and, in less than a minute, stopped outside room 226. He stood there for a moment, his heart pounding inside his chest. He took slow breaths, one after the other, willing his pulse to slow down. He peered inside.

Tricia Holloway appeared much the same as when he'd seen her before, days earlier, except now colorful plants and flower arrangements surrounded her bed, reminding him more of a funeral scene. The fresh blooms added their scents to the smell of sterile disinfectant in the room. He watched the frail figure on the hospital bed, studying her. She breathed in and out, slow and easy, much like he'd done outside her door. He recalled Stacy's tale of how the girl had said she'd been abused. Was that abuse connected to the drugs…or was it some weird coincidence? During his grad work, he learned abuse victims often turn to drugs.

"Thought you'd show up here pretty soon," said an almost hoarse voice behind him. Turning, Ken found himself looking into the bloodshot eyes of Henry Holloway. The man staring back wore a two-day stubble of beard and a relieved look on his face. "I called your sec'etary and told her the news 'bout Trish. She was really nice on the phone 'n said she would get a hold of ya. Said you be here this mornin'." As he talked, Holloway's bad breath spilled out.

"Yeah, thanks for giving me a call." Ken noted the change in the father's attitude from their first encounter. Henry Holloway's face held a kind of exhausted relief. Ken asked, "When did she come out of it?"

"She hasn't, at least not all the way," a female voice said. Ken turned as Clarese Holloway came up beside her husband, deep furrows evident on her cheeks. "She woke up 'n spoke to us 'bout eight this morning. The doctors think she might be okay. They're not sure but they don't think she'll have any brain damage." She sniffed a bit but held onto a small smile.

"Said she might have some amnesia for a while, though."

"I'm so relieved she'll be all right," Ken said. "Is there any chance I could ask her a few questions about the drugs?" He paused and the Holloways glanced at each other but neither one answered. Ken added, "Maybe we can get a lead on who's pushing this poison on our kids."

"It's likely she may not be able to respond," Dr. Alex Hardcastle called from a few steps down the hallway. The thin figure in the flapping lab coat covered the distance between them in large, easy strides, his hand ruffling his curling hair.

"Oh, hi, Dr. Hardcastle," said Clarese. "Mr. Parks, this is Tricia's doctor, or at least one of them."

Ken extended a hand. "Yeah, we already know each other. Hi, Alex, good to see you."

Hardcastle nodded once at Ken and turned back to the Holloways. "I came as quickly as I could when I got the word. How is she doing?"

"Trish woke up 'n spoke to us," answered Henry. "Jus' opened her eyes, said 'Daddy? Mommy?' 'n cried some. Trish asked where she was 'n what happened? So we told her and she cried some more. Then me 'n the missus cried too." He put one strong hairy arm around Clarese and squeezed her shoulders gently. His wife nodded and brought a small hankie to her nose.

"Then we talked fer a little more. Cryin' and just happy she was awake," Clarese continued the retelling. "She kept sayin' 'I'm sorry. I'm really sorry.' Then she said she was tired and needed t' rest some more. So we came out and the nurse called you, Dr. Hardcastle." She paused then added, "And we called your office, Mr.

Parks."

"That's fine, Mr. and Mrs. Holloway," replied the doctor. "I think I'll go in and have a look at her. Would you mind staying here?" Hardcastle didn't wait for a reply and went into the hospital room alone.

The other three watched from the hall as the tall, white-jacketed figure spoke in a hushed voice and Tricia's eyes fluttered open and she responded, but they couldn't hear any of the conversation. After a few minutes, the doctor returned to the hallway where the others waited.

"I think she's going to be all right," said Dr. Hardcastle. "It's going to take a little time for her to get all her faculties back. In no time, you'll be yelling at her to get off the phone."

This brought a smile to the faces of both Holloways, who exchanged relieved looks.

Ken asked, "Excuse me, Alex? Did you think she could possibly talk to me?"

Hardcastle turned to Ken, eyebrows narrowing.

Ken continued, "I apologize. I don't mean to intrude, but you know I'm trying to find out who's selling these drugs to our kids, and I was hoping Tricia might be able to tell me something."

Hardcastle said, "I don't know if she will be able to respond to what you ask." He shook his head. "Even though Tricia answered a little when I spoke with her, her answers were still muddled. She doesn't know me that well. Does she know you?"

"She knows who I am, but no, I don't know her well," Ken said.

"If she doesn't know you," Hardcastle said, "then you may not get much of an intelligent response, at least for a while."

Ken said, "It's just we think we're getting closer to the drug dealer and thought Tricia might hold a piece of the puzzle to help nail him—or her." Ken cleared his throat and stared at the other three adults. "Every night I go to sleep and pray I don't receive a call on another Tricia Holloway."

A prolonged silence hung in the air. Henry shifted his weight from one foot to the other and stared down at the abstract design in the hospital linoleum. Hardcastle consulted Tricia's chart in his hand. Only Clarese met Ken's gaze.

"Dr. Hardcastle," she asked without looking at him, "might Tricia be able to respond…if I ask her?"

Hardcastle glanced up from the chart. "I don't know, but you'd have a better chance."

Clarese gathered herself up. "Mr. Parks, jus' tell me what you want me to ask her 'n I will," she said, before either Ken or her husband could object. "Let's get in there." She walked into the hospital room and up to the bed of her daughter.

Chapter 54

Clarese Holloway reached down and grabbed her daughter's hand, giving it a gentle squeeze.

At her touch, Tricia opened her eyes. "Hi, Mommy."

As Ken walked up behind her, Clarese said, "Honey, I need to talk to you a minute. I gotta ask you some questions, some hard questions, and I want you to tell me the truth now, okay?"

Eyes wide, the acne face on the pillow nodded up and down.

Ken spoke into Clarese's ear. "Ask her if she remembers getting the drug tattoo."

"Tricia, honey, do you remember gettin' that tattoo, the one you put on your arm?" Clarese asked the question in a tone only mothers know, somewhere between a direct command and an anguished request.

The girl whispered, "Wolf's Head."

"Where did you get the Wolf's Head, Tricia?" Clarese asked.

"Got it from school," Tricia answered in straight, matter-of-fact manner.

Ken whispered, "Ask her who sold her the tattoo?"

Clarese pressed "Tricia, I want to know who you got the tattoo from?"

"It cost five dollars. I got the money out of your wallet, Dad. Sorry." Tricia said the last word so quietly she almost swallowed the sound.

"Honey, who sold you the tattoo, do you remember?" Clarese tried a softer tone.

"She said it would help me," the daughter sniffled. "Make me more relaxed. Said the boys would like me more. Said she understood because she was like me when she was younger."

Clarese looked toward Ken, a question in her eyes.

He gave a simple nod of his head, the plea in his eyes. He knew they were close. He could feel the answer. He laid a gentle hand on Clarese's shoulder.

"Tricia, who told you that?" Clarese asked.

The girl didn't answer and shut her eyes tight.

The mother asked, her voice more insistent, "Who sold that Wolf's Head tattoo to you?"

"I'm sorry. I don't remember," uttered Tricia. The teenager's voice sounded anguished, pain and fear slicing through each sound. The body on the bed began shaking, her eyes wide open with fright. "Help me, Mommy!" She started crying, long racking sobs. Clarese let go of her daughter's hand and wrapped her arms around the girl.

Alex Hardcastle stepped around Ken and came up beside Clarese. "That will be enough for now," he said to them both and he laid a gentle hand on the arm of his patient.

Ken pushed. "Alex, I need to hear Tricia's answer. I need to know who's selling drugs to our kids." Ken stood facing the doctor, shaking his head. He knew he sounded uncaring, but he felt desperate, more desperate than he'd ever been.

"I understand your problem, Ken," the doctor said, "but right now, I'm more concerned with my patient.

Tricia is agitated enough. I'll let you talk to her again when she's up to it. Now, please get out." With both hands, he ushered Ken and Henry Holloway out of the hospital room.

The strength of the doctor surprised Ken as he grabbed his forearm and used the grip to shove him out the doorway. With the answer a few feet away, Ken kept staring back over his shoulder at the weeping figure of the teen. When he finally turned around, he nearly ran into Everett O'Brien. The tall doctor stood, slouched in the doorway, almost blocking it.

"Hi, Ken. Hi, Mr. Holloway," said O'Brien, his voice conveying that hint of cultured professionalism. "I heard our patient is somewhat better this morning. Dr. Hardcastle?"

"Everett, would you step over here?" Alex said, as he escorted O'Brien to the other side of the hospital room, away from Tricia and her mother. Hardcastle talked in hushed tones and O'Brien nodded his head several times. Hardcastle handed his colleague the gray metal chart and O'Brien took it, studying the notes.

Staring at the tableau, two doctors, a worried mother, and a trembling patient, Ken realized he'd almost lost it…but he was so close.

Then, the wave of phobia began to drown him again, his fear and sense of failure rushing through the floodgates. Having lost his chance, Ken had to get out, out of the corridor, out of the ward, out of the hospital. He wished out of this whole debacle. He hustled down the corridor, first walking with short, rapid steps, then running all the way to the exit doors.

Chapter 55

Vivian caught Ken as he came through the doorway to his office. "Don't bother to take your coat off," she said as Ken started past her desk. "I just got off the phone with Bart. He's down at the station and wanted to know if you can get down there right away."

"God, it feels like I just left there," Ken said. The encounter at the hospital had drained him. Even his eyes hurt. "Did he say what it was about?"

"Yeah. He said they caught the—" she stopped mid-sentence, staring at her boss. "Ken, are you okay? You look like you've been hit by a truck."

"Gee thanks, Viv." Ken tried a weak stab at humor and, when his secretary started to apologize, he continued, "That's okay. That's about how I feel."

"Did you learn anything from Tricia?"

"Not much. Her mother talked to her and asked her about the drugs. Tricia said she bought the tattoo at school from a woman who told her 'boys would like her better.' "

Vivian's face clouded over. "You don't think Tricia meant she got the tattoo from Stacy? She said a woman?"

Ken shook his head. "I simply can't believe it could be Stacy. There are a lot of women in that building. But Tricia saying that sure doesn't help Stacy." He used one hand to wave away the idea.

"Anyway, when her mom tried to press her to tell us who this woman was, Tricia became hysterical, really terrified. Said she couldn't remember."

"Tricia give you anything on this woman?"

"No. Before I could get any more out of her, Dr. Hardcastle forced us out of the room. Said his patient was too upset. Viv, I was so desperate I was ready to beat it out of her."

A brief silence followed while Vivian stared across at Ken. He read the compassion in her kind eyes, grateful for her support. He perched on the edge of the large, wooden desk and faced her. "What were you saying about Bart?"

"Oh, yeah. Bart called and said they've picked up one of the kids who broke into the high school last week. Found two of the stolen computers right there in the truck. Caught him red handed."

Ken started to say something, but Vivian waved her slender fingers. "Bart said to tell you the suspect is Jack Clayton." Her grin broadened.

"James' brother? The gangly one at the high school?"

"The very same." The excitement in Vivian's voice climbed another rung. She was saving the best till last. "And Jack said he's ready to trade information about the drugs for a break on the burglary. Bart said you might want to hear what Jack has to say. He's waiting for you…and Jack's lawyer."

Ken got up off the desk, moving for the door. "Thanks, Viv," he called over his shoulder as he passed through the doorway.

"You're welcome. And Wally said he wanted to talk…to you."

****

Ken had been such a frequent visitor at the police station, the receptionist didn't even ask. She simply smiled and waved him through. He found Bart right where he expected, standing behind the two-way mirror, studying Jack Clayton as the teen paced inside the cramped interrogation room.

Looking up, Bart nodded. "Glad you could fit us into your schedule,"

"Very funny. I've been a tad busy."

"So I heard. What'd you learn from Tricia?"

"Not much." He retold the episode with the teen, the doctors, and his response. When he finished, he asked, "How about you?"

"Well, we may be a bit luckier here." Bart turned around and leaned his back against the glass. He pointed over his shoulder. "Mr. Jack Clayton in there was pulled over for speeding a little earlier this afternoon and got really nervous when he was questioned, you know. He said he didn't have his license with him, which was right because he doesn't have a license yet, only his temporary. When Tim Kelly—he pulled him over—called in and found out about the temp, it gave him cause and he searched the vehicle. When he checked behind the seat, he noticed some fairly new computer equipment. When Kelly asked about the computers, Jackie boy got spooked, so Kelly brought the truck and the kid into the station. When they checked the serial numbers on the computers, they found they match the ones taken from the high school and they called me. Professional courtesy, you know?"

"Vivian said Jack wants to trade some information

about the drugs. What's he got to trade?"

"Jack claims he has information about who's dealing the drugs, but he hasn't said anything yet. He wants assurance of getting off on the burglary beef and he's not making any deals till his lawyer gets here."

"How long is that going to be?" Ken asked.

"Shouldn't be long. Should be here any minute." Bart turned back and directed his attention again to the suspect in the interrogation room. Both men stared through the two-way mirror, studying the teenager like a prized specimen behind the glass.

Now walking around the perimeter of the room as if measuring the concrete floor for carpet, the lanky youth kept pacing. Then he had dumped himself into one of the three uncomfortable folding chairs around the table, tapping his right foot to some inaudible beat. Then he jumped up and walked over to the glass, preening in the mirror and admiring himself.

Ken's face only inches from the nervous adolescent, he struggled to control an impulse to reach through the glass and grab the kid by the neck. A short, fat man waddled into the interrogation room, interrupting Ken's fantasy.

The man, who stood less than five-foot-four and easily carried 280 pounds, wore a brown, wrinkled topcoat, Columbo style from the old TV series. As Ken and Bart watched, lawyer and client sat together and talked quietly, Jack's eyes darting up to the mirror several times, the brown orbs wider with each return.

Within a few minutes, the lawyer-client conference concluded, the squat, trench-coated figure got up from the table and joined Ken and Bart in the adjoining room. "Steven J. Hammond," he said in a low, hoarse voice. "I'm Jack Clayton's lawyer." He extended his hand and Bart and Ken took it, each in turn.

Ken found the lawyer's hand fleshy with short, stubby fingers and wet with perspiration. When he finished the handshake, Ken took out a handkerchief from his pocket to wipe off his hand. Bart did the introductions, explaining Ken was here representing the district.

"I've spoken with my client," Steven J. began, "and he's told me he's ready to cooperate fully with the police. Before I tell him to spill his guts, I need to know what you're willing to give me in exchange."

"Nothing," Bart said, the single word flippant.

Chapter 56

Both Ken and the lawyer stared at Bart. Ken couldn't believe what he heard, but he trusted his friend. So he held his tongue and waited. Hammond couldn't.

"Look Officer, uh…Callahan," the lawyer began, searching and finding the name badge on Bart's uniform. "My client might have the key to the biggest drug and murder case this town has ever seen, and *you* can't promise anything on the burglary beef. Maybe I better speak to the chief."

Bart appeared unimpressed, his slouched posture against the glass unchanged. "Mr. Hammond, your client and I have some history. He likes to shoot off his mouth, you know, but he often doesn't know anything. *If* he has information on who's dealing the drugs and *if* it helps us catch him or her, and *if* he's willing to testify in court, well, then we'll see about getting the theft charges dropped. If he simply wastes our time, then he can spend the next eighteen months in juvey."

Steven J. Hammond appeared to mull over the officer's words, rocking his head slightly from side to side, stray brown hairs doing a funny, electric dance. After a bit, he said, "Okay, let's do it," and then whirled his stout figure around to head back to the interrogation room.

After he left, Ken said, "Bart, I'd like to be in

there."

Bart glanced back and grinned. "Who's stopping you?"

One after the other, both men followed the lawyer inside, Bart taking the chair opposite the teen and Ken sliding to the corner behind Bart, the same corner where Stacy had stood weeping earlier. Resting his shoulders against the wall, Ken stared down at the teenager.

Fidgeting on the small, uneven metal chair, Jack Clayton's gaze darted from one face to another, from the cop to the school administrator to his lawyer. His hands grabbed the edge of the old metal table.

"Well, Jack, I understand you have a few things to tell us," Bart began.

His brown bloodshot eyes wide, the youth looked to his lawyer, who nodded, his fat head bouncing once. "What do ya wanna know?" Jack said, his voice squeaking.

"You know…everything," Bart said and grinned. "What do you know about the kids and the drugs?"

"I know the kids are gettin' the drugs at school." Jack paused a moment, glancing at the officer, and then added, "I mean, right there in the damn school building."

"Hey." Bart laughed. "You're not helping yourself, Jack. We already know that. Who's selling the drugs?"

"I dunno. Somebody in the school," Jack mumbled.

Bart said, "Look Jack, if you want to screw around, I got better things to do than sit here and keep you company, you know." Bart turned, starting to rise out of his seat. "I think you can take your chance with the judge."

"No, wait," cried the teen.

Halfway out of the seat, Bart stopped. He straightened and leaned across the table till his face was only two inches from the youth. As Ken watched, Bart's eyes narrowed and stared, unblinking, at the teen. Bart's words came out so quiet Ken had to strain to hear. "If you want to help yourself, we need to know who's selling these drugs to the kids."

"I can do a helluva lot better than that," said Jack Clayton, feigning a little bravado. "I can give ya the goddamn supplier." For a moment, the three men in the room simply looked at the teen and no one spoke. Then, sensing their disbelief, Clayton continued, "Ya know, the guy who's supplyin' the drugs to school."

"A name, Jack. You know, I need a name," said Bart, thumping the table.

"I don't know a name…not exactly," said the teenager, his voice squeaking a bit.

Bart threw both hands in the air. Ken took a step toward the lanky youth. Jack must've sensed an impending attack because he added, "I-I-I don't have a name, but the kids call him 'the doctor.' "

"Doctor what?" asked Bart.

"I don't know, they just call 'm the doctor," Jack answered, his words tumbling out.

"A real doctor like an M.D.?"

"I dunno, but that's what he's called…and he's the one who supplyin' all the drugs to the school."

"Well, Jack," Bart said, "that isn't good enough."

Jack's eyes flitted from the policeman to Ken, his irises now two tiny dots in seas of red and white.

Bart continued, "You're going to have to do a lot better than that. You see, we already know that too. So, unless you can give us something else, you can just take the eighteen months for the burglary."

Turning, Bart headed for the door. Taking the cue from his friend, Ken walked across the room toward the now open door.

"No, wait!" the high-pitched voice blurted out. Jack Clayton trembled in the folding chair, his hands rubbing together nervously. In the doorway, both Ken and Bart turned but neither said a word. The youth cleared his throat and stole a glance at his lawyer. Steven J. gave another slow nod. "What if I told you *how* the drugs are getting inside the school?"

"I'm listening." Bart still did not move from the doorway, but Ken moved back inside the room, to the side and out of the teen's view.

"What if I could give you the guy who's bringing the drugs onto school property?" Jack's voice was hesitant, uncertain.

"You mean the guy who's selling the drugs—" Bart started.

"I didn't say that," the youth snapped back. "I mean the guy who's transportin' the drugs onto school grounds. That oughta be worth somethin'."

For a while Bart said nothing. The teen's eyes darted from his lawyer to the officer, pleading for help. As if on cue, Steven J. pressed the point. "That should get my client some consideration, Officer Callahan."

Keeping his stare on the youth, Bart exhaled. He took a few steps back to the table and bent his torso till he was again only inches away from Jack's squirming face. A single bead of sweat rolled down the side of the teen's face and he choked back a sob. Jack released a nasty alcohol-tinged breath.

"This is your last chance," Bart said in a quiet

whisper. "You better not be jerking me around and you better give me a name."

"Yeah, okay," Jack said, lowering his face, avoiding Bart's stare. "He better not find out I gave him up or he'll beat the shit out of me."

"Who?" Bart shouted the single word directly in the teen's ear. Jack jumped in his seat.

"It's Earl. Okay, it's Earl!"

"The bus driver?" Bart's voice sounded incredulous.

"Yeah, Earl, the bus driver. He better not find out it was me."

Bart ignored the teenager's last comment. Instead, he turned to Ken and both men mouthed, "Earl, the car doctor?" With that, they both strode out of the room, slamming the door behind them.

Chapter 57

The sun hung low in the late afternoon, autumn sky, igniting the horizon in phosphorescence of reds and golds. The few trees still clothed in darkening leaves absorbed the dying sunlight and seemed to almost burst on fire. Ken glanced back as he jogged and realized against that background, Bart and he must've looked like mere silhouettes on the horizon to anyone watching. Their pace a steady rather than speedy gait, the two runners trotted side by side up the sidewalk, Ken glancing down at his feet for uneven concrete.

They ran in silence much of the way, the only sounds the occasional labored breathing between strides and the pounding of soles on the pavement. Bart, in dark sunglasses under a brown Portsmouth police cap, spoke first. "Why does this seem so hard today?"

"Probably because you're fat and out of shape." Ken answered, panting even harder than his partner. He snatched a breath and his voice got serious. "You sure we need to do it this way. I mean, it's a little elaborate."

Bart said, "It's the best I could come up with, you know? Remember, the case is officially closed." Panting slightly, he took three more strides to keep pace. "In case you've forgotten, I'm the idiot who's sticking his neck out for a friend, a neck that might just get chopped off."

Ken glanced ahead. "Let's finish at the firehouse

and start our cool down."

"Okay, wimp," Bart blurted out, sprinting the last quarter mile. Caught off guard, Ken hurried after him in a labored attempt to catch up. He didn't make it.

As soon as they crossed the imaginary finish line, both men slowed to a walk, struggling to return their breathing to a normal pace by the time they reached their real destination.

Between shortened breaths, Ken asked, "What is the big deal with Garcia? Why is he in such a hurry to put the chains on Stacy?"

"Like I told you before, he says he's convinced she's guilty." Bart stopped walking and faced his friend, hands on hips, bending at the waist. "Of course, it's probably a little more complicated than that. You know, if this mere cop was to speculate, I'd say Garcia is probably getting political heat from O'Brien and Walters to get this whole thing wrapped up and out of the headlines."

"Politics? Damn, we're talking about a woman's life here," Ken said. "What a screwed up system."

"I don't know, but that makes a whole lot more sense than some giant conspiracy between O'Brien, Walters, *and* Garcia."

"Man, I don't know."

"Well, something's going to break. I can feel it," Bart said, nodding toward the next property.

As their running shoes crunched the gravel under foot, Ken and Bart glanced up at the weathered marquee, creaking in the slight wind. Several letters in the title "Earl, the Car Doctor" were worn, almost unreadable. The two men picked their path carefully to avoid discarded auto parts, strewn about on the lot. Ken saw no other activity at the service station, and he thought maybe their luck was holding up. If this was going to work, they didn't need any witnesses.

In case their noisy footfalls didn't announce their arrival, Ken called "Hey, Earl! You around?"

In answer to his hail, the wheels of a crawler rolled from underneath the school bus parked in the garage. Earl took his time climbing off the dolly. When Ken saw the imposing figure a few feet in front of them, he wished Bart had his gun. He prayed they wouldn't need it.

"Oh hell, it's only you, Bart. I thought it was somebody important," Earl's voice boomed, and he barked a short laugh. Looking past Bart, Earl's head nodded. "Who's the fat boy behind you?"

"Very funny, Earl," Ken whined as he arrived at the garage, limping slightly, favoring his right leg.

"See, I keep telling you, Ken, you're carrying too much weight, you know," Bart said, chuckling. "Earl, I think the wimp here"—his thumb pointed back—"might have pulled something. Can he sit down somewhere, maybe rub it off?"

"Sure, sure," said Earl, leading them through the garage into his office.

Ken limped his way to the only chair and the other two stood watching him rub his calf.

"He simply can't handle the competition, you know." Bart shook his head and turned to the attendant. "Well, Earl, by the way, how's business?"

"Business is okay, just backed up as always," Earl said, leaning against the counter. His fingers flipped the pages of the girlie calendar from the Temple Tools Company. He held one page out for Bart's inspection.

"Not bad," Bart agreed. "But I'd think business must be really good. I saw you in the black Porsche, tooling around town. Jeez, you oughta be glad I didn't give you a ticket for simply driving the thing."

"I didn't know you got a new car, Earl," Ken said, his attention for the first time away from the leg he was massaging. "What'd you get?"

"A '95 Porsche 670," Earl boasted. "Got it out back. Wanna see it?"

"Not right now," Ken said, pointing to his leg where his hands continued to work the muscles. "A Porsche. Well, that must've cost a small mint. Wish I could afford something like that. Seems all my money goes to Steven's college."

Ken stopped his manipulations and looked up at Earl. "But you've got a couple of kids. Maybe I'm missing something. How can you afford it?"

"Gotta watch your expenses is all," Earl said.

"That's not what I heard," said Bart.

"Don't tell me Earl's holding back on me?" Ken asked, his tone joking.

"I ain't holding back on nothing," Earl snapped, his voice curt. His total attention seemed riveted on Miss November.

"I've heard Earl's got himself a second income. You know, a very lucrative one," said Bart.

"Maybe that's what I need," said Ken.

"Not this kind," Bart said.

"I don't know what you guys are talking about." Earl became intent on Miss December now, his pointy nose only a few inches away from her voluptuous breasts. Though his voice tried to feign disinterest, it rose slightly on him.

Bart removed his cap and brushed the sweat off his forehead with the sleeve of his shirt. "Earl, I thought you'd like to know, we had a long talk with Jack. You know, Jack Clayton," Bart said, feigning equal disinterest, studying the sweat-soaked cap in his hand. He fingered the bill.

"So?" Earl asked.

"Oh, nothing," Bart said. "You know, we caught him red handed with the stolen computers from the high school. You know that dumb shit had them in the back of the truck he was joy riding around town."

"What's that got to do with me?" Earl's interest piqued.

"Oh, when little Jack realized he was going to get sizzled on the burglary beef, he decided to be, you know, quite cooperative."

"So—" Earl started but Bart cut him off.

"And he told us he could ID the drug pusher at the school."

Ken pretended to stop his leg massage and stared at the two men standing. "What?" he asked. "Bart, why didn't you tell me?"

Bart continued, ignoring Ken. "And Jack told us the big drug pusher was none other than Earl, the car doctor."

The burly mechanic's reactions were so immediate and so physical, Ken flinched.

"I'll kill the lyin' piece of shit," Earl growled.

"I'm not so sure," Bart said. He remained cool, almost disinterested, Earl's sudden reaction seemingly lost on him.

"Of course, I know Jack would sell out his own mother and lie in the process to save his skin," Bart went on. "But not this time. Too much checks out. The doctor part. Your sudden new income. I found out you even drove the bus to take those kids to Camp Haven, you know, the dead ones. What you'd do? Slip the kids the tattoos when they got off the bus?"

Chapter 58

"You guys are out of your damn minds!" yelled Earl, his voice echoing in the office.

He started to walk out the doorway, but in a move so quick Ken barely caught it, Bart now stood in front of Earl, blocking his way. Even though Bart was the shorter of the two and had to look up at Earl, his stare and posture never flinched.

The two men stood, frozen in a standoff, neither one moving. From their earlier conversations, Ken knew Bart wasn't sure about the extent of Earl's involvement, but sitting and watching the scene unfold, he couldn't tell Bart's acting from reality. Once again, he felt woefully unequal to the task of unmasking the drug dealer. He was grateful and relieved to have Bart on his side.

From Earl's features, Ken could tell the mechanic didn't want to physically challenge Bart. Like flipping a switch, Earl altered his stance. He relaxed, dropping his shoulders and leaning his body into the corner formed by the desk and the wall, and changed his tact. He shook his head and grinned.

"Look, I dunno what you guys is talking about. Sure, Jack hangs around here sometimes, he and Vince, Vince Patrillo, but Bart, you know what a weasel Jack is. He'd say anything to save his hide. You don't have shit." His gaze, which had been focused on the floor, rose up and squinted at Bart, calling his bluff.

Cap still in hand, Bart nodded. "Well, Earl, most of the time, I'd agree with you, you know. But, not this time. You see that buddy of Jack's, Vince Patrillo, well, he corroborates Jack's whole story."

Ken realized they hadn't even known the name of Jack's accomplice till now and he was relieved Earl, his back halfway turned, couldn't read his own puzzled expression. Ken decided to study the soiled floor tile.

Bart said, "Garcia's known all along Thompson wasn't in this alone. He'll be glad to know, we've sniffed out her accomplice."

Swallowing hard at Bart's blatant accusation of Stacy, Ken held his tongue and waited. Bart hadn't shared this gambit, but Ken trusted his cop friend.

"Hell, Ken, you know I might even get a promotion out of this."

Ken glanced up to see the grin on Bart's face. And he noticed the spark in his friend's eyes.

Bart continued, "But it doesn't look like we're going to get anywhere here. I'll call a car and let them take you down to the station and you can spend a little time thinking about this in a waiting cell." He headed out the doorway.

"No, wait!" Earl's words erupted, half plea and half command. For the first time he turned to Ken. "You know me. Hell, I worked for the district for six years. Shit! You're the one who recruited me to be a bus driver. You can't believe I could be some big drug pusher. Tell him." One huge hand pointed to Bart.

Ken raised his gaze and met Earl's, shaking his head. "One thing I'm learning in all this is I'm not sure I know anyone anymore." Rising from the chair, he moved next to the doorway, dropping the charade with the leg. "Bart tells me once they take you to the station he can't help you. Garcia has you then." He walked out of the room and joined Bart in the garage bay.

Waiting only a few seconds, Earl bolted out the door of the small room and in a few steps came up beside Ken and Bart. "Jus' wait a minute," he said, as he hustled around the garage. He pushed a pair of buttons and the twin overhead garage doors descended, their openers groaning in protest. It took less than thirty seconds for Earl to reverse the signs, lock the doors, and fix the lights. Once they were closed up inside, Ken couldn't keep from inhaling the strong odors of grease and gasoline.

Earl said, "What I've got to say, I don't want nobody else to hear. Let's go back to my office." Moving ahead, he led them back to the small room and shut the door.

Ken checked the room, afraid Earl might try something, then realized that was not likely in the confined space. He watched Earl's hands, making sure he didn't reach for any weapons.

"Let's get something straight," Earl said, his narrowed eyes darting between Bart and Ken, "I ain't no drug dealer. If I tell you what I know, I need to know you're going to help me, Bart."

"I'm not giving any guarantees, Earl," Bart said, "but if you can prove you're not the dealer and help me catch the guy, I'll do what I can. But you better not jerk me around."

"First of all, I don't know no names, jus' the arrangements," Earl started, his voice tentative.

"Earl, I told you—" Bart cut in, his voice angry.

Hands in front of him, Earl backed away from Bart. "No wait," he blurted out, trying to defend himself, "lemme tell you about the arrangements."

"What arrangements?" barked the cop.

"Well, you know I take that girl for OT to the hospital everyday—" the mechanic said.

Stepping to the office phone, Bart had the receiver in his hand before Earl could finish the sentence. "Earl, I'm in no mood for one of your stories. If you want to tell stories, you can do it down at lock up."

"Okay, okay," Earl said in a panic, "lemme explain how the drugs is gettin' into the school."

"Yeah, because you're the one doing the drug pushing." Bart said, beginning to punch the numbers in.

In a quick stride, Earl stepped to the desk and his hand depressed the button. "Lemme finish, then you'll see."

Placing the receiver back on the phone, Bart turned, glaring at Earl, but said nothing.

Earl hurried on, "Like I was tryin' to tell you, I ain't no dealer, but I think I know how the drugs is gettin' into the school."

"You think you know?" Bart's tone expressed his doubt.

"Okay, okay, I know how they're gettin' to the school. 'Member I told you about my OT run to the hospital every day." Seeing the expression on Bart's face, he hurried on. "Well, sometimes, I get a special transportation request."

"From who?" Bart snapped back.

"I dunno."

"What do you mean? You know everybody in this town. You can probably tell who they are from their voice," the cop said.

"I told you I dunno 'cause I never talked to nobody 'cause nobody called me."

"You said you got a request. Then how?" Bart asked.

"That's how," Earl said, pointing to the black fax machine on the corner of the desk. When Bart's face still showed a question, Earl went on. "Like I was saying, I get this message on the fax that says to leave my bus at the hospital and go get a cup of coffee." Looking from Ken to Bart, he continued. "And then when I bring her back to school, I do the same thing." He stopped, waited, looking at the two men.

"Is that it?" Bart said, laughing a short laugh. "Well, that about wraps it up. Gee, thanks for the help, Earl." His hand was back on the phone again.

"That's how I got the extra money." Earl's urgency was back. "After each time when I git back in the bus, I'd check the first aid box and the money'd be there."

"How much?" Ken asked, shooting a glance at Bart.

"Two hundred dollars a time," Earl volunteered.

"How did you know what you were transporting?" Bart asked.

"I didn't, not exactly."

Bart scowl at the mechanic, so Earl hurried on.

"Well, well, not that I could swear to."

"You mean to tell me you didn't look inside on your return trip?" Bart asked.

"Hell, I was warned not to look…in the box."

"Earl-l-l?" the policeman asked.

"Okay, once," Earl blurted.

"And?" Bart's impatience was growing.

"And they was drugs. Some of them tattoos and some cocaine and other shit."

"And you probably just borrowed a few hits," Ken said.

"Hell no, man, that'd get me killed. I knew that. I ain't a total dumb shit."

"Let me see if I got this straight." Bart looked from Earl to Ken. "You get this mysterious fax and then you leave your bus unattended while you're at the hospital. Then, after you bring this kid back to school, you do the same thing. After that, money appears in the first aid box. And one of these times you take a look, even though you're not supposed to, and see it's drugs you're carrying." He shook his head. "That's a pretty far-fetched story, you know, Earl. I don't suppose you kept any of the faxes?"

"Nope. Burned 'em jus' like I was told."

Ken glanced from Bart to Earl. He had little doubt he saw real fear bloom in the mechanic's features. He wondered if Bart saw the same thing.

Bart continued, his words thick with sarcasm, "And you got no idea who put the drugs in the bus *or* who took them out when you were conveniently gone. Is that about it?" He shrugged. "Gee, Earl, that is so helpful, you know. I'm sure I can get them to drop all charges for your help."

Earl missed the sarcasm. "You think so?"

"No, stupid," Bart went on. "I think you made it all up to save your neck."

"No, I didn't. It's true. I swear it," Earl said, agitated. "Why would I tell you all that if it ain't true? I'm tellin' ya that's what happened."

For a while, no one spoke. Bart shook his head.

Finally, Ken decided to say something.

"Earl, I agree with Bart, that story's hard to believe," he said. "Besides, one thing doesn't make sense. You're right, I've known you for a long time. This doesn't sound like you, Earl. Why'd you do it?"

"The money, of course," Earl responded.

"I don't believe it," said Ken. "Oh, I saw your new sports car around the side all right. But you've been running this garage for how long? Ten years?"

"Fourteen," Earl said.

"And you're the best damn mechanic I've ever seen. Can fix almost anything. Could charge a lot more than what you do, but don't. And look at this place, it looks like a dump."

"Yeah, but I know right where everything is," Earl said and grinned. "Ken, you ain't as dumb as they say." Earl looked from Ken to Bart and then dropped his gaze. "The money was jus' part o' it. I didn't have no choice."

"What's that supposed to mean?" Bart barked.

"Well, they was holdin' somethin' over my head," said Earl.

"That's what I thought," Ken said. "What was it, Earl? Maybe I can help."

Earl said, "I don't think so."

"Look, Earl," Bart blurted out, "this is the first thing you've said that I believe. You'd better tell us the whole story or I'm going to run you in."

"Okay, okay," Earl said to the cop, but looked at Ken as he spoke. "Ya know that girl, Tricia, who lives at the end of my route?"

"Tricia Holloway?" asked Ken.

"The student in the hospital?" Bart interjected. Ken

nodded twice and Earl continued.

"Well, I kinda like her and since she was las' on my route we always talked and some. Well, over the time we got kinda friendly, if you know what I mean. Well, anyway, Tricia musta thought I got too friendly 'cause she told somebody and *they* found out."

That clicked for Ken and he remembered Stacy telling him how Tricia had come to her room upset but wouldn't talk. He was still convinced it couldn't be Stacy so Tricia must've talked to somebody, the wrong somebody. Maybe Stacy would have an idea and suddenly he needed to talk to Tricia and Stacy more than ever. He glanced over at Bart and could tell he was about to go for the kill. He wanted to kill the guy too, but he realized that was going to have to wait. He intervened.

"Earl, the next time they contact you, let us know," Ken said, already heading out the room, grabbing Bart as he went. Bart started to say something, when Earl's next words stopped them as they were halfway through the door.

"There ain't gonna be a next time. I told them I was through." Earl sounded proud.

"What about Tricia?" Ken asked.

"Oh, they said not to worry about her anymore," Earl said.

Ken hurried out the door, already sprinting across the gravel.

Bart yelled back to Earl, "Don't go anywhere. I'll be back to pick this up."

Without waiting for an answer, he ran, trying to catch up. As they sprinted side by side, Ken prayed it wasn't too late already.

Chapter 59

Tension hung around the Parks' breakfast table like a palpable fog. As he did most mornings, Ken had prepared a quick breakfast for the two of them, juice and protein drink for himself and her favorite coffee and an English muffin for his wife. When he passed the mug to Amanda, the pungent aroma tempted Ken, but he decided he was hyped up enough already. From the countertop radio, the soft rock station concluded a song by Michael Bolton and then issued a three-minute recap of the morning news.

He attempted a little conversation about the ceasefire in Ireland, but Amanda responded with only curt, one-word answers. Reaching for something, anything, he tried to talk with her about Tricia's death yesterday. "They're not sure what happened. She seemed to be improving and then the nurses found her not breathing. They tried to revive her, but had no luck." Shaking his head slowly, he said, "Another death tied to this damn drug."

Even that brought little reaction. Amanda stared at him and mumbled into her mug.

Ken said, "What?" but got no response.

She was upset and there little he could do about it, except give in. He would not do that. Over their twenty years together, at times like these, he tried to distract her, change the subject and get her mind on something else. Sometimes it worked. Not this morning.

Between clipped words and short responses, she stirred her coffee, peering into her cup, even refusing to look at Ken. In the small kitchen the only sound came from the radio, a love ballad by Amy Grant filling the air with tense irony.

"Can't we turn that damn thing off this morning?" Amanda snapped, an angry finger jutting toward the radio on the counter.

Married long enough to realize this was no request, Ken got up, walked to the counter, and hit the switch on top of the radio, banishing Amy Grant to silence. He moved back to his seat and began sipping his protein drink, the silence in the room deafening.

He tried something else. "You said you wanted to think about it. What do you think about my idea about us getting away…once this investigation is wrapped up? Maybe we can take a few days for ourselves. Heck, we could even swing by the college and see Steven. What do you say?"

He thought he saw her eyes brighten at his mention of their son, but she mumbled into her coffee cup.

Ken asked, "I didn't catch that. What do you think?"

Amanda looked across the space of the table. "Sometimes I think it'll never be *finished*."

Ken turned his head. "One way or the other, with what Bart and I learned, I think we're pretty close to exposing the whole thing. It'll be over soon…one way or the other."

Amanda shook her head. "That's not what I meant. If it's not this, it'll be something else *for the district*.

With you, it always is." She stirred her coffee twice and looked back up. "Like why does it have to be you? Why do you have to be the one to bail out *Stacy Thompson*? Where's her lawyer?"

"Look, I don't have to do it. It's something I want to do. Tom Arnold will be there, all right. I'm not doing this alone. But I want her to know the district is behind her."

"Hey, Ken, I've got a news break for you. The district isn't behind her. *You* are." She flashed her white teeth. "You told me O'Brien and Walters wanted to terminate her and now they're threatening to terminate *you.*" With each line, her gestures became more animated, index finger pointing across the table. "I really think you're going too far for this…this woman. What happens if it turns out that she is guilty and you're risking your job for her?"

"Not you, too. I figured I could count on you."

"Look, Ken, you can count on me, all right. I'm worried about you, about us, that's all," Amanda responded, her tone changing, her hands now flat on the table. "You know, they're going to hang you if Stacy gets convicted. O'Brien will be only too happy to sacrifice you for the good of Portsmouth Schools."

"Amanda, don't you think I know that?" Ken shook his head. "This woman has no family and right now very few friends. She needs support."

"What about this family? What about taking care of us, of me? All you think about is the damn district. Why does it have to be you, Ken? Why do you have to be the *savior* all the time?"

"Okay." Ken exhaled. "What do you want me to do?" He stared across at his wife and waited. Her eyes met his again, but she said nothing. "Do you need me for something?"

"Oh, no, I don't *need* you to do anything." She spit out each word. "I just don't understand why you're doing this."

"I'm doing it because it's the right thing." He shrugged. "Stacy's scared and needs some support. That's *all* I'm trying to do." He paused and waited, eyeing his wife. "And, after what happened when I was in college, I want to stop this damn pusher."

"Ken, let…it…go. It was twenty years ago, for God sakes. You were a kid. Ever since the students' deaths, you've been carrying your guilt from your brother's accident like you were some kind of *tragic hero*." She waved both hands in the air. "What's past is past. You can't undo it."

Ken didn't know how to respond, so he didn't.

"Hell, do what you want. I don't care." She glanced at the gold watch on her wrist. "Oh, Christ, look at the time. I've got to get going." Amanda took another gulp of coffee and spilled some as she slammed the cup down on the saucer. Without another glance at Ken, she snatched up her purse, got up, and headed out the door.

Ken watched her go. "Have a nice day," he mumbled. He rose and cleared the table, putting the butter back in the fridge and stacking the dishes in the dishwasher. The cleanup complete, he walked over to the wall phone and punched in the number for the office. "Hi, Viv, it's Ken. You're in awfully early this morning. I thought I'd get Sharon."

"Well, I'm simply trying to get things caught up here," his secretary replied. "Somebody's got to keep the district running."

"Very funny."

"Just trying a little humor to keep things in perspective. I can hear it in your tone. What's the matter?"

"Oh, nothing. Amanda and I argued and she stormed out." Ken released a long breath. "God, I hope all this ends soon and we can get back to normal."

"Me, too. Didn't you tell me you're picking up Stacy this morning?"

"Yes, that's what the argument was about. I'm heading over to the jail in a few minutes."

"Do you have the check for the bail?"

"Yes, Mom. You have the numbers where you can reach me. Any burning messages? Anything I need to take care of?"

"Let me see." Ken could hear Vivian flipping the papers she kept notes on. "Oh yeah, I have a note from Wally, says he needs to see you. It's important, he says."

"Okay, call him and ask him to come and see me before he starts work. Make it about 2:30. I'll be back long before that."

"Will do, boss. Anything else you need me to do?"

"Hell, Vivian, you know what needs to be done better than I do. Just keep things moving. If you need me, you know how to reach me."

"Count on it. Take care of yourself and tell Stacy at least some of us still believe in her."

"Thanks, Viv. I got to run. See ya."

Chapter 60

Amanda cussed aloud at the car that cut in front of her. She was in one of those moods. Only a day or two from that damn time of the month, she had one of her famous headaches. She knew all this and realized she had taken it out on Ken anyway. As she wove through the light morning traffic, she rode in the quiet car, the radio off. Normally, the quiet solitude helped her think, but this morning the silence only gave her an excuse to argue with herself. The light went red. She hit the brakes.

"Why did I yell at Ken? Could I be that jealous, after—" Both hands slammed the steering wheel.

Glancing to her right, she caught the driver of the car alongside staring at her. As she was about to let him know how she felt, the light changed and he sped away, leaving her behind. Even this stoked her anger. She'd been only too happy to let that guy know where to get off.

Before she could accelerate and maybe catch up with the idiot, a beeping eruption startled her. Distracted, her gaze darted from the street ahead to her purse on the seat and then back to the road. Barely in time, she glanced up and saw a dark-green minivan switch lanes, jumping in front of her. Jerking her foot over, she slammed on the brake. The Regal screeched to a halt, missing the minivan by inches.

Amanda swore aloud first at the driver, then at the device which beeped again. With little choice, she checked back over both shoulders—glad for once that she lived in a small, podunk town with little traffic—and she pulled over to a vacant parking space.

"Where is that damn thing?" She snatched her purse off the seat, as the device kept beeping. In desperation, she turned the bag upside down, dumping the contents onto the passenger seat. Her fingers skidded through lipstick, other keys, a note pad, a worn leather wallet, the hotel key, two pens, a small bottle of Advil, her perfume dispenser, and then finally found it, still beeping. She pushed the button on the bottom right corner and the pager went silent.

She had bought the pager, less than a month ago. At one of their "appointments," Alex had suggested it so they could keep in touch. To cover herself, she had given the number to Ken and the office, but she found herself holding her breath…praying for it to be Alex.

Her index finger depressed the tiny white triangle and a short message scrolled across the small screen in electronic black letters:

Meet me atop Spencer Mountain.
Important we get together.
Do not call. See you at 9:30.
-A

She pushed the white arrow again and the message disappeared. And just like that, her anger evaporated, her headache melting away at the warm anticipation of the man's touch. She grinned at the abrupt change in her fate. "Maybe there is a God after all," she said, taking in a long slow breath. Picking up the cell phone, she pushed the first memory button and, after waiting a few moments, said, "Georgia, I've got some personal business to take care of. Pick up my calls and I'll be in a little later."

Closing the phone, she tossed it back into her purse and then scooped up the rest of the items and jammed them, one after the other, inside the small black bag. When she came to the atomizer, she spritzed it on her neck, the sharp citrus scent filling the inside of the car. Grinning, she tossed the bottle into the purse, then set it back on the seat, checking the road to make sure it was clear. After a moment, she pulled out and accelerated, the car lunging ahead. She drove two blocks and then made a left onto Blake Road, which took her out of town and eventually to the foot of Spencer Mountain.

Spencer Mountain, what a name. It wasn't really a mountain, only a heavily wooded rise on the east end of town. Amanda had only been up on the mountain once, years before when an amorous young man had designs on her virtue—and came away disappointed. She smirked at the memory and at the thought that, if she were lucky, Alex would have less trouble separating her from her virtue today.

As she turned onto Spencer Road, her anticipation rose, and her hand gripped the steering wheel tighter. Even though her new Regal boasted fingertip handling, she found driving the narrow, gravel road that twisted up the hill a difficult maneuver and had to concentrate to steer the car around the sharp bends and up the incline.

The weeds bordering the road were high and, of course never cut, and even in November, most had survived the mild fall and stood like silent sentinels. Their presence cut visibility to almost nothing. The tall weeds combined with enough spindly trees to block her view of the next stretch of road beyond the bend. As she eased the car around each turn, she prayed no one was coming the other way.

"Pretty strange place for a rendezvous, Dr. Hard-On," Amanda mumbled aloud as she maneuvered the car. "But these unexpected things are what I love about you, as long as I can get to the…top of the hill."

As she finished these last words, the car climbed to the summit of the ridge and she saw the land flatten out in front of her. Releasing a breath, she eased the gold Regal onto a clearing, the weeds and saplings beaten down. No doubt the space had been made by other surreptitious lovers. Putting the gear into park, she scanned the area, disappointed to see no sign of Alex's car.

Pulling the pager from her crowded purse again, she pushed the button and reread the message.

Meet me atop Spencer Mountain.
Important we get together.
Do not call. See you at 9:30.
-A

Cryptic message. She wondered why it was important they get together, but decided any meeting would only lead to one thing. A broad smile crossed her lips. She checked her watch, 9:22. She was early. She slid the seat back as far as it would go—they'd need the room. She laid her head back and closed her eyes, easing her body into aroused anticipation.

Chapter 61

Ken was unprepared for what it took to bail Stacy out. In fact, he felt unprepared for much of what he'd handled lately. He assumed he'd put the check down and take her home. It turned out to be much more complicated.

But when he saw her walk from the cell area, the metal door clanging shut behind her, he decided it was all worth the hassle. Her bright, green eyes shone even under tired lids, and she was able to muster a small smile.

"Hi, Ken," she breathed and held her stare on him for a few seconds.

"Good morning, Mrs. Thompson. Are you ready for a little trip? Those of us who have had to keep working at Portsmouth Schools decided it was about time to end your, um…little vacation."

She chuckled. "Just when I was getting to enjoy these fine accommodations." She handed Ken the stack of books he'd brought for her a few days earlier.

"Please check to be sure all of your things you brought with you are there," interrupted Matron Washburn, handing Stacy the bulky manila envelope. As she turned the envelope upside down, the contents tumbled out, spilling onto the counter. She picked up her wallet and checked the items.

"Yes, I think this is all of it," she replied, as she

scooped up the items and dropped them into her small, beige purse the matron handed to her. She signed the paper Washburn shoved at her.

"Then you're free to go…for now," Garcia hollered from across the room. Stacy and Ken turned. "Don't plan to go anywhere or leave town."

"Thank you, Chief," Ken said and, his hand on her arm, guided Stacy out into the fresh autumn air. As they stepped through the doorway, he recalled the journal passage about his touch and he pulled his hand back. After his argument with Amanda, he didn't want to give Stacy the wrong idea.

As he held the station door for her and she stepped through, he didn't take her arm again and instead hurried ahead to unlock the Taurus. Holding the passenger door for her, he allowed her time to slide in before shutting the car door, walking around the car, and climbing behind the wheel. As he eased out of the parking spot, Ken glanced into the rearview mirror. He half expected to see Garcia come running out the door, yelling at them to come back. Instead, in the mirror, the small-town police station stared back, quiet and still.

"I can't thank you enough for posting bail for me," Stacy said, gazing at him.

"A lot of teachers contributed. I only helped with the rest."

As Ken drove, he glanced over at her and then quickly returned his eyes to the road. After time in that cell and the past experiences she shared, he expected Stacy to appear drained and frazzled. Instead, she flashed him a weary smile. *No makeup, days in jail and she still looks pretty good.* Too bad he was a happily married man and then, remembering the morning argument, he chuckled inwardly at his own sarcasm.

He forced his mind back to the topic at hand. "I worked with Robyn Boyle and the union to collect most of the money. I simply kicked in."

She said, "It was all so depressing. I cried more in the last few days than I have in the last few years. Thank you for getting me out, even though I know it's not over."

"I'm glad I could help. Would you like to get real food, now that you're a free woman?"

"Sounds wonderful. I might even be able to buy, since Portsmouth's finest gave me back my meager funds."

"How does the breakfast place over on Columbus sound?"

"Sounds great, but isn't it out of your way? I don't want to keep you from your work anymore than I already have."

"Work can wait a while longer. There isn't anything else I'd rather do right now." Ken's quick response surprised even himself. "Maybe I can go over what we've pieced together and see if you can add anything."

"Sounds like a plan."

Turning the Taurus, he headed out of town toward the bypass and the interstate connection, where the few eateries made up what Portsmouth residents called restaurant row.

"I am so starved I feel like I could eat about everything on the menu," Stacy announced, as soon as they settled into their booth. Her excited eyes alternated from the menu to Ken across the table. The smells of warm breakfast foods—crispy bacon, rich, roasted coffee, sweet maple syrup—floated across the cozy space.

"The pancakes look so good, especially with blueberries. Oh, and it's been so long since I had biscuits and gravy. Have you ever had their biscuits and gravy?" she asked, without waiting for an answer. "They are really good here. But let me see, the Belgian waffles also look tempting. I can't make up my mind."

Shaking his head, Ken grinned at the woman sitting across from him. "Well, it's nice to see jail didn't kill your appetite."

Stacy simply shrugged and then continued on, eyes darting down the plastic list of options, considering one item after the other.

Ken couldn't help it. In the small restaurant booth, he found himself again intrigued by the woman across from him in the booth. Of course, reading her private thoughts in her journal no doubt colored his perception. As she rambled on, he watched her, noticing how her smile had brightened and her eyes regained some sparkle. He trusted his instincts and this observation confirmed his intuition. This woman cared so much about children and life, she couldn't have had anything to do with the drugs…or the boys' deaths.

And he was determined to get her out of this, no matter what it took.

A few minutes later, the waitress showed up at their table. Her blonde hair up in a ball on top of her head, she stood one hand on a hip and a pencil with a half-chewed eraser behind her ear. Her checkered name badge proclaimed "Darlene S."

"Welcome to Jimmy's," Darlene S. said and stopped, staring at Stacy. "Oh, it's you. Well, uh…you know what you want yet?" she spit out and rolled the gum around in her mouth.

Looking across the table, Ken saw Stacy react, deflated by the deliberate surliness of the waitress. He shot her a quick, reassuring glance. "I think I'll take bacon and eggs and the fruit cup. What would you like, Stacy?"

The ploy worked and she answered, "I think I'll take the Belgian waffle with strawberries and maybe a cup of hot tea."

"Oh-key," the waitress said, letting her inflection rise on the second syllable.

She turned and headed back to the counter. Ken's gaze followed her path as two other waitresses materialized and the three began a clandestine conference, casting furtive glances in their direction.

This town, he thought. Even the waitresses have Stacy guilty.

"Stacy?" She raised her eyes off the empty table she was studying. "I want to say thanks for trusting me enough to tell me about your past problems." She started to say something but he stopped her. "What you've been through is horrible and I'm sorry for your pain. I promise to do whatever I can to help."

She released a long breath. "To tell you the truth, it felt good to tell someone the whole story. After all this time, I still have nightmares. Maybe some things you never get over, at least not completely." She shook her head. "That's why all this hurts so much. Other people have no idea. For me, this isn't only about the death of those poor boys. It's personal."

"Yeah, I-I-I know what you mean," Ken said.

Stacy must've caught something in his response.

She asked, "Ken, what is it?"

He gazed across the table and Stacy stared back at him, large, sympathetic eyes focused on his. This woman does not need his problems, he thought. "Oh, nothing."

For a minute, the silence hung between them. After a bit, Stacy said, "Ken, if you don't want to talk about it, it's okay. I've been there." She stopped, held Ken's gaze for a moment and finished, "But if you do, I'll listen."

Glancing around the near empty restaurant, Ken was relieved to see the idle waitresses had apparently lost interest in them. He studied the woman across the table, waiting, neither impatient nor bored. After what she had shared about her past secrets, he figured she'd understand.

"When I said I knew what you meant about this being personal, that's exactly what I meant. I have more than a few past nightmares of my own."

She sat across from him, her features softening, welcoming him to share—or so he thought. He told the story of his painful past, his voice quiet and reverent. She leaned closer as he spoke of his brother, Dick, and his death from a drug, not unlike this new drug.

When the entire story spilled out, the heart-wrenching details told between pauses and Stacy's occasional questions, her response surprised him. Unlike Amanda, she didn't try to convince him it couldn't have been his fault or try to absolve him from his guilt. Instead, when he finished, she whispered, "I'm sorry, Ken," and, reaching across the table, laid her hand on his. "I'm sorry this has resurrected such painful memories for you too. I guess we have more in common than I thought."

Ken shrugged. "Well, I suppose I wanted you to know. No one else knows…except Amanda, of course. That's why it hurts when people call me a martyr. I think what I'm really searching for is some kind of personal redemption."

She hesitated before answering. "Whatever else happens, I hope you find it."

"Thank you. I hope I can count on you to keep my ugly secret," Ken said.

"What are friends for?"

Chapter 62

Her eyes still closed and lost to her own erotic anticipation, Amanda heard the crunch of tires on gavel announcing his arrival. Though anxious, she kept her eyes shut and waited, her breaths shortening. At first, she enjoyed playing this game with Alex, as she had several times before, but after a while she became anxious. Just when she couldn't take it anymore and started to open her eyes, she heard the click of the passenger door handle.

How does Alex always have such perfect timing?

As she grinned at the thought, a familiar voice called, "It's good to know you're glad to see me," and then her lips tasted the distinctive combination of mint and masculinity she had come to enjoy. She returned the kiss with passion, all the while still squeezing tight her eyelids. She inhaled his musky aroma of the cologne that made her knees go weak. When she opened her eyes, the handsome form of Alex Hardcastle filled her vision, sitting on the soft leather seat, pressing close.

"Move over a little so I can get out from behind this steering wheel," she said.

He slid over, leaving just barely enough space for her to wedge her body next to his on the leather bucket seat.

Glancing past the one blond curl on his forehead

and into his dreamy blue eyes, she said, "Well, this is certainly the strangest place we've ever met, I'd have to admit."

"I couldn't agree more. Interesting…exciting." His right hand roamed up her blouse as he spoke, "And a little, um…daring. Right up here in broad daylight above all of Portsmouth *and* secluded at the same time. You are something else."

"I'm glad you noticed." Her fingers crawled toward his own very ready middle. Both too horny for any extended foreplay, they stripped in a few seconds, flinging their clothes about the car, and pressed their naked bodies together. Amanda wasn't sure if it were her mood or the tawdry atmosphere of the car, but she felt like a horny teenager, thrilled with the daring escapade. They made clumsy, hurried sex and, satisfied she couldn't be heard with the car windows closed and away from the rest of the world, Amanda let herself go and screamed, vocalizing her pleasure.

Afterward, they lay there quiet and breathless for a while, both grinning like…well, like adolescents. The car smelled of sweat and excitement, like sex, she thought. Still curled together, hot and wet, they exchanged glances and giggled. Without another word, they began to dress, arms searching the crevices of the car for undergarments and reaching over the seat back to snatch her blouse and his pants. Alex pulled on his boxers and gray slacks and leered at the sight of Amanda, who chose to put her bra on first, leaving the rest of her body shimmering in the diffused sunlight.

"Amanda, my dear, this was certainly different from our suite at the Marriott." He tugged on his dark nylon socks, then brushed the stray locks of blond hair.

"Yes, but definitely fun. I'd say we made the most of tight quarters." Her fingers reached for her panties strewn by the passenger door, skittering close to his tender middle. Glancing around, she noted a silver-white fog draping the glass of the car windows, looking for a moment like white icing from one of her childhood cakes.

This was even sweeter.

"Looks like we heated it up pretty good in here," Alex said, chuckling, as his head popped through the elastic circle of his undershirt.

"My morning was really going in the dumper." Amanda squirmed on the car seat to draw her panties up. "Your message could not have come at a better time. When that pager wouldn't stop beeping, I knew it had to be you." She smiled and batted her eyelashes. "As usual, you had perfect timing."

"Thanks for the compliment, gorgeous, but unless I'm missing something, I don't think I deserve it." Alex stopped buttoning his starched, white shirt, now a good deal more wrinkled, and stared at Amanda, his features creased. "Did you say *I* paged *you*?"

"Sure." Amanda stopped dressing and peered across. "Oh, come on. Stop kidding me. Here, I'll show you." She reached for her purse, which had gotten jammed beneath the front seat in the frenetic activity. Pulling it out, she fished around a bit and then extracted the pager. She pushed the message button, eyed the small gold screen, and handed it to Alex.

He took her pager and studied the electronic screen. As he sat there, staring at the message, he reached one long arm behind the seat and retrieved his suit coat from the back floor. Rifling through its pockets, he found his own matching unit. He pushed the display button, examined his message, and handed both pagers to Amanda.

She looked at both units, studying the screen on his now.

Meet me atop Spencer Mountain.
Important we get together.
Do not call. See you at 9:30.
-A

Her eyes darted from one unit to the other. "What the hell?" Then her frown turned to a mischievous grin. "Is this some kind of joke, Alex?"

"If it is, it's not mine." His fingers hurried to finish their task of buttoning.

"But both pagers have exactly the same message," she said, shoving them at him.

"I see that. I noticed the same thing." He reached down to slip his black oxfords on his feet.

"So what does it mean?" Amanda asked, the earlier playfulness gone from her voice.

Alex shook his head. "I don't know. Maybe it's a trap. Could your husband have done it?"

"Ken? Ha!" A short squeal of laughter escaped her throat. "I don't think so. *Mr. Martyr* is too busy bailing out Thompson this morning. Saving 'that poor woman' is the only thing on his mind lately. What about your wife?"

"No way. She's in Connecticut, visiting her mother. I talked to her this morning."

"Then who?" Her puzzlement morphed into concern.

Chapter 63

His own burden lightened by sharing, Ken's thoughts returned to the present. "Speaking of secrets, I've got a question. Is there anyone at work who would know about your past? Someone you might have told, anyone you confided in?"

Stacy shook her head. "Before you and before yesterday, I never told anyone. I mean anyone. I was too scared. I thought if anyone ever learned, I'd lose my job."

"Well, someone knows all right. I spoke with the reporter and the editor, that's Jacqueline's father, remember? Neither would tell me much, said they had to protect their sources. But reading between the lines, they gave me the impression they got a tip from someone at the school. You think it could be Jacqueline?"

"I don't know how. I've never told her…or anyone else at school. And it's not like we're friends."

"Well, if not Jacqueline, someone found out about it somehow, and that makes sense now."

"What does?" Stacy scrunched her brow.

"You see, when I became convinced you were being framed, the problem I had was, why you? Why did the drug dealer pick you to frame? The leak to the paper, and what you told me about…" Ken groped for the right word. "About the troubles you had, that explained it, or part of it. The way I figure, someone knew about your past and thought, once they revealed it, you'd be a logical suspect." He paused and then added, "And they're probably right on that count."

"Also, I was on the trip with the boys."

"That might have been planned, or only a coincidence. Whoever is selling the drugs certainly didn't plan to have the boys die. Dead customers don't buy any more drugs. After the boys died, they had to do some fast thinking."

The waitress returned with their order, cutting off any further discussion. Darlene S. made a big show of setting Ken's plate into perfect position. Then she dumped Stacy's plate onto the table, almost spilling the waffle in the process. She filled their glasses, flashed the veneer of a plastic smile, and scooted. Ken ignored the slight, inhaling the delightful aroma of the bacon and maple syrup.

After the waitress disappeared, Stacy took a bite of her waffle, dipping it into the amber pool, chewed, and swallowed, a contented smile crossing her lips, "So good." She cut a second piece, ready to repeat the process and stopped. "What do mean they had to hurry?"

Ken finished some of the eggs. "Well, when the boys died, he—or she—had to find a scapegoat, to throw suspicion off them. They only had a few days to set up the frame…so they must have known about your past beforehand."

Stacy hadn't taken the second bite, her fork still poised in the air. "You mean like a *file* on me." She shook her head and ate the triangle, taking her time. "Why? How'd they find out?"

"As to how they found out, you can find out almost anything on the internet. As to why, just in case, maybe. I don't know."

He glanced around, but no one seemed to take any more notice of them.

When she'd polished off more of the waffle, Stacy asked, "Have you learned anything more?"

"Not a lot, but we're getting closer. Bart and I have a few small pieces but every time I think we're getting somewhere, something happens, like with Tricia." Ken caught the puzzled look on her face and said, "Oh, God, you don't know about Tricia."

"Know what?"

"Tricia died yesterday afternoon in the hospital."

Stacy gasped. "Oh, God, no. How?"

"The hospital says complications from the drugs, but I'm not convinced."

"What do you mean?"

Ken said, "Well, yesterday morning Tricia came out of her coma and I talked with her for a little while. She said she got the drugs from a woman at school but wouldn't say who. I tried to push her hard to get a name but her doctor, Alex Hardcastle—do you know him?" Stacy shook her head and frowned.

"Well, he stopped me, said his patient needed to be left alone. Told me to come back later. Only now, there's no later. Her death is awfully convenient."

"Poor Tricia. How horrible! What her parents must be going through," Stacy said, on the verge of tears now.

Ken stopped, ashamed, Stacy's response reminding him of his callousness. "You're right. I was so sure Tricia was going to give us the dealer. Now…I don't know." He watched Stacy's features and didn't say anymore, letting the silence return, while they had a few more bites.

He took another sip of tea and continued, "Oh, and Wally says the kids talk about some guy named 'the doctor' as being behind the whole thing."

"Doctor who?"

"Who knows? Could be any doctor or only a nickname, but we think Wally's on the level. Oh yeah, and there's the great computer burglar."

"The what?" she asked, dabbing her lips with a napkin.

"The cops caught one of the kids who broke into the high school and stole the computer equipment. Caught him with the computer, right there in the back of a truck when they pulled him over for speeding."

"Sounds interesting, Ken, but what does that have to do with me?" She paused between the last few bites of the Belgian waffle.

"The kid they caught is Jack Clayton."

"James' brother?"

Ken nodded. "The very same."

"I remember him. He was a harder case than James. A real weasel of a kid."

"Well, he's still weaseling. When he was caught with the stolen merchandise, he said he had information to trade if the cops would drop the charges, information about the drugs. Bart said maybe and James told him the supplier to the school is none other than…Earl."

"Earl, the bus driver?" she asked, incredulous.

"Yeah, lovable Earl, the bus driver and 'car doctor.' So Bart and I pay him a quiet visit at his place and guess what? He confesses, but not to what you think. He tells us he's transporting the drugs inside the first aid kit on his trips between the hospital and Foster. Says he doesn't know who puts them in or who takes them out, gets his directions by fax, never even talked to them."

"I can't believe this. I always liked Earl. He's one of the nice bus drivers. Why would he do it?"

"Great question," Ken said. "Earl says he had no choice, says the drug pusher was blackmailing him."

"About what?"

"Tricia Hollaway."

"What?" she asked, scrunching her forehead.

"It turns out Earl was the one Tricia came to see you about."

At first, Stacy stared at Ken in puzzlement. Then her eyes blazed. "Earl was molesting Tricia?"

"To hear Earl tell it, Tricia was at the end of the route and he just got a *little friendly* with her."

"Oh my God!" She shook her head slowly back and forth. "What did Bart say?"

"Bart was planning to turn Earl and use him to trap the drug dealers, but then Earl told us the dealers weren't going to use him anymore. Said they were going to take care of his 'Tricia problem.' "

"And then Tricia dies in the hospital. Hell of a coincidence," she said.

"Bart's squeezing Earl some more today, but he thinks he's on the level."

"Whew, you guys have been busy. I'm glad you're on my side." Stacy polished off the last few bites of her breakfast.

Chapter 64

Alex Hardcastle announced, "I don't know what's going on but I'm not hanging around here to find out."

His last button buttoned, he threw his tie around his neck and gathered up his suit coat. Giving Amanda a hurried peck on the cheek, he slid across the seat and opened the passenger door. As he did, the cool air rushed into the car, chilling Amanda, who shivered in her underwear. He stuck his head out the opening and did a three-hundred-sixty. His head popped back in.

"Looks all clear for now, but who knows. Maybe someone is on their way up now." He nodded to the single lane that ended at the clearing. "Sorry, love, but I better run. I have a practice to protect. Best if we're not seen together. To be safe, why don't you give me a few minutes head start and follow. I'll call you."

He shut the door and was gone. Amanda listened to the sound of a car door opening and closing and then the familiar roar as his engine started. As she sat there in her underwear, she heard the gravel crunching that signaled his departure.

Twisting the rearview mirror, she examined her face, makeup slightly smeared. She grabbed her foundation from the purse and dabbed at her cheeks, muttering to herself, "What is it about you, Amanda, that men keep leaving you?" She tried a chuckle but it came out more self-derision than mirth. She turned the key to start the car, triggering the heater to warm the interior and clear the fogged glass. As the fan blew, making the temperature more tolerable, she continued pulling her clothes on. Some sixth sense told her to hurry as she fumbled with the final two buttons on her blouse.

By the time the windows cleared, Amanda, fully dressed, studied the entire landscape atop the rise. Her car sat alone in the clearing, the same as it had on her arrival. When a careful inspection through the tinted glass revealed no Peeping Tom's or private detectives about, her anxiety eased a bit. She released one long breath, her gaze still roaming from side to side. Jamming the few stray items back in her purse, she examined the message on the screen again.

She shook her head and then stared at the slight depression in the seat where Alex had reclined a few minutes ago. "I bet I'm going to find out this was some kind of joke by him. He has such a weird sense of humor." Her laugh held no conviction.

In a few moves, Amanda slid back behind the steering wheel, lowering it again to the height she liked. She shot another glance through the windshield at the area surrounding the car. All she saw were high weeds and small trees jutting up around the clearing. No one. She thought again about the matching messages on the pagers.

What the hell was going on?

She turned the steering wheel and spun the car one-hundred-eighty degrees, heading back down the hill. Amanda pressed hard on the accelerator, spinning the tires wildly and shooting gravel out behind the car. The tires grabbed and the Regal barreled off the hill onto the twisting road.

She needed to get out of here…and back to the office. She might need an alibi. She pondered a bit and decided she could say she'd agreed to meet an out-of-town client up on top of Spencer Mountain. Uh, he said he was interested in developing the area. She waited a while up here, but he never showed. She nodded and smiled to herself.

That would work.

The expensive tires grabbed and the Regal barreled off the hill onto the twisting road. Amanda was glad she'd talked Ken into paying for the better tires. She might need them to navigate her way back down this road. The seat belt signal dinged at her, and she shot a glance at the panel. She'd take care of that before she got into traffic. In a hurry, she pushed it, hitting the first curve fast, forcing her to take a sharp turn to set the car down the next straight stretch.

From that bend, the road descended quickly and she felt the car picking up speed as gravity and its powerful engine propelled it downhill. As she approached the next turn, Amanda realized she was coming in a little too fast. She slid her foot to the brake. Her concentration on steering the twisting road ahead, at first it didn't register. She dared to take her gaze off the road and look down at her feet before she understood. When her right foot depressed the brake, the pedal glided all the way to the floor. No friction. She pulled her foot back and slammed on the brake again. The pedal slid all the way down. Unbelieving, she pumped it, again and again.

There was nothing there.

She jerked her eyes back. The hairpin turn hurtled

at her. On instinct, she kept jamming on the pedal. *It was supposed to work.* She turned the wheel wildly. The big car shuddered as it tried to negotiate the turn. The two rear wheels slipped off the pavement, spinning in space. With the front wheel drive, the front two tires managed enough traction to catch. The car veered around the curve and headed down the next straight incline. The heavy vehicle rolled faster again as gravity pulled it down the hill.

Amanda's mind reeled. What was she supposed to do?

White knuckles gripped the steering wheel. Struggling desperately to force her mind to think, she tried to consider her options. It was all happening too quickly. The next treacherous turn came at her fast. She had no way to slow down. Her hands gripped the steering wheel even tighter.

The bend ahead showed a hard curve to the right, not quite as tight as the last one, but steeper. And she felt the car accelerating, though she hadn't touched the gas pedal. Right before the car hit the curve, Amanda spun the steering wheel. The car lurched around the bend. The driver side of the car lifted up. Halfway through the long bend, Amanda watched the hood tilt in the turn until it was almost vertical. No seat belt on, she was catapulted down the leather seat, crashing into the passenger door.

"Hell!" she cried, reaching to grab her bruised shoulder.

She froze as the two wheels still on the ground shuddered in the gravel, sliding off the small road. Slammed against the side door, she heard the tall weeds and low branches whip against the body. But the car didn't slow. Blood streamed from a gash on her forehead. For an instant she lay there stretched across the passenger door, holding her breath.

Then she sensed the car teetering. The front tire bumped something hard. Amanda stared, unbelieving, as the car began to flip. As the Regal made the first revolution, she screamed.

Chapter 65

Holding the passenger door open for Stacy, Ken heard the car phone chirp in its cradle. Sprinting around the car, he slid quickly into the driver's seat. As he rounded the car, his mind called out "Amanda." Even with all their problems lately, Ken still felt that bond with his wife, a bond stretched and strained, but not broken. Not yet, Ken thought. As he climbed behind the wheel, Stacy handed him the cell phone.

"Hello, Amanda?" he shouted into the receiver.

"No, Ken, it's me, Viv," said the shaken voice on the other end of the line. "I don't bother you on the car phone unless it's an emergency." Ken heard his secretary pause. "Well, this is."

"Viv, what is it?" Ken felt his own panic rose.

"It's, it's, it's…Amanda. Ken, she's been in an accident. Went off the road on Spencer's Mountain."

"Spencer's Mountain? What was she doing on Spencer's Mountain?"

"I don't know." Vivian's voice caught in her throat and Ken heard her swallow hard. "Her car slipped off the road up there and flipped several times. They're not really sure what happened. And Ken?" she continued, her voice choking.

"Yes?"

"It looks really bad. The car caught on fire."

"Oh, God," he cried as he felt the tears squeeze

from his eyes.

Vivian took an audible breath. "They're not sure she's going to make it. They air-flighted her over to Bethesda North."

"Okay. Okay, Viv, I'm on my way now." He used the sleeve of his jacket to wipe his cheeks. He set the phone on its cradle and turned toward Stacy. His fingers shook as he turned the key. "I've got to get you home right now."

"Ken, what is it?"

"It's Amanda. She's been in an accident. A bad one. Happened on Spencer Mountain." He struggled with the words, choking out each painful syllable. "They're not sure she's going to survive."

Stacy cried, "Oh, God, no!" and collapsed back into the seat.

Jamming the gearshift, Ken shoved the car in reverse, turned, and peeled out of the parking lot into the street. He slammed on the accelerator, speeding down the road.

He heard her whisper, "Someone close to you will die," and she began to sob.

While he drove, he prayed. Frantic, desperate, guilty prayers to an uncaring God.

Staring through the windshield, he felt more tears, tears of guilt stream down his cheeks. He mumbled, "What have I done? *What* have I done?"

Chapter 66

The pounding inside his head would not stop.

Ken turned over and tried to ignore it, rolling to the other side in an effort to deaden the hammering. It didn't work. He had no idea how long it had been going on, but his temple throbbed with each repetition. The thumping sounded erratic, coming and going in waves. Then, as the pounding forced its way into his consciousness, he could make out someone calling his name. A voice shouted, demanded. He pushed his body up into a sitting position. This movement sent new pains slicing through his brain.

Sitting there, hands on either side of his face, Ken shook his head, trying to clear it. Then he got it. The infernal pounding didn't emanate from inside his skull but came from the front door. Struggling to clear his vision, he did a slow blink of his eyes and shook his head. He stared across the semi-darkness of the room, the only light escaping from the adjacent bathroom. Ken tried to read the clock, but with his bloodshot eyes the clock face appeared fuzzy. His head hurt and his stomach clenched. He belched, an ugly, uncontrolled eruption, releasing the horrible stink of his nasty breath.

The pounding returned, unabated, jerking his attention to the front door. Bam! Bam! Bam! Then he could make out the words, "Ken, I know you're in there. Come and open this damn door."

Even in his stupor, the voice sounded familiar, its tone somewhere between angry and desperate. A brief pause, followed by hammering on the door again. Bam! Bam! Bam!

"Ken, look, I'm not going anywhere, so you might as well open this door. I'm just as stubborn as you are and if you don't come and open this damn door, I'm going to break it down."

"Oh, all right, I'm coming," Ken croaked, his voice hoarse from disuse. "Stop hitting the damn door."

When he rose to his feet, he swayed and had to grab hold of the arm of the couch. His legs weak and numb, he stumbled down the short hall, lurching from one handhold to the next. Not bothering to turn on a light, his fingers fumbled in the dark with the lock till he found it and turned the deadbolt. The moment the latch cleared, the door was thrown open, knocking him on his butt. In the opening, Ken could make out the silhouette of a tall figure, who stepped through and slammed the door behind him.

The man glanced down at Ken, sprawled on the floor, and extended a hand to help him get up. "Man! You look terrible."

From the floor, Ken stared up at the figure and squinted, trying to get his foggy brain to cooperate. The dizziness flooded back and he shook his head again in an effort to fight the vertigo. Squinting, he focused on the outline of the tall body standing over him. "Bart? What the hell are you doing here?"

"Oh, you know, I was simply out looking for a jogging partner. From how you look on the floor there, maybe I better look elsewhere."

"You got that right. Now, get the hell out of here

and leave me alone," Ken squealed, not moving from his prone position.

Ignoring Bart's outstretched hand, Ken rolled his body to one side and, using the end of the stair rail, struggled to drag himself up off the floor. When he made it to his feet again, Bart slid one strong arm under Ken's armpit to steady him and he helped him back to the family room and onto the crumpled couch.

"God, you stink, boy. Ever heard of a shower?"

Ken thought his words held more mirth than bite and tried to ignore him.

Bart reached and switched on the light, bathing the dark room in sudden brilliance from the three sixty-watt bulbs in the fixture.

The bright light blinded Ken and he raised his right arm to shield his eyes. "Bart, give me a break. Turn the damn light off."

"Jeez, look at this place." Bart said. "And look at you."

Ken's glance rolled down his body. His clothes, a once-starched white shirt and dark, dress slacks he'd worn to the funeral, were now creased with ragged wrinkles. His feet bare, two pink protrusions stuck out through the end of the black pants cuffs. His fingers rubbed the stubble on his chin and one hand went to a disheveled mop of hair, black tufts matted to his head.

Bart's gaze roamed around the room and Ken did his best to follow the stare. Bart took in Ken's suit coat, the one that once matched the rumpled slacks he still wore, tossed onto the coffee table. The cop's eyes lit on the more than ten empty bottles of booze, mostly cheap rum and bourbon bottles and one of a nondescript red wine, strewn at the foot of the couch. A dark red, oval stain on the gray carpet lay just beyond the neck of the empty wine bottle.

A buzzing sound erupted from elsewhere in the house and Bart stomped off in that direction. A beat later, Ken heard the clink of the phone receiver onto the cradle. The one he'd left *off* the hook. Bart strode back into the living room, where Ken still slouched on the couch, struggling to adapt his eyes, and his brain, to the bright light.

"No wonder I couldn't reach you. You know the phone was off the hook?"

"No shit, Sherlock. You should be a detective," Ken growled, his voice becoming a little less hoarse with each sentence. "Maybe, I didn't want to be disturbed,"

"Well, maybe, some of your friends were worried about you. That is, if you still have any friends." Bart shook his head. "Ken, I hadn't heard a word from you since the funeral, more than two weeks. I thought, you know, I was worried something had happened to you. Now look at you."

"As you can see, I'm fine." Sitting on the couch, hand gripping the armrest, Ken glared back at his friend.

"Oh yeah, you look fine all right." The cop removed his cap and used it to gesture around the room again. "And look at this place. It's a pigsty. And it smells like a strip club the morning after. You throw up in here?"

"Look, buddy—" The sudden ringing of the phone interrupted Ken, the sound erupting from the small table in the corner of the room. Two rings passed as Bart looked from Ken to the phone and back.

"Aren't you going to get it?"

Ring.

"Probably some stupid telemarketer."

Ring.

Bart said, "At 10:30 at night, I don't think so. I'll get it."

"Don't—"

"Hello, this is the Parks' residence," announced Amanda in a bright female voice. "Ken and I are busy and can't come to the phone right now, but if you'll leave your name and number and any message, we'll get back to you."

As the voice from the grave spoke, Ken buried his face behind his outstretched fingers. He felt the knife of his guilt saw at his insides, cutting into vital organs, making him bleed. Or that's what it felt like.

The recording was followed by a series of beeps and then a brief period of silence. "Ken, this is…Stacy," a hesitant voice came through the speaker. "Ken, I'm pretty sure you're there. If you are, I'd really like a chance to talk with you."

Another pause and the caller cleared her throat. Bart looked at Ken and then at the recorder. Ken shook his head and turned away.

"Ken, you were there for me…If you could use somebody to talk to, I'm here. Okay?" the caller continued.

Bart shot another glance at Ken and rushed across the room, snatching up the receiver. "Stacy, don't hang up," he blurted into the phone. "It's Bart. No, Ken's okay…well, pretty much okay. I know it's late, could you come over here? Yeah, right now. Okay, I'll see you in a few minutes."

Ken stood and faced Bart, the blood in his face pulsing. "You had no right to do that. I don't want her to see me like this. Hell, I don't want anyone to see me like this."

"Then I guess we'll have to do something about that."

Bart grabbed his friend by the elbow and strong-armed him around the corner into the small shower stall in the first-floor bathroom. Bart reached in and turned on both knobs, the water spraying from the faucet.

"Hey, what the hell," Ken yelled, as he tried to duck out of the way of the spray.

"Stay put." Bart shoved him back under the shower. "I'll come back to get you in a few minutes."

Bart closed the shower door as the steam began to drift up and fill the small bathroom.

A few minutes later, Bart returned with a towel and some clothes. "I've grabbed an old jogging outfit so you could put something on." He reached in and turned off the water and stood over Ken, who had slumped to the floor. "Pull yourself together. Get out of those damn wet clothes, dry off, and get dressed, so we can talk."

"Maybe I don't feel like talking."

"Well, I do, so you'll have to humor me."

"Look, Bart, I know you mean well but—"

The chime of the doorbell stopped Ken.

"That must be Stacy. I'll get it." Bart stepped out of the bathroom, shutting the door behind him.

Chapter 67

Pissed but acknowledging he had little choice, Ken stripped off his drenched clothes and dumped them into the shower stall. After toweling off, he dragged on the jogging suit, brushed down his hair a little, and looked in the small mirror. Hell.

How had he come to this?

He recalled the meeting with Walters and O'Brien, where they insisted he take a few weeks off "for his own health." He remembered the hollow, helpless feeling then and at the funeral. He couldn't even be there for his son, Steven. Most of all, he couldn't shake the dreadful sense of guilt for Amanda's death.

God, he needed another drink.

He stumbled out of the bathroom and heard the voices of his two uninvited visitors coming from the kitchen. He headed there.

Bart, still in uniform Ken now realized, sat at the drop-leaf table, his face unreadable as usual. He held a mug of almost black liquid. Stacy, dressed in an oversized sweatshirt and faded blue jeans, stood by the stove, fiddling with the tea kettle. Atop the counter next to the stove, three TV dinners lay half-eaten, the brown and yellow contents spilling out and hardening on the Formica top. Next to the stove sat the open trash can, overfilled with the remnants of his earlier analgesics, empty glass vodka bottles, several dark long necks, and even a tall empty bottle of bourbon, a few amber drops clinging to its side. The room stunk of decaying food and stale beer. It reeked of despair. Ken knew he should've been ashamed.

What did it matter? The pain of Amanda's death gnawed at his gut.

"How about a cup of tea?" Stacy asked, offering a small smile.

Ken looked into her face and saw in those small emerald eyes an echo of his pain and something else. Hope?

He eyed the bottles in the trash. "I'd like something a lot stronger." He relented. "As long as I'm here, might as well."

Stacy poured the steaming water over a tea bag in a mug she'd retrieved from the cabinet. The new cherry cabinets Amanda had just purchased...without him. Now she was gone. He never even got to tell her how much he liked the new wood look.

Stacy set the mug on the table in front of the head seat. Bringing over her own mug, she sat down in the chair opposite Bart. They had him covered from both sides. Glancing from one to the other, Ken shrugged and took the chair between the two of them.

"Guys, I really appreciate what you're trying to do, but I have to deal with this my own way," Ken said, after he had taken the first sip of his tea.

"Yeah, you're doing that so well," Bart said. "I've got news for you, buddy. This is no social call. You know, I got other things to do with my time. I just found out something I think you should know."

"I guess you haven't heard, Bart. I'm no longer in the investigation business." Ken turned. "Look, Stacy,

I'm sorry. I know you aren't behind the drugs, but I wasn't much help anyway."

Stacy started to say something, but Bart stopped her. "Stacy, wait." He turned and looked at his jogging partner. "Look, pal, I don't know how else to break this to you. Your wife's death was no accident."

"What are you talking about?" Ken blurted out, feeling the wound tearing open again.

"Because of the car fire, it took us a while to figure it out," Bart explained. "Somebody cut the brake and fuel lines on Amanda's car, from what we figured. Probably the first time she hit the brakes hard, the line ruptured and the brake fluid ran out. Voila! No brakes. There was no way she was going to get off that mountain road alive."

"Oh, God," Stacy gasped.

Bart said, "I'm sorry, friend, but I thought you needed to know."

Stunned, Ken stared at his cop friend. "What about the fuel lines?"

"Oh, yeah," Bart continued, "that's why we didn't figure the whole thing out till today. You see, the fuel leaked from a slash in the line and spilled onto the hot engine and ignited. The fire melted most of the brake lines under the car, which pretty much covered up the sabotage. It took a while, but the lab boys were able to figure it out."

He paused a bit, hesitating, then asked, "Do you have any idea what Amanda was doing on Spencer's Mountain?"

"No, I haven't a clue," Ken said. "When I talked to her secretary and the others at her office, they said they didn't have any idea."

"Well, we can't be sure, but we think she may have met someone up there."

"What makes you think so?" Ken asked.

"Well, the light rain had washed some of them away, you know, but we think we've found a second set of tracks next to Amanda's tire tracks on the top ridge," Bart said and then continued on, "Michelin, good ones, used on lots of expensive cars."

"So what does that mean?" Stacy asked.

"I don't know. Maybe Amanda was somehow mixed up in the whole mess—" Bart began.

"No way," Ken said. "Amanda had her faults, but come on."

"Or she could've been lured up there," Bart continued. "We're pretty sure it was set up so she would have to use her brakes hard in order for the line to rupture coming down that slope."

"But if she's not involved, what sense does it make? Why Amanda?" Stacy voiced the question Ken had been thinking.

"Well, let's say, I don't believe in coincidence," Bart continued. "Hell, I don't know, maybe the killers thought Amanda's death would distract Ken and throw everybody off."

"Those bastards," Ken hissed between clenched teeth. "What kind of cold-blooded animals kill an innocent woman and four kids?"

"Five," interjected Bart.

"Five?" Stacy asked.

"We're still investigating but, with what we learned from Earl, we don't think Tricia Holloway died from natural causes. We're performing an autopsy tomorrow."

"Those bastards," Ken repeated. "I don't care what I have to do, I will get them."

"Easy, boy," tempered Bart.

"Easy nothing," screamed Ken. "They killed my wife…as a goddamn distraction! Christ, I told my son I thought I was responsible for Amanda's death. Steven called twice and left messages while I was…out. I couldn't even bring myself to call him back." He shook his head. "It looks like I was responsible, only not in the way I thought."

"Ken, don't start blaming yourself." Stacy said, shaking her head. "You had it right the first time. Those *bastards* are responsible for the deaths of five innocent children. They killed your wife, not you." Her voice got quiet. "We've got to stop them before more children die."

"How? We don't even know who they are. Hell, we don't know anything," Ken yelled at Stacy, his own anguish escaping in angry words.

"That's where you're wrong, buddy," Bart said. "We know more than you think. First, we know the kids are getting the drugs from someone at school." He raised his index finger. "Second, if we can believe what Tricia told you before she died from mysterious circumstances, the students are getting the drugs from a woman, and probably someone they trust…and fear." He raised his second finger. "Third," he went on and raised his ring finger for emphasis, "we know the supplier is known as the doctor. And fourth," raising his pinkie, "we know the drugs were coming into the school from the hospital—that is, if we believe Earl."

"And you said it yourself, Ken," Stacy chimed in, "the key is in who framed me. I've been thinking a lot about that since I got out. I think there may be more answers there."

"I think you've got something there, Stacy," Bart said. "I've got an idea. Ken, get some shoes on and grab a jacket. It's cold out there."

"What for?" Ken asked.

"Stacy, can you drive?" Bart asked, ignoring his friend's question. "I don't think this guy is quite ready to yet and the squad car might be a bit obvious."

"Sure," Stacy responded, "but where are we going?"

"We're going back to the scene of the crime. Do either of you two have keys to get into Foster?"

"Yeah, I do," Stacy and Ken replied almost in unison, and both looked at each other.

Chapter 68

Trespassing. B & E.

That's what leaped into Ken's mind as he, Bart, and Stacy skulked down the darkened school hallway. Stacy worked here, Ken visited every week, and Bart was a regular here. Still, they felt like intruders, eyes glancing over shoulders and peering into shadows, searching for real or imagined villains. They kept the lights off so the only illumination came from the exit sign and the flashlight Bart carried. The lighted red letters cast an eerie glow down the corridor. Stacy led and they hustled down the hallway, keeping their steps quiet. When they reached Stacy's classroom, Ken let out a long breath and noticed Stacy and Bart with a similar look on their faces. Relieved not to have been discovered, after Stacy had the door open, he hurried inside and hustled them in as well, closing the door behind them.

Stacy flipped the light switch by the door, illuminating the room. "Okay, what are we doing here?"

"Yeah, Bart, what do you expect to learn here?" asked Ken, gesturing around the room with his hands.

"We'll. I'm not exactly sure, you know," hedged the cop, "but my gut tells me the answer is here somewhere."

"Sure," Ken said, the sarcasm returning to his

voice. "Stacy, quick, look into each desk to see if we can find a secret, coded message that tells us who the drug dealer is."

Bart ignored Ken's comment. "I want to check out a few things. Stacy, can you open your locker for us? I want to have another look at where the drug tattoos were found."

Stacy stepped into the adjoining workroom and flipped the light on. She bent down and twisted the dial to find the right combination, but it wouldn't move. Figuring she'd misdialed in her haste, Ken encouraged her to try again. She repeated her efforts but with the same result. Clearly exasperated, she made one more unsuccessful attempt before quitting.

"I don't get it. I'm sure I'm using the right combination. I've had the same one for more than ten years, 8-26-18. But it doesn't work." Stacy looked confused and turned toward Ken. "Do you remember what combination you used when you got my books out the other week?"

"No, but it doesn't matter." Ken glanced up at Bart and Stacy as the idea struck him. "Remember, I told you they keep the combinations in the front office, and how Martha simply went into Carla's office and got it. Well, they can simply change the combinations the way we do with the kids' lockers."

Bart picked it up. "That means that Martha or Carla...or Wally or any teacher really could get Stacy's combination, you know, and get into her locker to leave the drugs. Of course, there were no fingerprints on the tattoo packages and none in the locker, except Stacy's."

Stacy said, "Hey boys, I don't want to rain on your parade, but I don't see where that gets us. We just figured out almost anybody who knows their way around here could have planted the drugs."

"You're right there," Bart agreed.

"Could it be something about the condo?" Ken asked.

Much to his surprise, all this was…helping. For the first time in a week, he was thinking about something other than Amanda's death. And his guilt for it. Something other than his failures and not wanting to go on.

Of course, he'd been over this terrain before by himself and came up empty. He took a deep breath. He hoped the three together might see something he missed.

Bart explained, "Well, we know Stacy didn't buy the condo in Marco Island. After the agent couldn't identify her, even Garcia had to concede he couldn't prove she did. But someone did purchase the unit and we don't know who that is. I figured it was probably some woman hired for the job or one of the perps in disguise, you know."

Both Stacy and Ken looked at their police friend with a question.

"Perpetrators," he said and the other two nodded. "Anyway, thanks to some behind-the-scene investigation by yours truly, I think I figured out how it was done."

"How?" asked Ken and Stacy in the same breath and glanced at each other.

"Whoever pulled it off had to have help inside the bank, but you know with that, it was relatively easy." Bart leaned back against the wall. "Most of the safeguards at the bank are on taking money out of accounts, not putting money in, so it was relatively easy to put the extra funds into your account, Stacy. They simply had to have an account in the bank as well."

"Okay, I'll bite," said Ken. "Who else have accounts at that bank? Probably everybody, right?"

"Not as many as you might think." The cop pulled a tattered notebook from his back pocket and thumbed through the worn pages till he found what he wanted. "Two of the dead boys' families bank there, the Waycrosses and the Thortons *and* Wally, Martha, and Dawn have accounts or CD's there. And three more have active savings and checking accounts." He paused briefly and looked at the other two. "Rachel Bedinghaus, Carla Michaels, and Jacqueline Highstreet."

"Rachel Bedinghaus," Ken exclaimed, "I'd almost forgotten." He turned to Bart. "In their investigation, did you guys look at Rachel as a possible suspect?"

Bart shook his head. "Not that I heard. I mean she was on the list of staff that interacted with the kids the day they died, but I don't think it went further than that. Why?"

"Well, after Stacy was arrested and I was getting a few things for her, I ran into Rachel in the hallway. She was coming out of the restroom and almost bumped into me. Anyway, when I looked into her face, I could've sworn I saw the signs of cocaine use."

When Bart didn't say any more, Ken continued. "Her eyes were red and she was sniffling all the time, complaining she had a cold. Well, if she was using cocaine, wouldn't it make sense to at least check to see if she was involved with dealing these other drugs? And you just said she banks there."

Bart nodded. "Okay, you have a point. Let's keep her in mind. Maybe she's connected somehow."

Stacy said, "I don't get it. How did anyone get the money from my account to the agent in Marco Island and make it look like I bought the condo?"

"Also, not as hard as you think," answered Bart, "but let me ask you a question first. How carefully do you review your statement every month?"

"Well…" Stacy responded, tilting her head and gesturing with her left hand.

"That's what I thought," Bart continued. "If you go back and examine your statements, I'll bet you'll find a notation for the money going in and coming out, probably on the same day. If you caught it, you know, you would've most likely thought the bank had made a mistake. Anyway, all it would take is somebody on the inside of the bank to submit your 'code' and authorize the bank transfer. The bank's security system would have checked to make sure there was money in your account and then would've approved it."

"Sounds almost too simple," said Ken.

"I know, but if you got somebody on the inside, it's not that hard. I haven't yet figured out who, but I'm getting closer." Bart paused. "If you think about it, it makes sense. The drug dealers need somebody to help launder the money after all. Who better than somebody who works for the bank."

All three looked at each other and didn't speak for a while. Then Ken said, "I still don't see where that gets us."

"It gets us closer, but not there yet," responded Bart.

"Closer to what?" Ken quipped.

"Closer to knowing who the drug pusher is," Bart said and smiled his wry, cop smile.

Chapter 69

"I must be missing something. What else do we have?" Stacy asked.

"Well, Garcia's other piece of circumstantial evidence is the email messages," answered the DARE officer, "but I don't know enough about that techy stuff to be helpful."

Ken stared at his two friends. Bart shrugged and Stacy gestured with both hands, palm out. Ken said, "All right. God knows I'm no expert, but it's obvious I know more than the two of you combined."

He moved to the corner of the room where the computer sat on the beige metal stand and pulled the clear plastic cover off the machine. As he did, his action scattered gray dust particles in the air.

"Looks like maybe the sub hasn't had the students use the computer much." He pushed the start button and after a few seconds, the familiar logo of the district system came up with a color graphic of the school mascot behind the words. Ken typed a few keystrokes and turned to Stacy. "Okay, what's your user name?"

Stacy's only response was to close one eye and wrinkle her nose.

He should've been frustrated but her expression made him chuckle. "Stacy, what do you type in to get into the network?" Ken tried again, his tone a little pedantic.

"Oh, that. THOMPSONSA."

"No spaces. T-H-O-M-P-S-O-N-S-A." Ken hit the keys and the letters appeared on the screen. "Okay, Stacy what's your password?" He paused a bit. "You do remember your password, don't you?"

"Of course. My password is Brent. B-R-E-N-T."

As she spelled out each letter, Ken typed it on the keyboard and a series of X's appeared on the screen. All three waited, watching the green screen and the tiny picture of a man thinking. In a few seconds, the screen responded, displaying the words "UNAUTHORIZED PASSWORD" on the screen.

Ken stared at the small blinking cursor. "You sure that's your password? You sure you didn't change it and forget?"

"No, I didn't change it and forget," insisted Stacy. "Ken, I changed it not that long ago. And you know why I used that as my password. I'm sure that's my password. Or was, at least."

Ken leaned back in the chair and folded his arms across his chest. "Well, then, somebody has locked you out of the system."

"Why would they do that?" Stacy asked.

"I don't know, but I sure want to find out." Ken paused again and raised his index finger to his head, tapping his forehead. Let me try mine." He quickly typed the eight keys and the screen asked for his password. He paused a second to clear his head and it was Stacy's turn.

"Ken, you do remember your password, don't you?" Stacy said, mimicking his earlier words but grinning.

Sitting on the computer chair, Ken glanced back at

her. "Yes, Stacy," he said softly. "I had to think a bit because I have to change it so often. I changed it again two weeks ago." Then he smiled slightly and Stacy watched him hit six keys, S-T-A-C-Y-1, as the six X's appeared on the screen.

Stacy's gaze moved from the blinking screen to Ken's face. The surprise registered on her features, but neither spoke. A short bleep diverted their attention back to the screen.

When he glanced back at the computer, Ken saw the organized display of the network menu. Using the mouse, he highlighted the label "email" and clicked the mouse button with his finger. After another brief pause, the image changed again. Without taking his eyes off the computer screen, he spoke to Bart and Stacy. "When I started looking into the drugs, I made a copy of the email file the police confiscated from your computer. Then I sent the copy to my mailbox. It should still be there."

Using the mouse, he selected "Parks Mailbox" and pulled the menu down. Finding the "Inbox," he clicked the button again. A new box appeared on the screen containing dates and abbreviated titles. All three heads moved closer to the screen, peering at the lines of text. Ken moved his right hand to the screen and used his index finger to point to each line as he read the entries. He got about halfway down the screen before anyone spoke.

"I don't see any line with my name on it," Stacy said and turned to Ken. "Do you?"

"No," Ken said, "and it should be right here." As he pointed to the top half of the screen, Bart and Stacy leaned in closer. "These entries are listed chronologically, in the order in which they were received. You see I got this message on October 19th," Ken said, pointing to the first line of text. "I've kept it because it has some details about proficiency tests that I would need later." He moved his finger down the rows of entries. "These next messages are dated after November second. The ones from your email should be right here." He touched the screen for emphasis. "But they're not."

"Okay, I give," said Bart, clearly confused, "what does all that mean?"

"It means someone has gotten into my computer, used my password, and erased some file, these files." The tension in Ken's voice rose, his finger stabbing at the screen.

Bart asked "How did they do that? I thought you told me everybody's access is supposed to be private."

"That's the way the system is supposed to work, but obviously somebody has found a way around it." Ken's voice went pensive again. "All of a sudden, I'm really anxious to see those email files."

"If you want, we can head over to the station," Bart volunteered. "Garcia has a disk with them in the evidence locker."

"I don't think so, Bart. I want to have a look at the *original* files." Ken paused a second. "And I know where to find them, I think." As he spoke, Ken pointed his left index finger in the air and then turned and aimed it at Stacy. "Do you know where they keep the file server for your building's network?"

The same puzzled response Ken saw earlier showed on her face.

"You know, the main computer, the one the

school's programs are stored on, like your attendance program."

Stacy shrugged her shoulders and flashed a timid grin.

"You really don't know much about your building's technology, do you?"

Stacy shook her head and Bart interrupted, "What's the big deal, Ken? Why would you need the server anyway?"

"Oh, what a pair I have here? Welcome to the almost 21st century," Ken said. "The file server is the brains of the network, and, what's more important, it's the memory of the network. It has a system called a tape back-up that records all the files on the network. Unless somebody's messed with the tape, the original email files will still be stored there."

"Ken?" Stacy's asked, "Is the file server what the computer technician works on when the system crashes?"

"Yeah, sure. He has to get into the file server to get the system up and running."

"Then I know where it is," Stacy added. "Whenever the system crashes, Michaels complains because the technician has to be in her office. That must be where the file server is."

"Bingo. Let's go have a look." Ken's voice had gained a slight edge of optimism. He used the few commands needed to shut down the computer and then turned it off. Picking up the cover, Stacy replaced it, careful to leave the computer the same way they had found it. In a few more seconds, they were out the door, lights off, Stacy's key turning in the lock.

The three figures moved quietly down the hallway,

stealth returning to their movements in the corridor. Stacy's hushed whisper broke the silence. "Ken, I don't have a key to get into the office, do you?"

"I should." On reflex, he reached into the right pocket of his pants. "I might if I had my regular clothes on." Ken glared at Bart. "Right now at home on the floor of my shower stall is a ring of master keys, one of which has "Foster" engraved on it. A lot of good it will do us."

"Uh…um, could I help ya folks?"

All three figures jerked and spun around.

Chapter 70

Bart recovered first. "Wally! You scared the hell out of us. I didn't know you could move around so quietly."

Wally flashed a devilish grin in response. "Oh sure. I'm just full of surprises, ain't I, Mr. Parks?"

When he recognized the custodian, Ken relaxed and walked across the narrow hallway and Stacy joined him.

Wally's face lost its joviality. "Ken, I'm real sorry about the missus. I couldn't believe it when I heard about it. I didn't know the lady that well, but the few times I saw her, she was always nice to me. Anyway, my missus says to tell you she's real sorry too."

Ken nodded in response.

"Wally?" Stacy's soft voice interrupted, and she stepped in front of the janitor. "There is something you can do to help us. We need to get into the office to check out something on the server. Can you get us in?" Ken saw the twinkle in her eye and heard her plaintive tone. It worked on Wally.

"For you, Mrs. T, be glad to." Wally grinned as he moved his hand from where it had rested atop the broom handle and plunged it into his deep pocket, retrieving a monstrous ring of keys. As he swung them around they jingled, the sound reverberating down the darkened hallway. Both Ken and Bart glanced around, eyes darting down opposite sides of the hall, while Stacy smiled nervously at Wally. The custodian brought out a thin, pocket flashlight and shone it on the ring of keys. "Let's see. I know it's one of these here." Wally flipped each key on the ring as the small penlight hit it.

The custodian seemed to be enjoying the attention and took his time. Ken was used to his grandstanding, but tonight he was worried about being discovered. Even though Ken was still the Assistant Superintendent, he was supposed to be on leave. And Stacy had been suspended, pending the investigation and banned from school premises. And Bart? He glanced down the hall again, both ways. He didn't want to have to answer any difficult questions.

Three-fourths of the way around the ring, Wally found the one he wanted. "Here it is, I think." He inserted the selected key into the lock and opened the door, waving his arm ceremoniously.

Ken and Bart stepped through the doorway into the outer office. As Stacy followed then, she patted Wally's hand on the door handle and said, "Thanks." Then she walked through the office and joined her friends at an interior door.

The plaque on the door read "Carla Michaels, Principal. Knock before entering." Ken turned the handle, but found it locked too.

"Wally, do you have the key for this office?" Ken turned and asked the janitor who leaned on the outer doorframe.

"Nossir. Ain't nobody got keys to her office, 'cept Carla Michaels. Even have t' clean it durin' the day when she's there."

"Oh great, now what do we do?" asked Stacy.

"I got this," Bart said.

Nudging Ken out of the way, he stepped in front of the locked door. Reaching inside a pants pocket, he retrieved a small, slender metal tool that looked like a dental instrument or a crooked steel toothpick. He crouched down so his head was level with the door handle and brought the metal tool to the lock. He handed Ken the flashlight.

"Hold that on the lock so I can see what I'm doing." As Bart worked, he kept his eyes focused ahead and spoke. "None of you has seen this. That includes you, Wally." He turned and glanced back at the figure of the janitor, still in the doorframe.

"Seen what?" Wally said, the mischievous grin returning to his face. Bart smiled and turned his attention to the lock.

Ken asked, "Where'd you learn to do that? I didn't know they gave lessons in lock picking at the academy?"

"Hardly. But when you spend much of your time with the criminal element, you're bound to pick up a few bad habits, you know. And some of them can come in handy from time…to…time." As Bart came to the last word, he turned the handle and opened the door.

Ken stepped into the inner office, followed by Stacy and Bart. Wally, with the support of his push broom, moved from one office doorway to the next. Ken glanced around the space and eyed the file server stacked between the walnut credenza and a filing cabinet.

"No wonder I never noticed it. Carla put the cabinet alongside it."

He rolled the chair from behind Carla's large

wooden desk over to the server and sat down, turning on the computer. The series of graphics they'd seen before reappeared. After he entered his user name, Ken typed in ADMIN followed by his password and turned to face his two partners. "I'm authorized as a system administrator for the district and this way I can look at the network monitoring programs." Before he finished talking, the monitor changed and a blank screen appeared with a white, blinking box. He quickly typed "email.Thompsonsa" and the command appeared in white on the darkened screen. Below the typed line scrolled the word "password."

Stacy straightened up and spoke to Ken. "Oh great. So now what do we do? We don't have my new password."

Ken said, "No we don't, but we know somebody else found out your old password and changed it. If this was part of the attempt to frame you, maybe we can figure it out."

"How?" Bart asked.

"Well, when people pick a password, they usually pick some word from their lives, like Stacy picked 'Brent.' All we need to do is try to think like the real dealer and try to guess what password they might have chosen for Stacy."

"Like what?" asked a skeptical Bart.

"Um, let's try Marco," Ken said, as he punched the letters.

The computer's response was "invalid password." He sat at the keyboard, thinking, his fingers ready.

"How 'bout drugs?" called the custodian from the doorway. All three turned in unison. "Well, mebbe, the person doin' the framin' on Stacy would use that as part of it. Hell, I don't know. I'm jus' tryin' to help."

Ken typed the letters, hit return, but got the same response from the program. "No luck, but you got the idea, Wally." Ken nodded at the janitor.

"Okay," Bart offered "how about the obvious. Try money…or maybe Benjamins." Ken did, but the computer rejected both passwords.

"No, not drugs or money," Stacy said and paused, her finger on the bridge of her nose and her head tilted slightly to the left. "Try tattoo."

Ken did and as he typed, the six X's appeared on the screen. There was a momentary pause as they held their breath, and then the screen shifted, unveiling a log of Stacy's email entries. "Yes," Ken practically shouted.

He moved the mouse to highlight the menu labeled "mailbox" and then clicked on the "inbox." The grid on the screen showed about twelve lines and the three leaned in closer to the computer.

"I remember what the files look like," Ken said. "It's these two." Pointing to the two entries near the end of the list, he moved the mouse to highlight the first of the two. He clicked and the screen shifted again, displaying the first email message.

Masker@mail.grafton-internet-cafe.com
New Merchandise
To: Thompsonsa@mail.portsmouth.edu
On Tues 10 Oct 95 10:20 AM EST
The merchandise you ordered is in and will be delivered Wed. Also have a special shipment of foreign stamps available bundled at 100$. Grateful for your continued business.

Ken turned, trying to think of a simple way to

explain. "Whoever knew your password could get into your email and accept or send messages, *and* make it look like it was you." Then he turned and addressed Bart. "Did you guys ever figure out where these messages were coming from and who was sending then?"

"The tech expert at the station, Buckwater, checked it out and it turned out to be a dead end. You know, one of these places that book themselves as internet cafes. You can come in, have a cup of coffee and a bagel, and send or get email messages there. Absolutely no way to trace who this masker is, Buckwater said."

"It *wasn't me.* I've never been to an internet café. Looks like another dead end." Stacy jabbed at the screen. "And this makes it look like this masker is some partner of mine. You guys are not making me feel any better."

Using the mouse, Ken closed that window and returned to the email menu. He clicked on "outbox" and revealed an even shorter list. He peered at the computer and spoke without taking his eyes off the screen. "There's an entry here from you, Stacy, to this 'masker' guy on the fifth. That's the—"

Stacy broke in, "The day the boys died. Yeah. That date is kind of seared into my memory."

Ken clicked on the message and the screen shifted again, revealing another email. The three leaned in close and read the message together.

Thompsonsa@mail.portsmouth.edu
Next Shipment
To: Masker@mail.grafton-internet-cafe.com
On Thur 5 Oct 95 3:25 EST
The last set of stamps are a big hit. Sold out almost

immediately. Have more buyers ready. Let me know when they can be delivered.

"Maybe it's only me," Stacy said, "but I don't see the connection to drug dealing. Can one of you guys enlighten me?"

"According to Garcia," Bart answered, "the merchandise in the messages are drugs and the word 'stamps' is slang for the drug tattoos."

Stacy nodded, scanning the screen to reread the message. "Hey," she blurted, "I couldn't have sent this email."

"We know you didn't—" Ken began, but Stacy cut him off.

"I didn't say 'didn't send.' I said 'couldn't send!' Look at the time of this email message."

Both men stared at the screen and Ken said, "So?"

"Well according to the computer memory here, this message was sent at 15:35:14. 3:25 p.m., right?" Stacy said.

"Yeah. So?" Ken asked.

"Because at the time this was sent, I was on the road to Camp Haven, halfway between here and Collin Gorge. There is no way I could've sent the last message."

"But you were supposed to be here?" asked Ken.

"What?" Stacy said.

"At 3:25, you would normally be here at school still, wouldn't you?"

"Yeah, sure. The students are dismissed by 3:15 and staff have to stay till 3:45. But because Rachel got sick, I left around 3:00 to go up to Camp Haven to take her place."

"Who here at Foster knew about that? About you

leaving early?" Ken asked.

"Camp officials called Martha around 2:30, I think, and she asked me to go. She said Carla was at a meeting or something, and was due back later. So Dawn covered my class for me and I took off. Anyway, doesn't that prove I couldn't have sent that message?"

"It certainly does," Ken said, "but it may do more than that. It may tell us who is framing you."

An "ah-ha" moment hit him. He knew something that might actually make a difference. That possibility kicked his depression and anxiety aside.

Bart asked. "How? What are you driving at?"

Ken turned back to the computer, striking keys as he spoke. "When we installed this network, we set up several ways to monitor computer use. One of these monitoring systems keeps a record of what computer logs onto the system and when." As he spoke, his fingers danced across the keys, sending the program through several commands. "Stacy, give me your user name again."

"Thompsonsa." As she spoke, Ken entered the letters. A few seconds passed as the three watched and then a chart of numbers appeared on the screen.

"I know it looks complicated, but it's not." As Ken moved the mouse to scan down the list, the numbers scrolling past, the screen gave the momentary impression of rolling. When he saw what he wanted he clicked the mouse and stopped the display. "This is the record for the date we want to see—100595." He pointed to a line on the screen and Bart and Stacy leaned in closer again. "The numbers in these columns show your activity for that date—or whoever was logging on as you." Ken's index finger moved across the screen horizontally. "Here, this shows you logged into the system at 8:47," and he pointed to a number on the screen showing "084715."

"That's about right," Stacy said. "Tammy and Candice are usually the first students here in the morning and they always want to get on the computer. I usually turn it on about then and get them onto the network, so they can use the math program."

"Okay, and it shows here that you logged off the system at 2:33." As he spoke, Ken's index finger pointed to a number reading "143306." He turned and looked at his cop friend. "Am I going too fast for you?"

"Very funny. Just get to the rest of it," Bart said, rolling his hand.

"Okay," Ken laughed. He realized this was the first time he had felt even slightly normal since his wife's death. "This next column shows the node." Seeing the puzzled look on the faces of his two friends, he went on, "The node is the location on the network where you logged on, and the number indicates which computer you were on. It might look complicated, but the code is really simple," he explained, pointing to a number Bart and Stacy read over his shoulder as "158237." "The first three numbers—158—indicate the building, Foster, the first building with grades five through eight and the last three—237—would be your room number."

"It is."

"Anyway, that indicates the location read by the file server," Ken continued. "This next entry in your file shows that you logged off at 2:33 and then logged on again at 3:28."

"I already explained that's not possible. I was on the road to Camp Haven by then."

"Hold on to that, Stacy. I'm not done yet. According to the server, this time when 'you' logged on, you were at a different station. See, it shows the node as being 158110. Okay, whose room is 110?"

"You're asking me?" Stacy said. "I'm lucky to know my own room number."

Ken asked, "Could that be Rachel Bedinghaus' room number? Maybe she got your password somehow and sent the email?"

"I don't think so. Rachel's room is down the hall from mine so it would have to be two hundred something, I think. Besides, she'd gotten sick at Camp Haven and was heading home then. At least, she was supposed to be."

Ken said, "Maybe she came here and planned to set you up."

Bart said, "Let's go out in the hallway to find out." He stepped into the outer office, Stacy and Ken following, and they saw Wally still leaning against the doorframe. The three stopped in their tracks to look at the custodian. He flashed a wide grin.

"Well, Wally, whose room is it?" Bart asked.

"I wondered when you was going t' get t' me." He paused a second and looked back at the three. "You're standing in it."

Chapter 71

A momentary silence fell over the small group, then Bart said, "Holy shit."

"Carla?" exclaimed Stacy.

"Sure, it makes sense if you think about it," Ken explained. "She had access to all the kids on the edge, all the 'potential customers.' They show up in the principal's office every week. *That's* why James made sure he was sent to the principal's office every Friday." He smacked his head with one palm. "God, I am so dense. It was all staring me in the face."

Bart said, "Don't be too hard on yourself. You got us this far." He glanced over at Stacy. "And, as principal, I bet Carla would be in the best position to find out about your past."

"The kids are terrified of her anyway," Ken said. "I thought it was only her tough discipline stand, but maybe it was something else altogether. No wonder Tricia wouldn't say who it was."

Ken stopped and another thought dawned on him. "And she would have no trouble getting the drugs off the bus Earl drove. No one would have suspected anything seeing her checking out the bus."

"Oh my God," said Stacy. "I bet Tricia went to *her* after she came to me, and Carla got her to tell her who the molester was." She shook her head in disbelief and then a new recognition flickered in her eyes. "Maybe

Tricia wasn't just a random tattoo customer."

Bart said, "But Carla couldn't have had anything to do with Tricia's death—assuming it was murder—she never went to the hospital when Tricia was there. We were monitoring visitors."

"That must've been her accomplice," Ken said and the other two looked at him. "Someone had to put the drugs on the bus at the hospital, the 'doctor'—if we believe Earl."

"Who's her accomplice?" asked Stacy.

Ken shrugged. "I don't know."

Stacy snapped her fingers. "Oh, remember how Carla always bragged she knew more about our computer systems than anyone. If anybody could have gotten into the system and changed passwords, it would've been her."

Then her voice changed. "I've got it. I think I just figured out how she knew my password. A few weeks ago, she called me to her office and said the system was having trouble with my password. She told me I needed to change my password, which I did, right in front of her. She could easily have watched me type in BRENT."

"Wait a minute," cautioned Bart, "if she's such a technology whiz, how come she didn't know the system would record the log-in at a different location?"

"Simple," said Ken. "She's not cleared for administrator status for the system. She doesn't know how the network monitoring systems work. No one does, except me and Craig, the IT guy. She probably never gave it a thought we can track use and locations."

"Uh-um." Wally cleared his throat.

Ken glanced up at the custodian who was grinning,

still slouched in the doorway. "Okay, Wally what is it?"

All three heads now turned toward the janitor.

"Do you know something about this?" Bart asked.

"Ya could say that."

"Well, out with it," Ken blurted.

"I wan' an agreement first." Wally looked down at the floor and dragged the scarred toe of his work boot across the pattern. "If I tell ya what I know, I wanna be sure you'll protect me. I need to be sure I won't lose my job over this." He looked up, his stare moving from Bart to Ken.

"I'll do what I can—" began Ken.

"Not good enough. When this all comes down, I don't wanna git hit by the fallout. And I don't wan' my past used against me."

Ken said, "Okay, Wally, tell you what I'll do. If we get this unraveled and *you're not part of it*, I promise I'll do everything I can to protect your job."

Wally thought it over for a bit and must've decided it was enough. He nodded. "When ya said Carla, Stacy, it kinda made sense to me. I know I'm not s'posed to say this, but I never really liked the woman. Oh, I know, she's all sugar n' nice to the parents and all, but she can be downright sneaky. I seen it."

Wally started rambling. "I always thought there was somethin' about that woman. I can't tell ya how many times I'd go home at night n' tell the missus 'I jus' don't trust that woman.' "

"Wally?" Ken's one word conveyed more of an unspoken command than a question. The custodian got the message.

"Anyway, about two weeks ago, I think it was the night of the DARE awards assembly, I think it was that night, but so much has happened with your wife's death and all, Ken. Oh, sorry."

"Wally?" The inflection in Ken's voice rose.

"Okay, okay. I was cleanin' up after the assembly. You wouldn't believe what a mess those kids leave that auditorium in after that night. Programs, cups, napkins everywhere. Bunch of the kids even threw away their certificates, would ya believe?"

The other three simply stared at the janitor. "Anyways, I go to my cart t' get trash bags, t' put all this in and there ain't none there. Les musta used the last one up and didn't refill 'em. Lester can be the laziest guy sometime, ya know that?"

Stacy nodded, but Bart and Ken continued staring. Wally must've read their faces because he hurried on.

"We keep those bags in the janitors' closet by the teachers' lounge down your hallway, Stacy. While I'm down there, I decided I'll git myself a drink. So I git a Pepsi out of the pop machine in the lounge and sit down in that old, worn blue chair—for jus' a minute, mind you—and that's when I heard it."

He stopped, apparently waiting for their reaction. It didn't take long.

"Heard what?" Bart snapped.

"Well, I don't know…least, I didn't at the time. When you work the night shift as long as me, you get to know the sounds of the building. I heard somethin' out of place. Kinda sounded like a woman moanin', ya know." He raised both hands up. "Hey, with everything' happenin' 'round here, ya can't be too careful. Anyways, I go out into the hallway to check it out and I don't hear anymore. I'm jus' about ready to head back to the auditorium n' I see n' hear someone walkin' down the hallway toward the side exit. So I duck back into the area by the lounge door so they can't see me."

"Why'd you worry about them seeing you?" Bart asked.

Wally said, "I dunno. I had a feeling, is all."

"They. How many did you see?" Ken asked.

"Two. I seen two figures and heard two talkin', quiet like."

"Who were they? Could you tell who they were?" Ken pushed.

"Sure I could tell. When ya work at night all these years, ya get use t' seein' in the dark, jus' like a bat."

"Wally—" It was Bart, this time, though a little gentler.

"It was Carla alrighty n'…Doc O'Brien."

No one spoke for a moment, then Stacy said, "So what does that mean? Wasn't he at the DARE graduation? They could've merely been working on school business late."

"Mebbe, but I don't think so. They was working all right…but not on no school business." He winked at both men. "You know what I mean."

"Spell it out," Bart said.

Wally grinned again. "When they walked past the light of the exit sign, Carla looked all flushed and O'Brien was wiping sweat off his head and neck. An' both were smiling like a couple of foxes in a henhouse. Or maybe I should say cathouse." He blushed. "Excuse me, Stacy."

"Why not?" Bart responded. "You know, two consenting adults. And that would explain the pusher's nickname of the doctor."

"And that also might explain why the good Dr. O'Brien was so compassionate as to relieve me of my responsibilities on this investigation," Ken mumbled.

Stacy added, "Yeah, after he had your wife killed."

The mention of Amanda's death sobered them all, even Wally. Ken felt his gut clench again. No one spoke for a few minutes.

In a quiet voice, Stacy asked, "Okay, but where does that put us…er, me? What does all this prove?"

Bart shook his head. "Unfortunately it doesn't prove anything, at least not legally."

When Ken started to object, Bart continued. "Look, she could always claim somebody else came in and used her computer. And even if Wally is right about the rendezvous, it doesn't prove anything. Besides it would just be his word against the good doctor and the esteemed principal."

"Are you telling me, there's nothing we can do?" Stacy asked.

"No, I didn't say that. I said we don't have anything that will stand up in court…yet," Bart continued.

"I can almost see that cop brain working," Ken said. "Okay, what do you have in mind?"

"Well, it will take a little doing, but I think we can pull it off." Bart flashed the wry cop smile again. "I think it's time to catch us some really bad guys."

Chapter 72

Stacy sat in her own, comfortable chair—or at least, it used to be her chair—and she rocked slightly back and forth. Terrified now, she could hear her own breathing and her heart pounding in her ears and thought she might hyperventilate. Two hours ago, when Bart had gone over the plan, it sounded plausible, almost reasonable. He made her believe it would work. Now that she was here, it didn't seem so simple. Her stomach tightened further.

Why had she agreed? She was not cut out for this.

The waiting did her in. Each minute that crawled by she thought of a hundred ways this could go south. And none of them boded well for her. Her eyes darted around the darkened room, or at least what she could see in the shadows. She tried to practice the slow, measured yoga breathing she taught her students. It did little good.

She decided to leave and stood up. Too late. She heard the sounds.

As she strained to listen, she heard the footsteps get louder as someone approached the door, footfalls echoing in the empty corridor. Stacy sat and stared in the darkness, her gaze fixed on the door handle. Her concentration so intense, she jerked when the dull, brass handle began to turn.

"Stacy," called the familiar, syrupy-sweet voice as

the door edged open. "Are you here, dear?"

Stacy thought she could detect a hint of nervousness in the voice and that settled her a bit.

"Come on in, Mrs. Michaels," Stacy called back, fighting to keep her voice calm. Then, as she saw the hand stretch for the light switch, she added, "I'd rather you'd leave those off—at least for now."

Carla Michaels removed her hand and shoved the door all the way open. As she stood in the doorway, the hallway emergency lights silhouetted her figure in the opening, as if her body emanated darkness against the faint background of light.

"Well, okay, if you wish, dear. We're certainly melodramatic tonight," replied Michaels. "Are you okay? We were all so concerned about you when you were in jail. I was so glad when the teachers' organization took up donations so you could post bail. I went ahead and contributed, even though I'm not a member. I hope that was okay. I couldn't stand it to think of one of my people in one of those horrible cells."

Stacy watched as the principal slipped through the doorway and moved into the room, moving toward the desk where she sat.

"When you called, you said you had information on the drugs and you made it sound awfully urgent, so I came right away. So here I am, at 12:30 at night. It must be important if it couldn't wait till tomorrow morning." Michaels' tone sounded like that of an older sister who knows better but tolerates her younger sibling anyway.

"The information I have, I don't think you'll want *anyone else* to hear," Stacy said, gripping the arms of her chair to keep her composure.

"Whatever are you talking about, dear?"

Stacy wished she could see the woman's face in the darkness, but Bart had argued it would work better this way. She hoped he was right. Still, she thought she could hear Michaels' haughty confidence cracking around the edges of her words.

"Okay, Carla, you can cut the act. I know everything."

"I'm sure I don't know what you're talking about."

"Carla, cut the crap." Stacy's palm slapped the desk, and she heard Carla jump. Good. "It's only you and me here, so there's nobody to impress. And, if you play your cards right, I will be out of your hair forever."

"What is it that you think you know?" Michaels edged closer to the teacher's desk.

"Let's just say…hypothetically, I've discovered who's dealing drugs to the kids." Stacy paused a bit and rose from the chair. As she talked, she sidled away from the advancing Michaels. "Let's say, I even know who's the dealer's associate, or should I say, bed partner. And let's say, I even know how I was framed…hypothetically speaking." Stacy paused to stare into the other woman's face, or what she could make out of her features. "I thought this might be something the school officials and the cops would like to know."

"Who else might possess this 'hypothetical' knowledge?" Michaels tried to appear calm, but Stacy heard the surprise creep into her voice.

"So far, only me. You see, since I got out on bail, I've been busy."

"What about your friend, Parks?" Michaels asked.

"I don't know. Last I heard he was pretty devastated by the untimely death of his wife. Quite a coincidence, wouldn't you say?"

Michaels kept moving and Stacy could make out the whites of her eyes darting around the darkened classroom.

"Okay, Thompson, what do you want?"

Stacy didn't answer right away. She had to keep moving to stay away from Michaels. "Two things. First, I want what everybody wants, money and lots of it."

"And how much would we be talking about...hypothetically?" Michaels sounded almost sincere.

"I was thinking around $250,000. Oh, and I'll sign the deed of the new condo over to you. Something tells me I won't be able to make much use of it." Stacy grinned, though her insides churned. "Pretty sweet deal, I think."

"And what does this *investment* purchase?"

"My silence and my distance." Stacy worked to make her voice hard, cold, like a steely negotiator. If this was going to work, Carla had to believe her. "Look, the way I see it, no matter how this turns out, my reputation is shot here anyway. With a little nest egg, I can get away from here and start over. I've done it before."

"I know you have dear. I know all about your...troubles in Seattle."

Both women had kept moving, Michaels trying to crowd Stacy, Stacy edging away from her. By now they had switched positions. Stacy saw Carla glanced past her to the door and she turned her head.

"You said two things. What else?" Michaels asked.

Stacy turned back to face her. "Oh yeah. Well, the second's not as important, but I'd like to know something. Why me?"

"What?"

"Why me, Carla? You could have picked anybody, Chris, Rachel, Dawn, even Jacqueline. Why frame me?"

The woman's reaction to the question made Stacy shiver. Carla gave a laugh that began low and stretched into a long, throaty cackle. "Since you'll soon be gone, one way or the other, I guess it won't hurt to tell you. There were several reasons I picked you. First, you're a loner. No family and no real friends. Nobody to really care what happens to you. Sad state of affairs." Her smirk broadened. "Sorry, honey, but that's the truth."

Carla laughed again, and Stacy could tell she was enjoying herself. "Then, since I know you never pay that much attention to your bank statements—I overheard you sharing that little tidbit with Dawn—I figured out to make it look like you bought the condo, and gave you a huge motive."

Stacy realized Carla was simply toying with her, but for this to work she needed her to play along a little longer. Stacy prayed Bart's plan would work.

Michaels continued, "Oh, you know, I like to know *everything* I can about my teachers." She flashed an evil grin, two red lips Stacy could see in the dim light. "Well, I knew from your application you grew up in Seattle, but somehow never wanted to talk about it and that got me to thinking. So on a hunch, I did some research on the internet and did a search of a few years before you came here. It's amazing what you can learn on the web, don't you think?"

Michaels looked across for confirmation and when Stacy didn't react, she went on, her voice breathy with excitement. "Anyway, I accessed newspaper files from Seattle for before you joined our little family here at Portsmouth. The whole story was all there in the *Seattle Herald*—though I saw you changed your name. But your photo gave you away. When I found out all about your somewhat sordid past, well, the rest simply fell into place. I squirreled that little piece of information away for a rainy day. I've had you as my ace in the hole for a few years."

Michaels stopped moving and Stacy did the same. The principal laughed again, a sound that made Stacy's skin crawl.

Michaels continued, "Do you know what the best part of it was? Watching the reaction of everyone when they saw you taken away in handcuffs. I'm proud to say I got Garcia to do that. You, Ms. Do-Gooder herself, the teacher who *cares* about all her kids, who could reach kids nobody else could. That was the sweetest part."

Stacy should have seen it coming, but when it happened, it caught her completely off guard. As she'd moved to stay away from Michaels, Stacy stepped in front of the doorway, her back to the opening. One moment she was moving, shifting her feet to keep her distance, and the next she was frozen in place, caught in the ice-like grip of two huge hands. Stacy struggled but it did no good. She opened her mouth to scream. A hand clamped over it. The tight grip on her jaw made her wince and Stacy felt tears roll down her cheeks.

From behind her, a male voice spoke, "Now, isn't this sweet? Come back to visit your room one more time before leaving? Or perhaps just returning to the scene of the crime." Everett O'Brien added his own haughty laugh. "What do you think, my dear?"

"Maybe she came back for sentimental reasons," Michaels said. "I guess we could call the police since she was told to stay away from Foster as condition of her bail."

O'Brien's two large hands twisted Stacy's head toward him. "Did I hear you say all you wanted is a little money and you'll leave town?"

Stacy tried to nod her head yes, but his rough hands restrained her. After a bit, he dropped his hand from her face. "Go ahead and scream. There's nobody here. I already checked. Nobody will hear you."

Stacy prayed O'Brien was mistaken. She counted on Bart…and Ken. *He* wouldn't let her down.

Michaels had now moved in front of her. "Don't be too hard on her, Everett. All she wants is a mere $250,000. That's all."

Michaels' hand flew up and slapped Stacy hard across the face. Stacy staggered back and felt the sting of the hand on her skin. At the same time, O'Brien's hand gripped Stacy's left shoulder and the fingers of his other hand encircled her small neck from behind. Stacy couldn't move. The throbbing pain erupting from the back of her neck screamed at her to be very careful. Her eyes stared wide with fright. She had no need to fake it.

"So you worked this all out on your own, did you? Are you sure you haven't told anyone? Hatcher, Parks, anyone?" Carla's face hovered in front of Stacy, her blue eyes blazing.

"I haven't told anyone," Stacy mumbled and shut her eyes, cringing, waiting for the next hit.

"Can you believe this woman, Everett? Tsk, tsk, tsk."

Michaels shook her head slowly back and forth. Without warning, she rounded on Stacy and slapped her again. Stacy gasped and more tears rolled down her face.

"You are even dumber than I thought, Thompson, you know that. I picked the right idiot to frame, though I'd like to know how you figured it out."

"It's pretty clear that doesn't matter, Carla," interjected O'Brien. "She's not going to get a chance to tell anyone, because she's about to meet an untimely end." As Stacy watched, transfixed, his gaze roamed around the room and met his partner's eyes. "The question is, will she be in an unfortunate auto accident like the late Mrs. Parks or maybe her heart will give out on her like poor Tricia? What do you think, my dear?"

"I've been thinking about it, and I have a better idea. I think I may have the sad duty to report that I came into work here late at night and found a distraught Stacy Thompson so overcome with the guilt—" she paused as she carefully extracted a length of nylon rope from a bag she'd brought and went on "—so distraught she hung herself in her own classroom—and left a typed confession on her own computer."

Stacy stared at the white noose and gulped. Any time now, guys.

"Perfect, my dear, perfect. As always, your solutions are so creative. Now, exactly where shall the tragic event occur?" O'Brien laughed.

Chapter 73

O'Brien glanced around the darkened room and rough-handed Stacy. "Stupid bitch. Carla, turn on the damn lights so we can see what we're doing."

Stacy watched Michaels walk over to the still open door. Reaching for the light switch, the principal turned her head back toward O'Brien and said, "You know, Everett, my love, this is too perfect. Poor Mrs. Thompson will be out of the way, the police will wrap up the whole drug mystery, and we can go back to business as—hey!"

"I don't think so, Carla. Not in this lifetime." Bart stepped through the doorway and quickly snatched Carla's wrist before she reached the light switch.

Bart flipped on the bright overhead lights. At the same instant, Ken came around the corner of the workroom where he'd concealed himself in the darkness. He stood and faced O'Brien, who still had Stacy in a rough hold. Stacy glanced from one man to the other, Ken still wore the faded jogging outfit Bart had scrounged out of the closet and his hair hung in unruly tufts, never really combed out after the impromptu shower. O'Brien looked ever the professional, in a cream colored turtleneck and pressed blue Khakis. The clothes do *not* make the man.

The bright lights dazed O'Brien and Michaels, but Carla recovered first. "Oh, Bart and Ken, I'm so glad you're here." She reverted to the sweet, placating feminine voice.

She wore a bright red top that clung to her figure with a pair of stirrup pants, cream in color. Even now, in the middle of all this, her hair looked perfectly coifed and her makeup was perfect. Even now. Stacy couldn't believe it. "Dr. O'Brien and I were working late, and we heard a commotion in Stacy's room and came to find her distraught and suicidal…"

"Save your breath, Carla," Ken said.

Stacy watched the woman's features return to a snarl she'd seen earlier.

Ken continued, "You are some piece of work, lady. First, you deal drugs to the very students you're entrusted with and, when some of them die, you don't even care. Instead, you try to frame somebody else, so you can keep poisoning kids." Then he turned to the board president. "It's over, Everett. You might as well let her go."

O'Brien shoved Stacy roughly forward. She stumbled on a desk leg and fell into Ken's arms. He caught her and pulled her up, her face only a few inches from his, and they exchanged a momentary glance.

"Now, isn't that sweet? I think I'm going to vomit," barked O'Brien. He pointed at Ken. "Look, Parks, who do you think is going to take your word against mine? Hell, I'm president of the board. Not only will I come out of this, but I'll have your ass fired in the process."

Exchanging a glance, Ken and Bart began laughing, hard. Michaels and O'Brien stared at the two men.

"Funny." Still chuckling, Ken leaned against Bart

and called, "Hey, Wally, did you get all this?" and he looked up at the intercom box on the wall.

As all five people turned to stare at the gray mesh cover on the painted wall, a tense silence gripped the room.

"Wally, you there?" Bart called.

Ken and Bart exchanged a brief, worried glance and haughty smiles crept back to the faces of Michaels and O'Brien.

A loud, electronic beep erupted from the little box, making all five people jump.

"Sorry, Bart, I didn't mean that, but I ain't no electric wizard," Wally's tinny voice responded. "Yeah, I got every word on tape, up here at the office. You want me to play it back for ya?"

Stacy jumped up and hugged Ken.

"Not necessary, buddy. Did you make that call I asked for?" Bart asked.

"You betcha. Called the station a few minutes ago and they said backup is on the way."

"Thanks, Wally, we really appreciate the help," Ken added. "You got your deal. You've earned it."

"Okay, Carla and Everett," called Bart, "might as well get this over with."

His cop uniform a bit wrinkled, Bart walked over to the side wall of the classroom and gestured for the two to join him. Glancing at each other, both Michaels and O'Brien took their time before following him.

"Place your hands against the wall and slide your feet back. You probably know the drill." They did as instructed, moving slowly, Carla looking as if she were in pain. The policeman patted O'Brien in the appropriate places, his hands slapping O'Brien's ribs and hips. Satisfied, he glanced at Michaels and then turned. "Stacy, would you do the honors?" He pointed to Carla, leaning on the wall.

"It would be my pleasure," Stacy said, grinning, as she strolled up behind her former principal. Stacy used rough hands to pat her down.

"Hey, that hurts," Carla screamed out, turning her face toward Stacy.

"Oh, I'm so sorry," Stacy replied, her grin broadening, and walked back and stood beside Ken.

"Okay, you two, turn around and listen up," called Bart, pulling a laminated card from his breast pocket. "I'm placing you two under arrest for the murder of Amanda Parks, Tricia Holloway, and the other four students. You have the right to remain silent. You know anything you say can and will be used against you in a court of law…"

As Bart continued on, Stacy noticed that even though she'd heard the same chant countless times on TV shows, it sounded different here, in person. More chilling.

Neither Michaels nor O'Brien made any reaction to the speech.

"Do you understand these rights as I've read them to you?" Bart asked, but drew no response from his suspects. "Carla?" he called sharply, looking at her.

"Yeah," she snapped.

"Dr. O'Brien?"

"Of course."

"Officer Callahan, what's going on here?"

Everyone in the room turned to see the squat figure of Chief Tony Garcia, standing in the open doorway looking into the room with a puzzled look. His uniform perfect as if it had just come from the dry cleaners, he looked exactly like he had when he showed up at her classroom door to arrest her. Stacy froze.

"Yes, sir, everything's fine. These two suspects, Carla Michaels and Everett O'Brien, confessed to the murders of Amanda Parks and Tricia Holloway. And you know, they also admitted to being behind the drug ring at school."

"They did?" The chief's voice registered disbelief.

"Yes, sir, they did, and we have it all on tape, sir. Don't we Wally?" he added, without turning around.

Another loud, electronic beep bellowed out of the speaker on the wall followed by the tinny voice of the janitor. "You want me to play it now?"

"Never mind, Wally. Just bring me the tape, will you?" Bart called back.

"Sure."

"Nice work, Officer Callahan. Well, well, well. What a turn of events." Then the chief turned to Stacy. "Mrs. Thompson, I would like to formally apologize both for myself and the department. I am deeply sorry for what we put you through. Will you accept my apology?"

Stacy let out a long breath. "I've been waiting a while to hear that, but yes, of course, I will, Chief," Stacy said, "I—"

A groan from Carla on the other side of the room interrupted her. The others looked as the principal spun around, grabbing her chest. Her back now against the wall, she slid down the painted surface to the floor.

"My chest!" gasped Carla Michaels. "I-I-I can't breathe. Everett!"

O'Brien turned away from the wall and moved

next to her, kneeling on the floor and began checking her pulse.

"Carla? Carla? Can you hear me?" he called, each word getting louder as they all watched Carla's eyes glaze over. "Ken, call 911," he said over his shoulder.

Ken didn't budge, studying the scene before him.

O'Brien fumed, "Damn it, Parks. I think this woman is having a heart attack. She has a history of heart trouble, and I don't think anyone wants her to die right here!"

Chapter 74

Chief Tony Garcia studied the individuals in the room. He needed to decide exactly how he was going to play this. He barked, "Dr. O'Brien, this better be on the level."

"Tony, do you want to take the responsibility if this woman dies right here?" O'Brien pointed to Michaels, lying on the floor clutching her chest. Not waiting for an answer, he turned back and unbuttoned the top buttons of her blouse. "Carla," he said in a calm voice, "simply try to relax. It's Everett. I'll take care of you. You'll be all right." While he talked, he slid her body so she was lying flat on the floor, cushioning his hand behind her head. He leaned his ear down close to her mouth.

Garcia watched Parks glance at him, then at his officer, obviously unsure what to do.

Callahan kept his gaze on the two on the ground but jerked his head toward the office. "Go on, Ken. I'll keep an eye on things here."

Parks disappeared through the doorway and a burly custodian came through the opening, fingers holding a tape cartridge.

"Here ya go, Bart," the man called.

Before Garcia could say something, the janitor flipped the clear tape cassette at Bart, who caught it in midair.

"Nice catch." Wally chuckled.

"Watch it. That's evidence!" Bart said in mock horror and slapped him on the back.

Garcia started, "Bart, I'll take custody of—"

The custodian blurted out, "What's the matter? Somebody hit her?" One fat finger pointed to Michaels on the floor.

"No," Stacy said. "Dr. O'Brien says Mrs. Michaels may be having a heart attack."

The custodian crossed his arms. "After how she just got caught n' all, it ain't real surprising now, is it?"

O'Brien turned around. "Where the hell is that ambulance?"

"They're on their way, Dr. O'Brien," Garcia said. "You tend to your patient there. Bart, why don't you check on Mr. Parks…to make sure everything is okay. Let me—"

An ambulance entered the parking lot at high speed, its circling red lights strafing the classroom window, and screeched to a stop. Everyone froze. They stared at the parking lot as the two EMT's rolled a gurney out the back of the ambulance and in through the front door of the school.

"Down here," yelled Ken, who had returned and stood right outside the classroom. The frantic steps of the EMT's echoed off the walls as they ran down the hallway. The others in the room moved out of the way as the two rushed over to where Michaels was lying on the floor. Working under the direction of O'Brien, they had the woman up on the gurney and were rolling out the door in a few seconds.

Garcia had to think fast. He grabbed O'Brien's arm as he was passing. "Where are you taking her?"

"Uh, I don't know…Bethesda, I guess," O'Brien replied over his shoulder, hurrying to catch up with his patient.

"Well, you're not going anywhere without me." The chief turned to Callahan. "Bart, take these guys to the station and get their statements. Nice job. I'll make sure this is on the up and up. Send Shaffer to relieve me at the hospital." He went out the door and hollered, "Hey, hold the ambulance till I get there."

Garcia hustled out to the ambulance and, by the time he got there, they were sliding Carla Michaels through the opening.

O'Brien barked orders to the EMT's. "No one's going to take care of this lady but me. I'm Dr. O'Brien, her physician. You two can ride up front and you make damn sure we get there as quickly as you can."

Exchanging glances, the two medical workers looked at the police chief for confirmation.

Garcia said, "It's okay, fellows. He is her doctor and besides, I'll be back here the whole time."

The two shrugged their shoulders and walked to the front and climbed in, closing the doors behind them. Garcia and O'Brien jumped up and in through the back doors, then pulled them closed as the vehicle lurched sideways and began rolling. Lights flashing, the ambulance swung in a wide arc and headed out of the parking lot.

Inside the ambulance no one moved at first. Michaels lay still on the gurney, her face ashen. Garcia and O'Brien stared at each other, but neither spoke. After a few moments, O'Brien leaned down to his patient and whispered, "It's okay."

At the words, Carla's eyes popped open and stared

up at O'Brien. Then she raised her right arm and pulled the oxygen mask off her mouth. A broad grin on her face, she asked, "How'd I do?"

"Marvelous, dear. A performance truly deserving of an Oscar. Don't you agree, Tony?" O'Brien turned and laughed at Garcia, whose only reply was a grunt. Rising to a sitting position, Carla threw her arms around O'Brien and kissed him. O'Brien returned the kiss, wrapping his arms around her.

"Uh-um!" Garcia cleared his throat loudly enough to get their attention.

"Oh, all right," O'Brien said and extracted himself from Michaels. He reached inside the breast pocket of his jacket and pulled out a sealed, overstuffed white envelope and handed it to the police chief. "Equitable compensation for services rendered."

Garcia opened the envelope and fingered the bills inside.

"Oh, you can be sure it's all there. I trust it's what you want," O'Brien said.

"What I want," muttered Garcia, "is to never see your two sorry asses again."

"Oh, you can be sure of that, Chief. After tonight we'll be but a distant memory."

As Michaels unbuttoned O'Brien's dress shirt, she asked, "Our business arrangement around here has been very profitable, but all good things must change. Well, what next, Dr. O'Brien? What do we do for an encore, lover?" She kissed his neck and chest, her lips running down his exposed skin.

Garcia rolled his eyes.

"Well, dear…" O'Brien said, hesitating a little as his right arm reached into the breast pocket of his jacket.

In a soothing voice, O'Brien said, "Well, I think it's clear our fans all think you have suffered a heart attack and I don't think we should disappoint them."

Garcia watched as the doctor's fingers withdrew a small, amber-colored syringe from the pocket, keeping it out of view of Michaels. Before Garcia could react, O'Brien brought up the hypodermic and plunged it into Carla's neck.

In three seconds, the look on Michaels' face flashed from surprise, to shock, to pain. Releasing O'Brien, she grabbed her chest, gasping for breath. "Everett, why—" she cried as her eyes bulged. Perspiration covered her face, the sheen of the drops reflecting the lighting inside and her body convulsed with pain.

Glancing from Michaels' writhing body to Garcia sitting across the small space, O'Brien shrugged and grinned. "What can I say? No honor among thieves."

Garcia shook his head, slapping the full envelope in his hand.

As if on cue, the ambulance hit a bump, pulling into the emergency room parking lot. The driver jerked the vehicle to a stop. In five seconds, both EMT's opened the back doors with practiced, split-second precision.

"Hurry," O'Brien shouted, "this woman's just gone into full arrest." The medics accelerated their actions, pulling the gurney through the opening and dropping the wheels to the pavement. "Go on ahead and tell the emergency team to start. I'm going to scrub up and I'll join them." With that, the two men were off, racing through the hospital emergency doors.

O'Brien climbed out of the ambulance, followed by Garcia. For a moment they both stood on the paved lot, watching the EMT's hustle down the almost empty corridor. Turning to Garcia, O'Brien extended his hand and said, "Nice working with you, Tony."

Garcia simply stared at the hand. O'Brien shrugged again and flashed his charming smile. He turned and strolled between the cars of the parking lot, his lanky figure swallowed up by the darkness.

Garcia turned to head inside, trying to figure out what he was going to say. Concentrating, almost at the automatic doors, his attention was drawn to a commotion in the parking lot.

A familiar voice called, "Aren't you headed in the wrong direction, Doc?"

"Get off me, Callahan!" O'Brien yelled.

Winding his way around the parked cars, Garcia hurried toward the voices, his mind racing. How was he going to play this? He pulled up short. Callahan, Parks, and Thompson stood over O'Brien, who lay sprawled on his back against the asphalt.

His foot on O'Brien's stomach, Callahan looked up and said, "I saw this guy hightailing out of here. Ken and I chased him and"—he grinned—"well, we caught him."

Garcia stared at Callahan. "I thought I told you to take these two"—he pointed to Parks and Thompson—"to the station. They're material witnesses and we're going to need their statements."

Callahan said, "Well, Chief, I had a feeling about this one"—he shoved O'Brien to the asphalt with his foot—"and I figured he might try something."

From the ground, O'Brien growled, "Get off me

and let me up. I was just going to my car to get my, uh…scrubs." Then he turned his head toward Garcia, "Tony, tell your Gestapo to get off me. We had a—"

Garcia yelled, "O'Brien, you have a right to remain silent. I'd advise you to use it." Then he turned toward Callahan. "Good work, Officer. I was heading into the hospital to check on Michaels. O'Brien here gave her something in the ambulance but when they took her in, she didn't look good. I guess I lost track of the doctor."

Another voice called, "Okay, sir, I'm here. You want me posted outside the patient's room?"

Garcia turned to see Shaffer join the circle around O'Brien, still on the ground. Garcia said, "Bart, let Dr. O'Brien up. Shaffer, you stay on him like glue. I'm heading back in to see if I can get anything out of Michaels when she comes to." He jerked his head toward Parks and Thompson. "And get these guys to the station and take their statements. Where's the other one, the janitor?"

"Waiting in the car," Callahan said.

"Well, get on it."

Shaffer collected O'Brien, who rose up off the asphalt and started brushing off his blazer. He shepherded him toward the hospital. Callahan, Parks, and Thompson walked across three rows of cars to get to their vehicle. For a few seconds, Garcia stood there, watching, and then turned to head into the hospital.

He thought, what the hell do I do now?

Chapter 75

Six Months Later

Marco Island was warm for this time of the season, so Stacy wore the wide straw hat she'd discovered at a local shop as protection against the bright sun. This late in the afternoon, she had little company at the shore.

Picking up her beach chair, she moved it closer to the water, so, as the tide moved in, the lapping waves would cool and caress her bare legs. She stretched out in the chair, in her two-piece, the one the salesgirl at the boutique had called "stunning."

Having come here three months ago to try out "her" condo and think things through, she found, after a while she had little to do. Not that she didn't try. She ate at the best local spots. She did a good deal of walking on the beach. She even did a few of the tourist things like a dolphin cruise and the seashell museum. She enjoyed them all, but found her mind kept returning to what she'd left behind. With time on her hands, she picked up several books in the resort's quaint bookstore. She'd had little time for pleasure reading on the job. One of those, a popular romance novel, lay open on her lap. With the promise of romance and sex and lust on the title, she thought it might be just what she needed. Still, it didn't work. Probably not the writing. As she tried to focus, the words on the page blurred and she found her mind drifting back to her last days in Portsmouth.

A week after the arrests, she'd received a request from the superintendent "to come in and talk." Nervous, she sat across the expansive cherry desk and studied the man. He looked the same, still imposing in a black suit, pressed white shirt, and staid blue tie. But when he spoke, she found a very different Dr. Mark Walters—personable, compassionate, almost talkative.

"I cannot thank you enough for helping us get to the bottom of this terrible crime. I'm so glad it's over and we can concentrate on helping children learn again." She could still picture him, his tall form shifting uncomfortably on his posh, leather chair, brown eyes darting from the desktop to her and back down again. "I still can't believe the drug ring was going on right under my nose…with my own people. I don't know how I could have been so blind."

Stacy tried to reassure him, but Walters had more to say. "I'm especially sorry for Ken. He's been an invaluable assistant to me. For him to lose Amanda from all this, I'm not sure he'll ever recover…and I blame myself."

She anguished at the pain Ken must be going through.

Listening to Walters, Stacy pondered what compelled him to abandon his normal, stoic demeanor. She didn't have to wonder long.

"More than anything else, I want to apologize for everything *you* were put through. Ken shared enough with me that I realize what a traumatic ordeal this must have been for you. I know there's no way we can make it up to you, but I would like to extend an offer of indefinite leave *with pay* for as long as you need—for the rest of the school year even—to give you time to recover. *And* your job will be here, waiting for you whenever you're ready to return. I've already talked to the board, and they have agreed."

Even after all the sordid details had come out— headlines about the arrests filling the newspapers and eleven o'clock news—Stacy still got suspicious looks from some locals at the diner and the gas station. The encounter with Mrs. Vargas, the mother of one of her former students, still stung. Stacy had queued up behind the woman in the checkout line at the grocery. Stretching to place her items on the conveyor, she noticed Mrs. Vargas ahead of her and smiled. When the woman recognized her, her eyes got wide and she hissed, "I still think you had something to do with the whole sordid affair."

Stacy was too stunned to even respond. But she didn't forget it.

As much as she loved teaching and loved her kids, she realized she needed to get away, at least for a while. So, when Walters made the offer, Stacy seized it, shaking hands with her boss, his palm large and sweaty. The superintendent and board were no doubt terrified she might sue them. Several of her friends had urged her to do exactly that. She was sure that gossip made the rounds—no doubt to the board members as well. They didn't know her well enough to realize revenge wasn't her style. She was even willing to sign the legal papers.

Still, during her time away, she found she'd missed the kids, even the "rotten" ones, though that hardly surprised her. But the days she'd spent locked in that bleak, ugly jail cell had forced her to do some radical rethinking. She took the leave because she needed the time to decide what she was going to do with the rest of her life. Of course, having a luxurious condo on the Gulf coast of Florida—even temporarily—wasn't a bad place to do some contemplating.

She still hadn't arrived at any final decision.

As she lounged in the chair, toes cooling in the water, she remembered thanking Walters and strolling across the hall to Ken's office. He was on the phone again, helping out one of the principals from what she could hear. If she closed her eyes, here on the shore, she could still picture him. He looked great, seated behind his worn, oaken desk with stacks of papers and messages spread out in front of him, phone cradled on his shoulder. His pale-yellow shirt sleeves were rolled up and his colorful "Save the Children" tie pulled down. At first, concentrating so intently on the conversation, he didn't notice her in the doorway. Then he glanced up from the paper he was reading to the caller and saw her. A slow, broad smile spread across his handsome face. Gesturing to a chair, he said, "Tom, I'll call you back."

Then and there, she and Ken made comfortable small talk—talk about how busy he was, about the district's offer of leave for her, and about how Ken's son was handling Amanda's death. They talked for close to half an hour. She remembered them talking about different things…but not about what was really important.

Sitting alone on the stretch of beach, the pangs of regret struck her again. As her mind replayed the scene—Ken across the large wooden desk, with his strong shoulders, slightly graying hair, and warm, welcoming smile—she chided herself for not telling him how she felt.

But how could she? He had just lost his wife.

She rose to leave, and he turned toward her, gave a small wave, and smiled—she thought she read more in his eyes. But his secretary beeped in, announcing another caller, the new board president this time, and Ken jerked his focus back to the phone. Before she left, she studied him, as he spoke into the phone, animated and intense. She wanted to memorize his image.

What wouldn't she do to roll time back and have the chance to at least say…something.

With the breeze on her face, she inhaled the sweet, salt-water air, hoping it would help to soothe her heartache. Clinging onto the memory of that afternoon in Ken's office, she closed her eyes and listened to the calming, rhythmic sound of the waves lapping the shore, the water cooling her legs. She surrendered to the welcoming embrace of sleep.

She had no idea how long she slept, but she sensed something, some change, and opened her eyes. The moment she did, she had to blink them shut as she was looking directly at the bright circle of the sun hanging above the horizon. Raising her arm to shield her eyes from the glare, she watched a figure step into view, blocking the sun. She dropped her arm. Against the burning orange background, she could make out only a silhouette.

"Do you know where a guy can get something to eat around here?" asked a familiar voice.

"Ken?" Stacy squinted and asked, incredulous. She must be dreaming.

"In the flesh," Ken said.

She could hear that beautiful smile, hidden in the sun's rays, in the three words. Stacy jumped up and threw her arms around him, almost knocking him down. Then embarrassed a bit, she lowered her arms and stepped beside him out of the glare of the setting sun.

She said, "You came! It's so great to see you."

She watched Ken examine her, his glance taking in her figure from head to toe. She silently thanked the salesgirl for her swimwear suggestion.

"Same here." He grinned, his eyebrows dancing up and down once. "You look incredible, you know that? The Florida sun must agree with you."

"Thank you for noticing." Stacy turned for him, one side, then the other, but when his smile broadened, she felt her cheeks blush. She took a step toward the beach chair, reaching down to retrieve her cover up but Ken stopped her. He pulled her close, leaned in, and kissed her, long and hard, and she felt him stiffen against her.

When they broke apart, he took a quick breath and smiled. "I've been wanting to do that for a long time."

"Not as long as I've wanted it." She pulled his head down and kissed him again, her lips parting slightly. She wrapped both arms around him and finished the kiss breathlessly.

For a minute, neither said anything as he held her gaze. Then he said, "Glad to know we're on the same page."

"Me, too," she smirked. "But I can't wait to see how the rest of this book turns out."

Chapter 76

Hours later, as she lay atop him, Stacy felt Ken's strong arms envelop her, incredible comfort oozing from the touch of his skin next to hers. She collapsed into his chest, wonderfully exhausted, and heard the words she so craved. His lips a few inches from her ears, he whispered, "I love you."

"I know." Stacy smiled, laying her head sideways on his strong chest. She couldn't believe *she* could be this lucky, this happy. For the first time in a long while, she felt relaxed, protected, safe and at peace.

For a while, they both lay there, basking in their sensual afterglow, the only noise in the room the quiet whirl of the ceiling fan above.

"I have a confession to make," he said.

She slid off him and glanced back, her anxiety creeping back in. "What kind of confession?"

"I read some of the entries in your journal."

"Which entries?" She scrunched her nose.

"When I retrieved your things from your locker, I dropped the journal, and it flopped open to that page. When I saw my name written there, I couldn't help it. The entry drew me in. Then I had to read more." He looked down. "Will you forgive my intrusion?"

She smiled. "Maybe you were supposed to see what I wrote. What did you think?"

He said, "I was stunned. You'd never let on and I

didn't realize…" He must've seen something in her face because he hurried on. "I mean I cared for you. I felt something for you—respect, collegiality, friendship definitely. But I loved Amanda. We'd been married for twenty years, and I was determined to make it work. It wasn't till after she died and I found out…" he paused, as if he wasn't sure how to go on. "Anyway, it wasn't till after Amanda died that I even allowed myself to think of you as anything more than a good friend."

"I'm glad I had you as a friend and that you believed in me." She took a deep breath.

"I did, but it was more than that. When I became convinced you couldn't be the drug dealer, I knew the real pusher was still out there and would keep poisoning kids."

"Speak of the devil, what happened to O'Brien?" Stacy asked.

Ken said, "You mean you don't get the *Portsmouth Gazette* down here in Marco Island?"

"Somehow, the newsstand must not get copies of that fine publication."

"Well, after Carla died, the way she died, they did an autopsy on her body. Anyway, as reported by the award-winning journalist from the *Gazette*, the autopsy showed she did die of a heart attack, an attack induced by an injection of some drug."

"That's what we suspected," she said.

"Yeah. In his report, Garcia wrote he saw O'Brien inject her with something, but he thought it was something to stop the attack."

Stacy asked, "Do they have enough to convict O'Brien? I mean we got the two of them on tape, admitting they did the whole thing. But will that be enough to convict someone as connected as O'Brien?"

"Oh, yeah, you don't know." He turned to face her. "Bart got search warrants and when they searched O'Brien's office at home, they hit the motherlode. They found all these records of the drug peddling for the past five years. Names, amounts, dollars, for a network of small towns—the whole ball of wax. It took them a while but Bart and some of Portsmouth's finest worked with the county sheriff to round up most of the other pushers and break up the drug ring, they think. Several turned on O'Brien. The trials start next month."

"Did you say Bart got the search warrants? Wouldn't that be Garcia's turf?"

He smiled. "Oh, you have been out of touch. Garcia resigned."

"What?" She pushed herself up on her elbow.

"Two days after we caught Michaels and O'Brien, Garcia put in his report, turned in his resignation, and left town. Said he was going to head out west and do some fly-fishing."

"Just like that? Seems a little strange."

"Yeah, Bart thinks there might be more to the story, like maybe he was in on the whole thing. Bart wanted to investigate but, after all the bad press, the town fathers didn't want to look very closely. They simply accepted Garcia's resignation and said thanks for your service."

"I can understand they didn't think Portsmouth could stomach any more scandal. Hey, what about Earl? What happened to him?" She found that, after not thinking much about her home town for a while, she was anxious to learn what she'd missed.

"Oh, Earl, now there's a story." Ken slid his hand

to the small of her back. His touch felt great there. "With Tricia and Carla dead and O'Brien not talking— by order of his lawyer—the prosecutor said there wasn't much they could do to hold Earl. But Bart had other ideas."

"What'd he do?"

"He brought Earl in and did a number on him and finally got him to confess to rigging Amanda's car."

"Earl rigged Amanda's car?" Stacy asked.

"After talking with me, Bart found out Earl worked on Amanda's car the day before O'Brien had lured her up to the mountain. I didn't remember he had done any work on her car. Amanda must've arranged it herself. It turns out Earl was the one who fixed the car so the brakes would fail. He said he was ordered to."

Stacy moved her hand to the back of Ken's head and gently stroked his hairline.

"Anyway, after Bart figured it out, he brought Earl in, told him he needed his help to wrap up some things about O'Brien and Michaels. You know Bart, after he got Earl talking, he dropped the bomb on him about Amanda's car. Earl was so surprised, he confessed to the whole thing. Didn't even want a trial, just wanted it off his conscience, he told Bart. He pleaded guilty and got ten years."

"I'm glad he didn't get off after everything he did."

"When Bart figured out Earl was responsible for Amanda's death, he said there was no way he was going to let him walk. Bart's a good friend."

"We were both lucky to have him on our side."

Another silence followed. Right then, Stacy didn't want to say anything, preferring the quiet touch of his body next to hers to any other reality. She found the most contentment simply lying next to him in the large bed, nestled together under the rumpled covers.

She sighed. "Can we stay here forever?"

"I don't think so. Eventually, when the trials are over, you'll have to give back your condo."

She went silent again and curled up next to him, cradling her curves inside the warmth of his body.

In the darkness and silence, Ken asked, "Have you given any thought to what you're going to do next?" When she didn't answer right away, he asked, "Stacy, are you planning to come back to Portsmouth?"

"I don't know. I haven't figured that one out yet, though I know I want to teach again." She looked across at him, his eyes reflecting the shimmering lights from the town outside the window. "Do you want me to come back?"

"That's a silly question. What I want more than anything is to be with you, whether that's in Portsmouth or wherever."

"But your job—"

"There will be other jobs, but I'm convinced I'll never find another you. Anyway, I don't plan to risk finding out."

"Well, I don't know if I should tell you this now." She watched his eyes. "I've given this some thought. I'd like to go out west."

"West?"

"Yeah, Oregon. My folks are out there, and I haven't seen them in quite a while. Besides, I decided I want to look for Brent." She stopped.

"Would you like some company?"

"I'd love it." She kissed him again.

He said, "Besides, Oregon sounds good. Probably a

lot cooler than here."

"You think it's warm here?" she asked, her eyebrows arching. "Not as warm as it's going to be."

They both laughed, the sound echoing through the condo.

A word about the author…

Dr. Randy Overbeck is the author of the best-selling series, The Haunted Shores Mysteries, each a cold case murder mystery wrapped in ghost story served with a side romance, set in a beautiful resort location. His novels have garnered hundreds of five star reviews from critics and readers alike and have won ten national awards including the Gold Award (Literary Titan) Silver Award/Thriller of the Year (ReadersFavorite.com), Silver Award/Mystery of the Year (ReaderViews.com) and Crown Heart of Excellence (InD'tale Magazine). He is the host of the popular podcast, "Great Stories about Great Storytellers," which reveals the unusual backstories of famous authors, directors and poets and is available wherever you get your podcasts. A speaker in much demand, he has shared his programs, "Thanks Still Go Bump in the Night" and "A Few Favorite Haunts" with audiences all over the country. A member of Mystery Writers of America, Dr. Overbeck is an active member of the literary community contributing to a writers' critique group, serving as a mentor to emerging writers and participating in writing conferences. More info about his novels, blog, programs and podcast can be found at his website www.authorrandyoverbeck.com . Dr. Overbeck is always interested in connecting with his readers. You can reach him at randyoverbeck@authorrandyoverbeck.com or via the social media or other contacts below.

Facebook:
https://www.facebook.com/authorrandyoverbeck

Twitter:
https://twitter.com/OverbeckRandy/media

Instagram:
https://www.instagram.com/authorrandyoverbeck/

BookBub:
https://www.bookbub.com/authors/randy-overbeck

Goodreads:
https://www.goodreads.com/author/show/4825632.Randy_Overbeck

Amazon:
https://www.amazon.com/Randy-Overbeck/e/B07QQHW7DM?ref=sr_ntt_srch_lnk_1&qid=1658371317&sr=8-1

Thank you for purchasing
this publication of The Wild Rose Press, Inc.

For questions or more information
contact us at
info@thewildrosepress.com.

The Wild Rose Press, Inc.
www.thewildrosepress.com